THE WORLD'S CLASSICS

'TYPHOON' AND OTHER TALES

JOSEPH CONRAD was born Józef Teodor Konrad Korzeniowski in the Russian-held part of Poland in 1857. His parents were punished by the Russians for their Polish nationalist activities and both died while Conrad was still a child. In 1874 he left Poland for France and in 1878 began a career with the British merchant navy. He spent nearly twenty years as a sailor before becoming a full-time novelist. He became a British citizen in 1886 and settled permanently in England during the 1890s, marrying Jessie George in 1896.

Conrad is a writer of graphic richness and of extreme subtlety and sophistication; 'Heart of Darkness', *Lord Jim*, and *Nostromo* display technical complexities which have established Conrad as one of the first English 'Modernists'. He is also noted for the unprecedented vividness with which, in such works as *The Secret Agent*, *Under Western Eyes*, and *Victory*, he expresses a searching pessimism. Despite the immediate critical recognition that they received in his lifetime, Conrad's major novels did not sell well, and he lived in relative poverty until in 1914 the commercial success of *Chance* secured for him a wider public and an assured income. In 1923 he visited the United States, with great acclaim; and in England he was offered a knighthood (which he declined) shortly before his death in 1924. Since then his reputation has steadily grown, and he is now seen as a writer who greatly extended the resources of English fiction and offered prophetically intelligent insights into the problems and preoccupations of the twentieth century.

CEDRIC WATTS is a Professor of English at the University of Sussex. His books on Conrad include *Conrad's 'Heart of Darkness': A Critical and Contextual Discussion* (1977), *A Preface to Conrad* (1982), and *The Deceptive Text* (1984). He has edited *Joseph Conrad's Letters to R. B. Cunninghame Graham* (1969) and *Lord Jim* (1986).

THE WORLD'S CLASSICS

JOSEPH CONRAD

'Typhoon'
and Other Tales

Edited with an Introduction by
CEDRIC WATTS

Oxford   New York
OXFORD UNIVERSITY PRESS

Oxford University Press, Walton Street, Oxford OX2 6DP

Oxford New York Toronto
Delhi Bombay Calcutta Madras Karachi
Kuala Lumpur Singapore Hong Kong Tokyo
Nairobi Dar es Salaam Cape Town
Melbourne Auckland Madrid

and associated companies in
Berlin Ibadan

Oxford is a trade mark of Oxford University Press

British Library Cataloguing in Publication Data
Data available

Library of Congress Cataloging in Publication Data
Conrad, Joseph, 1857 1924.
Typhoon and other tales.
(The World's classics)
Bibliography: p.
Contents: Typhoon– Falk Amy Foster - [etc.]
I. Watts, Cedric Thomas. II. Title.
PR6005.04A6 1986 823'.912 86 2566
ISBN 0-19 281711-6 (pbk.)

5 7 9 10 8 6

Printed in Great Britain by
BPCC Hazells Ltd
Aylesbury, Bucks

CONTENTS

Acknowledgements   vi

Introduction   vii

Note on the Text   xxi

Select Bibliography   xxvii

A Chronology of Joseph Conrad   xxix

'Typhoon'   1

'Falk'   103

'Amy Foster'   201

'The Secret Sharer'   241

Explanatory Notes   297

Glossary   314

ACKNOWLEDGEMENTS

In preparing this edition, books which I found particularly useful were *Tait's Seamanship*, by James Tait, Master Mariner (Glasgow : James Brown & Son, 1902), Gershom Bradford's *A Glossary of Sea Terms* (London : Cassell, 1954), and Norman Sherry's *Conrad's Eastern World* (London : Cambridge University Press, 1966). I am also grateful for the help generously given by friends and colleagues, particularly Tony Inglis (who, on pp. 311–12, navigated me skilfully past Koh-ring), Hans van Marle, and Alan Sinfield.

INTRODUCTION

I

THE four tales in this volume illustrate both the diversity and the imaginative integrity of Joseph Conrad's work. They vary in location, situation, tone, texture, and intensity, but they all maintain characteristic Conradian preoccupations—with isolation and inadequate communication, with transient and beleaguered solidarity, and with the ordeal that tests character. Each tale offers a sympathetic view of an individual subjected not only to physical stress but also to prejudice and incomprehension : MacWhirr, the indomitable captain who is regarded as merely 'a stupid man'; Falk, the lonely survivor reviled as a bestial cannibal; Yanko Goorall, the castaway scorned as a pariah; and Leggatt, the intrepid seaman pursued as a murderer.

The earliest of the texts, 'Typhoon', was soon recognized as one of Conrad's finest descriptive pieces. Accounts of a ship's struggle with a storm have long been part of the stock-in-trade of sea-writers; but none of them has surpassed Conrad's description of the *Nan-Shan*'s battle with the typhoon. It's graphic, knowledgeable, dramatic; a wealth of vivid particulars—from the darkness that 'palpitated down' between the lightning to the water swallowed by Jukes ('sometimes . . . . . fresh and sometimes . . . . . salt')—bring the vessel's ordeal intensely to the imagination. Nevertheless, as Conrad said when recalling the incident on which the tale was based,

the interest . . . . . was, of course, not the bad weather but the extraordinary complication brought into the ship's life at a moment of exceptional stress by the human element below her deck . . . . . I felt that to bring out its deeper significance which was quite apparent to me, something other, something more was required; a leading motive that would harmonize all these violent noises, and a point of view that would put all that elemental fury into its proper place.

What was needed of course was Captain MacWhirr.[1]

The tale stresses that MacWhirr is stolid, unimaginative, and unsophisticated; and at first we may be tempted to patronize him as a semi-comic character. What the narrative does, progressively, is to reveal the peculiar integrity which his thick skin both conceals and preserves. He may not have the intelligence or professionalism to evade the typhoon, but he has the courage to take the ship and her crew through it; he may not understand Jukes's patriotic indignation at serving under a Siamese flag, but when Jukes is almost paralysed by fear, it is MacWhirr who sustains and encourages him.

Crucially important is MacWhirr's treatment of the coolies. Jukes adopts the familiar contemporaneous attitude of racial contempt for these labourers, and, when they panic and battle during the storm, his inclination is to ignore them. It is MacWhirr who insists that they be reduced to salutary order, and again, after the typhoon has passed, it is Mac-Whirr who takes pains to redistribute their money as equitably as possible. As he explains to Jukes:

'Had to do what's fair, for all—they are only Chinamen. Give them the same chance with ourselves . . . . . Bad enough to be shut up below in a gale . . . . . without being battered to pieces . . . . . Couldn't let that go on in my ship, if I knew she hadn't five minutes to live.'

In that gale-interrupted phrase, 'for all—they are only Chinamen', the predictable concession to commonplace racial assumptions is made; but the emphasis falls on Mac-Whirr's determination to preserve 'fair play' by treating them as fellow-humans. The same simple integrity that enables MacWhirr to captain the ship through the typhoon obliges him to enforce a humane order. The 'simple' ethic is

[1] 'Author's Note' [1919] to *Typhoon and Other Stories* (London: Dent, 1950), pp. v–vi,

eventually, in its implications and consequences, more considerate as well as more practical than Jukes's apparently intelligent outlook. When Jukes rushes about, mustering men with rifles, MacWhirr replies with exasperated common sense : 'For God's sake, Mr. Jukes . . . . . do take away these rifles from the men. Somebody's sure to get hurt before long if you don't.' At the end of a letter to his friend, Jukes says of MacWhirr : 'I think that he got out of it very well for such a stupid man'; and the irony is that the stupidity here is mainly Jukes's, for failing to see that MacWhirr's reticent simplicity has eventually approximated a model of humane practicality.

MacWhirr's wife impatiently skims the letters she receives, unable to imagine the ship's perils or to appreciate her husband's courage. The tale has taught us what she may never learn : of the ordeals faced, in the course of wage-earning, by those whose labours are taken for granted; and of the salutary integrity of obscure and unglamorous individuals whose heroism is not the less for its absence of egoistic eloquence.

It remains for the reader to decide whether Conrad's general presentation of the coolies is culturally patronizing, given that only a European can master their internecine panic, or plausibly consistent, given the thematic need to dramatize their confusion as a daunting challenge. Similarly, the reader may consider whether the tale's political implications are authoritarian, suggesting that a strong leader is needed to meet the threat of social anarchy, or democratic, given that the thick-skinned mariner from a humble background proves equal to a variety of responsibilities and becomes the mentor of his socially-advantaged first mate. Whatever the verdict, the linguistic richness of 'Typhoon' mocks the grey prose of a summary.

II

'Typhoon' was written between September 1900 and January 1901; and almost immediately afterwards, Conrad

wrote 'Falk : A Reminiscence', which he finished in May.
'Typhoon' had been based partly on hearsay, partly on
personal experience of purgatorial voyages through storms
(like the ordeal of the *Palestine*, which survived the tempest
to be destroyed by fire), and partly on Conrad's memory of
an actual Captain MacWhirr, skipper of the sailing-ship
Highland Forest.[2] The only vessel that Conrad himself ever
captained was the *Otago*, a beautiful barque of 346 tons
which was moored at Bangkok when he first joined her. This
Siamese location, coupled with the exhilaration and the cares
of a first command, proved peculiarly fruitful for Conrad's
imagination : the same setting is used for 'Falk', 'The Secret
Sharer' and part of *The Shadow-Line*.[3]

'Falk' is a lucid, leisurely, assured, and efficient tale; the
narrative and its themes are systematically and adroitly
managed. Falk's confession, when it comes, is an account of
horrific privation, of starvation, homicide, and cannibalism;
but the tale as a whole is sunlit, resilient, and affirmative, and
the predominant tone is one of gently humorous irony. The
narratorial control is proficient and even elegant, though we
pay a price for it. There are themes in this story which, elsewhere (as in 'An Outpost of Progress' and 'Heart of Darkness'), Conrad could explore with intensity and searching
complexity; here, the urbanity limits the tale's potential. In
at least two ways, however, that limitation can be seen as
polemical : as a deliberate challenge to expectations. The
first way is that material which we might expect Conrad to
use as the basis of a sombrely sceptical analysis of human
nature and civilized society is here firmly contained within a
social comedy which augments the author's tonal range. The
second way is that if the reader's reflexive response to the
idea of cannibalism is one of revulsion, Conrad mocks that

---

[2] MacWhirr appears as 'good Captain MacW——' in the autobio-
graphical *The Mirror of the Sea* (London : Dent, 1946), pp. 5–6.

[3] The *Otago* and the Siamese location are discussed in *The Mirror
of the Sea*, pp. 18–20, and figure briefly in *Lord Jim*, Chapter 19. The
same vessel appears in the tale 'A Smile of Fortune'.

reflex by attributing it to the mediocre Hermann.[4] 'Don't be shocked', says the narrator; and by a variety of devices the text seeks to allay orthodox misgivings; we are invited to understand and condone—even to approve—Falk's action. One device is the appeal to popularized Darwinism—to the aspect of Darwinism summed up in Herbert Spencer's phrase, 'This survival of the fittest'.[5] 'The best man had survived', says the narrator; 'I saw him before me as though preserved for a witness to the mighty truth of an unerring and eternal principle.' Another device is the appeal to Homeric primitivism : the suggestion that Falk is a survival of an elemental heroic type. In contrast to Hermann's bourgeois domesticity stands an example of primeval directness, force, and simplicity. On the battle between Falk and the carpenter, the narrator comments : 'both had displayed pitiless resolution, endurance, cunning and courage—all the qualities of classic heroism.' And, in stressing the 'Homeric' aspect of Falk, the narrator makes him seem an appropriate suitor to the statuesque and opulently bodied niece, who has 'a beauty of a rustic and olympian order' and induces 'a strain of pagan piety'. There is, however, some tension in the narrative between the sense that Falk's determination to survive, even by cannibalism, is laudable, and the sense that Falk deserves compassion because he is a man neurotically haunted by the horror of his past experience—a quality evoked by his face-wiping gesture, his ascetic, lined face, and his abhorrence of conventional meat-dishes.

Another challenge to delicate susceptibilities (and possibly an affront to feminists) is the narrator's suggestion that there is a clear relationship between Falk's previous craving for food and his present sexual craving for the young woman :

    [4] Conrad said that the basic idea of the tale was 'Contrast between common sentimentality and the clear viewpoint of a rather primitive man (Falk himself) who considers the preservation of life to be the supreme—and moral—law'. (*Lettres françaises*, ed. G. Jean-Aubry [Paris : Gallimard, 1929], p. 45. The original is in French.)

    [5] *The Principles of Biology*, Vol. I (London and Edinburgh : Williams and Norgate, 1864), pp. 444–5.

He was hungry for the girl, terribly hungry, as he had been terribly hungry for food.

Don't be shocked if I declare that in my belief it was the same need, the same pain, the same torture. We are in his case allowed to contemplate the foundation of all the emotions . . . . .

Thus, just as the gourmet's delight in an exquisite meal is a sophistication of a savage's glee at a bloody feast, so 'the infinite gradation in shades and in flavour of our discriminating love' is an evolutionary development of a basic sexual hunger that Falk displays with tragicomic clarity. And, in the tradition of tragicomedy, the whole tale contains affirmatively what elsewhere (in *The Secret Agent*, for example) would be the stuff of pessimism and nightmare.

III

'Pessimism and nightmare' are terms which might, indeed, sum up the main qualities of 'Amy Foster' (written in May and June 1901), that tale of the shipwrecked emigrant 'cast out mysteriously by the sea to perish in the supreme disaster of loneliness and despair'. It's a sombre story of a pious innocent who, in his native land, is deceived into emigration, and who, after narrowly surviving a shipwreck, is treated brutally and uncomprehendingly. ('If it hadn't been for the steel cross at Miss Swaffer's belt, he would not, he confessed, have known whether he was in a Christian country at all.') If Amy, at least, grants him charity, kindness, and eventually the sanctuary of marriage, the sanctuary is brief : terrified by his incomprehensible demands for water during his fever, she flees from him and leaves him to die. ' "Why?" he cried, in the penetrating and indignant voice of a man calling to a responsible Maker. A gust of wind and a swish of rain answered.'

There is no doubt that, as Bertrand Russell suggested,[6] in

---

[6] *The Autobiography of Bertrand Russell: 1872–1914* (London: Allen and Unwin, 1967), pp. 208–9.

this tale Conrad has precipitated some of his own deep fears and anxieties as a Polish exile living in an adopted country; a land where, in rural areas particularly, the inhabitants might have been slow to welcome a stranger who spoke with a marked foreign accent. ('I feel myself strangely growing into a sort of outcast. A mental and moral outcast', he once wrote.[7]) Furthermore, a revealingly unintentional commentary on 'Amy Foster' is provided by Jessie Conrad's recollections of her honeymoon with Joseph in 1896, during which he was ill with fever :

For a whole long week, the fever ran high and for most of the time J.C. was delirious. To see him lying in the white canopied bed, dark-faced, with gleaming teeth and shining eyes, was sufficiently impressive, but to hear him muttering to himself in a strange tongue (he thinks he must have been speaking Polish)[,] to be unable to penetrate the clouded mind or catch one intelligible word, was for a young inexperienced girl truly awful . . . . .[8]

The personal implications of the tale are evident, but that personal material has been carefully, even dourly, controlled and objectified. Yanko Goorall is no Korzeniowski but a holy fool, an innocent and ignorant Slavic peasant; and a variety of source material has contributed to the story. Ford Madox Ford claimed to have supplied its basis, for his chronicle *The Cinque Ports* told of a shipwrecked seaman from a German vessel who had wandered about near Romney in Kent, uncomprehended and unaided, before being found asleep in a pig-sty.[9] The character of Amy Foster was, according to Jessie Conrad,[10] based on that of the Conrads' servant-girl;

[7] G. Jean-Aubry, *Joseph Conrad: Life and Letters*, Vol. I (London: Heinemann, 1927), p. 317.

[8] *Personal Recollections of Joseph Conrad* (London: privately printed, 1924), pp. 25–6.

[9] F. M. Ford, *Joseph Conrad: A Personal Remembrance* (London: Duckworth, 1924), pp. 120, 132; F. M. Hueffer (later Ford), *The Cinque Ports* (Edinburgh and London: Blackwood, 1900), p.163.

[10] *Joseph Conrad as I Knew Him* (London: Heinemann, 1926), p. 118.

and the Kentish location was well known to them, since they were then living at Pent Farm, near Hythe. Other material was more literary: Jocelyn Baines[11] has seen a parallel between the villagers' response to Yanko Goorall and the treatment of the mysterious Gilliat in Victor Hugo's *Les Travailleurs de la mer*, while Elsa Nettels[12] suggests that Stephen Crane's tale 'The Monster' may have provided hints. Conrad had long studied Maupassant, whose tales offer grimly realistic depictions of tough villagers. And English readers will readily relate Conrad's story to the sombre side of the Romantic tradition, particularly to the depictions of rural harshness and suffering in Crabbe's *The Village* and *The Borough*, in some of Wordsworth's *Lyrical Ballads*, and eventually in Thomas Hardy's *Tess of the d'Urbervilles* and *Jude the Obscure*. 'Amy Foster' is a classic statement of Conradian pessimism; but, when the narrator describes the Kentish landscape, the tones of elegiac bleakness could be those of Hardy.

With the sun hanging low on its western limit, the expanse of the grass-lands framed in the counter-scarps of the rising ground took on a gorgeous and sombre aspect. A sense of penetrating sadness, like that inspired by a grave strain of music, disengaged itself from the silence of the fields. The men we met walked past, slow, unsmiling, with downcast eyes, as if the melancholy of an over-burdened earth had weighted their feet, bowed their shoulders, borne down their glances.

'Yes,' said the doctor . . . . . 'one would think the earth is under a curse, since of all her children these that cling to her the closest are uncouth in body and as leaden of gait as if their very hearts were loaded with chains.'

This is an eloquent mystification of the drudgery of rural work; yet mystification it remains, with its suggestion that

[11] *Joseph Conrad: A Critical Biography* (London: Weidenfeld and Nicolson, 1960), pp. 266–7.

[12] ' "Amy Foster" and Stephen Crane's "The Monster" ', *Conradiana* XV (1983), pp. 181–90.

the drudges partake of an enduring and seemingly irremediable 'curse' of 'an over-burdened earth'. To the reader who travels through Kent in a blossoming springtime, the tale's selectivity is apparent : those 'chains' are not so inexorable; yet in its dramatization of the ways in which ignorance and fear can generate national or racial prejudice, 'Amy Foster' imparts an indignation which resists the narrative's presentment of a condition so absolute that only a stoical sigh appears the proper response.

IV

'The Secret Sharer' was written towards the end of 1908. It is generally regarded as one of Conrad's finest tales, and has attracted numerous and diverse interpretations. It is lucid, concise, tense, exciting, and enigmatic; and in its morality there is a grittily resistant feature which may encourage critics to secrete around it the putative pearl of a smoothing exegesis. If a literary text has evident merit, the critic may be tempted to imply that it also has the astuteness to share his or her moral biases; but the text is under no such flattering obligation. Its merit may lie in its qualities of articulate intelligence, and its paraphrasable morality may be harsher than the critic would like it to be.

'The Secret Sharer' is a tale which succeeds in being at once satisfyingly straightforward and intriguingly mysterious. After the deceptive calm of the opening, there follows the shock of the unexpected visitant, the suspense aroused by the young captain's endeavour to conceal the fugitive, and the climactic suspense entailed by the captain's determination to take his ship perilously close to a rocky shore while the fugitive escapes. The narrative is terse and economical, and our interest is engaged by a relay-race of questions : Who is the fugitive? How can he be successfully concealed? Will the captain succeed in mastering the new ship while yet helping the law-breaker? And will the vessel finally survive the manoeuvre? Broadly, the central principle of suspense is that the evidence to support a reader's prediction of a successful outcome is almost evenly matched by evidence to support a prediction of a disastrous outcome. The story is well paced; every detail counts; numerous ironies are generated; and the sense of conspiratorial confinement (and, finally, of wilfully perilous navigation) is admirably evoked.

What makes the tale so tempting to read and re-read, and what makes it so seductive to commentators, is the fact that while, as narrative sequence, it is so straightforward, it generates a variety of enigmas, connotations, and problems. Obviously, it has the resonance of a work which extends the *Doppelgänger* tradition. This literary tradition burgeoned in the Romantic period and continued through the nineteenth century into the twentieth; representative texts include Poe's 'William Wilson', Dostoevsky's 'The Double', and Stevenson's 'Dr Jekyll and Mr Hyde'. The main convention in such texts is that an uncanny complicity is established between two apparently contrasting characters : their relationship is symbiotic. Sometimes the connection is supernatural, one character being an external manifestation of part of the other : thus, the whispering Mr Wilson represents the conscience of the debauched Mr Wilson, while Mr Hyde represents the depraved clandestine self of the respectable Dr Jekyll. In Conrad's tale there are various uncanny features: the captain and the fugitive are remarkably similar, in that both are former *Conway* boys, both are young 'gentlemen' who are socially superior to their respective crews, and one seems providentially placed to save the other; furthermore the captain is immediately sympathetic to the fugitive and has no hesitation in deciding to shelter him. Nevertheless, Conrad's treatment is predominantly secular and realistic: Leggatt is two years younger than the fictional narrator, is rather different in temperament (tougher, more impatient and decisive), and eventually goes his own way, leaving his former protector to an independent career. Albert Guerard's attempt to interpret Leggatt as some kind of Freudian 'id' or Jungian 'anima',[13] as a repressed part of the hero's psyche,

[13] *Conrad the Novelist* (Cambridge, Mass.: Harvard University Press, 1965), pp. 14–16, 25–6.

is resisted by the tale's predominant realism, which—Guerard conceded—establishes very fully (by means of the hue and cry, for example) the objective existence of Leggatt. Much more germane is Guerard's observation of a recurrent paradox in Conrad's work; namely, 'a deep commitment to order in society and in the self—doubled by [i.e. accompanied by] incorrigible sympathy for the outlaw, whether existing in society or the self'.[14] 'The Secret Sharer' offers a vivid illustration of this paradox.

Leggatt has killed a man while striving to set the sail. He believes himself to be entirely justified in his homicidal action, since the sail saved the imperilled ship. The hero of the tale, the anonymous young captain, promptly endorses Leggatt's view and successfully enables Leggatt to elude the laws of the land and of the sea. An unsavoury moral implication of the tale is clearly this: that some men constitute a bold élite with the right to override long-established moral and legal principles. Such men, it seems, may justifiably commit homicide if the act coincides with the survival of a ship, and the justification is not one which needs to be presented in court. Conrad's 'sympathy with the outlaw' is evident; and the paradox is completed when we see that this outlaw believes that he was a better defender of 'order' on the *Sephora* than her own master.

The bond between the hero and Leggatt is partly an irrational, instinctive one: they have an immediate, intuitive understanding. It is partly a matter of caste and class: they are both 'officers and gentlemen', middle-class ex-*Conway* trainees, socially more polished than their fellow-seamen, sharing the freemasonry of members of the same rather exclusive school or club. We may recall E. M. Forster's famous pronouncement: 'if I had to choose between betraying my country and betraying my friend, I hope I should have the guts to betray my country'.[15] The reference to Forster is doubly appropriate when we notice that 'The

14 Ibid., p. 58.
15 *Two Cheers for Democracy* (London: Arnold, 1951), p. 78.

Secret Sharer' has a mild, muted, homophile aspect. In the hero, the sense of intuitive comradeship modulates, very reticently, towards love: he stares fascinated as his 'other self' lies on the bed; and the long, lingering parting resembles that of lovers: 'Our eyes met; several seconds elapsed, till, our glances still mingled, I extended my hand and turned the lamp out.' During their final moments together, Leggatt seems to think that the hero is engaging him in some kind of embrace, which he has to fend off:

> We were in the sail-locker, scrambling on our knees over the sails . . . . . I snatched off my floppy hat and tried hurriedly in the dark to ram it on my other self. He dodged and fended off silently. I wonder what he thought had come to me before he understood and suddenly desisted. Our hands met gropingly, lingered united in a steady, motionless clasp for a second . . . . . No word was breathed by either of us when they separated.

Furthermore, the hero's insistence that Leggatt is his complement ('my other self', 'my double', 'the secret sharer of my life'), particularly in the remark, 'I felt less torn in two when I was with him', may recall to us Aristophanes' explanation of homosexuality: 'Man's original body having been thus cut in two, each half yearned for the half from which it had been severed.'[16]

The young captain's truest love, however, is for his ship, whereas the master of the *Sephora* has committed a kind of maritime infidelity by bringing his wife aboard *his* vessel. The hero's situation on his first command has some resemblance to that of a newly wed husband when, just at the start of the honeymoon, a fascinating male visitor arrives and by his presence causes numerous distractions and problems; but at length the intruder departs, and the delayed honeymoon can at last begin in earnest, its joys now the more fully to be savoured. As the narrator puts it:

[16] Plato, *The Symposium*, tr. W. Hamilton (Harmondsworth: Penguin, 1951), p. 61.

I did not know her. Would she do it? How was she to be handled?

. . . . . I was alone with her. Nothing! no one in the world should stand now between us, throwing a shadow on the way of silent knowledge and mute affection, the perfect communion of a seaman with his first command.

This is one of many symmetries or near-symmetries in the narrative: it begins with the hero's hopes of communion; interruption and distraction follow; and finally communion is restored. A related symmetry is that while a well-intentioned action by him introduced the initial crisis, another well-intentioned action resolves the final crisis. In order to get to know the ship better, the captain had taken on himself the duty of the first anchor-watch. This disrupted the formal routine of watch-setting, so that the ladder was left alongside instead of being drawn up; and it was this ladder that caused the fugitive to linger at the ship. Near the end of the story, when the fugitive is attempting to escape overboard, the captain impulsively puts his own floppy hat on Leggatt's head (so that it may later shield him from the tropical sun ashore); and the hat, falling into the sea, forms the salutary marker that helps the captain to avert shipwreck. A large irony is that while Leggatt had thought it right to kill a man in order to save a ship and her crew, the hero thinks it right to imperil a ship and her crew in order to save a man.

In so far as the narrative endorses Leggatt's conduct, it seems to commend a provocatively élitist and ruthless ethic. Other Conradian narratives (notably 'Heart of Darkness' and *Nostromo*) offer contrasting commendations. In 'The Secret Sharer', Conrad has chosen to dramatize a strange and lucid challenge to orthodox ideas of law and justice. But it remains a dramatization, not a manifesto; it is a fictional narrative, not a testament. There exists no encephalograph or cardiograph which can tell us precisely the extent to which, while we are experiencing a work of fiction, our sense of imaginative escape from real ethical problems is outweighed (if at all) by our sense that searching questions have been directed from the text towards that ethical actuality. The satisfyingly vivid descriptive texture of this tale may make it more seductively escapist or more provocatively challenging. For most readers, the appeal probably lies in its distinctive combination of both effects. 'The Secret Sharer' is a yarn and a rune; an imaginative sanctuary which proves to be a baited trap.

NOTE ON THE TEXT

THE specified copy-text of this edition is the Collected Edition of Conrad's work published by J. M. Dent & Sons (London) between 1946 and 1955. Thus the copy-text for 'Typhoon', 'Falk' and 'Amy Foster' is *Typhoon and Other Stories*, published (in a double volume with *The Nigger of the 'Narcissus'*) by Dent in 1950, while that for 'The Secret Sharer' is within *'Twixt Land and Sea: Three Tales*, published by Dent in 1947. According to Gordon Lindstrand and J. H. Stape, that Collected Edition derived from a new impression of the plates originally used for the Sun-Dial Edition issued by Doubleday of New York in 1920–21 and later used for the Uniform Edition (Dent, 1923–8).

'Typhoon' was first published as a serial in the *Pall Mall Magazine* (London) between January and March 1902. In book form, it was first issued (as *Typhoon*) by G. P. Putnam's Sons, New York, in September 1902, and subsequently (in *Typhoon and Other Stories*) by William Heinemann, London, in April 1903.

'Falk: A Reminiscence' was not serialized. Conrad recalled, 'I think the copy was shown to the editor of some magazine who rejected it indignantly on the sole ground that "the girl never says anything"' ('Author's Note', 1919, p. viii). 'Amy Foster' first appeared in the *Illustrated London News* on 14, 21, and 28 December 1901.

'The Secret Sharer' was originally published (as 'The Secret-Sharer') in *Harper's Monthly Magazine*, New York, in August and September 1910, before appearing in book form in the collection *'Twixt Land and Sea: Tales* (London: Dent, October 1912; New York: Doran, December 1912).

The present volume has not been commissioned as a critical edition, and therefore it offers a text which has been emended but not radically revised. My emendations of the copy-text are listed below. I have corrected misprints and spelling errors; and, when it seemed essential in order to clarify the sense, I have emended the punctuation. Conspicuous inconsistencies have been regularized (so that 'bo'ss'en', 'boss'n', 'boss'en' and 'bo's'n' become 'bosun'), but inconspicuous inconsistencies (like the widely-separated 'wagon' and 'waggon', or 'roadstead' and 'Roadstead') have been allowed to remain. A second list gives some samples of the differences between the magazine texts and the present texts.

List of Emendations

p.11, l.10:	bosun *for* bo'ss'en
20, 13:	country *for* county
41, 26:	gleam of *for* gleam on
46, 34:	over *for* ever
49, 31:	bosun *for* boss'n
49, 32:	bosun *for* boss'n
51, 4:	'tween-deck *for* 'tween deck
57, 11:	was as though *for* was though
59, 33:	Bosun *for* Boss'n
60, 1:	bosun *for* boss'n
60, 8:	bosun *for* boss'n
68, 34:	below, the *for* below the
81, 29:	"Had *for* Had
87, 10:	bosun *for* boss'en
100, 6:	bosun *for* boss'en
102, 23:	books.' *for* books.
106, 13:	Plate *for* Platte
106, 29–30:	forward were *for* were forward
113, 30:	opened hopefully, *for* opened, hopefully
116, 22:	world-proof *for* world proof
127, 35:	out— he *for* out-he
132, 1:	brought out the *for* brought the
132, 13–14:	unheard-of *for* unheard of
159, 23:	this, Schomberg *for* this Schomberg
172, 30:	called, vulgar *for* called vulgar
186, 4:	Break-down *for* Break down

189, 32 :   ropes' *for* rope's
204, 33 :   brick *for* black
209, 17 :   startled— glance *for* startled, glance
209, 26 :   blur *for* blurr
221, 19 :   found, a *for* found a
230, 1 :   seeing *for* see
238, 26 :   wicket-gate *for* wicker-gate
253, 15 :   *Conway for* Conway
253, 17 :   *Conway for* Conway
254, 24 :   yelling, "Look *for* yelling, Look
254, 31 :   forebitts *for* forebits
256, 31 :   L, the *for* L the
258, 25 :   *Conway for* Conway
271, 22 :   "Sui—cide ! *for* "Sui-cide !
273, 33 :   "*Sephora*'s *for* "*Sephora's*
279, 20 :   pâté *for* paté
281, 34 :   eyes, I *for* eyes I

Samples of Differences between the Magazine-Texts and the Book-Texts

Conrad was a diligent reviser of his works, and this fact accounts for many (though not all) of the differences between the magazine texts and the present texts of 'Typhoon', 'Amy Foster', and 'The Secret Sharer'. The main narratives remain unchanged, but there are numerous differences in detail. I give below some samples—samples only—of these. The present text is quoted first; the magazine version follows in square brackets.

'Typhoon'

p.61, l.30:   shop in the East-end of London. [shop.]
70, 24–7:   The water in the bilges thundered at each roll, and lumps of coal skipped to and fro, from end to end, rattling like an avalanche of pebbles on a slope of iron. [Lumps of coal skipped to and fro, from end to end, rattling like an avalanche on a slope of iron.]

73, 1 :   He waited. [He listened.]
73, 19 :   hands with you . . . , [hands . . . ,]
73, 21 :   do with them, [do with the hands,]
73, 28 :   a desperate leap. [a leap.]
84, 12 :   ever seen in his life. [ever seen.]
92, 7 :   by for a job— [by—]
94, 2–3 :   salary before. What was the matter now? [salary.]
101, 19 :   leave off jawing [leave off]
102, 24 :   he got out of it very well [he had not done badly]

'Amy Foster'

203, 19–20 :   squatting at the water's edge [squatting]
204, 25 :   the half-open door [the door left open]
205, 1 :   up to [up from a trot to]
205, 27 :   Isaac [Amos]
206, 6 :   rise near the road [rise]
206, 9 :   rose [rosy]
207, 1–2 :   her heart was of the kindest [her heart is of the kindest]
209, 33–5 :   A poor emigrant from Central Europe bound to America and washed ashore here in a storm. And [A poor emigrant. And]
211, 20 :   world, there is not one, it seems to me, that [world I have read of, not one, it seems to me]
213, 30–1 :   America straight away [America]
223, 6 (and subsequently) : Swaffer [Rigby]

'The Secret Sharer' ['The Secret-Sharer']

243, 23 :   Meinam [Mekong]
244, 1 :   monotonous [undistinguished]
244, 8 :   My eye followed [But presently my eye caught]
246, 18 :   infinitely. The ship [infinitely. We had been having scorpion at every meal, and the second mate's lip had been kept on the quiver all the time. The ship]

247, 7:	the crew [the men]
248, 30:	mysterious shades [impenetrable mysteriousness]
249, 7:	My action [It]
249, 11:	new captain [strange captain]
249, 25:	something elongated [something fish-like, elongated]
249, 35:	head. A headless corpse! The [head. The]
250, 31:	But, for [This impression remained, though for]
251, 13:	about his limbs [about him]
251, 18:	quietly [seriously]
252, 7:	called. [called and wander out of his berth to have a look at the weather.]
254, 24–5:	yelling, "Look out! look out!" [yelling.]
257, 7:	But that way was never used. [But that door was kept always locked.]
257, 22:	seven weeks [nine weeks]
268, 2:	smeary [intense]
268, 7:	I behaved with a politeness [I received him with an icy punctilious politeness]
272, 6:	Not heartily! [Heartily?]
272, 9:	Surlily? Yes, but surliness [Surliness]
272, 11:	punctilious [a chilly, distant]
273, 31 (and subsequently):	whiskers [mustaches]
274, 11–12:	and just saved myself by [but it was]
284, 17:	I know [you know]
290, 18:	flew [fled]
291, 14:	may [will]
294, 14:	strained [forced]
295, 5:	The stars [All the stars]

Note on Omissions

In quotations which appear in the Introduction, Notes, and Glossary, a row of five dots (. . . . .) represents an omission that I have made, whereas a row of three or four dots represents an ellipsis already present in the material being quoted.

Asterisks

An asterisk in the text indicates the availability of an explanatory note.

SELECT BIBLIOGRAPHY

DENT'S Collected Edition (1946–55) contains almost all Conrad's works except the fragment called *The Sisters*, the dramatizations, and a tale written in collaboration with Ford Madox Hueffer (who later became Ford Madox Ford), *The Nature of a Crime. Congo Diary and Other Uncollected Pieces* (ed. Zdzislaw Najder, 1978) contains Conrad's Congo notebooks, *The Sisters*, *The Nature of a Crime*, and other minor pieces. Cambridge University Press is preparing a scholarly edition of the canon.

Important editions of Conrad's letters are as follows: G. Jean-Aubry : *Joseph Conrad: Life and Letters* (2 vols., 1927); *Letters from Conrad, 1895 to 1924* (ed. Edward Garnett, 1928); *Letters of Joseph Conrad to Marguerite Poradowska* (tr. and ed. J. A. Gee and P. J. Sturm, 1940); and *Conrad's Polish Background* (ed. Z. Najder, 1964). There are further collections by Richard Curle (1928), G. Jean-Aubry (1930), William Blackburn (1958), D. B. J. Randall (1968), and Cedric Watts (1969). In 1983 appeared Volume I (ed. F. R. Karl and Laurence Davies) of *The Collected Letters of Joseph Conrad*; further volumes have been prepared.

Informative memoirs of Conrad include those by Ford Madox Ford (1924), Jessie Conrad (1926 and 1935), Richard Curle (1928), Bertrand Russell (1967), Borys Conrad (1970), and John Conrad (1981). Notable critical biographies have been written by Jocelyn Baines (1960), Bernard Meyer (a 'psycho-analytic' biography, 1967), Frederick Karl (1979), and Ian Watt (*Conrad in the Nineteenth Century*, 1980). An important scholarly account is Zdzisław Najder's *Joseph Conrad: A Chronicle* (1983).

Probably the most influential of the biographically-related studies which make substantial use of documentary material are : J. D. Gordan, *Joseph Conrad: The Making of a Novelist* (1940), and Norman Sherry, *Conrad's Eastern World* (1966) and *Conrad's Western World* (1971). There are further relevant studies by Richard Curle (1914), Edward Crankshaw (1936),

Gustav Morf (1930 and 1976), R. L. Mégroz (1931), J. H. Retinger (1941), Jerry Allen (1965), and Norman Sherry (1972).

Of the numerous critical books on Conrad, the following may be found fruitful: Douglas Hewitt, *Conrad: A Reassessment* (1952), Thomas Moser, *Joseph Conrad: Achievement and Decline* (1957), Albert Guerard, *Conrad the Novelist* (1958), R. W. Stallman (ed.), *The Art of Joseph Conrad* (1960), Eloise Knapp Hay, *The Political Novels of Joseph Conrad* (1963), Avrom Fleishman, *Conrad's Politics* (1967), C. B. Cox, *Joseph Conrad: The Modern Imagination* (1974), Jacques Berthoud, *Joseph Conrad: The Major Phase* (1978), and Cedric Watts, *A Preface to Conrad* (1982) and *The Deceptive Text* (1984). Other studies of interest are by Paul Kirschner (1968), Bruce Johnson (1971), and Jan Verleun (1978 and 1979). There are important essays on Conrad in F. R. Leavis, *The Great Tradition* (1948) and *'Anna Karenina' and Other Essays* (1967), J. Hillis Miller, *Poets of Reality* (1966), Norman Sherry (ed.), *Joseph Conrad: A Commemoration* (1976), and Tzvetan Todorov, *Les Genres du discours* (1978).

Early reviews of 'Typhoon', 'Falk', 'Amy Foster' and 'The Secret Sharer' are reprinted in *Conrad: The Critical Heritage* (1973). The magazine *Conradiana* (published thrice a year at Lubbock, Texas, by Texas Tech University) has featured various articles on these tales.

A CHRONOLOGY OF JOSEPH CONRAD

1857   3 December: born Józef Teodor Konrad Korzeniow-
        ski, of Polish parents in the Ukraine.

1861   His father, poet and translator Apollo Korzeniowski,
        arrested for patriotic conspiracy.

1862   Conrad's parents exiled to Vologda, Russia; their son
        accompanies them.

1865   Death of his mother.

1869   Death of Apollo Korzeniowski in Kraków; Conrad
        becomes the ward of his uncle, Tadeusz Bobrowski.

1874   Leaves Poland for Marseille to become a trainee sea-
        man with the French merchant navy.

1876   As a 'steward' on the *Saint-Antoine*, becomes
        acquainted with Dominic Cervoni (who appears in
        The Mirror of the Sea, *A Personal Record* and *The
        Arrow of Gold*, and who is a source for Nostromo and
        for Peyrol in *The Rover*).

1877   Possibly involved in smuggling arms from Marseille to
        the 'Carlists' (Spanish royalists).

1878   March: shoots himself in the chest but is not seriously
        injured; as a direct result of this suicide attempt his
        uncle clears his debts. April: joins his first British ship,
        the *Mavis*, and later in the year joins the *Skimmer
        of the Sea*.

1886   August: becomes a British citizen. (Formerly, as a
        Russian citizen and the son of a convict, Conrad was
        liable for Russian military service.) November: passes
        the examination for a Master's certificate.

1887   In hospital in Singapore with an injury sustained on
        the *Highland Forest*.

1887–8 Gets to know the Malay Archipelago as an officer of
        the *Vidar*.

1888   Master of the *Otago*, his only command. (The *Otago* voyages provided a basis of 'Falk', 'The Secret Sharer', *The Shadow-Line*, and 'A Smile of Fortune'.)

1889   Resigns from the *Otago*, settles briefly in London and begins to write *Almayer's Folly*. Begins a lasting friendship with Marguerite Poradowska.

1890   Works in the Belgian Congo for the Société Anonyme pour le Commerce du Haut-Congo.

1891–3   His pleasantest experience at sea, as an officer of the *Torrens*; meets John Galsworthy, who is among the passengers and becomes a loyal friend.

1893   Autumn : meets Jessie George.

1894   February : death of Tadeusz Bobrowski. October: *Almayer's Folly* accepted by Unwin. Meets Edward Garnett, Unwin's reader and an influential literary friend.

1895   *Almayer's Folly* published.

1896   *An Outcast of the Islands* published. Becomes acquainted with H. G. Wells. 24 March : marriage to Jessie George. Begins work on *The Rescue* and initiates correspondence with Henry James.

1897   Corresponds with R. B. Cunninghame Graham (to be a close friend and a source for Gould in *Nostromo*). *The Nigger of the 'Narcissus'* published.

1898   *Tales of Unrest* ('Karain', 'The Idiots', 'An Outpost of Progress', 'The Return', 'The Lagoon') published. Enters into collaboration with Ford Madox Ford (then surnamed Hueffer). Takes over from Ford the lease of a Kentish farmhouse, 'The Pent'. Friendship with Stephen Crane. Borys Conrad born.

1899   'Heart of Darkness' serialized in *Blackwood's Magazine*. J. B. Pinker becomes Conrad's literary agent.

1899–1900   *Lord Jim* serialized in *Blackwood's*.

1900   Stephen Crane dies. *Lord Jim* published as a book.

1901   *The Inheritors* (collaboration with Ford) published.

1902   *Youth: A Narrative; and Two Other Stories* ('Youth', 'Heart of Darkness', 'The End of the Tether') published. *Typhoon* published in New York.

1903 *Typhoon and Other Stories* ('Typhoon', 'Amy Foster', 'Falk', 'Tomorrow') and *Romance* (collaboration with Ford) published.

1904 Jessie Conrad injures her knees and is partially disabled for life. *Nostromo* published.

1906 Meets Arthur Marwood, who becomes a close friend. John Conrad born. *The Mirror of the Sea* published.

1907 The Conrads move to Someries, Luton Hoo. *The Secret Agent* published.

1908 *A Set of Six* ('Gaspar Ruiz', 'The Informer', 'The Brute', 'An Anarchist', 'The Duel', 'Il Conde') published.

1909 Quarrels with Ford over his contributions to *The English Review*. The Conrads move to a cottage at Aldington, near 'The Pent'.

1910 Completion of *Under Western Eyes* accompanied by a nervous breakdown; Conrad lies in bed holding 'converse with the characters' of the novel. On his recovery the Conrads move to Capel House, Orlestone.

1911 *Under Western Eyes* published.

1912 *A Personal Record* and *'Twixt Land and Sea* ('A Smile of Fortune', 'The Secret Sharer', 'Freya of the Seven Isles') published. *Chance* serialized in *New York Herald*.

1914 *Chance* has very good sales, especially in America; the earlier works now find a larger public. The Conrads visit Poland and are nearly trapped by the outbreak of war.

1915 *Within the Tides* ('The Planter of Malata', 'The Partner', 'The Inn of the Two Witches') and *Victory* published.

1917 *The Shadow-Line* published. Conrad begins to write 'Author's Notes' for a collected edition of his works.

1919 *The Arrow of Gold* published. The Conrads move to Oswalds, Bishopsbourne, near Canterbury.

1920   *The Rescue* published, 24 years after it was begun.

1921   Visit to Corsica for research on *Suspense*. Conrad in poor health. *Notes on Life and Letters* published.

1923   Conrad visits America and is lionized. *The Rover* published.

1924   May: declines the offer of a knighthood. 3 August: dies of a heart attack at Oswalds; buried at Canterbury. *The Nature of a Crime* (collaboration with Ford) published.

1925   *Tales of Hearsay* ('The Warrior's Soul', 'Prince Roman', 'The Tale', 'The Black Mate') and *Suspense* published.

1926   *Last Essays* published.

1928   *The Sisters* (fragment) published.

TYPHOON*

TYPHOON

I

CAPTAIN MACWHIRR, of the steamer *Nan-Shan*, had a physiognomy that, in the order of material appearances, was the exact counterpart of his mind: it presented no marked characteristics of firmness or stupidity; it had no pronounced characteristics whatever; it was simply ordinary, irresponsive, and unruffled.

The only thing his aspect might have been said to suggest, at times, was bashfulness; because he would sit, in business offices ashore, sunburnt and smiling faintly, with downcast eyes. When he raised them, they were perceived to be direct in their glance and of blue colour. His hair was fair and extremely fine, clasping from temple to temple the bald dome of his skull in a clamp as of fluffy silk. The hair of his face, on the contrary, carroty and flaming, resembled a growth of copper wire clipped short to the line of the lip; while, no matter how close he shaved, fiery metallic gleams passed, when he moved his head, over the surface of his cheeks. He was rather below the medium height, a bit round-shouldered, and so sturdy of limb that his clothes always looked a shade too tight for his arms and legs. As if unable to grasp what is due to the difference of latitudes, he wore a brown bowler hat, a complete suit of a brownish hue, and clumsy black boots. These harbour togs gave to his thick figure an air of stiff and uncouth smartness. A thin silver watch-

chain looped his waistcoat, and he never left his ship
for the shore without clutching in his powerful, hairy
fist an elegant umbrella of the very best quality, but
generally unrolled. Young Jukes, the chief mate, attending his commander to the gangway, would sometimes venture to say, with the greatest gentleness,
"Allow me, sir"—and possessing himself of the umbrella
deferentially, would elevate the ferule, shake the folds,
twirl a neat furl in a jiffy, and hand it back; going
through the performance with a face of such portentous
gravity, that Mr. Solomon Rout, the chief engineer,
smoking his morning cigar over the skylight, would
turn away his head in order to hide a smile. "Oh!
aye! The blessed gamp. . . . Thank 'ee, Jukes,
thank 'ee," would mutter Captain MacWhirr, heartily,
without looking up.

Having just enough imagination to carry him through
each successive day, and no more, he was tranquilly
sure of himself; and from the very same cause he was
not in the least conceited. It is your imaginative
superior who is touchy, overbearing, and difficult to
please; but every ship Captain MacWhirr commanded
was the floating abode of harmony and peace. It was,
in truth, as impossible for him to take a flight of fancy
as it would be for a watchmaker to put together a
chronometer with nothing except a two-pound hammer
and a whip-saw in the way of tools. Yet the uninteresting lives of men so entirely given to the actuality
of the bare existence have their mysterious side. It
was impossible in Captain MacWhirr's case, for instance, to understand what under heaven could have
induced that perfectly satisfactory son of a petty grocer
in Belfast to run away to sea. And yet he had done
that very thing at the age of fifteen. It was enough,
when you thought it over, to give you the idea of an

immense, potent, and invisible hand thrust into the ant-heap of the earth, laying hold of shoulders, knocking heads together, and setting the unconscious faces of the multitude towards inconceivable goals and in undreamt-of directions.

His father never really forgave him for this undutiful stupidity. "We could have got on without him," he used to say later on, "but there's the business. And he an only son, too!" His mother wept very much after his disappearance. As it had never occurred to him to leave word behind, he was mourned over for dead till, after eight months, his first letter arrived from Talcahuano. It was short, and contained the statement: "We had very fine weather on our passage out." But evidently, in the writer's mind, the only important intelligence was to the effect that his captain had, on the very day of writing, entered him regularly on the ship's articles as Ordinary Seaman. "Because I can do the work," he explained. The mother again wept copiously, while the remark, "Tom's an ass," expressed the emotions of the father. He was a corpulent man, with a gift for sly chaffing, which to the end of his life he exercised in his intercourse with his son, a little pityingly, as if upon a half-witted person.

MacWhirr's visits to his home were necessarily rare, and in the course of years he despatched other letters to his parents, informing them of his successive promotions and of his movements upon the vast earth. In these missives could be found sentences like this: "The heat here is very great." Or: "On Christmas day at 4 P. M. we fell in with some icebergs." The old people ultimately became acquainted with a good many names of ships, and with the names of the skippers who commanded them—with the names of Scots and

English shipowners—with the names of seas, oceans, straits, promontories—with outlandish names of lumber-ports, of rice-ports, of cotton-ports—with the names of islands—with the name of their son's young woman. She was called Lucy. It did not suggest itself to him to mention whether he thought the name pretty. And then they died.

The great day of MacWhirr's marriage came in due course, following shortly upon the great day when he got his first command.

All these events had taken place many years before the morning when, in the chart-room of the steamer *Nan-Shan*, he stood confronted by the fall of a barometer he had no reason to distrust. The fall—taking into account the excellence of the instrument, the time of the year, and the ship's position on the terrestrial globe—was of a nature ominously prophetic; but the red face of the man betrayed no sort of inward disturbance. Omens were as nothing to him, and he was unable to discover the message of a prophecy till the fulfilment had brought it home to his very door. "That's a fall, and no mistake," he thought. "There must be some uncommonly dirty weather knocking about."

The *Nan-Shan* was on her way from the southward to the treaty port of Fu-chau, with some cargo in her lower holds, and two hundred Chinese coolies returning to their village homes in the province of Fo-kien, after a few years of work in various tropical colonies. The morning was fine, the oily sea heaved without a sparkle, and there was a queer white misty patch in the sky like a halo of the sun. The fore-deck, packed with Chinamen, was full of sombre clothing, yellow faces, and pigtails, sprinkled over with a good many naked shoulders, for there was no wind, and the heat was close. The coolies lounged, talked, smoked, or stared over the rail; some, drawing water over the side, sluiced each other; a few slept on hatches, while several small parties of six sat on their heels surrounding iron trays with plates of rice and tiny teacups; and every single Celestial of them was carrying with him all he had in the world—a wooden chest with a ringing lock and brass on the corners, containing the savings of his labours: some clothes of ceremony, sticks of incense, a little opium maybe, bits of nameless rubbish of conventional value, and a small hoard of silver dollars, toiled for in coal lighters, won in gambling-houses or in petty trading, grubbed out of earth, sweated out in mines, on railway lines, in deadly jungle, under heavy burdens—amassed patiently, guarded with care, cherished fiercely.

A cross swell had set in from the direction of Formosa Channel about ten o'clock, without disturbing these passengers much, because the *Nan-Shan*, with her flat bottom, rolling chocks on bilges, and great breadth of beam, had the reputation of an exceptionally steady ship in a sea-way. Mr. Jukes, in moments of expansion on shore, would proclaim loudly that the "old girl was as good as she was pretty." It would never have occurred to Captain MacWhirr to express his favourable opinion so loud or in terms so fanciful.

She was a good ship, undoubtedly, and not old either. She had been built in Dumbarton less than three years before, to the order of a firm of merchants in Siam—Messrs. Sigg* and Son. When she lay afloat, finished in every detail and ready to take up the work of her life, the builders contemplated her with pride.

"Sigg has asked us for a reliable skipper to take her out," remarked one of the partners; and the other, after reflecting for a while, said: "I think MacWhirr is ashore just at present." "Is he? Then wire him at once. He's the very man," declared the senior, without a moment's hesitation.

Next morning MacWhirr stood before them unperturbed, having travelled from London by the midnight express after a sudden but undemonstrative parting with his wife. She was the daughter of a superior couple who had seen better days.

"We had better be going together over the ship, Captain," said the senior partner; and the three men started to view the perfections of the *Nan-Shan* from stem to stern, and from her keelson to the trucks of her two stumpy pole-masts.

Captain MacWhirr had begun by taking off his coat, which he hung on the end of a steam windlass embodying all the latest improvements.

"My uncle wrote of you favourably by yesterday's mail to our good friends—Messrs. Sigg, you know—and doubtless they'll continue you out there in command," said the junior partner. "You'll be able to boast of being in charge of the handiest boat of her size on the coast of China, Captain," he added.

"Have you? Thank 'ee," mumbled vaguely Mac-Whirr, to whom the view of a distant eventuality could appeal no more than the beauty of a wide landscape to a purblind tourist; and his eyes happening at the moment to be at rest upon the lock of the cabin door, he walked up to it, full of purpose, and began to rattle the handle vigorously, while he observed, in his low, earnest voice, "You can't trust the workmen nowadays. A brand-new lock, and it won't act at all. Stuck fast. See? See?"

As soon as they found themselves alone in their office across the yard: "You praised that fellow up to Sigg. What is it you see in him?" asked the nephew, with faint contempt.

"I admit he has nothing of your fancy skipper about him, if that's what you mean," said the elder man, curtly. "Is the foreman of the joiners on the *Nan-Shan* outside? . . . Come in, Bates. How is it that you let Tait's people put us off with a defective lock on the cabin door? The Captain could see directly he set eye on it. Have it replaced at once. The little straws, Bates . . . the little straws.* . . ."

The lock was replaced accordingly, and a few days afterwards the *Nan-Shan* steamed out to the East, without MacWhirr having offered any further remark as to her fittings, or having been heard to utter a single word hinting at pride in his ship, gratitude for his appointment, or satisfaction at his prospects.

With a temperament neither loquacious nor taciturn he found very little occasion to talk. There were matters of duty, of course—directions, orders, and so on; but the past being to his mind done with, and the future not there yet, the more general actualities of the day required no comment—because facts can speak for themselves with overwhelming precision.

Old Mr. Sigg liked a man of few words, and one that "you could be sure would not try to improve upon his instructions." MacWhirr, satisfying these requirements, was continued in command of the *Nan-Shan*, and applied himself to the careful navigation of his ship in the China seas. She had come out on a British register, but after some time Messrs. Sigg judged it expedient to transfer her to the Siamese flag.

At the news of the contemplated transfer Jukes grew restless, as if under a sense of personal affront. He went about grumbling to himself, and uttering short scornful laughs. "Fancy having a ridiculous Noah's Ark elephant in the ensign of one's ship," he said once at the engine-room door. "Dash me if I can stand it:

I'll throw up the billet. Don't it make *you* sick, Mr. Rout?" The chief engineer only cleared his throat with the air of a man who knows the value of a good billet.

The first morning the new flag floated over the stern of the *Nan-Shan* Jukes stood looking at it bitterly from the bridge. He struggled with his feelings for a while, and then remarked, "Queer flag for a man to sail under, sir."

"What's the matter with the flag?" inquired Captain MacWhirr. "Seems all right to me." And he walked across to the end of the bridge to have a good look.

"Well, it looks queer to me," burst out Jukes, greatly exasperated, and flung off the bridge.

Captain MacWhirr was amazed at these manners. After a while he stepped quietly into the chart-room, and opened his International Signal Code-book at the plate where the flags of all the nations are correctly figured in gaudy rows. He ran his finger over them, and when he came to Siam he contemplated with great attention the red field and the white elephant. Nothing could be more simple; but to make sure he brought the book out on the bridge for the purpose of comparing the coloured drawing with the real thing at the flag-staff astern. When next Jukes, who was carrying on the duty that day with a sort of suppressed fierceness, happened on the bridge, his commander observed:

"There's nothing amiss with that flag."

"Isn't there?" mumbled Jukes, falling on his knees before a deck-locker and jerking therefrom viciously a spare lead-line.

"No. I looked up the book. Length twice the breadth and the elephant exactly in the middle. I thought the people ashore would know how to make the local flag. Stands to reason. You were wrong, Jukes. . . ."

"Well, sir," began Jukes, getting up excitedly, "all I can say——" He fumbled for the end of the coil of line with trembling hands.

"That's all right." Captain MacWhirr soothed him, sitting heavily on a little canvas folding-stool he greatly affected. "All you have to do is to take care they don't hoist the elephant upside-down before they get quite used to it."

Jukes flung the new lead-line over on the fore-deck with a loud "Here you are, bosun—don't forget to wet it thoroughly," and turned with immense resolution towards his commander; but Captain MacWhirr spread his elbows on the bridge-rail comfortably.

"Because it would be, I suppose, understood as a signal of distress," he went on. "What do you think? That elephant there, I take it, stands for something in the nature of the Union Jack in the flag. . . ."

"Does it!" yelled Jukes, so that every head on the *Nan-Shan's* decks looked towards the bridge. Then he sighed, and with sudden resignation: "It would certainly be a dam' distressful sight," he said, meekly.

Later in the day he accosted the chief engineer with a confidential, "Here, let me tell you the old man's latest."

Mr. Solomon Rout (frequently alluded to as Long Sol, Old Sol, or Father Rout), from finding himself almost invariably the tallest man on board every ship he joined, had acquired the habit of a stooping, leisurely condescension. His hair was scant and sandy, his flat cheeks were pale, his bony wrists and long scholarly hands were pale, too, as though he had lived all his life in the shade.

He smiled from on high at Jukes, and went on smoking and glancing about quietly, in the manner of a kind uncle lending an ear to the tale of an excited schoolboy. Then, greatly amused but impassive, he asked:

"And did you throw up the billet?"

"No," cried Jukes, raising a weary, discouraged voice above the harsh buzz of the *Nan-Shan's* friction winches. All of them were hard at work, snatching slings of cargo, high up, to the end of long derricks, only, as it seemed, to let them rip down recklessly by the run. The cargo chains groaned in the gins, clinked on coamings, rattled over the side; and the whole ship quivered, with her long gray flanks smoking in wreaths of steam. "No," cried Jukes, "I didn't. What's the good? I might just as well fling my resignation at this bulkhead. I don't believe you can make a man like that understand anything. He simply knocks me over."

At that moment Captain MacWhirr, back from the shore, crossed the deck, umbrella in hand, escorted by a mournful, self-possessed Chinaman, walking behind in paper-soled silk shoes, and who also carried an umbrella.

The master of the *Nan-Shan*, speaking just audibly and gazing at his boots as his manner was, remarked that it would be necessary to call at Fu-chau this trip, and desired Mr. Rout to have steam up to-morrow afternoon at one o'clock sharp. He pushed back his hat to wipe his forehead, observing at the same time that he hated going ashore anyhow; while overtopping him Mr. Rout, without deigning a word, smoked austerely, nursing his right elbow in the palm of his left hand. Then Jukes was directed in the same subdued voice to keep the forward 'tween-deck clear of cargo. Two hundred coolies were going to be put down there. The Bun Hin Company were sending that lot home. Twenty-five bags of rice would be coming off in a sampan directly, for stores. All seven-years'-men they were, said Captain MacWhirr, with a camphor-wood chest to every man. The carpenter should be set to work nailing three-inch battens along the deck below, fore and aft, to keep these boxes from shifting in a sea-way. Jukes had better look to it at once. "D'ye hear, Jukes?" This Chinaman here was coming with the ship as far as Fu-chau—a sort of interpreter he would be. Bun Hin's clerk he was, and wanted to have a look at the space. Jukes had better take him forward. "D'ye hear, Jukes?"

Jukes took care to punctuate these instructions in proper places with the obligatory "Yes, sir," ejaculated without enthusiasm. His brusque "Come along, John; make look see" set the Chinaman in motion at his heels.

"Wanchee look see, all same look see can do," said Jukes, who having no talent for foreign languages mangled the very pidgin-English cruelly. He pointed at the open hatch. "Catchee number one piecie place to sleep in. Eh?"

He was gruff, as became his racial superiority, but not unfriendly. The Chinaman, gazing sad and speechless into the darkness of the hatchway, seemed to stand at the head of a yawning grave.

"No catchee rain down there—savee?" pointed out Jukes. "Suppose all'ee same fine weather, one piecie coolie-man come topside," he pursued, warming up imaginatively. "Make so—Phooooo!" He expanded his chest and blew out his cheeks. "Savee, John? Breathe—fresh air. Good. Eh? Washée him piecie pants, chow-chow top-side—see, John?"

With his mouth and hands he made exuberant motions of eating rice and washing clothes; and the Chinaman, who concealed his distrust of this pantomime under a collected demeanour tinged by a gentle and refined melancholy, glanced out of his almond eyes from Jukes to the hatch and back again. "Velly good," he murmured, in a disconsolate undertone, and hastened smoothly along the decks, dodging obstacles in his course. He disappeared, ducking low under a sling of ten dirty gunny-bags full of some costly merchandise and exhaling a repulsive smell.

Captain MacWhirr meantime had gone on the bridge, and into the chart-room, where a letter, commenced two days before, awaited termination. These long letters began with the words, "My darling wife," and the steward, between the scrubbing of the floors and the dusting of chronometer-boxes, snatched at every opportunity to read them. They interested him much more than they possibly could the woman for whose eye they were intended; and this for the reason that they related in minute detail each successive trip of the *Nan-Shan.*

Her master, faithful to facts, which alone his consciousness reflected, would set them down with painstaking care upon many pages. The house in a northern suburb to which these pages were addressed had a bit of garden before the bow-windows, a deep porch of good appearance, coloured glass with imitation lead frame in the front door. He paid five-and-forty pounds a year for it, and did not think the rent too high, because Mrs. MacWhirr (a pretentious person with a scraggy neck and a disdainful manner) was admittedly ladylike, and in the neighbourhood considered as "quite superior." The only secret of her life was her abject terror of the time when her husband would come home to stay for good. Under the same roof there dwelt also a daughter called Lydia and a son, Tom. These two were but slightly acquainted with their father. Mainly, they knew him as a rare but privileged visitor, who of an evening smoked his pipe in the dining-room and slept in the house. The lanky girl, upon the whole, was rather ashamed of him; the boy was frankly and utterly indifferent in a straightforward, delightful, unaffected way manly boys have.

And Captain MacWhirr wrote home from the coast of China twelve times every year, desiring quaintly to be "remembered to the children," and subscribing himself "your loving husband," as calmly as if the words so long used by so many men were, apart from their shape, worn-out things, and of a faded meaning.

The China seas north and south are narrow seas. They are seas full of every-day, eloquent facts, such as islands, sand-banks, reefs, swift and changeable currents—tangled facts that nevertheless speak to a seaman in clear and definite language. Their speech appealed to Captain MacWhirr's sense of realities so forcibly that he had given up his state-room below and practically lived all his days on the bridge of his ship, often having his meals sent up, and sleeping at night in the chart-room. And he indited there his home letters. Each of them, without exception, contained the phrase, "The weather has been very fine this trip," or some other form of a statement to that effect. And this statement, too, in its wonderful persistence, was of the same perfect accuracy as all the others they contained.

Mr. Rout likewise wrote letters; only no one on board knew how chatty he could be pen in hand, because the chief engineer had enough imagination to keep his desk locked. His wife relished his style greatly. They were a childless couple, and Mrs. Rout, a big, high-bosomed, jolly woman of forty, shared with Mr. Rout's toothless and venerable mother a little cottage near Teddington. She would run over her correspondence, at breakfast, with lively eyes, and scream out interesting passages in a joyous voice at the deaf old lady, prefacing each extract by the warning shout,

"Solomon* says!" She had the trick of firing off
Solomon's utterances also upon strangers, astonishing
them easily by the unfamiliar text and the unexpectedly
jocular vein of these quotations. On the day the new
curate called for the first time at the cottage, she found
occasion to remark, "As Solomon says: 'the engineers
that go down to the sea in ships behold the wonders of
sailor nature';" when a change in the visitor's countenance made her stop and stare.

"Solomon. . . . Oh! . . . Mrs. Rout," stut-
tered the young man, very red in the face, "I must
say . . . I don't. . . ."

"He's my husband," she announced in a great shout,
throwing herself back in the chair. Perceiving the
joke, she laughed immoderately with a handkerchief
to her eyes, while he sat wearing a forced smile, and,
from his inexperience of jolly women, fully persuaded
that she must be deplorably insane. They were excellent friends afterwards; for, absolving her from
irreverent intention, he came to think she was a very
worthy person indeed; and he learned in time to receive
without flinching other scraps of Solomon's wisdom.

"For my part," Solomon was reported by his wife
to have said once, "give me the dullest ass for a skipper
before a rogue. There is a way to take a fool; but a
rogue is smart and slippery." This was an airy gen-
eralization drawn from the particular case of Captain
MacWhirr's honesty, which, in itself, had the heavy
obviousness of a lump of clay. On the other hand, Mr.
Jukes, unable to generalize, unmarried, and unengaged,
was in the habit of opening his heart after another
fashion to an old chum and former shipmate, actually
serving as second officer on board an Atlantic liner.

First of all he would insist upon the advantages of
the Eastern trade, hinting at its superiority to the

Western ocean service. He extolled the sky, the seas, the ships, and the easy life*of the Far East. The *Nan-Shan*, he affirmed, was second to none as a sea-boat.

"We have no brass-bound uniforms, but then we are like brothers here," he wrote. "We all mess together and live like fighting-cocks. . . . All the chaps of the black-squad are as decent as they make that kind, and old Sol, the Chief, is a dry stick. We are good friends. As to our old man, you could not find a quieter skipper. Sometimes you would think he hadn't sense enough to see anything wrong. And yet it isn't that. Can't be. He has been in command for a good few years now. He doesn't do anything actually foolish, and gets his ship along all right without worrying anybody. I believe he hasn't brains enough to enjoy kicking up a row. I don't take advantage of him. I would scorn it. Outside the routine of duty he doesn't seem to understand more than half of what you tell him. We get a laugh out of this at times; but it is dull, too, to be with a man like this—in the long-run. Old Sol says he hasn't much conversation. Conversation! O Lord! He never talks. The other day I had been yarning under the bridge with one of the engineers, and he must have heard us. When I came up to take my watch, he steps out of the chart-room and has a good look all round, peeps over at the sidelights, glances at the compass, squints upwards at the stars. That's his regular performance. By-and-by he says: 'Was that you talking just now in the port alleyway?' 'Yes, sir.' 'With the third engineer?' 'Yes, sir.' He walks off to starboard, and sits under the dodger on a little camp-stool of his, and for half an hour perhaps he makes no sound, except that I heard him sneeze once. Then after a while I hear him getting up over there, and he strolls across to port, where I was. 'I can't understand what you can find to talk about,' says he. 'Two solid hours. I am not blaming you. I see people ashore at it all day long, and then in the evening they sit down and keep at it over the drinks. Must be saying the same things over and over again. I can't understand.'

"Did you ever hear anything like that? And he was so patient about it. It made me quite sorry for him. But he is exasperating, too, sometimes. Of course one would not do anything to vex him even if it were worth while. But it isn't. He's so jolly innocent that if you were to put your thumb to your nose and wave your fingers at him he would only wonder gravely to himself what got into you. He told me once quite simply that he found it very difficult to make out what made people always act so queerly. He's too dense to trouble about, and that's the truth."

Thus wrote Mr. Jukes to his chum in the Western ocean trade, out of the fulness of his heart and the liveliness of his fancy.

He had expressed his honest opinion. It was not worth while trying to impress a man of that sort. If the world had been full of such men, life would have probably appeared to Jukes an unentertaining and unprofitable business. He was not alone in his opinion. The sea itself, as if sharing Mr. Jukes' good-natured forbearance, had never put itself out to startle the silent man, who seldom looked up, and wandered innocently over the waters with the only visible purpose of getting food, raiment, and house-room for three people ashore. Dirty weather he had known, of course. He had been made wet, uncomfortable, tired in the usual way, felt at the time and presently forgotten. So that upon the whole he had been justified in reporting fine weather at home. But he had never been given a glimpse of immeasurable strength and of immoderate wrath, the wrath that passes exhausted but never appeased—the wrath and fury of the passionate sea. He knew it existed, as we know that crime and abominations exist; he had heard of it as a peaceable citizen in a town hears of battles, famines, and floods, and yet knows nothing of what these things mean—though, indeed, he may have been mixed up in a street row, have gone without his dinner once, or been soaked to the skin in a shower. Captain MacWhirr had sailed over the surface of the oceans as some men go skimming over the years of existence to sink gently into a placid grave, ignorant of life to the last, without ever having been made to see all it may contain of perfidy, of violence, and of terror. There are on sea and land such men thus fortunate—or thus disdained by destiny or by the sea.

II

OBSERVING the steady fall of the barometer, Captain MacWhirr thought, "There's some dirty weather knocking about." This is precisely what he thought. He had had an experience of moderately dirty weather —the term dirty as applied to the weather implying only moderate discomfort to the seaman. Had he been informed by an indisputable authority that the end of the world was to be finally accomplished by a catastrophic disturbance of the atmosphere, he would have assimilated the information under the simple idea of dirty weather, and no other, because he had no experience of cataclysms, and belief does not necessarily imply comprehension. The wisdom of his country had pronounced by means of an Act of Parliament that before he could be considered as fit to take charge of a ship he should be able to answer certain simple questions on the subject of circular storms such as hurricanes, cyclones, typhoons; and apparently he had answered them, since he was now in command of the *Nan-Shan* in the China seas during the season of typhoons. But if he had answered he remembered nothing of it. He was, however, conscious of being made uncomfortable by the clammy heat. He came out on the bridge, and found no relief to this oppression. The air seemed thick. He gasped like a fish, and began to believe himself greatly out of sorts.

The *Nan-Shan* was ploughing a vanishing furrow upon the circle of the sea that had the surface and the shimmer of an undulating piece of gray silk. The

sun, pale and without rays, poured down leaden heat
in a strangely indecisive light, and the Chinamen were
lying prostrate about the decks. Their bloodless,
pinched, yellow faces were like the faces of bilious
invalids. Captain MacWhirr noticed two of them
especially, stretched out on their backs below the
bridge. As soon as they had closed their eyes they
seemed dead. Three others, however, were quarrelling
barbarously away forward; and one big fellow, half
naked, with herculean shoulders, was hanging limply
over a winch; another, sitting on the deck, his knees
up and his head drooping sideways in a girlish attitude,
was plaiting his pigtail with infinite languor depicted in
his whole person and in the very movement of his
fingers. The smoke struggled with difficulty out of
the funnel, and instead of streaming away spread itself
out like an infernal sort of cloud, smelling of sulphur
and raining soot all over the decks.

"What the devil are you doing there, Mr. Jukes?"
asked Captain MacWhirr.

This unusual form of address, though mumbled
rather than spoken, caused the body of Mr. Jukes to
start as though it had been prodded under the fifth rib.
He had had a low bench brought on the bridge, and
sitting on it, with a length of rope curled about his
feet and a piece of canvas stretched over his knees, was
pushing a sail-needle vigorously. He looked up, and
his surprise gave to his eyes an expression of innocence
and candour.

"I am only roping some of that new set of bags we
made last trip for whipping up coals," he remonstrated,
gently. "We shall want them for the next coaling,
sir."

"What became of the others?"

"Why, worn out of course, sir."

Captain MacWhirr, after glaring down irresolutely at his chief mate, disclosed the gloomy and cynical conviction that more than half of them had been lost overboard, "if only the truth was known," and retired to the other end of the bridge. Jukes, exasperated by this unprovoked attack, broke the needle at the second stitch, and dropping his work got up and cursed the heat in a violent undertone.

The propeller thumped, the three Chinamen forward had given up squabbling very suddenly, and the one who had been plaiting his tail clasped his legs and stared dejectedly over his knees. The lurid sunshine cast faint and sickly shadows. The swell ran higher and swifter every moment, and the ship lurched heavily in the smooth, deep hollows of the sea.

"I wonder where that beastly swell comes from," said Jukes aloud, recovering himself after a stagger.

"North-east," grunted the literal MacWhirr, from his side of the bridge. "There's some dirty weather knocking about. Go and look at the glass."

When Jukes came out of the chart-room, the cast of his countenance had changed to thoughtfulness and concern. He caught hold of the bridge-rail and stared ahead.

The temperature in the engine-room had gone up to a hundred and seventeen degrees. Irritated voices were ascending through the skylight and through the fiddle of the stokehold in a harsh and resonant uproar, mingled with angry clangs and scrapes of metal, as if men with limbs of iron and throats of bronze had been quarrelling down there. The second engineer was falling foul of the stokers for letting the steam go down. He was a man with arms like a blacksmith, and generally feared; but that afternoon the stokers were answering him back recklessly, and slammed the furnace

doors with the fury of despair. Then the noise ceased
suddenly, and the second engineer appeared, emerging
out of the stokehold streaked with grime and soaking
wet like a chimney-sweep coming out of a well. As
soon as his head was clear of the fiddle he began to scold
Jukes for not trimming properly the stokehold ventilators; and in answer Jukes made with his hands dep-
recatory soothing signs meaning: No wind—can't be
helped—you can see for yourself. But the other
wouldn't hear reason. His teeth flashed angrily in his
dirty face. He didn't mind, he said, the trouble of
punching their blanked*heads down there, blank his
soul, but did the condemned sailors think you could
keep steam up in the God-forsaken boilers simply by
knocking the blanked stokers about? No, by George!
You had to get some draught, too—may he be everlastingly blanked for a swab-headed deck-hand if you
didn't! And the chief, too, rampaging before the
steam-gauge and carrying on like a lunatic up and
down the engine-room ever since noon. What did
Jukes think he was stuck up there for, if he couldn't
get one of his decayed, good-for-nothing deck-cripples
to turn the ventilators to the wind?

The relations of the "engine-room" and the "deck"
of the *Nan-Shan* were, as is known, of a brotherly
nature; therefore Jukes leaned over and begged the
other in a restrained tone not to make a disgusting ass
of himself; the skipper was on the other side of the
bridge. But the second declared mutinously that he
didn't care a rap who was on the other side of the bridge,
and Jukes, passing in a flash from lofty disapproval
into a state of exaltation, invited him in unflattering
terms to come up and twist the beastly things to please
himself, and catch such wind as a donkey of his sort
could find. The second rushed up to the fray. He

flung himself at the port ventilator as though he meant
to tear it out bodily and toss it overboard. All he did
was to move the cowl round a few inches, with an
enormous expenditure of force, and seemed spent in
the effort. He leaned against the back of the wheelhouse, and Jukes walked up to him.

"Oh, Heavens!" ejaculated the engineer in a feeble
voice. He lifted his eyes to the sky, and then let his
glassy stare descend to meet the horizon that, tilting
up to an angle of forty degrees, seemed to hang on a
slant for a while and settled down slowly. "Heavens!
Phew! What's up, anyhow?"

Jukes, straddling his long legs like a pair of com-
passes, put on an air of superiority. "We're going to
catch it this time," he said. "The barometer is tumbling down like anything, Harry. And you trying to
kick up that silly row. . . ."

The word "barometer" seemed to revive the second
engineer's mad animosity. Collecting afresh all his
energies, he directed Jukes in a low and brutal tone
to shove the unmentionable instrument down his gory
throat. Who cared for his crimson barometer? It
was the steam—the steam—that was going down;
and what between the firemen going faint and the chief
going silly, it was worse than a dog's life for him; he
didn't care a tinker's curse how soon the whole show
was blown out of the water. He seemed on the point
of having a cry, but after regaining his breath he muttered darkly, "I'll faint them," and dashed off. He
stopped upon the fiddle long enough to shake his fist
at the unnatural daylight, and dropped into the dark
hole with a whoop.

When Jukes turned, his eyes fell upon the rounded
back and the big red ears of Captain MacWhirr, who
had come across. He did not look at his chief officer,

but said at once, "That's a very violent man, that second engineer."

"Jolly good second, anyhow," grunted Jukes. "They can't keep up steam," he added, rapidly, and made a grab at the rail against the coming lurch.

Captain MacWhirr, unprepared, took a run and brought himself up with a jerk by an awning stanchion.

"A profane man," he said, obstinately. "If this goes on, I'll have to get rid of him the first chance."

"It's the heat," said Jukes. "The weather's awful. It would make a saint swear. Even up here I feel exactly as if I had my head tied up in a woollen blanket."

Captain MacWhirr looked up. "D'ye mean to say, Mr. Jukes, you ever had your head tied up in a blanket? What was that for?"

"It's a manner of speaking, sir," said Jukes, stolidly.

"Some of you fellows do go on! What's that about saints swearing? I wish you wouldn't talk so wild. What sort of saint would that be that would swear? No more saint than yourself, I expect. And what's a blanket got to do with it—or the weather either. . . . The heat does not make me swear—does it? It's filthy bad temper. That's what it is. And what's the good of your talking like this?"

Thus Captain MacWhirr expostulated against the use of images in speech, and at the end electrified Jukes by a contemptuous snort, followed by words of passion and resentment: "Damme! I'll fire him out of the ship if he don't look out."

And Jukes, incorrigible, thought: "Goodness me! Somebody's put a new inside to my old man. Here's temper, if you like. Of course it's the weather; what else? It would make an angel quarrelsome—let alone a saint."

All the Chinamen on deck appeared at their last gasp.

At its setting the sun had a diminished diameter and an expiring brown, rayless glow, as if millions of centuries elapsing since the morning had brought it near its end. A dense bank of cloud became visible to the northward; it had a sinister dark olive tint, and lay low and motionless upon the sea, resembling a solid obstacle in the path of the ship. She went floundering towards it like an exhausted creature driven to its death. The coppery twilight retired slowly, and the darkness brought out overhead a swarm of unsteady, big stars, that, as if blown upon, flickered exceedingly and seemed to hang very near the earth. At eight o'clock Jukes went into the chart-room to write up the ship's log.

He copied neatly out of the rough-book the number of miles, the course of the ship, and in the column for "wind" scrawled the word "calm" from top to bottom of the eight hours since noon. He was exasperated by the continuous, monotonous rolling of the ship. The heavy inkstand would slide away in a manner that suggested perverse intelligence in dodging the pen. Having written in the large space under the head of "Remarks" "Heat very oppressive," he stuck the end of the pen-holder in his teeth, pipe fashion, and mopped his face carefully.

"Ship rolling heavily in a high cross swell," he began again, and commented to himself, "Heavily is no word for it." Then he wrote: "Sunset threatening, with a low bank of clouds to N. and E. Sky clear overhead."

Sprawling over the table with arrested pen, he glanced out of the door, and in that frame of his vision he saw all the stars flying upwards between the teak-wood jambs on a black sky. The whole lot took flight together and disappeared, leaving only a blackness flecked with white flashes, for the sea was as black as the sky and speckled with foam afar. The stars that had flown to the roll came back on the return swing of the ship, rushing downwards in their glittering multitude, not of fiery points, but enlarged to tiny discs brilliant with a clear wet sheen.

Jukes watched the flying big stars for a moment, and then wrote: "8 P.M. Swell increasing. Ship labouring and taking water on her decks. Battened down the coolies for the night. Barometer still falling." He paused, and thought to himself, "Perhaps nothing whatever'll come of it." And then he closed resolutely his entries: "Every appearance of a typhoon coming on."

On going out he had to stand aside, and Captain Mac-Whirr strode over the doorstep without saying a word or making a sign.

"Shut the door, Mr. Jukes, will you?" he cried from within.

Jukes turned back to do so, muttering ironically: "Afraid to catch cold, I suppose." It was his watch below, but he yearned for communion with his kind; and he remarked cheerily to the second mate: "Doesn't look so bad, after all—does it?"

The second mate was marching to and fro on the bridge, tripping down with small steps one moment, and the next climbing with difficulty the shifting slope of the deck. At the sound of Jukes' voice he stood still, facing forward, but made no reply.

"Hallo! That's a heavy one," said Jukes, swaying to meet the long roll till his lowered hand touched the planks. This time the second mate made in his throat a noise of an unfriendly nature.

He was an oldish, shabby little fellow, with bad teeth and no hair on his face. He had been shipped in a hurry in Shanghai, that trip when the second officer brought from home had delayed the ship three hours

in port by contriving (in some manner Captain Mac-
Whirr could never understand) to fall overboard into
an empty coal-lighter lying alongside, and had to be
sent ashore to the hospital with concussion of the brain
and a broken limb or two.

Jukes was not discouraged by the unsympathetic
sound. "The Chinamen must be having a lovely time
of it down there," he said. "It's lucky for them the
old girl has the easiest roll of any ship I've ever been
in. There now! This one wasn't so bad."

"You wait," snarled the second mate.

With his sharp nose, red at the tip, and his thin
pinched lips, he always looked as though he were raging
inwardly; and he was concise in his speech to the point
of rudeness. All his time off duty he spent in his cabin
with the door shut, keeping so still in there that he was
supposed to fall asleep as soon as he had disappeared;
but the man who came in to wake him for his watch on
deck would invariably find him with his eyes wide open,
flat on his back in the bunk, and glaring irritably from a
soiled pillow. He never wrote any letters, did not
seem to hope for news from anywhere; and though he
had been heard once to mention West Hartlepool, it
was with extreme bitterness, and only in connection
with the extortionate charges of a boarding-house.
He was one of those men who are picked up at need in
the ports of the world. They are competent enough,
appear hopelessly hard up, show no evidence of any
sort of vice, and carry about them all the signs of manifest failure. They come aboard on an emergency, care
for no ship afloat, live in their own atmosphere of casual
connection amongst their shipmates who know nothing
of them, and make up their minds to leave at inconvenient times. They clear out with no words of leave-
taking in some God-forsaken port other men would fear

to be stranded in, and go ashore in company of a shabby sea-chest, corded like a treasure-box, and with an air of shaking the ship's dust off their feet.

"You wait," he repeated, balanced in great swings with his back to Jukes, motionless and implacable.

"Do you mean to say we are going to catch it hot?" asked Jukes with boyish interest.

"Say? . . . I say nothing. You don't catch me," snapped the little second mate, with a mixture of pride, scorn, and cunning, as if Jukes' question had been a trap cleverly detected. "Oh, no! None of you here shall make a fool of me if I know it," he mumbled to himself.

Jukes reflected rapidly that this second mate was a mean little beast, and in his heart he wished poor Jack Allen had never smashed himself up in the coal-lighter. The far-off blackness ahead of the ship was like another night seen through the starry night of the earth—the starless night of the immensities beyond the created universe, revealed in its appalling stillness through a low fissure in the glittering sphere of which the earth is the kernel.

"Whatever there might be about," said Jukes, "we are steaming straight into it."

"*You've* said it," caught up the second mate, always with his back to Jukes. "You've said it, mind—not I."

"Oh, go to Jericho!" said Jukes, frankly; and the other emitted a triumphant little chuckle.

"You've said it," he repeated.

"And what of that?"

"I've known some real good men get into trouble with their skippers for saying a dam' sight less," answered the second mate feverishly. "Oh, no! You don't catch me."

"You seem deucedly anxious not to give yourself away," said Jukes, completely soured by such absurdity. "I wouldn't be afraid to say what I think."

"Aye, to me   That's no great trick. I am nobody, and well I know it."

The ship, after a pause of comparative steadiness, started upon a series of rolls, one worse than the other, and for a time Jukes, preserving his equilibrium, was too busy to open his mouth. As soon as the violent swinging had quieted down somewhat, he said: "This is a bit too much of a good thing. Whether anything is coming or not I think she ought to be put head on to that swell. The old man is just gone in to lie down. Hang me if I don't speak to him."

But when he opened the door of the chart-room he saw his captain reading a book. Captain MacWhirr was not lying down: he was standing up with one hand grasping the edge of the bookshelf and the other holding open before his face a thick volume. The lamp wriggled in the gimbals, the loosened books toppled from side to side on the shelf, the long barometer swung in jerky circles, the table altered its slant every moment. In the midst of all this stir and movement Captain MacWhirr, holding on, showed his eyes above the upper edge, and asked, "What's the matter?"

"Swell getting worse, sir."

"Noticed that in here," muttered Captain MacWhirr. "Anything wrong?"

Jukes, inwardly disconcerted by the seriousness of the eyes looking at him over the top of the book, produced an embarrassed grin.

"Rolling like old boots," he said, sheepishly.

"Aye! Very heavy—very heavy. What do you want?"

At this Jukes lost his footing and began to flounder.

"I was thinking of our passengers," he said, in the manner of a man clutching at a straw.

"Passengers?" wondered the Captain, gravely. "What passengers?"

"Why, the Chinamen, sir," explained Jukes, very sick of this conversation.

"The Chinamen! Why don't you speak plainly? Couldn't tell what you meant. Never heard a lot of coolies spoken of as passengers before. Passengers, indeed! What's come to you?"

Captain MacWhirr, closing the book on his forefinger, lowered his arm and looked completely mystified. "Why are you thinking of the Chinamen, Mr. Jukes?" he inquired.

Jukes took a plunge, like a man driven to it. "She's rolling her decks full of water, sir. Thought you might put her head on perhaps—for a while. Till this goes down a bit—very soon, I dare say. Head to the eastward. I never knew a ship roll like this."

He held on in the doorway, and Captain MacWhirr, feeling his grip on the shelf inadequate, made up his mind to let go in a hurry, and fell heavily on the couch.

"Head to the eastward?" he said, struggling to sit up. "That's more than four points off her course."

"Yes, sir. Fifty degrees. . . . Would just bring her head far enough round to meet this. . . ."

Captain MacWhirr was now sitting up. He had not dropped the book, and he had not lost his place.

"To the eastward?" he repeated, with dawning astonishment. "To the . . . Where do you think we are bound to? You want me to haul a full-powered steamship four points off her course to make the Chinamen comfortable! Now, I've heard more than enough of mad things done in the world—but this. . . . If I didn't know you, Jukes, I would think you were in liquor. Steer four points off. . . . And what afterwards? Steer four points over the other way, I suppose, to make the course good. What put it into your head that I would start to tack a steamer as if she were a sailing-ship?"

"Jolly good thing she isn't," threw in Jukes, with bitter readiness. "She would have rolled every blessed stick out of her this afternoon."

"Aye! And you just would have had to stand and see them go," said Captain MacWhirr, showing a certain animation. "It's a dead calm, isn't it?"

"It is, sir. But there's something out of the common coming, for sure."

"Maybe. I suppose you have a notion I should be getting out of the way of that dirt," said Captain Mac-Whirr, speaking with the utmost simplicity of manner and tone, and fixing the oilcloth on the floor with a heavy stare. Thus he noticed neither Jukes' discomfiture nor the mixture of vexation and astonished respect on his face.

"Now, here's this book," he continued with deliberation, slapping his thigh with the closed volume. "I've been reading the chapter on the storms*there."

This was true. He had been reading the chapter on the storms. When he had entered the chart-room, it was with no intention of taking the book down. Some influence in the air—the same influence, probably, that caused the steward to bring without orders the Captain's sea-boots and oilskin coat up to the chart-room—had as it were guided his hand to the shelf; and without taking the time to sit down he had waded with a conscious effort into the terminology of the subject. He lost himself amongst advancing semi-circles, left- and right-hand quadrants, the curves of the tracks, the probable bearing of the centre, the shifts of wind and the readings of barometer. He tried to bring all these things into a definite relation to himself, and ended by becoming contemptuously angry with such a lot of words and with so much advice, all head-work and supposition, without a glimmer of certitude.

"It's the damnedest thing, Jukes," he said. "If a fellow was to believe all that's in there, he would be running most of his time all over the sea trying to get behind the weather."

Again he slapped his leg with the book; and Jukes opened his mouth, but said nothing.

"Running to get behind the weather! Do you understand that, Mr. Jukes? It's the maddest thing!" ejaculated Captain MacWhirr, with pauses, gazing at the floor profoundly. "You would think an old woman had been writing this. It passes me. If that thing means anything useful, then it means that I should at once alter the course away, away to the devil somewhere, and come booming down on Fu-chau from the northward at the tail of this dirty weather that's supposed to be knocking about in our way. From the north! Do you understand, Mr. Jukes? Three hundred extra miles to the distance, and a pretty coal bill to show. I couldn't bring myself to do that if every word in there was gospel truth, Mr. Jukes. Don't you expect me. . . ."

And Jukes, silent, marvelled at this display of feeling and loquacity.

"But the truth is that you don't know if the fellow is right, anyhow. How can you tell what a gale is made of till you get it? He isn't aboard here, is he? Very well. Here he says that the centre of them things bears eight points off the wind; but we haven't got any wind, for all the barometer falling. Where's his centre now?"

"We will get the wind presently," mumbled Jukes.

"Let it come, then," said Captain MacWhirr, with dignified indignation. "It's only to let you see, Mr. Jukes, that you don't find everything in books. All these rules for dodging breezes and circumventing the winds of heaven, Mr. Jukes, seem to me the maddest thing, when you come to look at it sensibly."

He raised his eyes, saw Jukes gazing at him dubiously, and tried to illustrate his meaning.

"About as queer as your extraordinary notion of dodging the ship head to sea, for I don't know how long, to make the Chinamen comfortable; whereas all we've got to do is to take them to Fu-chau, being timed to get there before noon on Friday. If the weather delays me—very well. There's your log-book to talk straight about the weather. But suppose I went swinging off my course and came in two days late, and they asked me: 'Where have you been all that time, Captain?' What could I say to that? 'Went around to dodge the bad weather,' I would say. 'It must've been dam' bad,' they would say. 'Don't know,' I would have to say; 'I've dodged clear of it.' See that, Jukes? I have been thinking it all out this afternoon."

He looked up again in his unseeing, unimaginative way. No one had ever heard him say so much at one time. Jukes, with his arms open in the doorway, was like a man invited to behold a miracle. Unbounded wonder was the intellectual meaning of his eye, while incredulity was seated in his whole countenance.

"A gale is a gale, Mr. Jukes," resumed the Captain, "and a full-powered steam-ship has got to face it. There's just so much dirty weather knocking about the world, and the proper thing is to go through it with none of what old Captain Wilson of the *Melita* calls 'storm strategy.' The other day ashore I heard him hold forth about it to a lot of shipmasters who came in and sat at a table next to mine. It seemed to me the greatest nonsense. He was telling them how he out-manœuvred, I think he said, a terrific gale, so that it never came nearer than fifty miles to him. A neat piece of head-work he called it. How he knew there was a terrific gale fifty miles off beats me altogether. It was like listening to a crazy man. I would have thought Captain Wilson was old enough to know better."

Captain MacWhirr ceased for a moment, then said, "It's your watch below, Mr. Jukes?"

Jukes came to himself with a start. "Yes, sir."

"Leave orders to call me at the slightest change," said the Captain. He reached up to put the book away, and tucked his legs upon the couch. "Shut the door so that it don't fly open, will you? I can't stand a door banging. They've put a lot of rubbishy locks into this ship, I must say."

Captain MacWhirr closed his eyes.

He did so to rest himself. He was tired, and he experienced that state of mental vacuity which comes at the end of an exhaustive discussion that had liberated some belief matured in the course of meditative years. He had indeed been making his confession of faith, had he only known it; and its effect was to make Jukes, on the other side of the door, stand scratching his head for a good while.

Captain MacWhirr opened his eyes.

He thought he must have been asleep. What was that loud noise? Wind? Why had he not been called? The lamp wriggled in its gimbals, the barometer swung in circles, the table altered its slant every moment; a pair of limp sea-boots with collapsed tops went sliding past the couch. He put out his hand instantly, and captured one.

Jukes' face appeared in a crack of the door: only his face, very red, with staring eyes. The flame of the lamp leaped, a piece of paper flew up, a rush of air enveloped Captain MacWhirr. Beginning to draw on the boot, he directed an expectant gaze at Jukes' swollen, excited features.

"Came on like this," shouted Jukes, "five minutes ago . . . . all of a sudden."

The head disappeared with a bang, and a heavy splash and patter of drops swept past the closed door as if a pailful of melted lead had been flung against the house. A whistling could be heard now upon the deep vibrating noise outside. The stuffy chart-room seemed as full of draughts as a shed. Captain MacWhirr collared the other sea-boot on its violent passage along the floor. He was not flustered, but he could not find at once the opening for inserting his foot. The shoes he had flung off were scurrying from end to end of the cabin, gambolling playfully over each other like puppies. As soon as he stood up he kicked at them viciously, but without effect.

He threw himself into the attitude of a lunging fencer, to reach after his oilskin coat; and afterwards he staggered all over the confined space while he jerked himself into it. Very grave, straddling his legs far apart, and stretching his neck, he started to tie deliberately the strings of his sou'-wester under his chin, with thick fingers that trembled slightly. He went through all the movements of a woman putting on her bonnet before a glass, with a strained, listening attention, as though he had expected every moment to hear the shout of his name in the confused clamour that had suddenly beset his ship. Its increase filled his ears while he was getting ready to go out and confront whatever it might mean. It was tumultuous and very loud—made up of the rush of the wind, the crashes of the sea, with that prolonged deep vibration of the air, like the roll of an immense and remote drum beating the charge of the gale.

He stood for a moment in the light of the lamp, thick, clumsy, shapeless in his panoply of combat, vigilant and red-faced.

"There's a lot of weight in this," he muttered.

As soon as he attempted to open the door the wind caught it. Clinging to the handle, he was dragged out over the doorstep, and at once found himself engaged with the wind in a sort of personal scuffle whose object was the shutting of that door. At the last moment a tongue of air scurried in and licked out the flame of the lamp.

Ahead of the ship he perceived a great darkness lying upon a multitude of white flashes; on the starboard beam a few amazing stars drooped, dim and fitful, above an immense waste of broken seas, as if seen through a mad drift of smoke.

On the bridge a knot of men, indistinct and toiling, were making great efforts in the light of the wheelhouse windows that shone mistily on their heads and backs. Suddenly darkness closed upon one pane, then on another. The voices of the lost group reached him after the manner of men's voices in a gale, in shreds and fragments of forlorn shouting snatched past the ear. All at once Jukes appeared at his side, yelling, with his head down.

"Watch—put in—wheelhouse shutters—glass—afraid—blow in."

Jukes heard his commander upbraiding.

"This—come—anything—warning—call me."

He tried to explain, with the uproar pressing on his lips.

"Light air—remained—bridge—sudden—north-east
—could turn—thought—you—sure—hear."

They had gained the shelter of the weather-cloth,
and could converse with raised voices, as people quarrel.

"I got the hands along to cover up all the ventilators.
Good job I had remained on deck. I didn't think you
would be asleep, and so . . . What did you say,
sir? What?"

"Nothing," cried Captain MacWhirr. "I said—all
right."

"By all the powers! We've got it this time," observed Jukes in a howl.

"You haven't altered her course?" inquired Captain
MacWhirr, straining his voice.

"No, sir. Certainly not. Wind came out right
ahead. And here comes the head sea."

A plunge of the ship ended in a shock as if she had
landed her forefoot upon something solid. After a
moment of stillness a lofty flight of sprays drove hard
with the wind upon their faces.

"Keep her at it as long as we can," shouted Captain
MacWhirr.

Before Jukes had squeezed the salt water out of his
eyes all the stars had disappeared.

III

JUKES was as ready a man as any half-dozen young mates that may be caught by casting a net upon the waters; and though he had been somewhat taken aback by the startling viciousness of the first squall, he had pulled himself together on the instant, had called out the hands and had rushed them along to secure such openings about the deck as had not been already battened down earlier in the evening. Shouting in his fresh, stentorian voice, "Jump, boys, and bear a hand!" he led in the work, telling himself the while that he had "just expected this."

But at the same time he was growing aware that this was rather more than he had expected. From the first stir of the air felt on his cheek the gale seemed to take upon itself the accumulated impetus of an avalanche. Heavy sprays enveloped the *Nan-Shan* from stem to stern, and instantly in the midst of her regular rolling she began to jerk and plunge as though she had gone mad with fright.

Jukes thought, "This is no joke." While he was exchanging explanatory yells with his captain, a sudden lowering of the darkness came upon the night, falling before their vision like something palpable. It was as if the masked lights of the world had been turned down. Jukes was uncritically glad to have his captain at hand. It relieved him as though that man had, by simply coming on deck, taken most of the gale's weight upon his shoulders. Such is the prestige, the privilege, and the burden of command.

Captain MacWhirr could expect no relief of that sort
from any one on earth. Such is the loneliness of command. He was trying to see, with that watchful manner of a seaman who stares into the wind's eye as if into
the eye of an adversary, to penetrate the hidden intention and guess the aim and force of the thrust. The
strong wind swept at him out of a vast obscurity; he
felt under his feet the uneasiness of his ship, and he
could not even discern the shadow of her shape. He
wished it were not so; and very still he waited, feeling
stricken by a blind man's helplessness.

To be silent was natural to him, dark or shine. Jukes,
at his elbow, made himself heard yelling cheerily in the
gusts, "We must have got the worst of it at once, sir."
A faint burst of lightning quivered all round, as if flashed
into a cavern—into a black and secret chamber of the
sea, with a floor of foaming crests.

It unveiled for a sinister, fluttering moment a ragged
mass of clouds hanging low, the lurch of the long outlines of the ship, the black figures of men caught on
the bridge, heads forward, as if petrified in the act of
butting. The darkness palpitated down upon all this,
and then the real thing came at last.

It was something formidable and swift, like the sudden smashing of a vial of wrath. It seemed to explode
all round the ship with an overpowering concussion
and a rush of great waters, as if an immense dam had
been blown up to windward. In an instant the men
lost touch of each other. This is the disintegrating
power of a great wind: it isolates one from one's kind.
An earthquake, a landslip, an avalanche, overtake a
man incidentally, as it were—without passion. A
furious gale attacks him like a personal enemy, tries
to grasp his limbs, fastens upon his mind, seeks to rout
his very spirit out of him.

Jukes was driven away from his commander. He fancied himself whirled a great distance through the air. Everything disappeared—even, for a moment, his power of thinking; but his hand had found one of the rail-stanchions. His distress was by no means alleviated by an inclination to disbelieve the reality of this experience. Though young, he had seen some bad weather, and had never doubted his ability to imagine the worst; but this was so much beyond his powers of fancy that it appeared incompatible with the existence of any ship whatever. He would have been incredulous about himself in the same way, perhaps, had he not been so harassed by the necessity of exerting a wrestling effort against a force trying to tear him away from his hold. Moreover, the conviction of not being utterly destroyed returned to him through the sensations of being half-drowned, bestially shaken, and partly choked.

It seemed to him he remained there precariously alone with the stanchion for a long, long time. The rain poured on him, flowed, drove in sheets. He breathed in gasps; and sometimes the water he swallowed was fresh and sometimes it was salt. For the most part he kept his eyes shut tight, as if suspecting his sight might be destroyed in the immense flurry of the elements. When he ventured to blink hastily, he derived some moral support from the green gleam of the starboard light shining feebly upon the flight of rain and sprays. He was actually looking at it when its ray fell upon the uprearing sea which put it out. He saw the head of the wave topple over, adding the mite of its crash to the tremendous uproar raging around him, and almost at the same instant the stanchion was wrenched away from his embracing arms. After a crushing thump on his back he found himself suddenly afloat and borne upwards. His first irresistible notion

was that the whole China Sea had climbed on the
bridge. Then, more sanely, he concluded himself gone
overboard. All the time he was being tossed, flung,
and rolled in great volumes of water, he kept on repeat-
ing mentally, with the utmost precipitation, the words:
"My God! My God! My God! My God!"

All at once, in a revolt of misery and despair, he
formed the crazy resolution to get out of that. And he
began to thresh about with his arms and legs. But
as soon as he commenced his wretched struggles he
discovered that he had become somehow mixed up
with a face, an oilskin coat, somebody's boots. He
clawed ferociously all these things in turn, lost them,
found them again, lost them once more, and finally was
himself caught in the firm clasp of a pair of stout arms.
He returned the embrace closely round a thick solid
body. He had found his captain.

They tumbled over and over, tightening their hug.
Suddenly the water let them down with a brutal bang;
and, stranded against the side of the wheelhouse, out of
breath and bruised, they were left to stagger up in the
wind and hold on where they could.

Jukes came out of it rather horrified, as though he
had escaped some unparalleled outrage directed at his
feelings. It weakened his faith in himself. He started
shouting aimlessly to the man he could feel near him
in that fiendish blackness, "Is it you, sir? Is it you,
sir?" till his temples seemed ready to burst. And he
heard in answer a voice, as if crying far away, as if
screaming to him fretfully from a very great distance,
the one word "Yes!" Other seas swept again over the
bridge. He received them defencelessly right over his
bare head, with both his hands engaged in holding.

The motion of the ship was extravagant. Her lurches
had an appalling helplessness: she pitched as if taking

a header into a void, and seemed to find a wall to hit
every time. When she rolled she fell on her side headlong, and she would be righted back by such a demol-
ishing blow that Jukes felt her reeling as a clubbed man
reels before he collapses. The gale howled and scuffled
about gigantically in the darkness, as though the entire
world were one black gully. At certain moments the
air streamed against the ship as if sucked through a
tunnel with a concentrated solid force of impact that
seemed to lift her clean out of the water and keep her
up for an instant with only a quiver running through
her from end to end. And then she would begin her
tumbling again as if dropped back into a boiling cauldron. Jukes tried hard to compose his mind and judge
things coolly.

The sea, flattened down in the heavier gusts, would
uprise and overwhelm both ends of the *Nan-Shan* in
snowy rushes of foam, expanding wide, beyond both
rails, into the night. And on this dazzling sheet, spread
under the blackness of the clouds and emitting a bluish
glow, Captain MacWhirr could catch a desolate glimpse
of a few tiny specks black as ebony, the tops of the
hatches, the battened companions, the heads of the
covered winches, the foot of a mast. This was all he
could see of his ship. Her middle structure, covered
by the bridge which bore him, his mate, the closed
wheelhouse where a man was steering shut up with the
fear of being swept overboard together with the whole
thing in one great crash—her middle structure was like
a half-tide rock awash upon a coast. It was like an
outlying rock with the water boiling up, streaming over,
pouring off, beating round—like a rock in the surf to
which shipwrecked people cling before they let go—
only it rose, it sank, it rolled continuously, without
respite and rest, like a rock that should have miracu-

lously struck adrift from a coast and gone wallowing upon the sea.

The *Nan-Shan* was being looted by the storm with a senseless, destructive fury: trysails torn out of the extra gaskets, double-lashed awnings blown away, bridge swept clean, weather-cloths burst, rails twisted, light-screens smashed—and two of the boats had gone already. They had gone unheard and unseen, melting, as it were, in the shock and smother of the wave. It was only later, when upon the white flash of another high sea hurling itself amidships, Jukes had a vision of two pairs of davits leaping black and empty out of the solid blackness, with one overhauled fall flying and an iron-bound block capering in the air, that he became aware of what had happened within about three yards of his back.

He poked his head forward, groping for the ear of his commander. His lips touched it—big, fleshy, very wet. He cried in an agitated tone, "Our boats are going now, sir."

And again he heard that voice, forced and ringing feebly, but with a penetrating effect of quietness in the enormous discord*of noises, as if sent out from some remote spot of peace beyond the black wastes of the gale; again he heard a man's voice—the frail and indomitable sound that can be made to carry an infinity of thought, resolution and purpose, that shall be pronouncing confident words on the last day,* when heavens fall, and justice is done*—again he heard it, and it was crying to him, as if from very, very far—"All right."

He thought he had not managed to make himself understood. "Our boats—I say boats—the boats, sir! Two gone!"

The same voice, within a foot of him and yet so remote, yelled sensibly, "Can't be helped."

Captain MacWhirr had never turned his face, but Jukes caught some more words on the wind.

"What can—expect—when hammering through—such—— Bound to leave—something behind—stands to reason."

Watchfully Jukes listened for more. No more came. This was all Captain MacWhirr had to say; and Jukes could picture to himself rather than see the broad squat back before him. An impenetrable obscurity pressed down upon the ghostly glimmers of the sea. A dull conviction seized upon Jukes that there was nothing to be done.

If the steering-gear did not give way, if the immense volumes of water did not burst the deck in or smash one of the hatches, if the engines did not give up, if way could be kept on the ship against this terrific wind, and she did not bury herself in one of these awful seas, of whose white crests alone, topping high above her bows, he could now and then get a sickening glimpse—then there was a chance of her coming out of it. Something within him seemed to turn over, bringing uppermost the feeling that the *Nan-Shan* was lost.

"She's done for," he said to himself, with a surprising mental agitation, as though he had discovered an un-expected meaning in this thought. One of these things was bound to happen. Nothing could be prevented now, and nothing could be remedied. The men on board did not count, and the ship could not last. This weather was too impossible.

Jukes felt an arm thrown heavily over his shoulders; and to this overture he responded with great intelligence by catching hold of his captain round the waist.

They stood clasped thus in the blind night, bracing each other against the wind, cheek to cheek and lip to

ear, in the manner of two hulks lashed stem to stern
together.

And Jukes heard the voice of his commander hardly
any louder than before, but nearer, as though, starting
to march athwart the prodigious rush of the hurricane,
it had approached him, bearing that strange effect of
quietness like the serene glow of a halo.

"D'ye know where the hands got to?" it asked,
vigorous and evanescent at the same time, overcoming
the strength of the wind, and swept away from Jukes
instantly.

Jukes didn't know. They were all on the bridge
when the real force of the hurricane struck the ship.
He had no idea where they had crawled to. Under
the circumstances they were nowhere, for all the use
that could be made of them. Somehow the Captain's
wish to know distressed Jukes.

"Want the hands, sir?" he cried, apprehensively.

"Ought to know," asserted Captain MacWhirr.
"Hold hard."

They held hard. An outburst of unchained fury, a
vicious rush of the wind absolutely steadied the ship;
she rocked only, quick and light like a child's cradle,
for a terrific moment of suspense, while the whole
atmosphere, as it seemed, streamed furiously past her,
roaring away from the tenebrous earth.

It suffocated them, and with eyes shut they tightened
their grasp. What from the magnitude of the shock
might have been a column of water running upright in
the dark, butted against the ship, broke short, and fell
on her bridge, crushingly, from on high, with a dead
burying weight.

A flying fragment of that collapse, a mere splash,
enveloped them in one swirl from their feet over their
heads, filling violently their ears, mouths and nostrils

with salt water. It knocked out their legs, wrenched
in haste at their arms, seethed away swiftly under their
chins; and opening their eyes, they saw the piled-up
masses of foam dashing to and fro amongst what looked
like the fragments of a ship. She had given way as if
driven straight in. Their panting hearts yielded, too,
before the tremendous blow; and all at once she sprang
up again to her desperate plunging, as if trying to
scramble out from under the ruins.

The seas in the dark seemed to rush from all sides
to keep her back where she might perish. There was
hate in the way she was handled, and a ferocity in the
blows that fell. She was like a living creature thrown
to the rage of a mob: hustled terribly, struck at, borne
up, flung down, leaped upon. Captain MacWhirr and
Jukes kept hold of each other, deafened by the noise,
gagged by the wind; and the great physical tumult
beating about their bodies, brought, like an unbridled
display of passion, a profound trouble to their souls.
One of these wild and appalling shrieks that are heard
at times passing mysteriously overhead in the steady
roar of a hurricane, swooped, as if borne on wings,
upon the ship, and Jukes tried to outscream it.

"Will she live through this?"

The cry was wrenched out of his breast. It was as
unintentional as the birth of a thought in the head, and
he heard nothing of it himself. It all became extinct
at once—thought, intention, effort—and of his cry the
inaudible vibration added to the tempest waves of the
air.

He expected nothing from it. Nothing at all. For
indeed what answer could be made? But after a while
he heard with amazement the frail and resisting voice
in his ear, the dwarf sound, unconquered in the giant
tumult.

"She may!"

It was a dull yell, more difficult to seize than a whisper. And presently the voice returned again, half submerged in the vast crashes, like a ship battling against the waves of an ocean.

"Let's hope so!" it cried—small, lonely and unmoved, a stranger to the visions of hope or fear; and it flickered into disconnected words: "Ship. . . . . This. . . . Never—Anyhow . . . for the best." Jukes gave it up.

Then, as if it had come suddenly upon the one thing fit to withstand the power of a storm, it seemed to gain force and firmness for the last broken shouts:

"Keep on hammering . . . builders . . . good men. . . . And chance it . . . engines. . . . Rout . . . good man."

Captain MacWhirr removed his arm from Jukes' shoulders, and thereby ceased to exist for his mate, so dark it was; Jukes, after a tense stiffening of every muscle, would let himself go limp all over. The gnawing of profound discomfort existed side by side with an incredible disposition to somnolence, as though he had been buffeted and worried into drowsiness. The wind would get hold of his head and try to shake it off his shoulders; his clothes, full of water, were as heavy as lead, cold and dripping like an armour of melting ice: he shivered—it lasted a long time; and with his hands closed hard on his hold, he was letting himself sink slowly into the depths of bodily misery. His mind became concentrated upon himself in an aimless, idle way, and when something pushed lightly at the back of his knees he nearly, as the saying is, jumped out of his skin.

In the start forward he bumped the back of Captain MacWhirr, who didn't move; and then a hand gripped

his thigh. A lull had come, a menacing lull of the
wind, the holding of a stormy breath—and he felt
himself pawed all over. It was the boatswain.
Jukes recognized these hands, so thick and enormous
that they seemed to belong to some new species of
man.

The boatswain had arrived on the bridge, crawling
on all fours against the wind, and had found the chief
mate's legs with the top of his head. Immediately he
crouched and began to explore Jukes' person upwards
with prudent. apologetic touches, as became an in-
ferior.

He was an ill-favoured, undersized, gruff sailor of
fifty, coarsely hairy, short-legged, long-armed, resembling an elderly ape. His strength was immense; and
in his great lumpy paws, bulging like brown boxing-
gloves on the end of furry forearms, the heaviest objects
were handled like playthings. Apart from the grizzled
pelt on his chest, the menacing · demeanour and the
hoarse voice, he had none of the classical attributes of
his rating. His good nature almost amounted to imbecility: the men did what they liked with him, and he
had not an ounce of initiative in his character, which
was easy-going and talkative. For these reasons Jukes
disliked him; but Captain MacWhirr, to Jukes' scornful disgust, seemed to regard him as a first-rate petty
officer.

He pulled himself up by Jukes' coat, taking that
liberty with the greatest moderation, and only so far
as it was forced upon him by the hurricane.

"What is it, bosun, what is it?" yelled Jukes, impatiently. What could that fraud of a bosun want
on the bridge? The typhoon had got on Jukes' nerves.
The husky bellowings of the other, though unintelli-
gible, seemed to suggest a state of lively satisfaction.

There could be no mistake. The old fool was pleased with something.

The boatswain's other hand had found some other body, for in a changed tone he began to inquire: "Is it you, sir? Is it you, sir?" The wind strangled his howls.

"Yes!" cried Captain MacWhirr.

IV

ALL that the boatswain, out of a superabundance of yells, could make clear to Captain MacWhirr was the bizarre intelligence that "All them Chinamen in the fore 'tween-deck have fetched away, sir."

Jukes to leeward could hear these two shouting within six inches of his face, as you may hear on a still night half a mile away two men conversing across a field. He heard Captain MacWhirr's exasperated "What? What?" and the strained pitch of the other's hoarseness. "In a lump . . . seen them myself. . . . Awful sight, sir . . . thought . . . tell you."

Jukes remained indifferent, as if rendered irresponsible by the force of the hurricane, which made the very thought of action utterly vain. Besides, being very young, he had found the occupation of keeping his heart completely steeled against the worst so engrossing that he had come to feel an overpowering dislike towards any other form of activity whatever. He was not scared; he knew this because, firmly believing he would never see another sunrise, he remained calm in that belief.

These are the moments of do-nothing heroics to which even good men surrender at times. Many officers of ships can no doubt recall a case in their experience when just such a trance of confounded stoicism would come all at once over a whole ship's company. Jukes, however, had no wide experience of men or storms. He conceived himself to be calm—inexorably calm; but as a matter of fact he was daunted; not abjectly, but only so far as a decent man may, without becoming loathsome to himself.

It was rather like a forced-on numbness of spirit. The long, long stress of a gale does it; the suspense of the interminably culminating catastrophe; and there is a bodily fatigue in the mere holding on to existence within the excessive tumult; a searching and insidious fatigue that penetrates deep into a man's breast to cast down and sadden his heart, which is incorrigible, and of all the gifts of the earth—even before life itself— aspires to peace.

Jukes was benumbed much more than he supposed. He held on—very wet, very cold, stiff in every limb; and in a momentary hallucination of swift visions (it is said that a drowning man thus reviews all his life) he beheld all sorts of memories altogether unconnected with his present situation. He remembered his father, for instance: a worthy business man, who at an unfortunate crisis in his affairs went quietly to bed and died forthwith in a state of resignation. Jukes did not recall these circumstances, of course, but remaining otherwise unconcerned he seemed to see distinctly the poor man's face; a certain game of nap played when quite a boy in Table Bay on board a ship, since lost with all hands; the thick eyebrows of his first skipper; and without any emotion, as he might years ago have walked listlessly into her room and found her sitting there with a book, he remembered his mother—dead, too, now—the resolute woman, left badly off, who had been very firm in his bringing up.

It could not have lasted more than a second, perhaps not so much. A heavy arm had fallen about his shoulders; Captain MacWhirr's voice was speaking his name into his ear.

"Jukes! Jukes!"

He detected the tone of deep concern. The wind had thrown its weight on the ship, trying to pin her down amongst the seas. They made a clean breach over her, as over a deep-swimming log; and the gathered weight of crashes menaced monstrously from afar. The breakers flung out of the night with a ghostly light on their crests—the light of sea-foam that in a ferocious, boiling-up pale flash showed upon the slender body of the ship the toppling rush, the downfall, and the seething mad scurry of each wave. Never for a moment could she shake herself clear of the water; Jukes, rigid, perceived in her motion the ominous sign of haphazard floundering. She was no longer struggling intelligently. It was the beginning of the end; and the note of busy concern in Captain MacWhirr's voice sickened him like an exhibition of blind and pernicious folly.

The spell of the storm had fallen upon Jukes. He was penetrated by it, absorbed by it; he was rooted in it with a rigour of dumb attention. Captain MacWhirr persisted in his cries, but the wind got between them like a solid wedge. He hung round Jukes' neck as heavy as a millstone, and suddenly the sides of their heads knocked together.

"Jukes! Mr. Jukes, I say!"

He had to answer that voice that would not be silenced. He answered in the customary manner: ". . . Yes, sir."

And directly, his heart, corrupted by the storm that breeds a craving for peace, rebelled against the tyranny of training and command.

Captain MacWhirr had his mate's head fixed firm in the crook of his elbow, and pressed it to his yelling lips mysteriously. Sometimes Jukes would break in, admonishing hastily: "Look out, sir!" or Captain MacWhirr would bawl an earnest exhortation to "Hold hard, there!" and the whole black universe seemed to reel together with the ship. They paused. She floated yet. And Captain MacWhirr would resume his shouts. ". . . . Says . . . whole lot . . . fetched away. . . . Ought to see . . . what's the matter."

Directly the full force of the hurricane had struck the ship, every part of her deck became untenable; and the sailors, dazed and dismayed, took shelter in the port alleyway under the bridge. It had a door aft, which they shut; it was very black, cold, and dismal. At each heavy fling of the ship they would groan all together in the dark, and tons of water could be heard scuttling about as if trying to get at them from above. The boatswain had been keeping up a gruff talk, but a more unreasonable lot of men, he said afterwards, he had never been with. They were snug enough there, out of harm's way, and not wanted to do anything, either; and yet they did nothing but grumble and complain peevishly like so many sick kids. Finally, one of them said that if there had been at least some light to see each other's noses by, it wouldn't be so bad. It was making him crazy, he declared, to lie there in the dark waiting for the blamed hooker to sink.

"Why don't you step outside, then, and be done with it at once?" the boatswain turned on him.

This called up a shout of execration. The boatswain found himself overwhelmed with reproaches of all sorts. They seemed to take it ill that a lamp was not instantly created for them out of nothing. They would whine after a light to get drowned by—anyhow! And though the unreason of their revilings was patent—since no one could hope to reach the lamp-room, which was forward—he became greatly distressed. He did not think it was decent of them to be nagging at him like

this. He told them so, and was met by general con-
tumely. He sought refuge, therefore, in an embittered
silence. At the same time their grumbling and sighing
and muttering worried him greatly, but by-and-by it
occurred to him that there were six globe lamps hung
in the 'tween-deck, and that there could be no harm in
depriving the coolies of one of them.

The *Nan-Shan* had an athwartship coal-bunker,
which, being at times used as cargo space, communi-
cated by an iron door with the fore 'tween-deck. It was
empty then, and its manhole was the foremost one in
the alleyway. The boatswain could get in, therefore,
without coming out on deck at all; but to his great
surprise he found he could induce no one to help him
in taking off the manhole cover. He groped for it all
the same, but one of the crew lying in his way refused
to budge.

"Why, I only want to get you that blamed light you
are crying for," he expostulated, almost pitifully.

Somebody told him to go and put his head in a bag.
He regretted he could not recognize the voice, and that
it was too dark to see, otherwise, as he said, he would
have put a head on *that* son of a sea-cook, anyway, sink
or swim. Nevertheless, he had made up his mind to
show them he could get a light, if he were to die for it.

Through the violence of the ship's rolling, every
movement was dangerous. To be lying down seemed
labour enough. He nearly broke his neck dropping
into the bunker. He fell on his back, and was sent
shooting helplessly from side to side in the dangerous
company of a heavy iron bar—a coal-trimmer's slice
probably—left down there by somebody. This thing
made him as nervous as though it had been a wild beast.
He could not see it, the inside of the bunker coated with
coal-dust being perfectly and impenetrably black; but

he heard it sliding and clattering, and striking here and
there, always in the neighbourhood of his head. It
seemed to make an extraordinary noise, too—to give
heavy thumps as though it had been as big as a bridge
girder. This was remarkable enough for him to notice
while he was flung from port to starboard and back
again, and clawing desperately the smooth sides of the
bunker in the endeavour to stop himself. The door
into the 'tween-deck not fitting quite true, he saw a
thread of dim light at the bottom.

Being a sailor, and a still active man, he did not want
much of a chance to regain his feet; and as luck would
have it, in scrambling up he put his hand on the iron
slice, picking it up as he rose. Otherwise he would have
been afraid of the thing breaking his legs, or at least
knocking him down again. At first he stood still.
He felt unsafe in this darkness that seemed to make the
ship's motion unfamiliar, unforeseen, and difficult to
counteract. He felt so much shaken for a moment that
he dared not move for fear of "taking charge again."
He had no mind to get battered to pieces in that bunker.

He had struck his head twice; he was dazed a little.
He seemed to hear yet so plainly the clatter and bangs
of the iron slice flying about his ears that he tightened
his grip to prove to himself he had it there safely in his
hand. He was vaguely amazed at the plainness with
which down there he could hear the gale raging. Its
howls and shrieks seemed to take on, in the emptiness
of the bunker, something of the human character, of
human rage and pain—being not vast but infinitely
poignant. And there were, with every roll, thumps,
too—profound, ponderous thumps, as if a bulk object
of five-ton weight or so had got play in the hold. But
there was no such thing in the cargo. Something on
deck? Impossible. Or alongside? Couldn't be.

He thought all this quickly, clearly, competently, like a seaman, and in the end remained puzzled. This noise, though, came deadened from outside, together with the washing and pouring of water on deck above his head. Was it the wind? Must be. It made down there a row like the shouting of a big lot of crazed men. And he discovered in himself a desire for a light, too—if only to get drowned by—and a nervous anxiety to get out of that bunker as quickly as possible.

He pulled back the bolt: the heavy iron plate turned on its hinges; and it was as though he had opened the door to the sounds of the tempest. A gust of hoarse yelling met him: the air was still; and the rushing of water overhead was covered by a tumult of strangled, throaty shrieks that produced an effect of desperate confusion. He straddled his legs the whole width of the doorway and stretched his neck. And at first he perceived only what he had come to seek: six small yellow flames swinging violently on the great body of the dusk.

It was stayed like the gallery of a mine, with a row of stanchions in the middle, and cross-beams overhead, penetrating into the gloom ahead—indefinitely. And to port there loomed, like the caving in of one of the sides, a bulky mass with a slanting outline. The whole place, with the shadows and the shapes, moved all the time. The boatswain glared: the ship lurched to starboard, and a great howl came from that mass that had the slant of fallen earth.

Pieces of wood whizzed past. Planks, he thought, inexpressibly startled, and flinging back his head. At his feet a man went sliding over, open-eyed, on his back, straining with uplifted arms for nothing: and another came bounding like a detached stone with his head between his legs and his hands clenched. His pigtail whipped in the air; he made a grab at the boat-swain's legs, and from his opened hand a bright white disc rolled against the boatswain's foot. He recognized a silver dollar, and yelled at it with astonishment. With a precipitated sound of trampling and shuffling of bare feet, and with guttural cries, the mound of writhing bodies piled up to port detached itself from the ship's side and sliding, inert and struggling, shifted to starboard, with a dull, brutal thump. The cries ceased. The boatswain heard a long moan through the roar and whistling of the wind; he saw an inextricable confusion of heads and shoulders, naked soles kicking upwards, fists raised, tumbling backs, legs, pigtails, faces.

"Good Lord!" he cried, horrified, and banged-to the iron door upon this vision.

This was what he had come on the bridge to tell. He could not keep it to himself; and on board ship there is only one man to whom it is worth while to unburden yourself. On his passage back the hands in the alley-way swore at him for a fool. Why didn't he bring that lamp? What the devil did the coolies matter to any-body? And when he came out, the extremity of the ship made what went on inside of her appear of little moment.

At first he thought he had left the alleyway in the very moment of her sinking. The bridge ladders had been washed away, but an enormous sea filling the after-deck floated him up. After that he had to lie on his stomach for some time, holding to a ring-bolt, getting his breath now and then, and swallowing salt water. He struggled farther on his hands and knees, too frightened and distracted to turn back. In this way he reached the after-part of the wheelhouse. In that comparatively sheltered spot he found the second mate.

The boatswain was pleasantly surprised—his impression being that everybody on deck must have been washed away a long time ago. He asked eagerly where the captain was.

The second mate was lying low, like a malignant little animal under a hedge.

"Captain? Gone overboard, after getting us into this mess." The mate, too, for all he knew or cared. Another fool. Didn't matter. Everybody was going by-and-by.

The boatswain crawled out again into the strength of the wind; not because he much expected to find anybody, he said, but just to get away from "that man." He crawled out as outcasts go to face an inclement world. Hence his great joy at finding Jukes and the Captain. But what was going on in the 'tween-deck was to him a minor matter by that time. Besides, it was difficult to make yourself heard. But he managed to convey the idea that the Chinaman had broken adrift together with their boxes, and that he had come up on purpose to report this. As to the hands, they were all right. Then, appeased, he subsided on the deck in a sitting posture, hugging with his arms and legs the stand of the engine-room telegraph—an iron casting as thick as a post. When that went, why, he expected he would go, too. He gave no more thought to the coolies.

Captain MacWhirr had made Jukes understand that he wanted him to go down below—to see.

"What am I to do then, sir?" And the trembling of his whole wet body caused Jukes' voice to sound like bleating.

"See first . . . Bosun . . . says . . . adrift."

"That bosun is a confounded fool," howled Jukes, shakily.

The absurdity of the demand made upon him revolted Jukes. He was as unwilling to go as if the moment he had left the deck the ship were sure to sink.

"I must know . . . can't leave. . . ."

"They'll settle, sir."

"Fight . . . bosun says they fight. . . . Why? Can't have . . . fighting . . . board ship. . . . Much rather keep you here . . . case . . . . I should . . . washed overboard myself. . . . Stop it . . . some way. You see and tell me . . . through engine-room tube. Don't want you . . . come up here . . . too often. Dangerous . . . moving about . . . deck."

Jukes, held with his head in chancery, had to listen to what seemed horrible suggestions.

"Don't want . . . you get lost . . . so long . . . ship isn't. . . . . Rout . . . Good man . . . Ship . . . may . . . through this . . . all right yet."

All at once Jukes understood he would have to go.

"Do you think she may?" he screamed.

But the wind devoured the reply, out of which Jukes heard only the one word, pronounced with great energy ". . . . Always. . . ."

Captain MacWhirr released Jukes, and bending over the boatswain, yelled "Get back with the mate." Jukes only knew that the arm was gone off his shoulders. He was dismissed with his orders—to do what? He was exasperated into letting go his hold carelessly, and on the instant was blown away. It seemed to him that nothing could stop him from being blown right over the stern. He flung himself down hastily, and the boatswain, who was following, fell on him.

"Don't you get up yet, sir," cried the boatswain. "No hurry!"

A sea swept over. Jukes understood the boatswain to splutter that the bridge ladders were gone. "I'll lower you down, sir, by your hands," he screamed. He shouted also something about the smoke-stack being as likely to go overboard as not. Jukes thought it very possible, and imagined the fires out, the ship helpless. . . . The boatswain by his side kept on yelling. "What? What is it?" Jukes cried distressfully; and the other repeated, "What would my old woman say if she saw me now?"

In the alleyway, where a lot of water had got in and splashed in the dark, the men were still as death, till Jukes stumbled against one of them and cursed him savagely for being in the way. Two or three voices then asked, eager and weak, "Any chance for us, sir?"

"What's the matter with you fools?" he said, brutally. He felt as though he could throw himself down amongst them and never move any more. But they seemed cheered; and in the midst of obsequious warnings, "Look out! Mind that manhole lid, sir," they lowered him into the bunker. The boatswain tumbled down after him, and as soon as he had picked himself up he remarked, "She would say, 'Serve you right, you old fool, for going to sea.'"

The boatswain had some means, and made a point of alluding to them frequently. His wife—a fat woman —and two grown-up daughters kept a greengrocer's shop in the East-end of London.

In the dark, Jukes, unsteady on his legs, listened to a faint thunderous patter. A deadened screaming went on steadily at his elbow, as it were; and from above the louder tumult of the storm descended upon these near sounds. His head swam. To him, too, in that bunker, the motion of the ship seemed novel and menacing, sapping his resolution as though he had never been afloat before.

He had half a mind to scramble out again; but the remembrance of Captain MacWhirr's voice made this impossible. His orders were to go and see. What was the good of it, he wanted to know. Enraged, he told himself he would see—of course. But the boatswain, staggering clumsily, warned him to be careful how he opened that door; there was a blamed fight going on. And Jukes, as if in great bodily pain, desired irritably to know what the devil they were fighting for.

"Dollars! Dollars, sir. All their rotten chests got burst open. Blamed money skipping all over the place, and they are tumbling after it head over heels—tearing and biting like anything. A regular little hell in there."

Jukes convulsively opened the door. The short boatswain peered under his arm.

One of the lamps had gone out, broken perhaps. Rancorous, guttural cries burst out loudly on their ears, and a strange panting sound, the working of all these straining breasts. A hard blow hit the side of the ship: water fell above with a stunning shock, and in the forefront of the gloom, where the air was reddish and thick, Jukes saw a head bang the deck violently, two thick calves waving on high, muscular arms twined round a naked body, a yellow-face, open-mouthed and with a set wild stare, look up and slide away. An empty chest clattered turning over; a man fell head first with a jump, as if lifted by a kick; and farther off, indistinct, others streamed like a mass of rolling stones down a bank, thumping the deck with their feet and flourishing their arms wildly. The hatchway ladder was loaded with coolies swarming on it like bees on a branch. They hung on the steps in a crawling, stirring cluster, beating madly with their fists the underside of the battened hatch, and the headlong rush of the water above was heard in the intervals of their yelling. The ship heeled over more, and they began to drop off: first one, then two, then all the rest went away together, falling straight off with a great cry.

Jukes was confounded. The boatswain, with gruff anxiety, begged him, "Don't you go in there, sir."

The whole place seemed to twist upon itself, jumping incessantly the while; and when the ship rose to a sea Jukes fancied that all these men would be shot upon him in a body. He backed out, swung the door to, and with trembling hands pushed at the bolt. . . .

As soon as his mate had gone Captain MacWhirr, left alone on the bridge, sidled and staggered as far as the wheelhouse. Its door being hinged forward, he had to fight the gale for admittance, and when at last he managed to enter, it was with an instantaneous clatter and a bang, as though he had been fired through the wood. He stood within, holding on to the handle.

The steering-gear leaked steam, and in the confined space the glass of the binnacle made a shiny oval of light in a thin white fog. The wind howled, hummed, whistled, with sudden booming gusts that rattled the doors and shutters in the vicious patter of sprays. Two coils of lead-line and a small canvas bag hung on a long lanyard, swung wide off, and came back clinging to the bulkheads. The gratings underfoot were nearly afloat; with every sweeping blow of a sea, water squirted violently through the cracks all round the door, and the man at the helm had flung down his cap, his coat, and stood propped against the gear-casing in a striped cotton shirt open on his breast. The little brass wheel in his hands had the appearance of a bright and fragile toy. The cords of his neck stood hard and lean, a dark patch lay in the hollow of his throat, and his face was still and sunken as in death.

Captain MacWhirr wiped his eyes. The sea that had nearly taken him overboard had, to his great annoyance, washed his sou'-wester hat off his bald head. The fluffy, fair hair, soaked and darkened, resembled a mean skein of cotton threads festooned round his bare skull. His face, glistening with sea-water, had been made crimson with the wind, with the sting of sprays. He looked as though he had come off sweating from before a furnace.

"You here?" he muttered, heavily.

The second mate had found his way into the wheel-house some time before. He had fixed himself in a corner with his knees up, a fist pressed against each temple; and this attitude suggested rage, sorrow, resignation, surrender, with a sort of concentrated unforgiveness. He said mournfully and defiantly, "Well, it's my watch below now: ain't it?"

The steam gear clattered, stopped, clattered again; and the helmsman's eyeballs seemed to project out of a hungry face as if the compass card behind the binnacle glass had been meat. God knows how long he had been left there to steer, as if forgotten by all his shipmates. The bells had not been struck; there had been no reliefs; the ship's routine had gone down wind; but he was trying to keep her head north-north-east. The rudder might have been gone for all he knew, the fires out, the engines broken down, the ship ready to roll over like a corpse. He was anxious not to get muddled and lose control of her head, because the compass-card swung far both ways, wriggling on the pivot, and sometimes seemed to whirl right round. He suffered from mental stress. He was horribly afraid, also, of the wheelhouse going. Mountains of water kept on tumbling against it. When the ship took one of her desperate dives the corners of his lips twitched.

Captain MacWhirr looked up at the wheelhouse clock. Screwed to the bulk-head, it had a white face on which the black hands appeared to stand quite still. It was half-past one in the morning.

"Another day," he muttered to himself.

The second mate heard him, and lifting his head as one grieving amongst ruins, "You won't see it break," he exclaimed. His wrists and his knees could be seen to shake violently. "No, by God! You won't. . . ."

He took his face again between his fists.

The body of the helmsman had moved slightly, but his head didn't budge on his neck,—like a stone head fixed to look one way from a column. During a roll that all but took his booted legs from under him, and in the very stagger to save himself, Captain Mac-Whirr said austerely, "Don't you pay any attention to what that man says." And then, with an indefinable change of tone, very grave, he added, "He isn't on duty."

The sailor said nothing.

The hurricane boomed, shaking the little place, which seemed air-tight; and the light of the binnacle flickered all the time.

"You haven't been relieved," Captain MacWhirr went on, looking down. "I want you to stick to the helm, though, as long as you can. You've got the hang of her. Another man coming here might make a mess of it. Wouldn't do. No child's play. And the hands are probably busy with a job down below. . . . Think you can?"

The steering-gear leaped into an abrupt short clatter, stopped smouldering like an ember; and the still man, with a motionless gaze, burst out, as if all the passion in him had gone into his lips: "By Heavens, sir! I can steer for ever*if nobody talks to me."

"Oh! aye! All right. . . ." The Captain lifted his eyes for the first time to the man, ". . . Hackett."

And he seemed to dismiss this matter from his mind. He stooped to the engine-room speaking-tube, blew in, and bent his head. Mr. Rout below answered, and at once Captain MacWhirr put his lips to the mouthpiece.

With the uproar of the gale around him he applied alternately his lips and his ear, and the engineer's voice mounted to him, harsh and as if out of the heat of an engagement. One of the stokers was disabled, the others had given in, the second engineer and the donkey-man were firing-up. The third engineer was standing by the steam-valve. The engines were being tended by hand. How was it above?

"Bad enough. It mostly rests with you," said Captain MacWhirr. Was the mate down there yet? No? Well, he would be presently. Would Mr. Rout let him talk through the speaking-tube?—through the deck speaking-tube, because he—the Captain—was going out again on the bridge directly. There was some trouble amongst the Chinamen. They were fighting, it seemed. Couldn't allow fighting anyhow. . . .

Mr. Rout had gone away, and Captain MacWhirr could feel against his ear the pulsation of the engines, like the beat of the ship's heart. Mr. Rout's voice down there shouted something distantly. The ship pitched headlong, the pulsation leaped with a hissing tumult, and stopped dead. Captain MacWhirr's face was impassive, and his eyes were fixed aimlessly on the crouching shape of the second mate. Again Mr. Rout's voice cried out in the depths, and the pulsating beats recommenced, with slow strokes—growing swifter.

Mr. Rout had returned to the tube. "It don't matter much what they do," he said, hastily; and then, with irritation, "She takes these dives as if she never meant to come up again."

"Awful sea," said the Captain's voice from above.

"Don't let me drive her under," barked Solomon Rout up the pipe.

"Dark and rain. Can't see what's coming," uttered the voice. "Must—keep—her—moving—enough to steer—and chance it," it went on to state distinctly.

"I am doing as much as I dare."

"We are—getting—smashed up—a good deal up here," proceeded the voice mildly. "Doing—fairly well—though. Of course, if the wheelhouse should go. . . ."

Mr. Rout, bending an attentive ear, muttered peevishly something under his breath.

But the deliberate voice up there became animated to ask: "Jukes turned up yet?" Then, after a short wait, "I wish he would bear a hand. I want him to be done and come up here in case of anything. To look after the ship. I am all alone. The second mate's lost. . . ."

"What?" shouted Mr. Rout into the engine-room, taking his head away. Then up the tube he cried, "Gone overboard?" and clapped his ear to.

"Lost his nerve," the voice from above continued in a matter-of-fact tone. "Damned awkward circumstance."

Mr. Rout, listening with bowed neck, opened his eyes wide at this. However, he heard something like the sounds of a scuffle and broken exclamations coming down to him. He strained his hearing; and all the time Beale, the third engineer, with his arms uplifted, held between the palms of his hands the rim of a little black wheel projecting at the side of a big copper pipe.

He seemed to be poising it above his head, as though it were a correct attitude in some sort of game.

To steady himself, he pressed his shoulder against the white bulkhead, one knee bent, and a sweat-rag tucked in his belt hanging on his hip. His smooth cheek was begrimed and flushed, and the coal dust on his eyelids, like the black pencilling of a make-up, enhanced the liquid brilliance of the whites, giving to his youthful face something of a feminine, exotic and fascinating aspect. When the ship pitched he would with hasty movements of his hands screw hard at the little wheel.

"Gone crazy," began the Captain's voice suddenly in the tube. "Rushed at me. . . . Just now. Had to knock him down. . . . This minute. You heard, Mr. Rout?"

"The devil!" muttered Mr. Rout. "Look out, Beale!"

His shout rang out like the blast of a warning trumpet, between the iron walls of the engine-room. Painted white, they rose high into the dusk of the skylight, sloping like a roof; and the whole lofty space resembled the interior of a monument, divided by floors of iron grating, with lights flickering at different levels, and a mass of gloom lingering in the middle, within the columnar stir of machinery under the motionless swelling of the cylinders. A loud and wild resonance, made up of all the noises of the hurricane, dwelt in the still warmth of the air. There was in it the smell of hot metal, of oil, and a slight mist of steam. The blows of the sea seemed to traverse it in an unringing, stunning shock, from side to side.

Gleams, like pale long flames, trembled upon the polish of metal; from the flooring below, the enormous crank-heads emerged in their turns with a flash of

brass and steel—going over; while the connecting-rods,
big-jointed, like skeleton limbs, seemed to thrust them
down and pull them up again with an irresistible precision. And deep in the half-light other rods dodged
deliberately to and fro, crossheads nodded, discs of
metal rubbed smoothly against each other, slow and
gentle, in a commingling of shadows and gleams.

Sometimes all those powerful and unerring movements would slow down simultaneously, as if they had
been the functions of a living organism, stricken suddenly by the blight of languor; and Mr. Rout's eyes
would blaze darker in his long sallow face. He was
fighting this fight in a pair of carpet slippers. A
short shiny jacket barely covered his loins, and his
white wrists protruded far out of the tight sleeves, as
though the emergency had added to his stature, had
lengthened his limbs, augmented his pallor, hollowed
his eyes.

He moved, climbing high up, disappearing low down,
with a restless, purposeful industry, and when he stood
still, holding the guard-rail in front of the starting-gear,
he would keep glancing to the right at the steam-gauge,
at the water-gauge, fixed upon the white wall in the
light of a swaying lamp. The mouths of two speaking-
tubes gaped stupidly at his elbow, and the dial of the
engine-room telegraph resembled a clock of large diameter, bearing on its face curt words instead of figures.
The grouped letters stood out heavily black, around the
pivot-head of the indicator, emphatically symbolic
of loud exclamations: AHEAD, ASTERN, SLOW, HALF,
STAND BY; and the fat black hand pointed downwards
to the word FULL, which, thus singled out, captured
the eye as a sharp cry secures attention.

The wood-encased bulk of the low-pressure cylinder,
frowning portly from above, emitted a faint wheeze

at every thrust, and except for that low hiss the engines worked their steel limbs headlong or slow with a silent, determined smoothness. And all this, the white walls, the moving steel, the floor plates under Solomon Rout's feet, the floors of iron grating above his head, the dusk and the gleams, uprose and sank continuously, with one accord, upon the harsh wash of the waves against the ship's side. The whole loftiness of the place, booming hollow to the great voice of the wind, swayed at the top like a tree, would go over bodily, as if borne down this way and that by the tremendous blasts.

"You've got to hurry up," shouted Mr. Rout, as soon as he saw Jukes appear in the stokehold doorway.

Jukes' glance was wandering and tipsy; his red face was puffy, as though he had overslept himself. He had had an arduous road, and had travelled over it with immense vivacity, the agitation of his mind corresponding to the exertions of his body. He had rushed up out of the bunker, stumbling in the dark alleyway amongst a lot of bewildered men who, trod upon, asked "What's up, sir?" in awed mutters all round him;—down the stokehold ladder, missing many iron rungs in his hurry, down into a place deep as a well, black as Tophet, tipping over back and forth like a see-saw. The water in the bilges thundered at each roll, and lumps of coal skipped to and fro, from end to end, rattling like an avalanche of pebbles on a slope of iron.

Somebody in there moaned with pain, and somebody else could be seen crouching over what seemed the prone body of a dead man; a lusty voice blasphemed; and the glow under each fire-door was like a pool of flaming blood radiating quietly in a velvety blackness.

A gust of wind struck upon the nape of Jukes' neck and next moment he felt it streaming about his wet ankles. The stokehold ventilators hummed: in front of the six fire-doors two wild figures, stripped to the waist, staggered and stooped, wrestling with two shovels.

"Hallo! Plenty of draught now," yelled the second engineer at once, as though he had been all the time looking out for Jukes. The donkeyman, a dapper little chap with a dazzling fair skin and a tiny, gingery moustache, worked in a sort of mute transport. They were keeping a full head of steam, and a profound rumbling, as of an empty furniture van trotting over a bridge, made a sustained bass to all the other noises of the place.

"Blowing off all the time," went on yelling the second.* With a sound as of a hundred scoured saucepans, the orifice of a ventilator spat upon his shoulder a sudden gush of salt water, and he volleyed a stream of curses upon all things on earth including his own soul, ripping and raving, and all the time attending to his business. With a sharp clash of metal the ardent pale glare of the fire opened upon his bullet head, showing his spluttering lips, his insolent face, and with another clang closed like the white-hot wink of an iron eye.

"Where's the blooming ship? Can you tell me? blast my eyes! Under water—or what? It's coming down here in tons. Are the condemned cowls gone to Hades? Hey? Don't you know anything—you jolly sailor-man you . . . ?"

Jukes, after a bewildered moment, had been helped by a roll to dart through; and as soon as his eyes took in the comparative vastness, peace and brilliance of the engine-room, the ship, setting her stern heavily in the water, sent him charging head down upon Mr. Rout.

The chief's arm, long like a tentacle, and straightening as if worked by a spring, went out to meet him, and deflected his rush into a spin towards the speaking-tubes. At the same time Mr. Rout repeated earnestly:

"You've got to hurry up, whatever it is."

Jukes yelled "Are you there, sir?" and listened. Nothing. Suddenly the roar of the wind fell straight into his ear, but presently a small voice shoved aside the shouting hurricane quietly.

"You, Jukes?—Well?"

Jukes was ready to talk: it was only time that seemed to be wanting. It was easy enough to account for everything. He could perfectly imagine the coolies battened down in the reeking 'tween-deck, lying sick and scared between the rows of chests. Then one of these chests—or perhaps several at once—breaking loose in a roll, knocking out others, sides splitting, lids flying open, and all these clumsy Chinamen rising up in a body to save their property. Afterwards every fling of the ship would hurl that tramping, yelling mob here and there, from side to side, in a whirl of smashed wood, torn clothing, rolling dollars. A struggle once started, they would be unable to stop themselves. Nothing could stop them now except main force. It was a disaster. He had seen it, and that was all he could say. Some of them must be dead, he believed. The rest would go on fighting. . . .

He sent up his words, tripping over each other, crowding the narrow tube. They mounted as if into a silence of an enlightened comprehension dwelling alone up there with a storm. And Jukes wanted to be dismissed from the face of that odious trouble intruding on the great need of the ship.

V

HE WAITED. Before his eyes the engines turned with slow labour, that in the moment of going off into a mad fling would stop dead at Mr. Rout's shout, "Look out, Beale!" They paused in an intelligent immobility, stilled in mid-stroke, a heavy crank arrested on the cant, as if conscious of danger and the passage of time. Then, with a "Now, then!" from the chief, and the sound of a breath expelled through clenched teeth, they would accomplish the interrupted revolution and begin another.

There was the prudent sagacity of wisdom and the deliberation of enormous strength in their movements. This was their work—this patient coaxing of a distracted ship over the fury of the waves and into the very eye of the wind. At times Mr. Rout's chin would sink on his breast, and he watched them with knitted eyebrows as if lost in thought.

The voice that kept the hurricane out of Jukes' ear began: "Take the hands with you . . . ," and left off unexpectedly.

"What could I do with them, sir?"

A harsh, abrupt, imperious clang exploded suddenly. The three pairs of eyes flew up to the telegraph dial to see the hand jump from FULL to STOP, as if snatched by a devil. And then these three men in the engine-room had the intimate sensation of a check upon the ship, of a strange shrinking, as if she had gathered herself for a desperate leap.

"Stop her!" bellowed Mr. Rout.

Nobody—not even Captain MacWhirr, who alone on deck had caught sight of a white line of foam coming on at such a height that he couldn't believe his eyes—nobody was to know the steepness of that sea and the awful depth of the hollow the hurricane had scooped out behind the running wall of water.

It raced to meet the ship, and, with a pause, as of girding the loins,* the *Nan-Shan* lifted her bows and leaped. The flames in all the lamps sank, darkening the engine-room. One went out. With a tearing crash and a swirling, raving tumult, tons of water fell upon the deck, as though the ship had darted under the foot of a cataract.

Down there they looked at each other, stunned.

"Swept from end to end, by God!" bawled Jukes.

She dipped into the hollow straight down, as if going over the edge of the world. The engine-room toppled forward menacingly, like the inside of a tower nodding in an earthquake. An awful racket, of iron things falling, came from the stokehold. She hung on this appalling slant long enough for Beale to drop on his hands and knees and begin to crawl as if he meant to fly on all fours out of the engine-room, and for Mr. Rout to turn his head slowly, rigid, cavernous, with the lower jaw dropping. Jukes had shut his eyes, and his face in a moment became hopelessly blank and gentle, like the face of a blind man.

At last she rose slowly, staggering, as if she had to lift a mountain with her bows.

Mr. Rout shut his mouth; Jukes blinked; and little Beale stood up hastily.

"Another one like this, and that's the last of her," cried the chief.

He and Jukes looked at each other, and the same thought came into their heads. The Captain! Every-

thing must have been swept away. Steering-gear gone
—ship like a log. All over directly.

"Rush!" ejaculated Mr. Rout thickly, glaring with
enlarged, doubtful eyes at Jukes, who answered him
by an irresolute glance.

The clang of the telegraph gong soothed them instantly. The black hand dropped in a flash from STOP
to FULL.

"Now then, Beale!" cried Mr. Rout.

The steam hissed low. The piston-rods slid in and
out. Jukes put his ear to the tube. The voice was
ready for him. It said: "Pick up all the money.
Bear a hand now. I'll want you up here." And that
was all.

"Sir?" called up Jukes. There was no answer.

He staggered away like a defeated man from the
field of battle. He had got, in some way or other, a cut
above his left eyebrow—a cut to the bone. He was not
aware of it in the least: quantities of the China Sea,
large enough to break his neck for him, had gone over
his head, had cleaned, washed, and salted that wound.
It did not bleed, but only gaped red; and this gash over
the eye, his dishevelled hair, the disorder of his clothes,
gave him the aspect of a man worsted in a fight with
fists.

"Got to pick up the dollars." He appealed to Mr.
Rout, smiling pitifully at random.

"What's that?" asked Mr. Rout, wildly. "Pick up
. . . ? I don't care. . . ." Then, quivering in
every muscle, but with an exaggeration of paternal
tone, "Go away now, for God's sake. You deck
people'll drive me silly. There's that second mate been
going for the old man. Don't you know? You fellows
are going wrong for want of something to do. . . ."

At these words Jukes discovered in himself the

beginnings of anger. Want of something to do—indeed. . . . Full of hot scorn against the chief, he turned to go the way he had come. In the stokehold the plump donkeyman toiled with his shovel mutely, as if his tongue had been cut out; but the second was carrying on like a noisy, undaunted maniac, who had preserved his skill in the art of stoking under a marine boiler.

"Hallo, you wandering officer! Hey! Can't you get some of your slush-slingers to wind up a few of them ashes? I am getting choked with them there. Curse it! Hallo! Hey! Remember the articles: *Sailors and firemen to assist each other.* Hey! D'ye hear?"

Jukes was climbing out frantically, and the other, lifting up his face after him, howled, "Can't you speak? What are you poking about here for? What's your game, anyhow?"

A frenzy possessed Jukes. By the time he was back amongst the men in the darkness of the alleyway, he felt ready to wring all their necks at the slightest sign of hanging back. The very thought of it exasperated him. *He* couldn't hang back. They shouldn't.

The impetuosity with which he came amongst them carried them along. They had already been excited and startled at all his comings and goings—by the fierceness and rapidity of his movements; and more felt than seen in his rushes, he appeared formidable—busied with matters of life and death that brooked no delay. At his first word he heard them drop into the bunker one after another obediently, with heavy thumps.

They were not clear as to what would have to be done. "What is it? What is it?" they were asking each other. The boatswain tried to explain; the sounds of a great scuffle surprised them: and the

mighty shocks, reverberating awfully in the black
bunker, kept them in mind of their danger. When the
boatswain threw open the door it seemed that an eddy
of the hurricane, stealing through the iron sides of the
ship, had set all these bodies whirling like dust: there
came to them a confused uproar, a tempestuous tumult,
a fierce mutter, gusts of screams dying away, and the
tramping of feet mingling with the blows of the sea.

For a moment they glared amazed, blocking the
doorway. Jukes pushed through them brutally. He
said nothing, and simply darted in. Another lot of
coolies on the ladder, struggling suicidally to break
through the battened hatch to a swamped deck, fell off
as before, and he disappeared under them like a man
overtaken by a landslide.

The boatswain yelled excitedly: "Come along. Get
the mate out. He'll be trampled to death. Come on."

They charged in, stamping on breasts, on fingers, on
faces, catching their feet in heaps of clothing, kicking
broken wood; but before they could get hold of him
Jukes emerged waist deep in a multitude of clawing
hands. In the instant he had been lost to view, all the
buttons of his jacket had gone, its back had got split up
to the collar, his waistcoat had been torn open. The
central struggling mass of Chinamen went over to the
roll, dark, indistinct, helpless, with a wild gleam of
many eyes in the dim light of the lamps.

"Leave me alone—damn you. I am all right,"
screeched Jukes. "Drive them forward. Watch your
chance when she pitches. Forward with 'em. Drive
them against the bulkhead. Jam 'em up."

The rush of the sailors into the seething 'tween-deck
was like a splash of cold water into a boiling cauldron.
The commotion sank for a moment.

The bulk of Chinamen were locked in such a compact

scrimmage that, linking their arms and aided by an appalling dive of the ship, the seamen sent it forward in one great shove, like a solid block. Behind their backs small clusters and loose bodies tumbled from side to side.

The boatswain performed prodigious feats of strength. With his long arms open, and each great paw clutching at a stanchion, he stopped the rush of seven entwined Chinamen rolling like a boulder. His joints cracked; he said, "Ha!" and they flew apart. But the carpenter showed the greater intelligence. Without saying a word to anybody he went back into the alley-way, to fetch several coils of cargo gear he had seen there—chain and rope. With these life-lines were rigged.

There was really no resistance. The struggle, however it began, had turned into a scramble of blind panic. If the coolies had started up after their scattered dollars they were by that time fighting only for their footing. They took each other by the throat merely to save themselves from being hurled about. Whoever got a hold anywhere would kick at the others who caught at his legs and hung on, till a roll sent them flying together across the deck.

The coming of the white devils was a terror. Had they come to kill? The individuals torn out of the ruck became very limp in the seamen's hands: some, dragged aside by the heels, were passive, like dead bodies, with open, fixed eyes. Here and there a coolie would fall on his knees as if begging for mercy; several, whom the excess of fear made unruly, were hit with hard fists between the eyes, and cowered; while those who were hurt submitted to rough handling, blinking rapidly without a plaint. Faces streamed with blood; there were raw places on the shaven heads, scratches, bruises, torn wounds, gashes. The broken porcelain out of the chests was mostly responsible for the latter. Here and there a Chinaman, wild-eyed, with his tail unplaited, nursed a bleeding sole.

They had been ranged closely, after having been shaken into submission, cuffed a little to allay excitement, addressed in gruff words of encouragement that sounded like promises of evil. They sat on the deck in ghastly, drooping rows, and at the end the carpenter, with two hands to help him, moved busily from place to place, setting taut and hitching the life-lines. The boatswain, with one leg and one arm embracing a stanchion, struggled with a lamp pressed to his breast, trying to get a light, and growling all the time like an industrious gorilla. The figures of seamen stooped repeatedly, with the movements of gleaners, and everything was being flung into the bunker: clothing, smashed wood, broken china, and the dollars, too, gathered up in men's jackets. Now and then a sailor would stagger towards the doorway with his arms full of rubbish; and dolorous, slanting eyes followed his movements.

With every roll of the ship the long rows of sitting Celestials would sway forward brokenly, and her headlong dives knocked together the line of shaven polls from end to end. When the wash of water rolling on the deck died away for a moment, it seemed to Jukes, yet quivering from his exertions, that in his mad struggle down there he had overcome the wind somehow: that a silence had fallen upon the ship, a silence in which the sea struck thunderously at her sides.

Everything had been cleared out of the 'tween-deck —all the wreckage, as the men said. They stood erect and tottering above the level of heads and drooping shoulders. Here and there a coolie sobbed for his

breath. Where the high light fell, Jukes could see the
salient ribs of one, the yellow, wistful face of another;
bowed necks; or would meet a dull stare directed at his
face. He was amazed that there had been no corpses;
but the lot of them seemed at their last gasp, and they
appeared to him more pitiful than if they had been all
dead.

Suddenly one of the coolies began to speak. The
light came and went on his lean, straining face; he threw
his head up like a baying hound. From the bunker
came the sounds of knocking and the tinkle of some
dollars rolling loose; he stretched out his arm, his
mouth yawned black, and the incomprehensible
guttural hooting sounds, that did not seem to belong to
a human language, penetrated Jukes with a strange
emotion as if a brute had tried to be eloquent.

Two more started mouthing what seemed to Jukes
fierce denunciations; the others stirred with grunts and
growls. Jukes ordered the hands out of the 'tween-
decks hurriedly. He left last himself, backing through
the door, while the grunts rose to a loud murmur and
hands were extended after him as after a malefactor.
The boatswain shot the bolt, and remarked uneasily,
"Seems as if the wind had dropped, sir."

The seamen were glad to get back into the alleyway.
Secretly each of them thought that at the last moment
he could rush out on deck—and that was a comfort.
There is something horribly repugnant in the idea of
being drowned under a deck. Now they had done with
the Chinamen, they again became conscious of the
ship's position.

Jukes on coming out of the alleyway found himself
up to the neck in the noisy water. He gained the
bridge, and discovered he could detect obscure shapes
as if his sight had become preternaturally acute. He

saw faint outlines. They recalled not the familiar aspect of the *Nan-Shan*, but something remembered—an old dismantled steamer he had seen years ago rotting on a mudbank. She recalled that wreck.

There was no wind, not a breath, except the faint currents created by the lurches of the ship. The smoke tossed out of the funnel was settling down upon her deck. He breathed it as he passed forward. He felt the deliberate throb of the engines, and heard small sounds that seemed to have survived the great uproar: the knocking of broken fittings, the rapid tumbling of some piece of wreckage on the bridge. He perceived dimly the squat shape of his captain holding on to a twisted bridge-rail, motionless and swaying as if rooted to the planks. The unexpected stillness of the air oppressed Jukes.

"We have done it, sir," he gasped.

"Thought you would," said Captain MacWhirr.

"Did you?" murmured Jukes to himself.

"Wind fell all at once," went on the Captain.

Jukes burst out: "If you think it was an easy job——"

But his captain, clinging to the rail, paid no attention. "According to the books the worst is not over yet."

"If most of them hadn't been half dead with sea-sickness and fright, not one of us would have come out of that 'tween-deck alive," said Jukes.

"Had to do what's fair by them," mumbled MacWhirr, stolidly. "You don't find everything in books."

"Why, I believe they would have risen on us if I hadn't ordered the hands out of that pretty quick," continued Jukes with warmth.

After the whisper of their shouts, their ordinary

tones, so distinct, rang out very loud to their ears in the
amazing stillness of the air. It seemed to them they
were talking in a dark and echoing vault.

Through a jagged aperture in the dome of clouds the
light of a few stars fell upon the black sea, rising and
falling confusedly. Sometimes the head of a watery
cone would topple on board and mingle with the rolling
flurry of foam on the swamped deck; and the *Nan-Shan*
wallowed heavily at the bottom of a circular cistern of
clouds. This ring of dense vapours, gyrating madly
round the calm of the centre, encompassed the ship like
a motionless and unbroken wall of an aspect incon-
ceivably sinister. Within, the sea, as if agitated by an
internal commotion, leaped in peaked mounds that
jostled each other, slapping heavily against her sides;
and a low moaning sound, the infinite plaint of the
storm's fury, came from beyond the limits of the
menacing calm. Captain MacWhirr remained silent,
and Jukes' ready ear caught suddenly the faint, long-
drawn roar of some immense wave rushing unseen under
that thick blackness, which made the appalling boun-
dary of his vision.

"Of course," he started resentfully, "they thought
we had caught at the chance to plunder them. Of
course! You said—pick up the money. Easier said
than done. They couldn't tell what was in our heads.
We came in, smash—right into the middle of them.
Had to do it by a rush."

"As long as it's done . . . ," mumbled the
Captain, without attempting to look at Jukes. "Had
to do what's fair."

"We shall find yet there's the devil to pay when this
is over," said Jukes, feeling very sore. "Let them only
recover a bit, and you'll see. They will fly at our
throats, sir. Don't forget, sir, she isn't a British ship

now. These brutes know it well, too. The damned Siamese flag."

"We are on board, all the same," remarked Captain MacWhirr.

"The trouble's not over yet," insisted Jukes, prophetically, reeling and catching on. "She's a wreck," he added, faintly.

"The trouble's not over yet," assented Captain MacWhirr, half aloud. . . . "Look out for her a minute."

"Are you going off the deck, sir?" asked Jukes, hurriedly, as if the storm were sure to pounce upon him as soon as he had been left alone with the ship.

He watched her, battered and solitary, labouring heavily in a wild scene of mountainous black waters lit by the gleams of distant worlds. She moved slowly, breathing into the still core of the hurricane the excess of her strength in a white cloud of steam—and the deep-toned vibration of the escape was like the defiant trumpeting of a living creature of the sea impatient for the renewal of the contest. It ceased suddenly. The still air moaned. Above Jukes' head a few stars shone into a pit of black vapours. The inky edge of the cloud-disc frowned upon the ship under the patch of glittering sky. The stars, too, seemed to look at her intently, as if for the last time, and the cluster of their splendour sat like a diadem on a lowering brow.

Captain MacWhirr had gone into the chart-room. There was no light there; but he could feel the disorder of that place where he used to live tidily. His armchair was upset. The books had tumbled out on the floor: he scrunched a piece of glass under his boot. He groped for the matches, and found a box on a shelf with a deep ledge. He struck one, and puckering the corners of his eyes, held out the little flame towards the barometer whose glittering top of glass and metals nodded at him continuously.

It stood very low—incredibly low, so low that Captain MacWhirr grunted. The match went out, and hurriedly he extracted another, with thick, stiff fingers.

Again a little flame flared up before the nodding glass and metal of the top. His eyes looked at it narrowed with attention, as if expecting an imperceptible sign. With his grave face he resembled a booted and mis-shapen pagan burning incense before the oracle of a Joss. There was no mistake. It was the lowest reading he had ever seen in his life.

Captain MacWhirr emitted a low whistle. He forgot himself till the flame diminished to a blue spark, burnt his fingers and vanished. Perhaps something had gone wrong with the thing!

There was an aneroid glass screwed above the couch. He turned that way, struck another match, and discovered the white face of the other instrument looking at him from the bulkhead, meaningly, not to be gainsaid, as though the wisdom of men were made unerring by the indifference of matter. There was no room for doubt now. Captain MacWhirr pshawed at it, and threw the match down.

The worst was to come, then—and if the books were right this worst would be very bad. The experience of the last six hours had enlarged his conception of what heavy weather could be like. "It'll be terrific," he pronounced, mentally. He had not consciously looked at anything by the light of the matches except at the barometer; and yet somehow he had seen that his water-bottle and the two tumblers had been flung out of their stand. It seemed to give him a more intimate knowledge of the tossing the ship had gone through. "I wouldn't have believed it," he thought. And his table had been

cleared, too; his rulers, his pencils, the inkstand—all
the things that had their safe appointed places—they
were gone, as if a mischievous hand had plucked them
out one by one and flung them on the wet floor. The
hurricane had broken in upon the orderly arrangements of his privacy. This had never happened before,
and the feeling of dismay reached the very seat of his
composure. And the worst was to come yet! He was
glad the trouble in the 'tween-deck had been discovered
in time. If the ship had to go after all, then, at least,
she wouldn't be going to the bottom with a lot of
people in her fighting teeth and claw. That would have
been odious. And in that feeling there was a humane
intention and a vague sense of the fitness of things.

These instantaneous thoughts were yet in their
essence heavy and slow, partaking of the nature of the
man. He extended his hand to put back the matchbox
in its corner of the shelf. There were always matches
there—by his order. The steward had his instructions
impressed upon him long before. "A box . . .
just there, see? Not so very full . . . where I can
put my hand on it, steward. Might want a light in a
hurry. Can't tell on board ship *what* you might want
in a hurry. Mind, now."

And of course on his side he would be careful to put
it back in its place scrupulously. He did so now, but
before he removed his hand it occurred to him that perhaps he would never have occasion to use that box any
more. The vividness of the thought checked him and
for an infinitesimal fraction of a second his fingers
closed again on the small object as though it had been
the symbol of all these little habits that chain us to the
weary round of life. He released it at last, and letting
himself fall on the settee, listened for the first sounds of
returning wind.

Not yet. He heard only the wash of water, the heavy splashes, the dull shocks of the confused seas boarding his ship from all sides. She would never have a chance to clear her decks.

But the quietude of the air was startlingly tense and unsafe, like a slender hair holding a sword suspended over his head.* By this awful pause the storm penetrated the defences of the man and unsealed his lips. He spoke out in the solitude and the pitch darkness of the cabin, as if addressing another being awakened within his breast.

"I shouldn't like to lose her," he said half aloud.

He sat unseen, apart from the sea, from his ship, isolated, as if withdrawn from the very current of his own existence, where such freaks as talking to himself surely had no place. His palms reposed on his knees, he bowed his short neck and puffed heavily, surrendering to a strange sensation of weariness he was not enlightened enough to recognize for the fatigue of mental stress.

From where he sat he could reach the door of a washstand locker. There should have been a towel there. There was. Good. . . . He took it out, wiped his face, and afterwards went on rubbing his wet head. He towelled himself with energy in the dark, and then remained motionless with the towel on his knees. A moment passed, of a stillness so profound that no one could have guessed there was a man sitting in that cabin. Then a murmur arose.

"She may come out of it yet."

When Captain MacWhirr came out on deck, which he did brusquely, as though he had suddenly become conscious of having stayed away too long, the calm had lasted already more than fifteen minutes—long enough to make itself intolerable even to his imagination. Jukes, motionless on the forepart of the bridge, began to speak at once. His voice, blank and forced as though he were talking through hard-set teeth, seemed to flow away on all sides into the darkness, deepening again upon the sea.

"I had the wheel relieved. Hackett began to sing out that he was done. He's lying in there alongside the steering-gear with a face like death. At first I couldn't get anybody to crawl out and relieve the poor devil. That bosun's worse than no good, I always said. Thought I would have had to go myself and haul out one of them by the neck."

"Ah, well," muttered the Captain. He stood watchful by Jukes' side.

"The second mate's in there, too, holding his head. Is he hurt, sir?"

"No—crazy," said Captain MacWhirr, curtly.

"Looks as if he had a tumble, though."

"I had to give him a push," explained the Captain.

Jukes gave an impatient sigh.

"It will come very sudden," said Captain MacWhirr, "and from over there, I fancy. God only knows though. These books are only good to muddle your head and make you jumpy. It will be bad, and there's an end. If we only can steam her round in time to meet it. . . ."

A minute passed. Some of the stars winked rapidly and vanished.

"You left them pretty safe?" began the Captain abruptly, as though the silence were unbearable.

"Are you thinking of the coolies, sir? I rigged life-lines all ways across that 'tween-deck."

"Did you? Good idea, Mr. Jukes."

"I didn't . . . think you cared to . . . know," said Jukes—the lurching of the ship cut his speech as though somebody had been jerking him around while he talked—"how I got on with . . . that infernal job. We did it. And it may not matter in the end."

"Had to do what's fair, for all—they are only Chinamen. Give them the same chance with ourselves—hang it all. She isn't lost yet. Bad enough to be shut up below in a gale——"

"That's what I thought when you gave me the job, sir," interjected Jukes, moodily.

"——without being battered to pieces," pursued Captain MacWhirr with rising vehemence. "Couldn't let that go on in my ship, if I knew she hadn't five minutes to live. Couldn't bear it, Mr. Jukes."

A hollow echoing noise, like that of a shout rolling in a rocky chasm, approached the ship and went away again. The last star, blurred, enlarged, as if returning to the fiery mist of its beginning, struggled with the colossal depth of blackness hanging over the ship—and went out.

"Now for it!" muttered Captain MacWhirr. "Mr. Jukes."

"Here, sir."

The two men were growing indistinct to each other.

"We must trust her to go through it and come out on the other side. That's plain and straight. There's no room for Captain Wilson's storm-strategy here."

"No, sir."

"She will be smothered and swept again for hours," mumbled the Captain. "There's not much left by this time above deck for the sea to take away—unless you or me."

"Both, sir," whispered Jukes, breathlessly.

"You are always meeting trouble half way, Jukes," Captain MacWhirr remonstrated quaintly. "Though it's a fact that the second mate is no good. D'ye hear, Mr. Jukes? You would be left alone if. . . ."

Captain MacWhirr interrupted himself, and Jukes, glancing on all sides, remained silent.

"Don't you be put out by anything," the Captain continued, mumbling rather fast. "Keep her facing it. They may say what they like, but the heaviest seas run with the wind. Facing it—always facing it—that's the way to get through. You are a young sailor Face it. That's enough for any man. Keep a cool head."

"Yes, sir," said Jukes, with a flutter of the heart.

In the next few seconds the Captain spoke to the engine-room and got an answer.

For some reason Jukes experienced an access of confidence, a sensation that came from outside like a warm breath, and made him feel equal to every demand. The distant muttering of the darkness stole into his ears. He noted it unmoved, out of that sudden belief in himself, as a man safe in a shirt of mail would watch a point.

The ship laboured without intermission amongst the black hills of water, paying with this hard tumbling the price of her life. She rumbled in her depths, shaking a white plummet of steam into the night, and Jukes' thought skimmed like a bird through the engine-room, where Mr. Rout—good man—was ready. When the rumbling ceased it seemed to him that there was a pause of every sound, a dead pause in which Captain MacWhirr's voice rang out startlingly.

"What's that? A puff of wind?"—it spoke much louder than Jukes had ever heard it before—"On the bow. That's right. She may come out of it yet."

The mutter of the winds drew near apace. In the forefront could be distinguished a drowsy waking plaint passing on, and far off the growth of a multiple clamour, marching and expanding. There was the throb as of many drums in it, a vicious rushing note, and like the chant of a tramping multitude.

Jukes could no longer see his captain distinctly. The darkness was absolutely piling itself upon the ship. At most he made out movements, a hint of elbows spread out, of a head thrown up.

Captain MacWhirr was trying to do up the top button of his oilskin coat with unwonted haste. The hurricane, with its power to madden the seas, to sink ships, to uproot trees, to overturn strong walls and dash the very birds of the air to the ground, had found this taciturn man in its path, and, doing its utmost, had managed to wring out a few words. Before the renewed wrath of winds swooped on his ship, Captain MacWhirr was moved to declare, in a tone of vexation, as it were: "I wouldn't like to lose her."

He was spared that annoyance.

VI

On a bright sunshiny day, with the breeze chasing
her smoke far ahead, the *Nan-Shan* came into Fu-chau.
Her arrival was at once noticed on shore, and the seamen in harbour said: "Look! Look at that steamer.
What's that? Siamese—isn't she? Just look at her!"

She seemed, indeed, to have been used as a running
target for the secondary batteries of a cruiser. A hail
of minor shells could not have given her upper works a
more broken, torn, and devastated aspect: and she had
about her the worn, weary air of ships coming from the
far ends of the world—and indeed with truth, for in her
short passage she had been very far; sighting, verily,
even the coast of the Great Beyond, whence no ship
ever returns to give up her crew to the dust of the
earth. She was incrusted and gray with salt to the
trucks of her masts and to the top of her funnel; as
though (as some facetious seaman said) "the crowd on
board had fished her out somewhere from the bottom
of the sea and brought her in here for salvage." And
further, excited by the felicity of his own wit, he offered
to give five pounds for her—"as she stands."

Before she had been quite an hour at rest, a meagre
little man, with a red-tipped nose and a face cast in an
angry mould, landed from a sampan on the quay of the
Foreign Concession, and incontinently turned to shake
his fist at her.

A tall individual, with legs much too thin for a rotund
stomach, and with watery eyes, strolled up and remarked, "Just left her—eh? Quick work."

He wore a soiled suit of blue flannel with a pair of dirty cricketing shoes; a dingy gray moustache drooped from his lip, and daylight could be seen in two places between the rim and the crown of his hat.

"Hallo! what are you doing here?" asked the ex-second-mate of the *Nan-Shan*, shaking hands hurriedly.

"Standing by for a job—chance worth taking—got a quiet hint," explained the man with the broken hat, in jerky, apathetic wheezes.

The second shook his fist again at the *Nan-Shan*. "There's a fellow there that ain't fit to have the command of a scow," he declared, quivering with passion, while the other looked about listlessly.

"Is there?"

But he caught sight on the quay of a heavy seaman's chest, painted brown under a fringed sailcloth cover, and lashed with new manila line. He eyed it with awakened interest.

"I would talk and raise trouble if it wasn't for that damned Siamese flag. Nobody to go to—or I would make it hot for him. The fraud! Told his chief engineer—that's another fraud for you—I had lost my nerve. The greatest lot of ignorant fools that ever sailed the seas. No! You can't think . . ."

"Got your money all right?" inquired his seedy acquaintance suddenly.

"Yes. Paid me off on board," raged the second mate. "'Get your breakfast on shore,' says he."

"Mean skunk!" commented the tall man, vaguely, and passed his tongue on his lips. "What about having a drink of some sort?"

"He struck me," hissed the second mate.

"No! Struck! You don't say?" The man in blue began to bustle about sympathetically. "Can't possibly talk here. I want to know all about it.

Struck—eh? Let's get a fellow to carry your chest. I know a quiet place where they have some bottled beer. . . ."

Mr. Jukes, who had been scanning the shore through a pair of glasses, informed the chief engineer afterwards that "our late second mate hasn't been long in finding a friend. A chap looking uncommonly like a bummer. I saw them walk away together from the quay."

The hammering and banging of the needful repairs did not disturb Captain MacWhirr. The steward found in the letter he wrote, in a tidy chart-room, passages of such absorbing interest that twice he was nearly caught in the act. But Mrs. MacWhirr, in the drawing-room of the forty-pound house, stifled a yawn—perhaps out of self-respect—for she was alone.

She reclined in a plush-bottomed and gilt hammock-chair near a tiled fireplace, with Japanese fans on the mantel and a glow of coals in the grate. Lifting her hands, she glanced wearily here and there into the many pages. It was not her fault they were so prosy, so completely uninteresting—from "My darling wife" at the beginning, to "Your loving husband" at the end. She couldn't be really expected to understand all these ship affairs. She was glad, of course, to hear from him, but she had never asked herself why, precisely.

". . . They are called typhoons . . . The mate did not seem to like it . . . Not in books . . . Couldn't think of letting it go on. . . ."

The paper rustled sharply. ". . . . A calm that lasted more than twenty minutes," she read perfunctorily; and the next words her thoughtless eyes caught, on the top of another page, were: "see you and the children again. . . ." She had a movement of

impatience. He was always thinking of coming home.
He had never had such a good salary before. What was
the matter now?

It did not occur to her to turn back overleaf to look.
She would have found it recorded there that between 4
and 6 A. M. on December 25th, Captain MacWhirr did
actually think that his ship could not possibly live another hour in such a sea, and that he would never see
his wife and children again. Nobody was to know this
(his letters got mislaid so quickly)—nobody whatever
but the steward, who had been greatly impressed by
that disclosure. So much so, that he tried to give
the cook some idea of the "narrow squeak we all had"
by saying solemnly, "The old man himself had a dam'
poor opinion of our chance."

"How do you know?" asked, contemptuously, the
cook, an old soldier. "He hasn't told you, maybe?"

"Well, he did give me a hint to that effect," the
steward brazened it out.

"Get along with you! He will be coming to tell
me next," jeered the old cook, over his shoulder.

Mrs. MacWhirr glanced farther, on the alert.
". . . Do what's fair. . . . Miserable objects
. . . . Only three, with a broken leg each, and
one . . . Thought had better keep the matter
quiet . . . hope to have done the fair
thing. . . ."

She let fall her hands. No: there was nothing more
about coming home. Must have been merely expressing a pious wish. Mrs. MacWhirr's mind was set
at ease, and a black marble clock, priced by the
local jeweller at £3 18s. 6d., had a discreet stealthy
tick.

The door flew open, and a girl in the long-legged,
short-frocked period of existence, flung into the room.

A lot of colourless, rather lanky hair was scattered over
her shoulders. Seeing her mother, she stood still,
and directed her pale prying eyes upon the letter.

"From father," murmured Mrs. MacWhirr. "What
have you done with your ribbon?"

The girl put her hands up to her head and pouted.

"He's well," continued Mrs. MacWhirr, languidly.
"At least I think so. He never says." She had a little
laugh. The girl's face expressed a wandering indifference, and Mrs. MacWhirr surveyed her with fond
pride.

"Go and get your hat," she said after a while. "I
am going out to do some shopping. There is a sale at
Linom's."

"Oh, how jolly!" uttered the child, impressively, in
unexpectedly grave vibrating tones, and bounded out
of the room.

It was a fine afternoon, with a gray sky and dry
sidewalks. Outside the draper's Mrs. MacWhirr smiled
upon a woman in a black mantle of generous proportions
armoured in jet and crowned with flowers blooming falsely above a bilious matronly countenance.
They broke into a swift little babble of greetings and
exclamations both together, very hurried, as if the
street were ready to yawn open and swallow all that
pleasure before it could be expressed.

Behind them the high glass doors were kept on the
swing. People couldn't pass, men stood aside waiting
patiently, and Lydia was absorbed in poking the end
of her parasol between the stone flags. Mrs. MacWhirr
talked rapidly.

"Thank you very much. He's not coming home yet.
Of course it's very sad to have him away, but it's such
a comfort to know he keeps so well." Mrs. MacWhirr
drew breath. "The climate there agrees with him,"

she added, beamingly, as if poor MacWhirr had been away touring in China for the sake of his health.

Neither was the chief engineer coming home yet. Mr. Rout knew too well the value of a good billet.

"Solomon says wonders will never cease," cried Mrs. Rout joyously at the old lady in her armchair by the fire. Mr. Rout's mother moved slightly, her withered hands lying in black half-mittens on her lap.

The eyes of the engineer's wife fairly danced on the paper. "That captain of the ship he is in—a rather simple man, you remember, mother?—has done something rather clever, Solomon says."

"Yes, my dear," said the old woman meekly, sitting with bowed silvery head, and that air of inward stillness characteristic of very old people who seem lost in watching the last flickers of life. "I think I remember."

Solomon Rout, Old Sol, Father Sol, the Chief, "Rout, good man"—Mr. Rout, the condescending and paternal friend of youth, had been the baby of her many children—all dead by this time. And she remembered him best as a boy of ten—long before he went away to serve his apprenticeship in some great engineering works in the North. She had seen so little of him since, she had gone through so many years, that she had now to retrace her steps very far back to recognize him plainly in the mist of time. Sometimes it seemed that her daughter-in-law was talking of some strange man.

Mrs. Rout junior was disappointed. "H'm. H'm." She turned the page. "How provoking! He doesn't say what it is. Says I couldn't understand how much there was in it. Fancy! What could it be so very clever? What a wretched man not to tell us!"

She read on without further remark soberly, and at last sat looking into the fire. The chief wrote just a word or two of the typhoon; but something had moved him to express an increased longing for the companionship of the jolly woman. "If it hadn't been that mother must be looked after, I would send you your passage-money to-day. You could set up a small house out here. I would have a chance to see you sometimes then. We are not growing younger. . . ."

"He's well, mother," sighed Mrs. Rout, rousing herself.

"He always was a strong healthy boy," said the old woman, placidly.

But Mr. Jukes' account was really animated and very full. His friend in the Western Ocean trade imparted it freely to the other officers of his liner. "A chap I know writes to me about an extraordinary affair that happened on board his ship in that typhoon—you know—that we read of in the papers two months ago. It's the funniest thing! Just see for yourself what he says. I'll show you his letter."

There were phrases in it calculated to give the impression of light-hearted, indomitable resolution. Jukes had written them in good faith, for he felt thus when he wrote. He described with lurid effect the scenes in the 'tween-deck. ". . . It struck me in a flash that those confounded Chinamen couldn't tell we weren't a desperate kind of robbers. 'Tisn't good to part the Chinaman from his money if he is the stronger party. We need have been desperate indeed to go thieving in such weather, but what could these beggars know of us? So, without thinking of it twice, I got the hands away in a jiffy. Our work was done—that the old man had set his heart on. We cleared out without staying to inquire how they felt. I am convinced that if they had not been so unmercifully shaken, and afraid—each individual one of them—to stand up, we would have been torn to pieces. Oh! It was pretty complete, I can

tell you; and you may run to and fro across the Pond to
the end of time before you find yourself with such a job
on your hands."

After this he alluded professionally to the damage
done to the ship, and went on thus:

"It was when the weather quieted down that the
situation became confoundedly delicate. It wasn't
made any better by us having been lately transferred to
the Siamese flag; though the skipper can't see that it
makes any difference—'as long as *we* are on board'—
he says. There are feelings that this man simply
hasn't got—and there's an end of it. You might just
as well try to make a bedpost understand. But apart
from this it is an infernally lonely state for a ship to
be going about the China seas with no proper consuls,
not even a gunboat of her own anywhere, nor a body to
go to in case of some trouble.

"My notion was to keep these Johnnies under
hatches for another fifteen hours or so; as we weren't
much farther than that from Fu-chau. We would find
there, most likely, some sort of a man-of-war, and once
under her guns we were safe enough; for surely any
skipper of a man-of-war—English, French or Dutch—
would see white men through as far as row on board
goes. We could get rid of them and their money afterwards by delivering them to their Mandarin or Taotai,
or whatever they call these chaps in goggles you see
being carried about in sedan-chairs through their stink-
ing streets.

"The old man wouldn't see it somehow. He wanted
to keep the matter quiet. He got that notion into his
head, and a steam windlass couldn't drag it out of him.
He wanted as little fuss made as possible, for the sake of
the ship's name and for the sake of the owners—'for the
sake of all concerned,' says he, looking at me very hard.

It made me angry hot. Of course you couldn't keep a thing like that quiet; but the chests had been secured in the usual manner and were safe enough for any earthly gale, while this had been an altogether fiendish business I couldn't give you even an idea of.

"Meantime, I could hardly keep on my feet. None of us had a spell of any sort for nearly thirty hours, and there the old man sat rubbing his chin, rubbing the top of his head, and so bothered he didn't even think of pulling his long boots off.

"'I hope, sir,' says I, 'you won't be letting them out on deck before we make ready for them in some shape or other.' Not, mind you, that I felt very sanguine about controlling these beggars if they meant to take charge. A trouble with a cargo of Chinamen is no child's play. I was dam' tired, too. 'I wish,' said I, 'you would let us throw the whole lot of these dollars down to them and leave them to fight it out amongst themselves, while we get a rest.'

"'Now you talk wild, Jukes,' says he, looking up in his slow way that makes you ache all over, somehow. 'We must plan out something that would be fair to all parties.'

"I had no end of work on hand, as you may imagine, so I set the hands going, and then I thought I would turn in a bit. I hadn't been asleep in my bunk ten minutes when in rushes the steward and begins to pull at my leg.

"'For God's sake, Mr. Jukes, come out! Come on deck quick, sir. Oh, do come out!'

"The fellow scared all the sense out of me. I didn't know what had happened: another hurricane—or what. Could hear no wind.

"'The Captain's letting them out. Oh, he is letting them out! Jump on deck, sir, and save us. The chief engineer has just run below for his revolver.'

"That's what I understood the fool to say. However, Father Rout swears he went in there only to get a clean pocket-handkerchief. Anyhow, I made one jump into my trousers and flew on deck aft. There was certainly a good deal of noise going on forward of the bridge. Four of the hands with the bosun were at work abaft. I passed up to them some of the rifles all the ships on the China coast carry in the cabin, and led them on the bridge. On the way I ran against Old Sol, looking startled and sucking at an unlighted cigar.

"'Come along,' I shouted to him.

"We charged, the seven of us, up to the chart-room. All was over. There stood the old man with his sea-boots still drawn up to the hips and in shirt-sleeves—got warm thinking it out, I suppose. Bun-hin's dandy clerk at his elbow, as dirty as a sweep, was still green in the face. I could see directly I was in for something.

"'What the devil are these monkey tricks, Mr Jukes?' asks the old man, as angry as ever he could be. I tell you frankly it made me lose my tongue. 'For God's sake, Mr. Jukes,' says he, 'do take away these rifles from the men. Somebody's sure to get hurt before long if you don't. Damme, if this ship isn't worse than Bedlam! Look sharp now. I want you up here to help me and Bun-hin's Chinaman to count that money. You wouldn't mind lending a hand, too, Mr. Rout, now you are here. The more of us the better.'

"He had settled it all in his mind while I was having a snooze. Had we been an English ship, or only going to land our cargo of coolies in an English port, like Hong-Kong, for instance, there would have been no end of inquiries and bother, claims for damages and so on. But these Chinamen know their officials better than we do.

"The hatches had been taken off already, and they were all on deck after a night and a day down below. It made you feel queer to see so many gaunt, wild faces together. The beggars stared about at the sky, at the sea, at the ship, as though they had expected the whole thing to have been blown to pieces. And no wonder! They had had a doing that would have shaken the soul out of a white man. But then they say a Chinaman has no soul. He has, though, something about him that is deuced tough. There was a fellow (amongst others of the badly hurt) who had had his eye all but knocked out. It stood out of his head the size of half a hen's egg. This would have laid out a white man on his back for a month: and yet there was that chap elbowing here and there in the crowd and talking to the others as if nothing had been the matter. They made a great hubbub amongst themselves, and whenever the old man showed his bald head on the foreside of the bridge, they would all leave off jawing and look at him from below.

"It seems that after he had done his thinking he made that Bun-hin's fellow go down and explain to them the only way they could get their money back. He told me afterwards that, all the coolies having worked in the same place and for the same length of time, he reckoned he would be doing the fair thing by them as near as possible if he shared all the cash we had picked up equally among the lot. You couldn't tell one man's dollars from another's, he said, and if you asked each man how much money he brought on board he was afraid they would lie, and he would find himself a long way short. I think he was right there. As to giving up the money to any Chinese official he could scare up in Fu-chau, he said he might just as well put the lot in his own pocket at once for all the good it would be to them. I suppose they thought so, too.

"We finished the distribution before dark. It was rather a sight: the sea running high, the ship a wreck to look at, these Chinamen staggering up on the bridge one by one for their share, and the old man still booted, and in his shirt-sleeves, busy paying out at the chart-room door, perspiring like anything, and now and then coming down sharp on myself or Father Rout about one thing or another not quite to his mind. He took the share of those who were disabled himself to them on the No. 2 hatch. There were three dollars left over, and these went to the three most damaged coolies, one to each. We turned-to afterwards, and shovelled out on deck heaps of wet rags, all sorts of fragments of things without shape, and that you couldn't give a name to, and let them settle the ownership themselves.

"This certainly is coming as near as can be to keeping the thing quiet for the benefit of all concerned. What's your opinion, you pampered mail-boat swell? The old chief says that this was plainly the only thing that could be done. The skipper remarked to me the other day, 'There are things you find nothing about in books.' I think that he got out of it very well for such a stupid man."

FALK

FALK

A REMINISCENCE

SEVERAL of us, all more or less connected with the sea,* were dining in a small river-hostelry not more than thirty miles from London, and less than twenty from that shallow and dangerous puddle to which our coasting men give the grandiose name of "German Ocean." And through the wide windows we had a view of the Thames; an enfilading view down the Lower Hope Reach. But the dinner was execrable, and all the feast was for the eyes.

That flavour of salt-water which for so many of us had been the very water of life permeated our talk. He who hath known the bitterness of the Ocean shall have its taste for ever in his mouth. But one or two of us, pampered by the life of the land, complained of hunger.* It was impossible to swallow any of that stuff. And indeed there was a strange mustiness in everything. The wooden dining-room stuck out over the mud of the shore like a lacustrine dwelling; the planks of the floor seemed rotten; a decrepid old waiter tottered pathetically to and fro before an antediluvian and worm-eaten sideboard; the chipped plates might have been disinterred from some kitchen midden near an inhabited lake; and the chops recalled times more ancient still, They brought forcibly to one's mind the night of ages when the primeval man, evolving the first rudiments of cookery from his dim consciousness, scorched lumps of flesh at a fire of sticks in the company of other good

fellows; then, gorged and happy, sat him back among
the gnawed bones to tell his artless tales of experience—
the tales of hunger and hunt—and of women, perhaps!

But luckily the wine happened to be as old as the
waiter. So, comparatively empty, but upon the whole
fairly happy, we sat back and told our artless tales.
We talked of the sea and all its works. The sea never
changes, and its works for all the talk of men are
wrapped in mystery. But we agreed that the times
were changed. And we talked of old ships, of sea-
accidents, of break-downs, dismastings; and of a man
who brought his ship safe to Liverpool all the way from
the River Plate under a jury rudder. We talked of
wrecks, of short rations and of heroism—or at least of
what the newspapers would have called heroism at sea—
a manifestation of virtues quite different from the
heroism of primitive times. And now and then falling
silent all together we gazed at the sights of the river.

A P. & O. boat passed bound down. "One gets jolly
good dinners on board these ships," remarked one of our
band. A man with sharp eyes read out the name on
her bows: *Arcadia*. "What a beautiful model of a
ship!" murmured some of us. She was followed by a
small cargo-steamer, and the flag they hauled down
aboard while we were looking showed her to be a
Norwegian. She made an awful lot of smoke, and before it had quite blown away, a high-sided, short, wooden
barque, in ballast and towed by a paddle-tug, appeared in front of the windows. All her hands forward
were busy setting up the headgear; and aft a woman
in a red hood, quite alone with the man at the wheel,
paced the length of the poop back and forth, with the
gray wool of some knitting work in her hands.

"German I should think," muttered one. "The
skipper has his wife on board," remarked another;

and the light of the crimson sunset all ablaze behind the
London smoke, throwing a glow of Bengal light upon
the barque's spars, faded away from the Hope Reach.

Then one of us, who had not spoken before, a man
of more than ,fifty,* that had commanded ships for a
quarter of a century, looking after the barque now
gliding far away, all black on the lustre of the river,
said:

This reminds me of an absurd episode in my life,
now many years ago, when I got first the command of
an iron barque, loading then in a certain Eastern seaport. It was also the capital of an Eastern kingdom,*
lying up a river as might be London lies up this old
Thames of ours. No more need be said of the place;
for this sort of thing might have happened anywhere
where there are ships, skippers, tugboats, and orphan
nieces of indescribable splendour. And the absurdity
of the episode concerns only me, my enemy Falk, and
my friend Hermann.

There seemed to be something like peculiar emphasis
on the words "My friend Hermann," which caused one
of us (for we had just been speaking of heroism at sea)
to say idly and nonchalantly:

"And was this Hermann a hero?"

Not at all, said our grizzled friend. No hero at all.
He was a Schiff-führer: Ship-conductor. That's how
they call a Master Mariner in Germany. I prefer our
way. The alliteration is good, and there is something
in the nomenclature that gives to us as a body the
sense of corporate existence: Apprentice, Mate, Master, in the ancient and honourable craft of the sea. As
to my friend Hermann, he might have been a con-
summate master of the honourable craft, but he was
called officially Schiff-führer, and had the simple, heavy
appearance of a well-to-do farmer, combined with the

good-natured shrewdness of a small shopkeeper. With his shaven chin, round limbs, and heavy eyelids he did not look like a toiler, and even less like an adventurer of the sea. Still, he toiled upon the seas, in his own way, much as a shopkeeper works behind his counter. And his ship was the means by which he maintained his growing family.

She was a heavy, strong, blunt-bowed affair, awakening the ideas of primitive solidity, like the wooden plough of our forefathers. And there were, about her, other suggestions of a rustic and homely nature. The extraordinary timber projections which I have seen in no other vessel made her square stern resemble the tail end of a miller's waggon. But the four stern ports of her cabin, glazed with six little greenish panes each, and framed in wooden sashes painted brown, might have been the windows of a cottage in the country. The tiny white curtains and the greenery of flower-pots behind the glass completed the resemblance. On one or two occasions when passing under her stern I had detected from my boat a round arm in the act of tilting a watering-pot, and the bowed sleek head of a maiden whom I shall always call Hermann's niece, because as a matter of fact I've never heard her name, for all my intimacy with the family.

This, however, sprang up later on. Meantime in common with the rest of the shipping in that Eastern port, I was left in no doubt as to Hermann's notions of hygienic clothing. Evidently he believed in wearing good stout flannel next his skin. On most days little frocks and pinafores could be seen drying in the mizzen rigging of his ship, or a tiny row of socks fluttering on the signal halyards; but once a fortnight the family washing was exhibited in force. It covered the poop entirely. The afternoon breeze would incite to a weird and flabby activity all that crowded mass of clothing, with its vague suggestions of drowned, mutilated and flattened humanity. Trunks without heads waved at you arms without hands; legs without feet kicked fantastically with collapsible flourishes; and there were long white garments, that taking the wind fairly through their neck openings edged with lace, became for a moment violently distended as by the passage of obese and invisible bodies. On these days you could make out that ship at a great distance by the multi-coloured grotesque riot going on abaft her mizzen-mast.

She had her berth just ahead of me, and her name was *Diana*,—Diana not of Ephesus* but of Bremen. This was proclaimed in white letters a foot long spaced widely across the stern (somewhat like the lettering of a shop-sign) under the cottage windows. This ridiculously unsuitable name struck one as an impertinence towards the memory of the most charming of goddesses; for, apart from the fact that the old craft was physically incapable of engaging in any sort of chase, there was a gang of four children belonging to her. They peeped over the rail at passing boats and occasionally dropped various objects into them. Thus, sometime before I knew Hermann to speak to, I received on my hat a horrid rag-doll belonging to Hermann's eldest daughter. However, these youngsters were upon the whole well behaved. They had fair heads, round eyes, round little knobby noses, and they resembled their father a good deal.

This *Diana* of Bremen was a most innocent old ship, and seemed to know nothing of the wicked sea, as there are on shore households that know nothing of the corrupt world. And the sentiments she suggested were unexceptionable and mainly of a domestic order. She was a home. All these dear children had learned

to walk on her roomy quarter-deck. In such thoughts
there is something pretty, even touching. Their teeth,
I should judge, they cut on the ends of her running
gear. I have many times observed the baby Hermann
(Nicholas) engaged in gnawing the whipping of the
fore-royal brace. Nicholas' favourite place of residence
was under the main fife-rail. Directly he was let loose
he would crawl off there, and the first seaman who came
along would bring him, carefully held aloft in tarry
hands, back to the cabin door. I fancy there must have
been a standing order to that effect. In the course of
these transportations the baby, who was the only pep-
pery person in the ship, tried to smite these stalwart
young German sailors on the face.

Mrs. Hermann, an engaging, stout housewife, wore
on board baggy blue dresses with white dots. When,
as happened once or twice, I caught her at an elegant
little wash-tub rubbing hard on white collars, baby's
socks, and Hermann's summer neck-ties, she would
blush in girlish confusion, and raising her wet hands
greet me from afar with many friendly nods. Her
sleeves would be rolled up to the elbows, and the gold
hoop of her wedding ring glittered among the soap-
suds. Her voice was pleasant, she had a serene brow,
smooth bands of very fair hair, and a good-humoured expression of the eyes. She was motherly and moderately talkative. When this simple matron smiled,
youthful dimples broke out on her fresh broad cheeks.
Hermann's niece, on the other hand, an orphan and very
silent, I never saw attempt a smile. This, however,
was not gloom on her part but the restraint of youthful
gravity.

They had carried her about with them for the last
three years, to help with the children and be company
for Mrs. Hermann, as Hermann mentioned once to me.

It had been very necessary while they were all little,
he had added in a vexed manner. It was her arm and
her sleek head that I had glimpsed one morning,
through the stern-windows of the cabin, hovering over
the pots of fuchsias and mignonette; but the first time I
beheld her full length I surrendered to her proportions.
They fix her in my mind, as great beauty, great intelligence, quickness of wit or kindness of heart might
have made some other woman memorable.

. With her it was form and size. It was her physical
personality that had this imposing charm. She might
have been witty, intelligent, and kind to an exceptional
degree. I don't know, and this is not to the point. All
I know is that she was built on a magnificent scale.
Built is the only word. She was constructed, she was
erected, as it were, with regal lavishness. It staggered
you to see this reckless expenditure of material upon a
chit of a girl. She was youthful and also perfectly
mature, as though she had been some fortunate im-
mortal. She was heavy, too, perhaps, but that's nothing. It only added to that notion of permanence.
She was barely nineteen. But such shoulders! Such
round arms! Such a shadowing forth of mighty limbs
when with three long strides she pounced across the
deck upon the overturned Nicholas—it's perfectly
indescribable! She seemed a good, quiet girl, vigilant
as to Lena's needs, Gustav's tumbles, the state of Karl's
dear little nose—conscientious, hardworking, and all
that. But what magnificent hair she had! Abundant,
long, thick, of a tawny colour. It had the sheen of
precious metals. She wore it plaited tightly into one
single tress hanging girlishly down her back; and its end
reached down to her waist. The massiveness of it
surprised you. On my word it reminded one of a club.
Her face was big, comely, of an unruffled expression.

She had a good complexion, and her blue eyes were so
pale that she appeared to look at the world with the
empty white candour of a statue. You could not call
her good-looking. It was something much more
impressive. The simplicity of her apparel, the opulence
of her form, her imposing stature, and the extraordinary
sense of vigorous life that seemed to emanate from her
like a perfume exhaled by a flower, made her beautiful
with a beauty of a rustic and olympian order. To
watch her reaching up to the clothes-line with both arms
raised high above her head, caused you to fall a musing
in a strain of pagan piety. Excellent Mrs. Hermann's
baggy cotton gowns had some sort of rudimentary frills
at neck and bottom, but this girl's print frocks hadn't
even a wrinkle; nothing but a few straight folds in the
skirt falling to her feet, and these, when she stood still,
had a severe and statuesque quality. She was inclined
naturally to be still whether sitting or standing. However, I don't mean to say she was statuesque. She was
too generously alive; but she could have stood for an
allegoric statue of the Earth. I don't mean the worn-
out earth of our possession, but a young Earth, a
virginal planet undisturbed by the vision of a future
teeming with the monstrous forms of life, clamorous
with the cruel battles of hunger and thought.

The worthy Hermann himself was not very enter-
taining, though his English was fairly comprehensible.
Mrs. Hermann, who always let off one speech at least
at me in an hospitable, cordial tone (and in Platt-
Deutsch I suppose) I could not understand. As to
their niece, however satisfactory to look upon (and she
inspired you somehow with a hopeful view as to the
prospects of mankind) she was a modest and silent
presence, mostly engaged in sewing, only now and then,
as I observed, falling over that work into a state of

maidenly meditation. Her aunt sat opposite her, sewing also, with her feet propped on a wooden footstool. On the other side of the deck Hermann and I would get a couple of chairs out of the cabin and settle down to a smoking match, accompanied at long intervals by the pacific exchange of a few words. I came nearly every evening. Hermann I would find in his shirt-sleeves. As soon as he returned from the shore on board his ship he commenced operations by taking off his coat; then he put on his head an embroidered round cap with a tassel, and changed his boots for a pair of cloth slippers. Afterwards he smoked at the cabin-door, looking at his children with an air of civic virtue, till they got caught one after another and put to bed in various staterooms. Lastly, we would drink some beer in the cabin, which was furnished with a wooden table on cross legs, and with black straight-backed chairs—more like a farm kitchen than a ship's cuddy. The sea and all nautical affairs seemed very far removed from the hospitality of this exemplary family.

And I liked this because I had a rather worrying time on board my own ship. I had been appointed ex-officio by the British Consul to take charge of her after a man who had died suddenly,* leaving for the guidance of his successor some suspiciously unreceipted bills, a few dry-dock estimates hinting at bribery, and a quantity of vouchers for three years' extravagant expenditure; all these mixed up together in a dusty old violin-case lined with ruby velvet. I found besides a large account-book, which, when opened hopefully, turned out to my infinite consternation to be filled with verses—page after page of rhymed doggerel of a jovial and improper character, written in the neatest minute hand I ever did see. In the same fiddle-case a photograph of my predecessor, taken lately in Saigon,

represented in front of a garden view, and in company of
a female in strange draperies, an elderly, squat, rugged
man of stern aspect in a clumsy suit of black broad-
cloth, and with the hair brushed forward above the
temples in a manner reminding one of a boar's tusks.
Of a fiddle, however, the only trace on board was the
case, its empty husk as it were; but of the two last
freights the ship had indubitably earned of late, there
were not even the husks left. It was impossible to say
where all that money had gone to. It wasn't on
board. It had not been remitted home; for a letter
from the owners, preserved in a desk evidently by the
merest accident, complained mildly enough that they
had not been favoured by a scratch of the pen for the
last eighteen months.* There were next to no stores on
board, not an inch of spare rope or a yard of canvas.
The ship had been run bare, and I foresaw no end of
difficulties before I could get her ready for sea.

As I was young then—not thirty yet—I took myself
and my troubles very seriously. The old mate, who had
acted as chief mourner at the captain's funeral, was not
particularly pleased at my coming.* But the fact is
the fellow was not legally qualified for command, and
the Consul was bound, if at all possible, to put a
properly certificated man on board. As to the second
mate, all I can say his name was Tottersen, or something like that. His practice was to wear on his head,
in that tropical climate, a mangy fur cap. He was,
without exception, the stupidest man I had ever seen
on board ship. And he looked it, too. He looked so
confoundedly stupid that it was a matter of surprise
for me when he answered to his name.

I drew no great comfort from their company, to say
the least of it; while the prospect of making a long sea
passage with those two fellows was depressing. And

my other thoughts in solitude could not be of a gay
complexion. The crew was sickly,* the cargo was
coming very slow; I foresaw I would have lots of trouble
with the charterers, and doubted whether they would
advance me enough money for the ship's expenses.
Their attitude towards me was unfriendly. Altogether
I was not getting on. - I would discover at odd times
(generally about midnight) that I was totally inexperienced, greatly ignorant of business, and hopelessly
unfit for any sort of command; and when the steward
had to be taken to the hospital ill with choleraic symptoms I felt bereaved of the only decent person at the
after end of the ship. He was fully expected to recover,
but in the meantime had to be replaced by some sort
of servant. And on the recommendation of a certain
Schomberg,* the proprietor of the smaller of the two
hotels in the place, I engaged a Chinaman. Schomberg, a brawny, hairy Alsatian, and an awful gossip,
assured me that it was all right. "First-class boy that.
Came in the *suite* of his Excellency Tseng the Com-
missioner—you know. His Excellency Tseng lodged
with me here for three weeks."

He mouthed the Chinese Excellency at me with
great unction, though the specimen of the "*suite*" did
not seem very promising. At the time, however, I did
not know what an untrustworthy humbug Schomberg
was. The "boy" might have been forty or a hundred
and forty for all you could tell—one of those Chinamen
of the death's-head type of face and completely inscrutable. Before the end of the third day he had revealed himself as a confirmed opium-smoker, a gambler,
a most audacious thief, and a first-class sprinter.* When
he departed at the top of his speed with thirty-two
golden sovereigns of my own hard-earned savings it was
the last straw. I had reserved that money in case my

difficulties came to the worst. Now it was gone I felt as poor and naked as a fakir. I clung to my ship, for all the bother she caused me, but what I could not bear were the long lonely evenings in her cuddy, where the atmosphere, made smelly by a leaky lamp, was agitated by the snoring of the mate. That fellow shut himself up in his stuffy cabin punctually at eight, and made gross and revolting noises like a water-logged trombone. It was odious not to be able to worry oneself in comfort on board one's own ship. Everything in this world, I reflected, even the command of a nice little barque, may be made a delusion and a snare for the unwary spirit of pride in man.

From such reflections I was glad to make my escape on board that Bremen *Diana*. There apparently no whisper of the world's iniquities had ever penetrated. And yet she lived upon the wide sea: and the sea tragic and comic, the sea with its horrors and its peculiar scandals, the sea peopled by men and ruled by iron necessity is indubitably a part of the world. But that patriarchal old tub, like some saintly retreat, echoed nothing of it. She was world-proof. Her venerable innocence apparently put a restraint on the roaring lusts of the sea. And yet I have known the sea too long to believe in its respect for decency. An elemental force is ruthlessly frank. It may, of course, have been Hermann's skilful seamanship, but to me it looked as if the allied oceans had refrained from smashing these high bulwarks, unshipping the lumpy rudder, frightening the children, and generally opening this family's eyes out of sheer reticence. It looked like reticence. The ruthless disclosure was, in the end, left for a man to make; a man strong and elemental enough and driven to unveil some secrets of the sea by the power of a simple and elemental desire.

This, however, occurred much later, and meantime I took sanctuary in that serene old ship early every evening. The only person on board that seemed to be in trouble was little Lena, and in due course I perceived that the health of the rag-doll was more than delicate. This object led a sort of "in extremis" existence in a wooden box placed against the starboard mooring-bitts tended and nursed with the greatest sympathy and care by all the children, who greatly enjoyed pulling long faces and moving with hushed footsteps. Only the baby—Nicholas—looked on with a cold, ruffianly leer, as if he had belonged to another tribe altogether. Lena perpetually sorrowed over the box, and all of them were in deadly earnest. It was wonderful the way these children would work up their compassion for that bedraggled thing I wouldn't have touched with a pair of tongs. I suppose they were exercising and developing their racial sentimentalism by the means of that dummy. I was only surprised that Mrs. Hermann let Lena cherish and hug that bundle of rags to that extent, it was so disreputably and completely unclean. But Mrs. Hermann would raise her fine womanly eyes from her needlework to look on with amused sympathy, and did not seem to see it, somehow, that this object of affection was a disgrace to the ship's purity. Purity, not cleanliness, is the word. It was pushed so far that I seemed to detect in this, too, a sentimental excess, as if dirt had been removed in very love. It is impossible to give you an idea of such a meticulous neatness. It was as if every morning that ship had been arduously explored with—with toothbrushes. Her very bowsprit three times a week had its toilette made with a cake of soap and a piece of soft flannel. Arrayed—I *must* say arrayed—arrayed artlessly in dazzling white paint as to wood and dark green as to ironwork the simple-minded distribution of these colours evoked the images of guileless peace, of arcadian felicity; and the childish comedy of disease and sorrow struck me sometimes as an abominably real blot upon that ideal state.

I enjoyed it greatly, and on my part I brought a little mild excitement into it. Our intimacy arose from the pursuit of that thief. It was in the evening, and Hermann, who, contrary to his habits, had stayed on shore late that day, was extricating himself backwards out of a little gharry on the river bank, opposite his ship, when the hunt passed. Realizing the situation as though he had eyes in his shoulder-blades, he joined us with a leap and took the lead. The Chinaman fled silent like a rapid shadow on the dust of an extremely oriental road. I followed. A long way in the rear my mate whooped like a savage. A young moon threw a bashful light on a plain like a monstrous waste ground: the architectural mass of a Buddhist temple far away projected itself in dead black on the sky. We lost the thief of course; but in my disappointment I had to admire Hermann's presence of mind. The velocity that stodgy man developed in the interests of a complete stranger earned my warm gratitude—there was something truly cordial in his exertions.

He seemed as vexed as myself at our failure, and would hardly listen to my thanks. He said it was "nothings," and invited me on the spot to come on board his ship and drink a glass of beer with him. We poked sceptically for a while amongst the bushes, peered without conviction into a ditch or two. There was not a sound: patches of slime glimmered feebly amongst the reeds. Slowly we trudged back, drooping under the thin sickle of the moon, and I heard him mutter to himself, "Himmel! Zwei und dreissig Pfund!" He was impressed by the figure of my loss. For a long time we had ceased to hear the mate's whoops and yells.

Then he said to me, "Everybody has his troubles," and as we went on remarked that he would never have known anything of mine hadn't he by an extraordinary chance been detained on shore by Captain Falk. He didn't like to stay late ashore—he added with a sigh. The something doleful in his tone I put to his sympathy with my misfortune, of course.

On board the *Diana* Mrs. Hermann's fine eyes expressed much interest and commiseration. We had found the two women sewing face to face under the open skylight in the strong glare of the lamp. Hermann walked in first, starting in the very doorway to pull off his coat, and encouraging me with loud, hospitable ejaculations: "Come in! This way! Come in, captain!" At once, coat in hand, he began to tell his wife all about it. Mrs. Hermann put the palms of her plump hands together; I smiled and bowed with a heavy heart: the niece got up from her sewing to bring Hermann's slippers and his embroidered calotte, which he assumed pontifically, talking (about me) all the time. Billows of white stuff lay between the chairs on the cabin floor; I caught the words "Zwei und dreissig Pfund" repeated several times, and presently came the beer, which seemed delicious to my throat, parched with running and the emotions of the chase.

I didn't get away till well past midnight, long after the women had retired. Hermann had been trading in the East for three years or more, carrying freights of rice and timber mostly. His ship was well known in all the ports from Vladivostok to Singapore. She was his own property. The profits had been moderate, but the trade answered well enough while the children were small yet. In another year or so he hoped he would be

able to sell the old *Diana* to a firm in Japan for a fair
price. He intended to return home, to Bremen, by
mail boat, second class, with Mrs. Hermann and the
children. He told me all this stolidly, with slow puffs at
his pipe. I was sorry when knocking the ashes out he
began to rub his eyes. I would have sat with him till
morning. What had I to hurry on board my own ship
for? To face the broken rifled drawer in my stateroom. Ugh! The very thought made me feel unwell.

I became their daily guest, as you know. I think
that Mrs. Hermann from the first looked upon me as a
romantic person. I did not, of course, tear my hair
coram populo over my loss, and she took it for lordly
indifference. Afterwards, I daresay, I did tell them
some of my adventures—such as they were—and they
marvelled greatly at the extent of my experience.
Hermann would translate what he thought the most
striking passages. Getting upon his legs, and as if
delivering a lecture on a phenomenon, he addressed
himself, with gestures, to the two women, who would
let their sewing sink slowly on their laps. Meantime I
sat before a glass of Hermann's beer, trying to look
modest. Mrs. Hermann would glance at me quickly,
emit slight "Ach's!" The girl never made a sound.
Never. But she, too, would sometimes raise her pale
eyes to look at me in her unseeing, gentle way. Her
glance was by no means stupid; it beamed out soft and
diffuse as the moon beams upon a landscape—quite
differently from the scrutinizing inspection of the stars.
You were drowned in it, and imagined yourself to appear blurred. And yet this same glance when turned
upon Christian Falk must have been as efficient as the
searchlight of a battle-ship.

Falk was the other assiduous visitor on board, but
from his behaviour he might have been coming to see

the quarter-deck capstan. He certainly used to stare
at it a good deal when keeping us company outside the
cabin door, with one muscular arm thrown over the
back of the chair, and his big shapely legs, in very tight
white trousers, extended far out and ending in a pair of
black shoes as roomy as punts. On arrival he would
shake Hermann's hand with a mutter, bow to the
women, and take up his careless and misanthropic
attitude by our side. He departed abruptly, with a
jump, going through the performance of grunts, hand-
shakes, bow, as if in a panic. Sometimes, with a
sort of discreet and convulsive effort, he approached
the women and exchanged a few low words with them,
half a dozen at most. On these occasions Hermann's
usual stare became positively glassy and Mrs. Hermann's kind countenance would colour up. The girl
herself never turned a hair.

Falk was a Dane or perhaps a Norwegian, I can't
tell now. At all events he was a Scandinavian of some
sort, and a bloated monopolist to boot. It is possible
he was unacquainted with the word, but he had a clear
perception of the thing itself. His tariff of charges for
towing ships in and out was the most brutally incon-
siderate document of the sort I had ever seen. He was
the commander and owner of the only tug-boat on the
river, a very trim white craft of 150 tons or more, as
elegantly neat as a yacht, with a round wheelhouse
rising like a glazed turret high above her sharp bows,
and with one slender varnished pole mast forward. I
daresay there are yet a few shipmasters afloat who
remember Falk and his tug very well. He extracted
his pound and a half of flesh*from each of us merchant-
skippers with an inflexible sort of indifference which
made him detested and even feared. Schomberg used
to remark: "I won't talk about the fellow. I don't

think he has six drinks from year's end to year's end in my place. But my advice is, gentlemen, don't you have anything to do with him, if you can help it."

This advice, apart from unavoidable business relations, was easy to follow because Falk intruded upon no one. It seems absurd to compare a tug-boat skipper to a centaur: but he reminded me somehow of an engraving in a little book I had as a boy, which represented centaurs at a stream, and there was one especially, in the foreground, prancing bow and arrows in hand, with regular severe features and an immense curled wavy beard, flowing down his breast. Falk's face reminded me of that centaur. Besides, he was a composite creature. Not a man-horse, it is true, but a man-boat. He lived on board his tug, which was always dashing up and down the river from early morn till dewy eve. In the last rays of the setting sun,* you could pick out far away down the reach his beard borne high up on the white structure, foaming up stream to anchor for the night. There was the white-clad man's body, and the rich brown patch of the hair, and nothing below the waist but the 'thwart-ship white lines of the bridge-screens, that led the eye to the sharp white lines of the bows cleaving the muddy water of the river.

Separated from his boat, to me at least he seemed incomplete. The tug herself without his head and torso on the bridge looked mutilated as it were. But he left her very seldom. All the time I remained in harbour I saw him only twice on shore. On the first occasion it was at my charterers, where he came in misanthropically to get paid for towing out a French barque the day before. The second time I could hardly believe my eyes, for I beheld him reclining under his beard in a cane-bottomed chair in the billiard-room of Schomberg's hotel.

It was very funny to see Schomberg ignoring him pointedly. The artificiality of it contrasted strongly with Falk's natural unconcern. The big Alsatian talked loudly with his other customers, going from one little table to the other, and passing Falk's place of repose with his eyes fixed straight ahead. Falk sat there with an untouched glass at his elbow. He must have known by sight and name every white man in the room, but he never addressed a word to anybody. He acknowledged my presence by a drop of his eyelids, and that was all. Sprawling there in the chair, he would, now and again, draw the palms of both his hands down his face, giving at the same time a slight, almost imperceptible, shudder.

It was a habit he had, and of course I was perfectly familiar with it, since you could not remain an hour in his company without being made to wonder at such a passionate and inexplicable gesture breaking some long period of stillness. He used to make it at all sorts of times; as likely as not after he had been listening to little Lena's chatter about the suffering doll, for instance. The Hermann children always besieged him about his legs closely, though, in a gentle way, he shrank from them a little. He seemed, however, to feel a great affection for the whole family. For Hermann himself especially. He sought his company. In this case, for instance, he must have been waiting for him, because as soon as he appeared Falk rose hastily, and they went out together. Then Schomberg expounded in my hearing to three or four people his theory that Falk was after Captain Hermann's niece, and asserted confidently that nothing would come of it. It was the same last year when Captain Hermann was loading here, he said.

Naturally, I did not believe Schomberg, but I own

that for a time I observed closely what went on. All I
discovered was some impatience on Hermann's part.
At the sight of Falk, stepping over the gangway, the
excellent man would begin to mumble and chew between his teeth something that sounded like German
swear-words. However, as I've said, I'm not familiar
with the language, and Hermann's soft, round-eyed
countenance remained unchanged. Staring stolidly
ahead he greeted him with, "Wie geht's," or in English,
"How are you?" with a throaty enunciation. The
girl would look up for an instant and move her lips
slightly: Mrs. Hermann let her hands rest on her lap to
talk volubly to him for a minute or so in her pleasant
voice before she went on with her sewing again. Falk
would throw himself into a chair, stretch his big legs, as
like as not draw his hands down his face passionately.
As to myself, he was not pointedly impertinent: it was
rather as though he could not be bothered with such
trifles as my existence; and the truth is that being a
monopolist he was under no necessity to be amiable.
He was sure to get his own extortionate terms out of
me for towage whether he frowned or smiled. As a
matter of fact, he did neither: but before many days
went by he managed to astonish me not a little and to
set Schomberg's tongue clacking more than ever.

It came about in this way. There was a shallow bar
at the mouth of the river which ought to have been
kept down, but the authorities of the State were
piously busy gilding afresh the great Buddhist Pagoda
just then, and had no money to spare for dredging
operations. I don't know how it may be now, but at
the time I speak of that sandbank was a great nuisance
to the shipping. One of its consequences was that
vessels of a certain draught of water, like Hermann's
or mine, could not complete their loading in the river.

After taking in as much as possible of their cargo, they had to go outside to fill up. The whole procedure was an unmitigated bore. When you thought you had as much on board as your ship could carry safely over the bar, you went and gave notice to your agents. They, in their turn, notified Falk that so-and-so was ready to go out. Then Falk (ostensibly when it fitted in with his other work, but, if the truth were known, simply when his arbitrary spirit moved him), after ascertaining carefully in the office that there was enough money to meet his bill, would come along unsympathetically, glaring at you with his yellow eyes from the bridge, and would drag you out dishevelled as to rigging, lumbered as to the decks, with unfeeling haste, as if to execution. And he would force you, too, to take the end of his own wire hawser, for the use of which there was of course an extra charge. To your shouted remonstrances against this extortion this towering trunk with one hand on the engine-room telegraph only shook its bearded head above the splash, the racket and the clouds of smoke, in which the tug, backing and filling in the smother of churning paddle-wheels behaved like a ferocious and impatient creature. He had her manned by the cheekiest gang of lascars I ever did see, whom he allowed to bawl at you insolently, and, once fast, he plucked you out of your berth as if he did not care what he smashed. Eighteen miles down the river you had to go behind him, and then three more along the coast to where a group of uninhabited rocky islets enclosed a sheltered anchorage. There you would have to lie at single anchor with your naked spars showing to seaward over these barren fragments of land scattered upon a very intensely blue sea. There was nothing to look at besides but a bare coast, the muddy edge of the brown plain with the sinuosities of the river you had left, traced in dull green, and the Great Pagoda* uprising lonely and massive with shining curves and pinnacles like the gorgeous and stony efflorescence of tropical rocks. You had nothing to do but to wait fretfully for the balance of your cargo, which was sent out of the river with the greatest irregularity. And it was open to you to console yourself with the thought that, after all, this stage of bother meant that your departure from these shores was indeed approaching at last.

We both had to go through that stage, Hermann and I, and there was a sort of tacit emulation between the ships as to which should be ready first. We kept on neck and neck almost to the finish, when I won the race by going personally to give notice in the forenoon; whereas Hermann, who was very slow in making up his mind to go ashore, did not get to the agents' office till late in the day. They told him there that my ship was first on turn for next morning, and I believe he told them he was in no hurry. It suited him better to go the day after.

That evening, on board the *Diana*, he sat staring with his plump knees well apart and puffing at the curved mouthpiece of his pipe. Presently he spoke with some impatience to his niece about putting the children to bed. Mrs. Hermann, who was talking to Falk, stopped short and looked at her husband uneasily, but the girl got up at once and drove the children before her into the cabin. In a little while Mrs. Hermann had to leave us to quell what, from the sounds inside, must have been a dangerous mutiny. At this Hermann grumbled to himself. For half an hour longer Falk left alone with us fidgeted on his chair, sighed lightly, then at last, after drawing his hands down his face, got up, and as if renouncing the hope of making himself understood (he hadn't opened his

mouth once) he said in English: "Well . . . Good-
night, Captain Hermann." He stopped for a moment
before my chair and looked down fixedly, I may even
say he glared, and he went so far as to make a deep
noise in his throat. All this was so marked that for the
first time in our limited intercourse of nods and grunts
he excited in me something like interest. But next
moment he disappointed me—for he strode away
hastily without a nod even.

His manner was usually odd it is true, and I certainly did not pay much attention to it; but that sort of
obscure intention, which seemed to lurk in his noncha-
lance like a wary old carp in a pond, had never before
come so near the surface. He had distinctly aroused
my expectations. I would have been unable to say
what it was I expected, but at all events I did not expect the absurd developments he sprung upon me no
later than the break of the very next day.

I remember only that there was, on that evening,
enough point in his behaviour to make me, after he had
fled, wonder audibly what he might mean.* To this
Hermann, crossing his legs with a swing and settling
himself viciously away from me in his chair, said:
"That fellow don't know himself what he means."

There might have been some insight in such a remark. I said nothing, and, still averted, Hermann
added: "When I was here last year he was just the
same." An eruption of tobacco smoke enveloped his
head as if his temper had exploded like gunpowder.

I had half a mind to ask him point blank whether he,
at least, didn't know why Falk, a notoriously unsociable
man, had taken to visiting his ship with such assiduity.
After all, I reflected suddenly, it was a most remarkable
thing. I wonder now what Hermann would have said.
As it turned out—he didn't let me ask. Forgetting all

about Falk apparently, he started a monologue on his plans for the future: the selling of the ship, the going home; and falling into a reflective and calculating mood he mumbled between regular jets of smoke about the expense. The necessity of disbursing passage-money for all his tribe seemed to disturb him in a manner that was the more striking because otherwise he gave no signs of a miserly disposition. And yet he fussed over the prospect of that voyage home in a mail-boat like a sedentary grocer who has made up his mind to see the world. He was racially thrifty I suppose, and for him there must have been a great novelty in finding himself obliged to pay for travelling—for sea travelling which was the normal state of life for the family—from the very cradle for most of them. I could see he grudged prospectively every single shilling which must be spent so absurdly. It was rather funny. He would become doleful over it, and then again, with a fretful sigh, he would suppose there was nothing for it now but to take three second-class tickets—and there were the four children to pay for besides. A lot of money that to spend at once. A big lot of money.

I sat with him listening (not for the first time) to these heart-searchings till I grew thoroughly sleepy, and then I left him and turned in on board my ship. At daylight I was awakened by a yelping of shrill voices, accompanied by a great commotion in the water, and the short, bullying blasts of a steam-whistle. Falk with his tug had come for me.

I began to dress. It was remarkable that the answering noise on board my ship together with the patter of feet above my head ceased suddenly. But I heard more remote guttural cries which seemed to express surprise and annoyance. Then the voice of my mate reached me howling expostulations to somebody at a distance. Other voices joined, apparently indignant; a chorus of something that sounded like abuse replied. Now and then the steam-whistle screeched.

Altogether that unnecessary uproar was distracting, but down there in my cabin I took it calmly. In another moment, I thought, I should be going down that wretched river, and in another week at the most I should be totally quit of the odious place and all the odious people in it.

Greatly cheered by the idea, I seized the hair-brushes and looking at myself in the glass began to use them. Suddenly a hush fell upon the noise outside, and I heard (the ports of my cabin were thrown open)—I heard a deep calm voice, not on board my ship, however, hailing resolutely in English, but with a strong foreign twang, "Go ahead!"

There may be tides in the affairs of men which taken at the flood . . . and so on.* Personally I am still on the look-out for that important turn. I am, however, afraid that most of us are fated to flounder for ever in the dead water of a pool the shores of which are arid indeed. But I know that there are often in men's affairs unexpectedly—even irrationally—illuminating moments when an otherwise insignificant sound, perhaps only some perfectly commonplace gesture, suffices to reveal to us all the unreason, all the fatuous unreason, of our complacency. "Go ahead" are not particularly striking words even when pronounced with a foreign accent; yet they petrified me in the very act of smiling at myself in the glass. And then, refusing to believe my ears, but already boiling with indignation, I ran out of the cabin and up on deck.

It was incredibly true. It was perfectly true. I had no eyes for anything but the *Diana*. It was she that was being taken away. She was already out of her berth and shooting athwart the river. "The way this loonatic plucked that ship out is a caution," said the awed voice of my mate close to my ear. "Hey! Hallo! Falk! Hermann! What's this infernal trick?" I yelled in a fury.

Nobody heard me. Falk certainly could not hear me. His tug was turning at full speed away under the other bank. The wire hawser between her and the *Diana*, stretched as taut as a harpstring, vibrated alarmingly.

The high black craft careened over to the awful strain. A loud crack came out of her, followed by the tearing and splintering of wood. "There!" said the awed voice in my ear. "He's carried away their towing chock." And then, with enthusiasm, "Oh! Look! Look, sir! Look at them Dutchmen skipping out of the way on the forecastle. I hope to goodness he'll break a few of their shins before he's done with 'em."

I yelled my vain protests. The rays of the rising sun coursing level along the plain warmed my back, but I was hot enough with rage. I could not have believed that a simple towing operation could suggest so plainly the idea of abduction, of rape. Falk was simply running off with the *Diana*.

The white tug careered out into the middle of the river. The red floats of her paddle-wheels revolving with mad rapidity tore up the whole reach into foam. The *Diana* in mid-stream waltzed round with as much grace as an old barn, and flew after her ravisher. Through the ragged fog of smoke driving headlong upon the water I had a glimpse of Falk's square motion-less shoulders under a white hat as big as a cart-wheel, of his red face, his yellow staring eyes, his great beard. Instead of keeping a look-out ahead, he was deliber-ately turning his back on the river to glare at his tow.

The tall heavy craft, never so used before in her life,
seemed to have lost her senses; she took a wild sheer
against her helm, and for a moment came straight at
us, menacing and clumsy, like a runaway mountain.
She piled up a streaming, hissing, boiling wave halfway
up her blunt stem, my crew let out one great howl,—
and then we held our breaths. It was a near thing.
But Falk had her! He had her in his clutch. I
fancied I could hear the steel hawser ping as it surged
across the Diana's forecastle, with the hands on board
of her bolting away from it in all directions. It was a
near thing. Hermann, with his hair rumpled, in a
snuffy flannel shirt and a pair of mustard-coloured
trousers, had rushed to help with the wheel. I saw his
terrified round face; I saw his very teeth uncovered by
a sort of ghastly fixed grin; and in a great leaping
tumult of water between the two ships the Diana
whisked past so close that I could have flung a hair-
brush at his head, for, it seems, I had kept them in my
hands all the time. Meanwhile Mrs. Hermann sat
placidly on the skylight, with a woollen shawl on her
shoulders. The excellent woman in response to my
indignant gesticulations fluttered a handkerchief, nodding and smiling in the kindest way imaginable. The
boys, only half-dressed, were jumping about the poop
in great glee, displaying their gaudy braces; and Lena
in a short scarlet petticoat, with peaked elbows and thin
bare arms, nursed the rag-doll with devotion. The
whole family passed before my sight as if dragged
across a scene of unparalleled violence. The last I saw
was Hermann's niece with the baby Hermann in her
arms standing apart from the others. Magnificent in
her close-fitting print frock, she displayed something so
commanding in the manifest perfection of her figure that
the sun seemed to be rising for her alone. The flood of

light brought out the opulence of her form and the vigour
of her youth in a glorifying way. She went by perfectly
motionless and as if lost in meditation; only the hem of
her skirt stirred in the draught; the sun rays broke on
her sleek tawny hair; that bald-headed ruffian, Nicholas,
was whacking her on the shoulder. I saw his tiny fat
arm rise and fall in a workmanlike manner. And then
the four cottage windows of the *Diana* came into view
retreating swiftly down the river. The sashes were up,
and one of the white calico curtains fluttered straight
out like a streamer above the agitated water of the
wake.

To be thus tricked out of one's turn was an unheard-
of occurrence. In my agent's office, where I went to
complain at once, they protested with apologies they
couldn't understand how the mistake arose: but
Schomberg, when I dropped in later to get some tiffin,
though surprised to see me, was perfectly ready with an
explanation. I found him seated at the end of a long
narrow table, facing his wife*—a scraggy little woman,
with long ringlets and a blue tooth, who smiled abroad
stupidly and looked frightened when you spoke to her.
Between them a waggling punkah fanned twenty vacant
cane-bottomed chairs and two rows of shiny plates.
Three Chinamen in white jackets loafed with napkins in
their hands around that desolation. Schomberg's pet
table-d'hôte was not much of a success that day. He
was feeding himself furiously and seemed to overflow
with bitterness.

He began by ordering in a brutal voice the chops
to be brought back for me, and turning in his chair:
"Mistake they told you? Not a bit of it! Don't you
believe it for a moment, captain! Falk isn't a man to
make mistakes unless on purpose." His firm conviction
was that Falk had been trying all along to curry favour

on the cheap with Hermann. "On the cheap—mind you! It doesn't cost him a cent to put that insult upon you, and Captain Hermann gets in a day ahead of your ship. Time's money! Eh? You are very friendly with Captain Hermann I believe, but a man is bound to be pleased at any little advantage he may get. Captain Hermann is a good business man, and there's no such thing as a friend in business. Is there?" He leaned forward and began to cast stealthy glances as usual. "But Falk is, and always was, a miserable fellow. I would despise him."

I muttered, grumpily, that I had no particular respect for Falk.

"I would despise him," he insisted, with an appearance of anxiety which would have amused me if I had not been fathoms deep in discontent. To a young man fairly conscientious and as well-meaning as only the young be, the current ill-usage of life comes with a peculiar cruelty. Youth that is fresh enough to believe in guilt, in innocence, and in itself, will always doubt whether it have not perchance deserved its fate. Sombre of mind and without appetite, I struggled with the chop while Mrs. Schomberg sat with her everlasting stupid grin and Schomberg's talk gathered way like a slide of rubbish.

"Let me tell you. It's all about that girl. I don't know what Captain Hermann expects, but if he asked me I could tell him something about Falk. He's a miserable fellow. That man is a perfect slave. That's what I call him. A slave. Last year I started this *table-d'hôte*, and sent cards out—you know. You think he had one meal in the house? Give the thing a trial? Not once. He has got hold now of a Madras cook—a blamed fraud that I hunted out of my cookhouse with a rattan. He was not fit to cook for white men. No, not for the white men's dogs either; but see, any damned native that can boil a pot of rice is good enough for Mr. Falk. Rice and a little fish he buys for a few cents from the fishing-boats outside is what he lives on. You would hardly credit it—eh? A white man, too. . . ."

He wiped his lips, using the napkin with indignation, and looking at me. It flashed through my mind in the midst of my depression that if all the meat in the town was like these *table-d'hôte* chops, Falk wasn't so much to blame. I was on the point of saying this, but Schomberg's stare was intimidating. "He's a vegetarian, perhaps," I murmured instead.

"He's a miser. A miserable miser," affirmed the hotel-keeper with great force. "The meat here is not so good as at home—of course. And dear, too. But look at me. I only charge a dollar for the tiffin, and one dollar and fifty cents for the dinner. Show me anything cheaper. Why am I doing it? There's little profit in this game. Falk wouldn't look at it. I do it for the sake of a lot of young white fellows here that hadn't a place where they could get a decent meal and eat it decently in good company. There's first-rate company always at my table."

The convinced way he surveyed the empty chairs made me feel as if I had intruded upon a tiffin of ghostly Presences.

"A white man should eat like a white man, dash it all," he burst out impetuously. "Ought to eat meat, must eat meat. I manage to get meat for my patrons all the year round. Don't I? I am not catering for a dam' lot of coolies: Have another chop, captain. . . . No? You, boy—take away!"

He threw himself back and waited grimly for the curry. The half-closed jalousies darkened the room

pervaded by the smell of fresh whitewash; a swarm of
flies buzzed and settled in turns, and poor Mrs. Schomberg's smile seemed to express the quintessence of all
the imbecility that had ever spoken, had ever breathed,
had ever been fed on infamous buffalo meat within
these bare walls. Schomberg did not open his lips till
he was ready to thrust therein a spoonful of greasy
rice. He rolled his eyes ridiculously before he swallowed the hot stuff, and only then broke out afresh.

"It is the most degrading thing. They take the
dish up to the wheelhouse for him with a cover on it,
and he shuts both the doors before he begins to eat.
Fact! Must be ashamed of himself. Ask the engineer.
He can't do without an engineer—don't you see—and
as no respectable man can be expected to put up with
such a table, he allows them fifteen dollars a month
extra mess money. I assure you it is so! You just
ask Mr. Ferdinand da Costa. That's the engineer he
has now. You may have seen him about my place, a
delicate dark young man, with very fine eyes and a little
moustache. He arrived here a year ago from Calcutta.
Between you and me, I guess the money-lenders there
must have been after him. He rushes here for a meal
every chance he can get, for just please tell me what
satisfaction is that for a well-educated young fellow to
feed all alone in his cabin—like a wild beast? That's
what Falk expects his engineers to put up with for fifteen
dollars extra. And the rows on board every time a
little smell of cooking gets about the deck! You
wouldn't believe! The other day da Costa got the
cook to fry a steak for him—a turtle steak it was, too,
not beef at all—and the fat caught or something.
Young da Costa himself was telling me of it here in
this room. 'Mr. Schomberg'—says he—'if I had let
a cylinder cover blow off through my negligence Captain

Falk couldn't have been more savage. He frightened the cook so that he won't put anything on the fire for me now.' Poor da Costa had tears in his eyes. Only try to put yourself in his place, captain: a sensitive, gentlemanly young fellow. Is he expected to eat his food raw? But that's your Falk all over. Ask any one you like. I suppose the fifteen dollars extra he has to give keep on rankling—in there."

And Schomberg tapped his manly breast. I sat half stunned by his irrelevant babble. Suddenly he gripped my forearm in an impressive and cautious manner, as if to lead me into a very cavern of confidence.

"It's nothing but enviousness," he said in a lowered tone, which had a stimulating effect upon my wearied hearing. "I don't suppose there is one person in this town that he isn't envious of. I tell you he's dangerous. Even I myself am not safe from him. I know for certain he tried to poison . . . ."

"Oh, come now," I cried, disgusted.

"But I know for certain. The people themselves came and told me of it. He went about saying everywhere I was a worse pest to this town than the cholera. He had been talking against me ever since I opened this hotel. And he poisoned Captain Hermann's mind, too. Last time the *Diana* was loading here Captain Hermann used to come in every day for a drink or a cigar. This time he hasn't been here twice in a week. How do you account for that?"

He squeezed my arm till he extorted from me some sort of mumble.

"Falk makes ten times the money I do. I've another hotel to fight against, and there is no other tug on the river. I am not in his way, am I? He wouldn't be fit to run an hotel if he tried. But that's just his nature. He can't bear to think I am making a living.

I only hope it makes him properly wretched. He's like that in everything. He would like to keep a decent table well enough. But no—for the sake of a few cents. Can't do it. It's too much for him. That's what I call being a slave to it. But he's mean enough to kick up a row when his nose gets tickled a bit. See that? That just paints him. Miserly and envious. You can't account for it any other way. Can you? I have been studying him these three years."

He was anxious I should assent to his theory. And indeed on thinking it over it would have been plausible enough if there hadn't been always the essential false-ness of irresponsibility in Schomberg's chatter. How-ever, I was not disposed to investigate the psychology of Falk. I was engaged just then in eating despondently a piece of stale Dutch cheese, being too much crushed to care what I swallowed myself, let alone bothering my head about Falk's ideas of gastronomy. I could expect from their study no clue to his conduct in matters of business, which seemed to me totally unre-strained by morality or even by the commonest sort of decency. How insignificant and contemptible I must appear, for the fellow to dare treat me like this—I re-flected suddenly, writhing in silent agony. And I consigned Falk and all his peculiarities to the devil with so much mental fervour as to forget Schomberg's existence, till he grabbed my arm urgently. "Well, you may think and think till every hair of your head falls off, captain; but you can't explain it in any other way."

For the sake of peace and quietness I admitted hurriedly that I couldn't; persuaded that now he would leave off. But the only result was to make his moist face shine with the pride of cunning. He removed his hand for a moment to scare a black mass of flies off the sugar-basin, and caught hold of my arm again.

"To be sure. And in the same way everybody is aware he would like to get married. Only he can't. Let me quote you an instance. Well, two years ago a Miss Vanlo, a very ladylike girl, came from home to keep house for her brother, Fred, who had an engineering shop for small repairs by the waterside. Suddenly Falk takes to going up to their bungalow after dinner and sitting for hours in the verandah saying nothing. The poor girl couldn't tell for the life of her what to do with such a man, so she would keep on playing the piano and singing to him evening after evening till she was ready to drop. And it wasn't as if she had been a strong young woman either. She was thirty, and the climate had been playing the deuce with her. Then— don't you see—Fred had to sit up with them for propriety, and during whole weeks on end never got a chance to get to bed before midnight. That was not pleasant for a tired man—was it? And besides Fred had worries then because his shop didn't pay and he was dropping money fast. He just longed to get away from here and try his luck somewhere else, but for the sake of his sister he hung on and on till he ran himself into debt over his ears—I can tell you. I, myself, could show a handful of his chits for meals and drinks in my drawer. I could never find out tho' where Fred found all the money at last. Can't be but he must have got something out of that brother of his, a coal merchant in Port Said. Anyhow he paid everybody before he left, but the girl nearly broke her heart. Disappointment, of course, and at her age, don't you know. . . Mrs. Schomberg here was very friendly with her, and she could tell you. Awful despair. Fainting fits. It was a scandal. A notorious scandal. To that extent that old Mr. Siegers—not your present charterer, but Mr. Siegers, the father, the old gentleman who retired from business on a fortune and got buried at sea going home, *he* had to interview Falk in his private office. He was a man who could speak like a Dutch Uncle, and, besides, Messrs. Siegers had been helping Falk with a good bit of money from the start. In fact, you may say they made him as far as that goes. It so happened that just at the time he turned up here, their firm was chartering a lot of sailing-ships every year, and it suited their business that there should be good towing facilities on the river. See? . . . Well—there's always an ear at the keyhole—isn't there? In fact," he lowered his tone confidentially, "in this case it was a good friend of mine; a man you can see here any evening; only they conversed rather low. Anyhow my friend's certain that Falk was trying to make all sorts of excuses, and old Mr. Siegers was coughing a lot. And yet Falk wanted all the time to be married, too. Why! It's notorious the man has been longing for years to make a home for himself. Only he can't face the expense. When it comes to putting his hand in his pocket—it chokes him off. That's the truth and no other. I've always said so, and everybody agrees with me by this time. What do you think of that—eh?"

He appealed confidently to my indignation, but having a mind to annoy him I remarked, "that it seemed to me very pitiful—if true."

He bounced in his chair as if I had run a pin into him. I don't know what he might have said, only at that moment we heard through the half-open door of the billiard-room the footsteps of two men entering from the verandah, a murmur of two voices; at the sharp tapping of a coin on a table Mrs. Schomberg half rose irresolutely. "Sit still," he hissed at her, and then, in an hospitable, jovial tone, contrasting amazingly with the angry glance that had made his wife sink in her chair, he cried very loud: "Tiffin still going on in here, gentlemen."

There was no answer, but the voices dropped suddenly. The head Chinaman went out. We heard the clink of ice in the glasses, pouring sounds, the shuffling of feet, the scraping of chairs. Schomberg, after wondering in a low mutter who the devil could be there at this time of the day, got up napkin in hand to peep through the doorway cautiously. He retreated rapidly on tip-toe, and whispering behind his hand informed me that it was Falk, Falk himself who was in there, and what's more, he had Captain Hermann with him.

The return of the tug from the outer Roads was unexpected but possible, for Falk had taken away the *Diana* at half-past five, and it was now two o'clock. Schomberg wished me to observe that neither of these men would spend a dollar on a tiffin, which they must have wanted. But by the time I was ready to leave the dining-room Falk had gone. I heard the last of his big boots on the planks of the verandah. Hermann was sitting quite alone in the large, wooden room with the two lifeless billiard tables shrouded in striped covers, mopping his face diligently. He wore his best go-ashore clothes, a stiff collar, black coat, large white waistcoat, gray trousers. A white cotton sunshade with a cane handle reposed between his legs, his side whiskers were neatly brushed, his chin had been freshly shaved; and he only distantly resembled the dishevelled and terrified man in a snuffy night shirt and ignoble old trousers I had seen in the morning hanging on to the wheel of the *Diana*.

He gave a start at my entrance, and addressed me at once in some confusion, but with genuine eagerness. He was anxious to make it clear he had nothing to do with what he called the "tam pizness" of the morning.

It was most inconvenient. He had reckoned upon another day up in town to settle his bills and sign certain papers. There were also some few stores to come, and sundry pieces of "my ironwork," as he called it quaintly, landed for repairs, had been left behind. Now he would have to hire a native boat to take all this out to the ship. It would cost five to six dollars perhaps. He had had no warning from Falk. Nothing. . . . He hit the table with his dumpy fist. . . . Der verfluchte Kerl came in the morning like a "tam' ropper," making a great noise, and took him away. His mate was not prepared, his ship was moored fast—he protested it was shameful to come upon a man in that way. Shameful! Yet such was the power Falk had on the river that when I suggested in a chilling tone that he might have simply refused to have his ship moved, Hermann was quite startled at the idea. I never realized so well before that this is an age of steam. The exclusive possession of a marine boiler had given Falk the whip hand of us all. Hermann, recovering, put it to me appealingly that I knew very well how unsafe it was to contradict that fellow. At this I only smiled distantly.

"Der Kerl!" he cried. He was sorry he had not refused. He was indeed. The damage! The damage! What for all that damage! There was no occasion for damage. Did I know how much damage he had done? It gave me a certain satisfaction to tell him that I had heard his old waggon of a ship crack fore and aft as she went by. "You passed close enough to me," I added, significantly.

He threw both his hands up to heaven at the recollection. One of them grasped by the middle the white parasol, and he resembled curiously a caricature of a shopkeeping citizen in one of his own German comic

papers. "Ach! That was dangerous," he cried. I
was amused. But directly he added with an appearance of simplicity, "The side of your iron ship would
have been crushed in like—like this matchbox."

"Would it?" I growled, much less amused now;
but by the time I had decided that this remark was not
meant for a dig at me he had worked himself into a high
state of resentfulness against Falk. The inconvenience,
the damage, the expense! Gottferdam! Devil take
the fellow. Behind the bar Schomberg, with a cigar in
his teeth, pretended to be writing with a pencil on a large
sheet of paper; and as Hermann's excitement increased
it made me comfortingly aware of my own calmness and
superiority. But it occurred to me while I listened to
his revilings, that after all the good man had come up in
the tug. There perhaps—since he must come to town
—he had no option. But evidently he had had a drink
with Falk, either accepted or offered. How was that?
So I checked him by saying loftily that I hoped he
would make Falk pay for every penny of the damage.

"That's it! That's it! Go for him," called out
Schomberg from the bar, flinging his pencil down and
rubbing his hands.

We ignored his noise. But Hermann's excitement
suddenly went off the boil as when you remove a sauce-
pan from the fire. I urged on his consideration that he
had done now with Falk and Falk's confounded tug.
He, Hermann, would not, perhaps, turn up again in
this part of the world for years to come, since he was
going to sell the *Diana* at the end of this very trip ("Go
home passenger in a mail-boat," he murmured mechanically). He was therefore safe from Falk's malice. All
he had to do was to race off to his consignees and stop
payment of the towage bill before Falk had the time to
get in and lift the money.

Nothing could have been less in the spirit of my advice than the thoughtful way in which he set about to make his parasol stay propped against the edge of the table.

While I watched his concentrated efforts with astonishment he threw at me one or two perplexed, half-shy glances. Then he sat down. "That's all very well," he said, reflectively.

It cannot be doubted that the man had been thrown off his balance by being hauled out of the harbour against his wish. His stolidity had been profoundly stirred, else he would never have made up his mind to ask me unexpectedly whether I had not remarked that Falk had been casting eyes upon his niece. "No more than myself," I answered with literal truth. The girl was of the sort one necessarily casts eyes at in a sense. She made no noise, but she filled most satisfactorily a good bit of space.

"But you, captain, are not the same kind of man," observed Hermann.

I was not, I am happy to say, in a position to deny this. "What about the lady?" I could not help asking. At this he gazed for a time into my face, earnestly, and made as if to change the subject. I heard him beginning to mutter something unexpected, about his children growing old enough to require schooling. He would have to leave them ashore with their grandmother when he took up that new command he expected to get in Germany.

This constant harping on his domestic arrangements was funny. I suppose it must have been like the prospect of a complete alteration in his life. An epoch. He was going, too, to part with the *Diana!* He had served in her for years. He had inherited her. From an uncle, if I remember rightly. And the future loomed

big before him, occupying his thought exclusively with
all its aspects as on the eve of a venturesome enterprise. He sat there frowning and biting his lip, and
suddenly he began to fume and fret.

I discovered to my momentary amusement that he
seemed to imagine I could, should or ought, have caused
Falk in some way to declare himself. Such a hope
was incomprehensible, but funny. Then the contact
with all this foolishness irritated me. I said crossly
that I had seen no symptoms, but if there were any—
since he, Hermann, was so sure—then it was still
worse. What pleasure Falk found in humbugging
people in just that way I couldn't say. It was, however, my solemn duty to warn him. It had lately, I
said, come to my knowledge that there was a man (not
a very long time ago either) who had been taken in
just like this.

All this passed in undertones, and at this point
Schomberg, exasperated at our secrecy, went out of
the room slamming the door with a crash that positively
lifted us in our chairs. This, or else what I had said,
huffed my Hermann. He supposed, with a contemptuous toss of his head towards the door which trembled
yet, that I had got hold of some of that man's silly
tales. It looked, indeed, as though his mind had been
thoroughly poisoned against Schomberg. "His tales
were—they were," he repeated, seeking for the word—
"trash." They were trash, he reiterated and moreover
I was young yet . . .

This horrid aspersion (I regret I am no longer exposed to that sort of insult) made me huffy, too. I
felt ready in my own mind to back up every assertion of
Schomberg's and on any subject. In a moment,
devil only knows why, Hermann and I were looking at
each other most inimically. He caught up his hat

without more ado and I gave myself the pleasure of
calling after him:

"Take my advice and make Falk pay for breaking
up your ship. You aren't likely to get anything else
out of him."

When I got on board my ship, the old mate, who was
very full of the events of the morning, remarked:

"I saw the tug coming back from the outer Roads
just before two P. M." (He never by any chance used
the words morning or afternoon. Always P. M. or A. M.,
log-book style.) "Smart work that. Man's always in
a state of hurry. He's a regular chucker-out, ain't he,
sir? There's a few pubs I know of in the East-end of
London that would be all the better for one of his sort
around the bar." He chuckled at his joke. "A
regular chucker-out. Now he has fired out that
Dutchman head over heels, I suppose our turn's coming
to-morrow morning."

We were all on deck at break of day (even the sick
—poor devils—had crawled out) ready to cast off in
the twinkling of an eye. Nothing came. Falk did not
come. At last, when I began to think that probably
something had gone wrong in his engine-room, we
perceived the tug going by, full pelt, down the river, as
if we hadn't existed. For a moment I entertained the
wild notion that he was going to turn round in the next
reach. Afterwards, I watched his smoke appear above
the plain, now here, now there, according to the windings of the river. It disappeared. Then without a
word I went down to breakfast. I just simply went
down to breakfast.

Not one of us uttered a sound till the mate, after
imbibing—by means of suction out of a saucer—his
second cup of tea, exclaimed: "Where the devil is the
man gone to?"

"Courting!" I shouted, with such a fiendish laugh that the old chap didn't venture to open his lips any more.

I started to the office perfectly calm. Calm with excessive rage. Evidently they knew all about it already, and they treated me to a show of consternation. The manager, a soft-footed, obese man, breathing short, got up to meet me, while all round the room the young clerks, bending over their desks, cast glances in my direction. The fat man, without waiting for my complaint, wheezing heavily and in a tone as if he himself were incredulous, conveyed to me the news that Falk—Captain Falk—had declined—had absolutely declined—to tow my ship—to have anything to to with my ship—this day or any other day. Never!

I did my best to preserve a cool appearance, but, all the same, I must have shown how much taken aback I was. We were talking in the middle of the room. Suddenly, behind my back some ass blew his nose with a great noise and at the same time another quill-driver got up and went out on the landing hastily. It occurred to me I was cutting a foolish figure there. I demanded angrily to see the principal in his private room.

The skin of Mr. Siegers' head showed dead white between the iron gray streaks of hair lying plastered cross-wise from ear to ear over the top of his skull in the manner of a bandage. His narrow sunken face was of an uniform and permanent terra-cotta colour, like a piece of pottery. He was sickly, thin, and short, with wrists like a boy of ten. But from that debile body there issued a bullying voice, tremendously loud, harsh and resonant, as if produced by some powerful mechanical contrivance in the nature of a fog-horn. I do not know what he did with it in the private life of his home, but in the larger sphere of business it presented the advantage of overcoming arguments without the slightest mental effort, by the mere volume of sound. We had had several passages of arms. It took me all I knew to guard the interest of my owners—whom, *nota bene*, I had never seen—while Siegers (who had made their acquaintance some years before, during a business tour in Australia) pretended to the knowledge of their innermost minds, and, in the character of "our very good friends," threw them perpetually at my head.

He looked at me with a jaundiced eye (there was no love lost between us), and declared at once that it was strange, very strange. His pronunciation of English was so extravagant that I can't even attempt to reproduce it. For instance, he said "Fferie strantch." Combined with the bellowing intonation it made the language of one's childhood sound weirdly startling, and even if considered purely as a kind of unmeaning noise it filled you with astonishment at first. "They had," he continued, "been acquainted with Captain Falk for very many years, and never had any reason. . . ."

"That's why I come to you, of course," I interrupted. "I've the right to know the meaning of this infernal nonsense." In the half-light of the room, which was greenish, because of the tree-tops screening the window, I saw him writhe his meagre shoulders. It came into my head, as disconnected ideas will come at all sorts of times into one's head, that this, most likely, was the very room where, if the tale were true, Falk had been lectured by Mr. Siegers, the father. Mr. Siegers' (the son's) overwhelming voice, in brassy blasts, as though he had been trying to articulate words through a trumpet, was expressing his great regret at conduct characterized by a very marked want of discre-

tion . . . As I lived I was being lectured, too!
His deafening gibberish was difficult to follow, but it
was *my* conduct—mine!—that . . . Damn! I
wasn't going to stand this.

"What on earth are you driving at?" I asked in a
passion. I put my hat on my head (he never offered a
seat to anybody), and as he seemed for the moment
struck dumb by my irreverence, I turned my back on
him and marched out. His vocal arrangements blared
after me a few threats of coming down on the ship for
the demurrage of the lighters, and all the other expenses
consequent upon the delays arising from my frivolity.

Once outside in the sunshine my head swam. It
was no longer a question of mere delay. I perceived
myself involved in hopeless and humiliating absurdities
that were leading me to something very like a disaster.
"Let us be calm," I muttered to myself, and ran into
the shade of a leprous wall. From that short side-
street I could see the broad main thoroughfare ruinous
and gay, running away, away between stretches of decaying masonry, bamboo fences, ranges of arcades of brick
and plaster, hovels of lath and mud, lofty temple gates
of carved timber, huts of rotten mats—an immensely
wide thoroughfare, loosely packed as far as the eye
could reach with a barefooted and brown multitude
paddling ankle deep in the dust. For a moment
I felt myself about to go out of my mind with worry
and desperation.

Some allowance must be made for the feelings of a
young man new to responsibility. I thought of my
crew. Half of them were ill, and I really began to
think that some of them would end by dying on board if
I couldn't get them out to sea soon. Obviously I
should have to take my ship down the river, either
working under canvas or dredging with the anchor

down; operations which, in common with many modern
sailors, I only knew theoretically. And I almost
shrank from undertaking them shorthanded and without local knowledge of the river bed, which is so necessary for the confident handling of a ship. There were
no pilots, no beacons, no buoys of any sort; but there
was a very devil of a current for anybody to see, no end
of shoal places, and at least two obviously awkward
turns of the channel between me and the sea. But how
dangerous these turns were I could not tell. I didn't
even know what my ship was capable of! I had never
handled her in my life. A misunderstanding between
a man and his ship, in a difficult river with no room to
make it up, is bound to end in trouble for the man. On
the other hand, it must be owned I had not much reason
to count upon a general run of good luck. And suppose I had the misfortune to pile her up high and dry
on some beastly shoal? That would have been the
final undoing of that voyage. It was plain that if Falk
refused to tow me out he would also refuse to pull me
off. This meant—what? A day lost at the very best;
but more likely a whole fortnight of frizzling on some
pestilential mudflat, of desperate work, of discharging
cargo; more than likely it meant borrowing money at
an exorbitant rate of interest—from the Siegers' gang,
too, at that. They were a power in the port. And that
elderly seaman of mine, Gambril,* had looked pretty
ghastly when I went forward to dose him with quinine
that morning. *He* would certainly die—not to speak
of two or three others that seemed nearly as bad, and of
the rest of them just ready to catch any tropical disease
going. Horror, ruin and everlasting remorse. And no
help. None. I had fallen amongst a lot of unfriendly
lunatics!

At any rate, if I must take my ship down myself it

was my duty to procure if possible some local knowledge. But that was not easy. The only person I could think of for that service was a certain Johnson, formerly captain of a country ship, but now spliced to a country wife and gone utterly to the bad. I had only heard of him in the vaguest way, as living concealed in the thick of two hundred thousand natives, and only emerging into the light of day for the purpose of hunting up some brandy. I had a notion that if I could lay my hands on him I would sober him on board my ship and use him for a pilot. Better than nothing. Once a sailor always a sailor—and he had known the river for years. But in our Consulate (where I arrived dripping after a sharp walk) they could tell me nothing. The excellent young men on the staff, though willing to help me, belonged to a sphere of the white colony for which that sort of Johnson does not exist. Their suggestion was that I should hunt the man up myself with the help of the Consulate's constable—an ex-sergeant-major of a regiment of Hussars.

This man, whose usual duty apparently consisted in sitting behind a little table in an outer room of Consular offices, when ordered to assist me in my search for Johnson displayed lots of energy and a marvellous amount of local knowledge of a sort. But he did not conceal an immense and sceptical contempt for the whole business. We explored together on that afternoon an infinity of infamous grog shops, gambling dens, opium dens. We walked up narrow lanes where our gharry—a tiny box of a thing on wheels, attached to a jibbing Burmah pony—could by no means have passed. The constable seemed to be on terms of scornful intimacy with Maltese, with Eurasians, with Chinamen, with Klings, and with the sweepers belonging to a temple, with whom he talked at the gate. We interviewed also through a grating in a

mud wall closing a blind alley an immensely corpulent
Italian, who, the ex-sergeant-major remarked to me
perfunctorily, had "killed another man last year."
Thereupon he addressed him as "Antonio" and "Old
Buck," though that bloated carcase, apparently more
than half filling the sort of cell wherein it sat, recalled
rather a fat pig in a stye. Familiar and never unbend-
ing, the sergeant chucked—absolutely chucked—under
the chin a horribly wrinkled and shrivelled old hag
propped on a stick, who had volunteered some sort of
information: and with the same stolid face he kept up
an animated conversation with the groups of swathed
brown women, who sat smoking cheroots on the door-
steps of a long range of clay hovels. We got out of
the gharry and clambered into dwellings airy like
packing crates, or descended into places sinister like
cellars. We got in, we drove on, we got out again for
the sole purpose, as it seemed, of looking behind a heap
of rubble. The sun declined; my companion was curt
and sardonic in his answers, but it appears we were just
missing Johnson all along. At last our conveyance
stopped once more with a jerk, and the driver jumping
down opened the door.

A black mudhole blocked the lane. A mound of
garbage crowned with the dead body of a dog arrested
us not. An empty Australian beef tin bounded cheerily
before the toe of my boot. Suddenly we clambered
through a gap in a prickly fence. . . .

It was a very clean native compound: and the big
native woman, with bare brown legs as thick as bed-
posts, pursuing on all fours a silver dollar that came
rolling out from somewhere, was Mrs. Johnson herself.
"Your man's at home," said the ex-sergeant, and
stepped aside in complete and marked indifference to
anything that might follow. Johnson—at home—

stood with his back to a native house built on posts and with its walls made of mats. In his left hand he held a banana. Out of the right he dealt another dollar into space. The woman captured this one on the wing, and there and then plumped down on the ground to look at us with greater comfort.

"My man" was sallow of face, grizzled, unshaven, muddy on elbows and back; where the seams of his serge coat yawned you could see his white nakedness. The vestiges of a paper collar encircled his neck. He looked at us with a grave, swaying surprise. "Where do you come from?" he asked. My heart sank. How could I have been stupid enough to waste energy and time for this?

But having already gone so far I approached a little nearer and declared the purpose of my visit. He would have to come at once with me, sleep on board my ship, and to-morrow, with the first of the ebb, he would give me his assistance in getting my ship down to the sea, without steam. A six-hundred-ton barque, drawing nine feet aft. I proposed to give him eighteen dollars for his local knowledge; and all the time I was speaking he kept on considering attentively the various aspects of the banana, holding first one side up to his eye, then the other.

"You've forgotten to apologize," he said at last with extreme precision. "Not being a gentleman yourself, you don't know apparently when you intrude upon a gentleman. I am one. I wish you to understand that when I am in funds I don't work, and now . . ."

I would have pronounced him perfectly sober had he not paused in great concern to try and brush a hole off the knee of his trousers.

"I have money—and friends. Every gentleman has. Perhaps you would like to know my friend? His

name is Falk. You could borrow some money. Try
to remember. F-A-L-K. Falk." Abruptly his tone
changed. "A noble heart," he said, muzzily.

"Has Falk been giving you some money?" I asked,
appalled by the detailed finish of the dark plot.

"Lent me, my good man, not given me," he corrected,
suavely. "Met me taking the air last evening, and
being as usual anxious to oblige—— Hadn't you better
go to the devil out of my compound?"

And upon this, without other warning, he let fly with
the banana, which missed my head and took the constable just under the left eye. He rushed at the
miserable Johnston, stammering with fury. They fell.
. . . But why dwell on the wretchedness, the
breathlessness, the degradation, the senselessness, the
weariness, the ridicule and humiliation and—and—the
perspiration, of these moments? I dragged the ex-
hussar off. He was like a wild beast. It seems he
had been greatly annoyed at losing his free afternoon
on my account. The garden of his bungalow required
his personal attention, and at the slight blow of the
banana the brute in him had broken loose. We left
Johnson on his back still black in the face, but beginning to kick feebly. Meantime, the big woman had
remained sitting on the ground, apparently paralyzed
with extreme terror.

For half an hour we jolted inside our rolling box,
side by side, in profound silence. The ex-sergeant
was busy staunching the blood of a long scratch on his
cheek. "I hope you're satisfied," he said, suddenly.
"That's what comes of all that tomfool business. If
you hadn't quarrelled with that tugboat skipper over
some girl or other, all this wouldn't have happened."

"You heard *that* story?" I said.

"Of course I heard. And I shouldn't wonder if the

Consul-General himself doesn't come to hear of it. How am I to go before him to-morrow with that thing on my cheek—I want to know. It's *you* who ought to have got this!"

After that, till the gharry stopped and he jumped out without leave-taking, he swore to himself steadily, horribly; muttering great, purposeful, trooper oaths, to which the worst a sailor can do is like the prattle of a child. For my part I had just the strength to crawl into Schomberg's coffee-room, where I wrote at a little table a note to the mate instructing him to get everything ready for dropping down the river next day. I couldn't face my ship. Well! she had a clever sort of skipper and no mistake—poor thing! What a horrid mess! I took my head between my hands. At times the obviousness of my innocence would reduce me to despair. What had I done? If I had done something to bring about the situation I should at least have learned not to do it again. But I felt guiltless to the point of imbecility. The room was empty yet; only Schomberg prowled round me goggle-eyed and with a sort of awed respectful curiosity. No doubt he had set the story going himself; but he was a good-hearted chap, and I am really persuaded he participated in all my troubles. He did what he could for me. He ranged aside the heavy matchstand, set a chair straight, pushed a spittoon slightly with his foot—as you show small attentions to a friend under a great sorrow—sighed, and at last, unable to hold his tongue:

"Well! I warned you, captain. That's what comes of running your head against Mr. Falk. Man'll stick at nothing."

I sat without stirring, and after surveying me with a sort of commiseration in his eyes, he burst out in a hoarse whisper: "But for a fine lump of a girl, she's a

fine lump of a girl." He made a loud smacking noise
with his thick lips. "The finest lump of a girl that I
ever . . ." he was going on with great unction, but
for some reason or other broke off. I fancied myself
throwing something at his head. "I don't blame you,
captain. Hang me if I do," he said with a patronizing
air.

"Thank you," I said, resignedly. It was no use
fighting against this false fate. I don't know even if I
was sure myself where the truth of the matter began.
The conviction that it would end disastrously had been
driven into me by all the successive shocks my sense of
security had received. I began to ascribe an extraordinary potency to agents in themselves powerless.
It was as if Schomberg's baseless gossip had the power
to bring about the thing itself or the abstract enmity
of Falk could put my ship ashore.

I have already explained how fatal this last would
have been. For my further action, my youth, my inexperience, my very real concern for the health of my
crew must be my excuse. The action itself, when it
came, was purely impulsive. It was set in movement
quite undiplomatically and simply by Falk's appearance
in the doorway of the coffee-room.

The room was full by then and buzzing with voices.
I had been looked at with curiosity by everyone, but
how am I to describe the sensation produced by the
appearance of Falk himself blocking the doorway?
The tension of expectation could be measured by the
profundity of the silence that fell upon the very click of
the billiard balls. As to Schomberg, he looked extremely frightened; he hated mortally any sort of row
(*fracas* he called it) in his establishment. *Fracas* was
bad for business, he affirmed; but in truth, this specimen of portly, middle-aged manhood was of a timid

disposition. I don't know what, considering my presence in the place, they all hoped would come of it. A sort of stag fight, perhaps. Or they may have supposed Falk had come in only to annihilate me completely. As a matter of fact, Falk had come in because Hermann had asked him to inquire after the precious white cotton parasol which, in the worry and excitement of the previous day, he had forgotten at the table where we had held our little discussion.

It was this that gave me my opportunity. I don't think I would have gone to seek Falk out. No. I don't think so. There are limits. But there was an opportunity and I seized it—I have already tried to explain why. Now I will merely state that, in my opinion, to get his sickly crew into the sea air and secure a quick despatch for his ship a skipper would be justified in going to any length, short of absolute crime. He should put his pride in his pocket; he may accept confidences; he must explain his innocence as if it were a sin; he may take advantage of misconceptions, of desires and of weaknesses; he ought to conceal his horror and other emotions, and, if the fate of a human being, and that human being a magnificent young girl, is strangely involved—why, he should contemplate that fate (whatever it might seem to be) without turning a hair. And all these things I have done; the explaining, the listening, the pretending—even to the discretion—and nobody, not even Hermann's niece, I believe, need throw stones at me now. Schomberg at all events needn't, since from first to last, I am happy to say there was not the slightest "*fracas.*"

Overcoming a nervous contraction of the windpipe, I had managed to exclaim "Captain Falk!" His start of surprise was perfectly genuine, but afterwards he neither smiled nor scowled. He simply waited. Then,

when I had said, "I must have a talk with you," and
had pointed to a chair at my table, he moved up to me,
though he didn't sit down. Schomberg, however, with
a long tumbler in his hand, was making towards us
prudently, and I discovered then the only sign of weakness in Falk. He had for Schomberg a repulsion
resembling that sort of physical fear some people
experience at the sight of a toad. Perhaps to a man so
essentially and silently concentrated upon himself
(though he could talk well enough, as I was to find out
presently) the other's irrepressible loquacity, embracing
every human being within range of the tongue, might
have appeared unnatural, disgusting, and monstrous.
He suddenly gave signs of restiveness—positively like a
horse about to rear, and, muttering hurriedly as if in
great pain, "No. I can't stand that fellow," seemed
ready to bolt. This weakness of his gave me the
advantage at the very start. "Verandah," I suggested,
as if rendering him a service, and walked him out by the
arm. We stumbled over a few chairs; we had the feeling of open space before us, and felt the fresh breath of
the river—fresh, but tainted. The Chinese theatres
across the water made, in the sparsely twinkling
masses of gloom an Eastern town presents at night,
blazing centres of light, and of a distant and howling uproar. I felt him become suddenly tractable again like
an animal, like a good-tempered horse when the object
that scares him is removed. Yes. I felt in the darkness there how tractable he was, without my conviction
of his inflexibility—tenacity, rather, perhaps—being
in the least weakened. His very arm abandoning itself
to my grasp was as hard as marble—like a limb of iron.
But I heard a tumultuous scuffling of boot-soles within.
The unspeakable idiots inside were crowding to the
windows, climbing over each other's backs behind the

blinds, billiard cues and all. Somebody broke a
window-pane, and with the sound of falling glass, so
suggestive of riot and devastation, Schomberg reeled
out after us in a state of funk which had prevented him
from parting with his brandy and soda. He must have
trembled like an aspen leaf. The piece of ice in the
long tumbler he held in his hand tinkled with an effect
of chattering teeth. "I beg you, gentlemen," he
expostulated, thickly. "Come! Really, now, I must
insist . . ."

How proud I am of my presence of mind! "Hallo,"
I said instantly in a loud and naïve tone, "somebody's
breaking your windows, Schomberg. Would you
please tell one of your boys to bring out here a pack of
cards and a couple of lights? And two long drinks.
Will you?"

To receive an order soothed him at once. It was
business. "Certainly," he said in an immensely relieved tone. The night was rainy, with wandering
gusts of wind, and while we waited for the candles Falk
said, as if to justify his panic, "I don't interfere in
anybody's business. I don't give any occasion for
talk. I am a respectable man. But this fellow is
always making out something wrong, and can never
rest till he gets somebody to believe him."

This was the first of my knowledge of Falk. This
desire of respectability, of being like everybody else,
was the only recognition he vouchsafed to the organization of mankind. For the rest he might have been
the member of a herd, not of a society. Self-preservation was his only concern. Not selfishness, but mere
self-preservation. Selfishness presupposes consciousness, choice, the presence of other men; but his instinct
acted as though he were the last of mankind nursing
that law like the only spark of a sacred fire. I don't

mean to say that living naked in a cavern would have satisfied him. Obviously he was the creature of the conditions to which he was born. No doubt self-preservation meant also the preservation of these conditions. But essentially it meant something much more simple, natural, and powerful. How shall I express it? It meant the preservation of the five senses of his body—let us say—taking it in its narrowest as well as in its widest meaning. I think you will admit before long the justice of this judgment. However, as we stood there together in the dark verandah I had judged nothing as yet—and I had no desire to judge—which is an idle practice anyhow. The light was long in coming.

"Of course," I said in a tone of mutual understanding, "it isn't exactly a game of cards I want with you."

I saw him draw his hands down his face—the vague stir of the passionate and meaningless gesture; but he waited in silent patience. It was only when the lights had been brought out that he opened his lips. I understood his mumble to mean that "he didn't know any card-games."

"Like this, Schömberg and all the other fools will have to keep off," I said, tearing open the pack. "Have you heard that we are universally supposed to be quarrelling about a girl? You know who—of course. I am really ashamed to ask, but is it possible that you do me the honour to think me dangerous?"

As I said these words I felt how absurd it was and also I felt flattered—for, really, what else could it be? His answer, spoken in his usual dispassionate undertone, made it clear that it was so, but not precisely as flattering as I supposed. He thought me dangerous with Hermann, more than with the girl herself; but, as to quarrelling, I saw at once how inappropriate the

word was. We had no quarrel. Natural forces are
not quarrelsome. You can't quarrel with the wind that
inconveniences and humiliates you by blowing off your
hat in a street full of people. He had no quarrel with
me. Neither would a boulder, falling on my head,
have had. He fell upon me in accordance with the
law by which he was moved—not of gravitation, like a
detached stone, but of self-preservation. Of course
this is giving it a rather wide interpretation. Strictly
speaking, he had existed and could have existed without
being married. Yet he told me that he had found it
more and more difficult to live alone. Yes. He told
me this in his low, careless voice, to such a pitch of
confidence had we arrived at the end of half an
hour.

It took me just about that time to convince him that
I had never dreamed of marrying Hermann's niece.
Could any necessity have been more extravagant? And
the difficulty was the greater because he was so hard
hit himself that he couldn't imagine anybody else being
able to remain in a state of indifference. Any man with
eyes in his head, he seemed to think, could not help
coveting so much bodily magnificence. This profound
belief was conveyed by the manner he listened sitting
sideways to the table and playing absently with a few
cards I had dealt to him at random. And the more I
saw into him the more I saw of him. The wind swayed
the lights so that his sunburnt face, whiskered to the
eyes, seemed to successively flicker crimson at me and
to go out. I saw the extraordinary breadth of the high
cheek-bones, the perpendicular style of the features, the
massive forehead, steep like a cliff, denuded at the top,
largely uncovered at the temples. The fact is I had
never before seen him without his hat; but now, as if my
fervour had made him hot, he had taken it off and laid

it gently on the floor. Something peculiar in the shape
and setting of his yellow eyes gave them the provoking
silent intensity which characterized his glance. But the
face was thin, furrowed, worn; I discovered this through
the bush of his hair, as you may detect the gnarled
shape of a tree trunk in a dense undergrowth. These
overgrown cheeks were sunken. It was an anchorite's
bony head fitted with a Capuchin's beard and adjusted
to a herculean body. I don't mean athletic. Hercules,
I take it, was not an athlete. He was a strong man,
susceptible to female charms, and not afraid of dirt.
And thus with Falk, who was a strong man. He was
extremely strong, just as the girl (since I must think of
them together) was magnificently attractive by the
masterful power of flesh and blood, expressed in shape,
in size, in attitude—that is by a straight appeal to the
senses. His mind meantime, preoccupied with respectability, quailed before Schomberg's tongue and seemed
absolutely impervious to my protestations; and I went
so far as to protest that I would just as soon think of
marrying my mother's (dear old lady!) faithful female
cook as Hermann's niece. Sooner, I protested, in my
desperation, much sooner; but it did not appear that he
saw anything outrageous in the proposition, and in his
sceptical immobility he seemed to nurse the argument
that at all events the cook was very, very far away. It
must be said that, just before, I had gone wrong by
appealing to the evidence of my manner whenever I
called on board the *Diana*. I had never attempted to
approach the girl, or to speak to her, or even to look at
her in any marked way. Nothing could be clearer.
But, as his own idea of—let us say—courting, seemed
to consist precisely in sitting silently for hours in the
vicinity of the beloved object, that line of argument
inspired him with distrust. Staring down his extended

legs he let out a grunt—as much as to say, "That's all very fine, but you can't throw dust in *my* eyes."

As last I was exasperated into saying, "Why don't you put the matter at rest by talking to Hermann?" and I added, sneeringly: "You don't expect me perhaps to speak for you?"

To this he said, very loud for him, "Would you?"

And for the first time he lifted his head to look at me with wonder and incredulity. He lifted his head so sharply that there could be no mistake. I had touched a spring. I saw the whole extent of my opportunity, and could hardly believe in it.

"Why! Speak to . . . Well, of course," I proceeded very slowly, watching him with great attention, for, on my word, I feared a joke. "Not, perhaps, to the young lady herself. I can't speak German, you know. But . . ."

He interrupted me with the earnest assurance that Hermann had the highest opinion of me; and at once I felt the need for the greatest possible diplomacy at this juncture. So I demurred just enough to draw him on. Falk sat up, but except for a very noticeable enlargement of the pupils, till the irises of his eyes were reduced to two narrow yellow rings, his face, I should judge, was incapable of expressing excitement. "Oh, yes! Hermann did have the greatest . . ."

"Take up your cards. Here's Schomberg peeping at us through the blind!" I said.

We went through the motions of what might have been a game of écarté. Presently the intolerable scandalmonger withdrew, probably to inform the people in the billiard-room that we two were gambling on the verandah like mad.

We were not gambling, but it was a game; a game

in which I felt I held the winning cards. The stake, roughly speaking, was the success of the voyage—for me; and he, I apprehended, had nothing to lose. Our intimacy matured rapidly, and before many words had been exchanged I perceived that the excellent Hermann had been making use of me. That simple and astute Teuton had been, it seems, holding me up to Falk in the light of a rival. I was young enough to be shocked at so much duplicity. "Did he tell you that in so many words?" I asked with indignation.

Hermann had not. He had given hints only; and of course it had not taken very much to alarm Falk; but, instead of declaring himself, he had taken steps to remove the family from under my influence. He was perfectly straightforward about it—as straightforward as a tile falling on your head. There was no duplicity in that man; and when I congratulated him on the perfection of his arrangements—even to the bribing of the wretched Johnson against me—he had a genuine movement of protest. Never bribed. He knew the man wouldn't work as long as he had a few cents in his pocket to get drunk on, and, naturally (he said—"*naturally*") he let him have a dollar or two. He was himself a sailor, he said, and anticipated the view another sailor, like myself, was bound to take. On the other hand, he was sure that I should have to come to grief. He hadn't been knocking about for the last seven years up and down that river for nothing. It would have been no disgrace to me—but he asserted confidently I would have had my ship very awkwardly ashore at a spot two miles below the Great Pagoda. . . .

And with all that he had no ill-will. That was evident. This was a crisis in which his only object had been to gain time—I fancy. And presently he mentioned that he had written for some jewellery, real good jewellery—had written to Hong-Kong for it. It would arrive in a day or two.

"Well, then," I said, cheerily, "everything is all right. All you've got to do is to present it to the lady together with your heart, and live happy ever after."

Upon the whole he seemed to accept that view as far as the girl was concerned, but his eyelids drooped. There was still something in the way. For one thing Hermann disliked him so much. As to me, on the contrary, it seemed as though he could not praise me enough. Mrs. Hermann, too. He didn't know why they disliked him so. It made everything most difficult.

I listened impassive, feeling more and more diplomatic. His speech was not transparently clear. He was one of those men who seem to live, feel, suffer in a sort of mental twilight. But as to being fascinated by the girl and possessed by the desire of home life with her—it was as clear as daylight. So much being at stake, he was afraid of putting it to the hazard of the declaration. Besides, there was something else. And with Hermann being so set against him . . .

"I see," I said, thoughtfully, while my heart beat fast with the excitement of my diplomacy. "I don't mind sounding Hermann. In fact, to show you how mistaken you were, I am ready to do all I can for you in that way."

A light sigh escaped him. He drew his hands down his face, and it emerged, bony, unchanged of expression, as if all the tissues had been ossified. All the passion was in those big brown hands. He was satisfied. Then there was that other matter. If there were anybody on earth it was I who could persuade Hermann to take a reasonable view! I had a knowledge of the world and lots of experience. Hermann admitted this himself. And then I was a sailor, too. Falk thought that a sailor would be able to understand certain things best. . . .

He talked as if the Hermanns had been living all their life in a rural hamlet, and I alone had been capable, with my practice in life, of a large and indulgent view of certain occurrences. That was what my diplomacy was leading me to. I began suddenly to dislike it.

"I say, Falk," I asked quite brusquely, "you haven't already a wife put away somewhere?"

The pain and disgust of his denial were very striking. Couldn't I understand that he was as respectable as any white man hereabouts; earning his living honestly. He was suffering from my suspicion, and the low undertone of his voice made his protestations sound very pathetic. For a moment he shamed me, but, my diplomacy notwithstanding, I seemed to develop a conscience, as if in very truth it were in my power to decide the success of this matrimonial enterprise. By pretending hard enough we come to believe anything—anything to our advantage. And I had been pretending very hard, because I meant yet to be towed safely down the river. But, through conscience or stupidity, I couldn't help alluding to the Vanlo affair. "You acted rather badly there. Didn't you?" was what I ventured actually to say—for the logic of our conduct is always at the mercy of obscure and unforeseen impulses.

His dilated pupils swerved from my face, glancing at the window with a sort of scared fury. We heard behind the blinds the continuous and sudden clicking of ivory, a jovial murmur of many voices, and Schomberg's deep manly laugh.

"That confounded old woman of a hotel-keeper then would never, never let it rest!" Falk exclaimed. Well,

yes! It had happened two years ago. When it came
to the point he owned he couldn't make up his mind to
trust Fred Vanlo—no sailor, a bit of a fool, too. He
could not trust him, but, to stop his row, he had lent
him enough money to pay all his debts before he left. I
was greatly surprised to hear this. Then Falk could not
be such a miser after all. So much the better for the
girl. For a time he sat silent; then he picked up a card
and while looking at it he said:

"You need not think of anything bad. It was an
accident. I've been unfortunate once."

"Then in heaven's name say nothing about it."

As soon as these words were out of my mouth I
fancied I had said something immoral. He shook his
head negatively. It had to be told. He considered it
proper that the relations of the lady should know. No
doubt—I thought to myself—had Miss Vanlo not been
thirty and damaged by the climate he would have found
it possible to entrust Fred Vanlo with this confidence.
And then the figure of Hermann's niece appeared before
my mind's eye, with the wealth of her opulent form, her
rich youth, her lavish strength. With that powerful
and immaculate vitality, her girlish form must have
shouted aloud of life to that man, whereas poor Miss
Vanlo could only sing sentimental songs to the strum-
ming of a piano.

"And that Hermann hates me, I know it!" he cried
in his undertone, with a sudden recrudescence of
anxiety. "I must tell them. It is proper that they
should know. You would say so yourself."

He then murmured an utterly mysterious allusion to
the necessity for peculiar domestic arrangements.
Though my curiosity was excited I did not want to hear
any of his confidences. I feared he might give me a
piece of information that would make my assumed *rôle*

of match-maker odious—however unreal it was. I
was aware that he could have the girl for the asking;
and keeping down a desire to laugh in his face, I expressed a confident belief in my ability to argue away
Hermann's dislike for him. "I am sure I can make it
all right," I said. He looked very pleased.

And when we rose not a word had been said about
towage! Not a word! The game was won and the
honour was safe. Oh! blessed white cotton umbrella!
We shook hands, and I was holding myself with difficulty from breaking into a dance of joy when he came
back, striding all the length of the verandah, and said
doubtfully:

"I say, captain, I have your word? You—you—
won't turn round?"

Heavens! The fright he gave me. Behind his tone
of doubt there was something desperate and menacing.
The infatuated ass. But I was equal to the situation.

"My dear Falk," I said, beginning to lie with a glib-
ness and effrontery that amazed me even at the time—
"confidence for confidence." (He had made no confidences.) "I will tell you that I am already engaged to
an extremely charming girl at home, and so you understand . . ."

He caught my hand and wrung it in a crushing grip.

"Pardon me. I feel it every day more difficult to
live alone . . ."

"On rice and fish," I interrupted smartly, giggling
with the sheer nervousness of escaped danger.

He dropped my hand as if it had become suddenly
red hot. A moment of profound silence ensued, as
though something extraordinary had happened.

"I promise you to obtain Hermann's consent," I
faltered out at last, and it seemed to me that he could
not help seeing through that humbugging promise. "If

there's anything else to get over I shall endeavour to stand by you," I conceded further, feeling somehow defeated and overborne; "but you must do your best yourself."

"I have been unfortunate once," he muttered, unemotionally, and turning his back on me he went away, thumping slowly the plank floor as if his feet had been shod with iron.

Next morning, however, he was lively enough as man-boat, a combination of splashing and shouting; of the insolent commotion below with the steady overbearing glare of the silent head-piece above. He turned us out most unnecessarily at an ungodly hour, but it was nearly eleven in the morning before he brought me up a cable's length from Hermann's ship. And he did it very badly, too, in a hurry, and nearly contriving to miss altogether the patch of good holding ground, because, forsooth, he had caught sight of Hermann's niece on the poop. And so did I; and probably as soon as he had seen her himself. I saw the modest, sleek glory of the tawny head, and the full, gray shape of the girlish print frock she filled so perfectly, so satisfactorily, with the seduction of unfaltering curves—a very nymph of Diana the Huntress. And *Diana* the ship sat, high-walled and as solid as an institution, on the smooth level of the water, the most uninspiring and respectable craft upon the seas, useful and ugly, devoted to the support of domestic virtues like any grocer's shop on shore. At once Falk steamed away; for there was some work for him to do. He would return in the evening.

He ranged close by us, passing out dead slow, without a hail. The beat of the paddle-wheels reverberating amongst the stony islets, as if from the ruined walls of a vast arena, filled the anchorage confusedly with the

clapping sounds as of a mighty and leisurely applause.
Abreast of Hermann's ship Falk stopped the engines;
and a profound silence reigned over the rocks, the shore
and the sea, for the time it took him to raise his hat
aloft before the nymph of the gray print frock. I had
snatched up my binoculars, and I can answer for it she
didn't stir a limb, standing by the rail shapely and
erect, with one of her hands grasping a rope at the
height of her head, while the way of the tug carried
slowly past her the lingering and profound homage of
the man. There was for me an enormous significance
in the scene, the sense of having witnessed a solemn
declaration. The die was cast. After such a manifestation he couldn't back out. And I reflected that it
was nothing whatever to me now. With a rush of
black smoke belching suddenly out of the funnel, and a
mad swirl of paddle-wheels provoking a burst of weird
and precipitated clapping, the tug shot out of the
desolate arena. The rocky islets lay on the sea like the
heaps of a cyclopean ruin on a plain; the centipedes and
scorpions lurked under the stones; there was not a
single blade of grass in sight anywhere, not a single
lizard sunning himself on a boulder by the shore. When
I looked again at Hermann's ship the girl had disappeared. I could not detect the smallest dot of a bird
on the immense sky, and the flatness of the land continued the flatness of the sea to the naked line of the
horizon.

This is the setting now inseparably connected with
my knowledge of Falk's misfortune. My diplomacy
had brought me there, and now I had only to wait the
time for taking up the *rôle* of an ambassador. My
diplomacy was a success; my ship was safe; old Gambril would probably live; a feeble sound of a tapping
hammer came intermittently from the *Diana*. During

the afternoon I looked at times at the old homely ship,
the faithful nurse of Hermann's progeny, or yawned
towards the distant temple of Buddha, like a lonely
hillock on the plain, where shaven priests cherish the
thoughts of that Annihilation which is the worthy reward of us all.* Unfortunate! He had been unfortunate once. Well, that was not so bad as life goes.
And what the devil could be the nature of that misfortune? I remembered that I had known a man before who had declared himself to have fallen, years
ago, a victim to misfortune; but this misfortune, whose
effects appeared permanent (he looked desperately hard
up) when considered dispassionately, seemed indis-
tinguishable from a breach of trust. Could it be something of that nature? Apart, however, from the utter
improbability that he would offer to talk of it even to
his future uncle-in-law I had a strange feeling that
Falk's physique unfitted him for that sort of delin-
quency. As the person of Hermann's niece exhaled the
profound physical charm of feminine form, so her
adorer's big frame embodied to my senses the hard,
straight masculinity that would conceivably kill but
would not condescend to cheat. The thing was ob-
vious. I might just as well have suspected the girl of a
curvature of the spine. And I perceived that the sun
was about to set.

The smoke of Falk's tug hove in sight, far away at
the mouth of the river. It was time for me to assume
the character of an ambassador, and the negotiation
would not be difficult except in the matter of keeping
my countenance. It was all too extravagantly non-
sensical, and I conceived that it would be best to
compose for myself a grave demeanour. I practised
this in my boat as I went along, but the bashfulness
that came secretly upon me the moment I stepped on

the deck of the *Diana* is inexplicable. As soon as we
had exchanged greetings Hermann asked me eagerly if
I knew whether Falk had found his white parasol.

"He's going to bring it to you himself directly," I
said with great solemnity. "Meantime, I am charged
with an important message for which he begs your
favourable consideration. He is in love with your
niece. . . ."

"*Ach so!*" he hissed with an animosity that made
my assumed gravity change into the most genuine concern. What meant this tone? And I hurried on.

"He wishes, with your consent of course, to ask her
to marry him at once—before you leave here, that is.
He would speak to his Consul."

Hermann sat down and smoked violently. Five
minutes passed in that furious meditation, and then,
taking the long pipe out of his mouth, he burst into a
hot diatribe against Falk—against his cupidity, his
stupidity (a fellow that can hardly be got to say "yes"
or "no" to the simplest question)—against his outrageous treatment of the shipping in port (because he
saw they were at his mercy)—and against his manner
of walking, which to his (Hermann's) mind showed a
conceit positively unbearable. The damage to the
old *Diana* was not forgotten, of course, and there was
nothing of any nature said or done by Falk (even to
the last offer of refreshment in the hotel) that did not
seem to have been a cause of offence. "Had the cheek"
to drag him (Hermann) into that coffee-room; as though
a drink from him could make up for forty-seven dollars
and fifty cents of damage in the cost of wood alone—not
counting two days' work for the carpenter. Of course
he would not stand in the girl's way. He was going
home to Germany. There were plenty of poor girls
walking about in Germany.

"He's very much in love," was all I found to say.

"Yes," he cried. "And it is time, too, after making himself and me talked about ashore the last voyage I was here, and then now again; coming on board every evening unsettling the girl's mind, and saying nothing. What sort of conduct is that?"

The seven thousand dollars the fellow was always talking about did not, in his opinion, justify such behaviour. Moreover, nobody had seen them. He (Hermann) seriously doubted if Falk possessed seven thousand cents, and the tug, no doubt, was mortgaged up to the top of the funnel to the firm of Siegers. But let that pass. He wouldn't stand in the girl's way. Her head was so turned that she had become no good to them of late. Quite unable even to put the children to bed without her aunt. It was bad for the children; they got unruly; and yesterday he actually had to give Gustav a thrashing.

For that, too, Falk was made responsible apparently. And looking at my Hermann's heavy, puffy, good-natured face, I knew he would not exert himself till greatly exasperated, and, therefore, would thrash very hard, and being fat would resent the necessity. How Falk had managed to turn the girl's head was more difficult to understand. I supposed Hermann would know. And then hadn't there been Miss Vanlo? It could not be his silvery tongue, or the subtle seduction of his manner; he had no more of what is called "manner" than an animal—which, however, on the other hand, is never, and can never be called, vulgar. Therefore it must have been his bodily appearance, exhibiting a virility of nature as exaggerated as his beard, and resembling a sort of constant ruthlessness. It was seen in the very manner he lolled in the chair. He meant no offence, but his intercourse was characterized by that sort of frank disregard of susceptibilities a tall man, living in a world of dwarfs, would naturally assume, without in the least wishing to be unkind. But amongst men of his own stature, or nearly, this frank use of his advantages, in such matters as the awful towage bills for instance, caused much impotent gnashing of teeth. When attentively considered it seemed appalling at times. He was a strange beast. But maybe women liked it. Seen in that light he was well worth taming, and I suppose every woman at the bottom of her heart considers herself as a tamer of strange beasts. But Hermann arose with precipitation to carry the news to his wife. I had barely the time, as he made for the cabin door, to grab him by the seat of his inexpressibles. I begged him to wait till Falk in person had spoken with him. There remained some small matter to talk over as I understood.

He sat down again at once, full of suspicion.

"What matter?" he said, surlily. "I have had enough of his nonsense. There's no matter at all, as he knows very well; the girl has nothing in the world. She came to us in one thin dress when my brother died, and I have a growing family."

"It can't be anything of that kind," I opined. "He's desperately enamoured of your niece. I don't know why he did not say so before. Upon my word, I believe it is because he was afraid to lose, perhaps, the felicity of sitting near her on your quarter-deck."

I intimated my conviction that Falk's love was so great as to be in a sense cowardly. The effects of a great passion are unaccountable. It has been known to make a man timid. But Hermann looked at me as if I had raved; and the twilight was dying out rapidly.

"You don't believe in passion, do you, Hermann?" I continued, cheerily. "The passion of fear will make a

cornered rat courageous. Falk's in a corner. He will
take her off your hands in one thin frock just as she
came to you. And after ten years' service it isn't a bad
bargain," I added.

Far from taking offence, he resumed his air of civic
virtue. The sudden night came upon him while he
stared placidly along the deck, bringing in contact with
his thick lips, and taking away again after a jet of
smoke, the curved mouthpiece fitted to the stem of his
pipe. The night came upon him and buried in haste
his whiskers, his globular eyes, his puffy pale face, his
fat knees and the vast flat slippers on his fatherly feet.
Only his short arms in respectable white shirt-sleeves
remained very visible, propped up like the flippers of
seal reposing on the strand.

"Falk wouldn't settle anything about repairs. Told
me to find out first how much wood I should require
and he would see," he remarked; and after he had spat
peacefully in the dusk we heard over the water the beat
of the tug's floats. There is, on a calm night, nothing
more suggestive of fierce and headlong haste than the
rapid sound made by the paddle-wheels of a boat thresh-
ing her way through a quiet sea; and the approach of
Falk towards his fate seemed to be urged by an impatient and passionate desire. The engines must have
been driven to the very utmost of their revolutions.
We heard them slow down at last, and, vaguely, the
white hull of the tug appeared moving against the
black islets, whilst a slow and rhythmical clapping as of
thousands of hands rose on all sides. It ceased all at
once, just before Falk brought her up. A single brusque splash was followed by the long-drawn rumbling of
iron links running through the hawse pipe. Then a
solemn silence fell upon the Roadstead.

"He will soon be here," I murmured, and after that

we waited for him without a word. Meantime, raising my eyes, I beheld the glitter of a lofty sky above the *Diana's* mastheads. The multitude of stars gathered into clusters, in rows, in lines, in masses, in groups, shone all together, unanimously—and the few isolated ones, blazing by themselves in the midst of dark patches, seemed to be of a superior kind and of an inextinguishable nature. But long striding footsteps were heard hastening along the deck; the high bulwarks of the *Diana* made a deeper darkness. We rose from our chairs quickly, and Falk, appearing before us, all in white, stood still.

Nobody spoke at first, as though we had been covered with confusion. His arrival was fiery, but his white bulk, of indefinite shape and without features, made him loom up like a man of snow.

"The captain here has been telling me . . ." Hermann began in a homely and amicable voice; and Falk gave a low, nervous laugh. His cool, negligent undertone had no inflexions, but the strength of a powerful emotion made him ramble in his speech. He had always desired a home. It was difficult to live alone, though he was not answerable. He was domestic; there had been difficulties; but since he had seen Hermann's niece he found that it had become at last impossible to live by himself. "I mean—impossible," he repeated with no sort of emphasis and only with the slightest of pauses, but the word fell into my mind with the force of a new idea.

"I have not said anything to her yet," Hermann observed, quietly. And Falk dismissed this by a "That's all right. Certainly. Very proper." There was a necessity for perfect frankness—in marrying, especially. Hermann seemed attentive, but he seized the first opportunity to ask us into the cabin. "And

by-the-by, Falk," he said, innocently, as we passed in,
"the timber came to no less than forty-seven dollars
and fifty cents."

Falk, uncovering his head, lingered in the passage.
"Some other time," he said; and Hermann nudged me
angrily—I don't know why. The girl alone in the
cabin sat sewing at some distance from the table.
Falk stopped short in the doorway. Without a word,
without a sign, without the slightest inclination of his
bony head, by the silent intensity of his look alone, he
seemed to lay his herculean frame at her feet. Her
hands sank slowly on her lap, and raising her clear eyes,
she let her soft, beaming glance enfold him from head to
foot like a slow and pale caress. He was very hot when
he sat down; she, with bowed head, went on with her
sewing; her neck was very white under the light of the
lamp; but Falk, hiding his face in the palms of his hands,
shuddered faintly. He drew them down, even to his
beard, and his uncovered eyes astonished me by their
tense and irrational expression—as though he had just
swallowed a heavy gulp of alcohol. It passed away
while he was binding us to secrecy. Not that he cared,
but he did not like to be spoken about; and I looked at
the girl's marvellous, at her wonderful, at her regal hair,
plaited tight into that one astonishing and maidenly
tress. Whenever she moved her well-shaped head it
would stir stiffly to and fro on her back. The thin
cotton sleeve fitted the irreproachable roundness of her
arm like a skin; and her very dress, stretched on her
bust, seemed to palpitate like a living tissue with the
strength of vitality animating her body. How good her
complexion was, the outline of her soft cheek and the
small convoluted conch of her rosy ear! To pull her
needle she kept the little finger apart from the others;
it seemed a waste of power to see her sewing—eternally

sewing—with that industrious and precise movement of her arm, going on eternally upon all the oceans, under all the skies, in innumerable harbours. And suddenly I heard Falk's voice declare that he could not marry a woman unless she knew of something in his life that had happened ten years ago. It was an accident. An unfortunate accident. It would affect the domestic arrangements of their home, but, once told, it need not be alluded to again for the rest of their lives. "I should want my wife to feel for me," he said. "It has made me unhappy." And how could he keep the knowledge of it to himself—he asked us—perhaps through years and years of companionship? What sort of companionship would that be? He had thought it over. A wife must know. Then why not at once? He counted on Hermann's kindness for presenting the affair in the best possible light. And Hermann's countenance, mystified before, became very sour. He stole an inquisitive glance at me. I shook my head blankly. Some people thought, Falk went on, that such an experience changed a man for the rest of his life. He couldn't say. It was hard, awful, and not to be forgotten, but he did not think himself a worse man than before. Only he talked in his sleep now, he believed. . . . At last I began to think he had accidentally killed someone, perhaps a friend—his own father maybe; when he went on to say that probably we were aware he never touched meat. Throughout he spoke English, of course on my account.

He swayed forward heavily.

The girl, with her hands raised before her pale eyes, was threading her needle. He glanced at her and his mighty trunk overshadowed the table, bringing nearer to us the breadth of his shoulders, the thickness of his neck, and that incongruous, anchorite head, burnt in

the desert, hollowed and lean as if by excesses of vigils
and fasting. His beard flowed imposingly downwards,
out of sight, between the two brown hands gripping the
edge of the table, and his persistent glance made sombre
by the wide dilations of the pupils, fascinated.

"Imagine to yourselves," he said in his ordinary
voice, "that I have eaten man."

I could only ejaculate a faint "Ah!" of complete
enlightenment. But Hermann, dazed by the excessive
shock, actually murmured, "Himmel! What for?"

"It was my terrible misfortune to do so," said Falk
in a measured undertone. The girl, unconscious, sewed
on. Mrs. Hermann was absent in one of the staterooms, sitting up with Lena, who was feverish; but
Hermann suddenly put both his hands up with a jerk.
The embroidered calotte fell, and, in the twinkling of an
eye, he had rumpled his hair all ends up in a most extravagant manner. In this state he strove to speak;
with every effort his eyes seemed to start further out of
their sockets; his head looked like a mop. He choked,
gasped, swallowed, and managed to shriek out the one
word, "Beast!"

From that moment till Falk went out of the cabin the
girl, with her hands folded on the work lying in her lap,
never took her eyes off him. His own, in the blindness
of his heart, darted all over the cabin, only seeking to
avoid the sight of Hermann's raving. It was ridiculous,
and was made almost terrible by the stillness of every
other person present. It was contemptible, and was
made appalling by the man's overmastering horror of
this awful sincerity, coming to him suddenly, with the
confession of such a fact. He walked with great strides;
he gasped. He wanted to know from Falk how dared
he to come and tell him this? Did he think himself a
proper person to be sitting in this cabin where his wife

and children lived? Tell his niece! Expected him to
tell his niece! His own brother's daughter! Shameless! Did I ever hear tell of such impudence?—he
appealed to me. "This man here ought to have gone
and hidden himself out of sight instead of . . ."

"But it's a great misfortune for me. But it's a great
misfortune for me," Falk would ejaculate from time to
time.

However, Hermann kept on running frequently
against the corners of the table. At last he lost a slipper, and crossing his arms on his breast, walked up with
one stocking foot very close to Falk, in order to ask him
whether he did think there was anywhere on earth a
woman abandoned enough to mate with such a monster. "Did he? Did he? Did he?" I tried to restrain him. He tore himself out of my hands; he found
his slipper, and, endeavouring to put it on, stormed
standing on one leg—and Falk, with a face unmoved
and averted eyes, grasped all his mighty beard in one
vast palm.

"Was it right then for me to die myself?" he asked,
thoughtfully. I laid my hand on his shoulder.

"Go away," I whispered, imperiously, without any
clear reason for this advice, except that I wished to
put an end to Hermann's odious noise. "Go away."

He looked searchingly for a moment at Hermann before he made a move. I left the cabin, too, to see him
out of the ship. But he hung about the quarter-deck.

"It is my misfortune," he said in a steady voice.

"You were stupid to blurt it out in such a manner.
After all, we don't hear such confidences every day."

"What does the man mean?" he mused in deep
undertones. "Somebody had to die—but why me?"

He remained still for a time in the dark—silent;
almost invisible. All at once he pinned my elbows to

my sides. I felt utterly powerless in his grip, and his voice, whispering in my ear, vibrated.

"It's worse than hunger. Captain, do you know what that means? And I could kill then—or be killed. I wish the crowbar had smashed my skull ten years ago. And I've got to live now. Without her. Do you understand? Perhaps many years. But how? What can be done? If I had allowed myself to look at her once I would have carried her off before that man in my hands—like this."

I felt myself snatched off the deck, then suddenly dropped—and I staggered backwards, feeling bewildered and bruised. What a man! All was still; he was gone. I heard Hermann's voice declaiming in the cabin, and went in.

I could not at first make out a single word, but Mrs. Hermann, who, attracted by the noise, had come in some time before, with an expression of surprise and mild disapproval depicted broadly on her face, was giving now all the signs of profound, helpless agitation. Her husband shot a string of guttural words at her, and instantly putting out one hand to the bulkhead as if to save herself from falling, she clutched the loose bosom of her dress with the other. He harangued the two women extraordinarily, with much of his shirt hanging out of his waistbelt, stamping his foot, turning from one to the other, sometimes flinging both his arms straight up above his rumpled hair and keeping them in that position while he uttered a passage of loud denunciation; at others folding them tight across his breast—and then he hissed with indignation, elevating his shoulders and protruding his head. The girl was crying.

She had not changed her attitude. From her steady eyes that, following Falk in his retreat, had remained fixed wistfully on the cabin door, the tears fell rapid, thick, on her hands, on the work in her lap, warm and gentle like a shower in spring. She wept without grimacing, without noise—very touching, very quiet, with something more of pity than of pain in her face, as one weeps in compassion rather than grief—and Hermann, before her, declaimed. I caught several times the word "Mensch," man; and also "Fressen," which last I looked up afterwards in my dictionary. It means "Devour." Hermann seemed to be requesting an answer of some sort from her; his whole body swayed. She remained mute and perfectly still; at last his agitation gained her; she put the palms of her hands together, her full lips parted, no sound came. His voice scolded shrilly, his arms went like a windmill— suddenly he shook his thick fist at her. She burst out into loud sobs. He seemed stupefied.

Mrs. Hermann rushed forward babbling rapidly.

The two women fell on each other's necks, and, with an arm round her niece's waist, she led her away. Her own eyes were simply streaming, her face was flooded. She shook her head back at me negatively, I wonder why to this day. The girl's head dropped heavily on her shoulder. They disappeared together.

Then Hermann sat down and stared at the cabin floor.

"We don't know all the circumstances," I ventured to break the silence. He retorted tartly that he didn't want to know of any. According to his ideas no circumstances could excuse a crime—and certainly not such a crime. This was the opinion generally received. The duty of a human being was to starve. Falk therefore was a beast, an animal; base, low, vile, despicable, shameless, and deceitful. He had been deceiving him since last year. He was, however, inclined to think

that Falk must have gone mad quite recently; for no
sane person, without necessity, uselessly, for no earthly
reason, and regardless of another's self-respect and
peace of mind, would own to having devoured human
flesh. "Why tell?" he cried. "Who was asking him?"
It showed Falk's brutality because after all he had
selfishly caused him (Hermann) much pain. He would
have preferred not to know that such an unclean
creature had been in the habit of caressing his children.
He hoped I would say nothing of all this ashore, though.
He wouldn't like it to get about that he had been intimate
with an eater of men—a common cannibal. As to the
scene he had made (which I judged quite unnecessary)
he was not going to inconvenience and restrain himself
for a fellow that went about courting and upsetting
girls' heads, while he knew all the time that no decent
housewifely girl would think of marrying him. At
least he (Hermann) could not conceive how any girl
could. "Fancy Lena! . . . No, it was impossible.
The thoughts that would come into their heads every
time they sat down to a meal. Horrible! Horrible!"

"You are too squeamish, Hermann," I said.

He seemed to think it was eminently proper to be
squeamish if the word meant disgust at Falk's conduct;
and turning up his eyes sentimentally he drew my
attention to the horrible fate of the victims—the
victims of that Falk. I said that I knew nothing about
them. He seemed surprised. Could not anybody
imagine without knowing? He—for instance—felt he
would like to avenge them. But what if—said I—there
had not been any? They might have died as it were,
naturally—of starvation. He shuddered. But to be
eaten—after death! To be devoured! He gave another
deep shudder, and asked suddenly, "Do you think it is
true?"

His indignation and his personality together would have been enough to spoil the reality of the most authentic thing. When I looked at him I doubted the story—but the remembrance of Falk's words, looks, gestures, invested it not only with an air of reality but with the absolute truth of primitive passion.

"It is true just as much as you are able to make it; and exactly in the way you like to make it. For my part, when I hear you clamouring about it, I don't believe it is true at all."

And I left him pondering. The men in my gig lying at the foot of *Diana's* side-ladder, told me that the captain of the tug had gone away in his boat some time ago.

I let my fellows pull an easy stroke; because of the heavy dew the clear sparkle of the stars seemed to fall on me cold and wetting. There was a sense of lurking gruesome horror somewhere in my mind, and it was mingled with clear and grotesque images. Schomberg's gastronomic tittle-tattle was responsible for these; and I half hoped I should never see Falk again. But the first thing my anchor-watchman told me was that the captain of the tug was on board. He had sent his boat away and was now waiting for me in the cuddy.

He was lying full length on the stern settee, his face buried in the cushions. I had expected to see it discomposed, contorted, despairing. It was nothing of the kind; it was just as I had seen it twenty times, steady and glaring from the bridge of the tug. It was immovably set and hungry, dominated like the whole man by the singleness of one instinct.

He wanted to live. He had always wanted to live. So we all do—but in us the instinct serves a complex conception, and in him this instinct existed alone. There is in such simple development a gigantic force, and like the pathos of a child's naïve and uncontrolled desire. He wanted that girl, and the utmost that can be said for him was that he wanted that particular girl alone. I think I saw then the obscure beginning, the seed germinating in the soil of an unconscious need, the first shoot of that tree bearing now for a mature mankind the flower and the fruit, the infinite gradation in shades and in flavour of our discriminating love. He was a child. He was as frank as a child, too. He was hungry for the girl, terribly hungry, as he had been terribly hungry for food.

Don't be shocked if I declare that in my belief it was the same need, the same pain, the same torture. We are in his case allowed to contemplate the foundation of all the emotions—that one joy which is to live, and the one sadness at the root of the innumerable torments. It was made plain by the way he talked. He had never suffered so. It was gnawing, it was fire; it was there, like this! And after pointing below his breastbone, he made a hard wringing motion with his hands. And I assure you that, seen as I saw it with my bodily eyes, it was anything but laughable. And again, as he was presently to tell me (alluding to an early incident of the disastrous voyage when some damaged meat had been flung overboard), he said that a time soon came when his heart ached (that was the expression he used), and he was ready to tear his hair out at the thought of all that rotten beef thrown away.

I heard all this; I witnessed his physical struggles, seeing the working of the rack and hearing the true voice of pain. I witnessed it all patiently, because the moment I came into the cuddy he had called upon me to stand by him—and this, it seems, I had diplomatically promised.

His agitation was impressive and alarming in the

little cabin, like the floundering of a great whale driven into a shallow cove in a coast. He stood up; he flung himself down headlong; he tried to tear the cushion with his teeth; and again hugging it fiercely to his face he let himself fall on the couch. The whole ship seemed to feel the shock of his despair; and I contemplated with wonder the lofty forehead, the noble touch of time on the uncovered temples, the unchanged hungry character of the face—so strangely ascetic and so incapable of portraying emotion.

What should he do? He had lived by being near her. He had sat—in the evening—I knew?—all his life! She sewed. Her head was bent—so. Her head—like this—and her arms. Ah! Had I seen? Like this.

He dropped on a stool, bowed his powerful neck whose nape was red, and with his hands stitched the air, ludicrous, sublimely imbecile and comprehensible.

And now he couldn't have her? No! That was too much. After thinking, too, that . . . What had he done? What was my advice? Take her by force? No? Mustn't he? Who was there to stop him? For the first time I saw one of his features move; a fighting teeth-baring curl of the lip. . . . "Not Hermann, perhaps." He lost himself in thought as though he had fallen out of the world.

I may note that the idea of suicide apparently did not enter his head for a single moment. It occurred to me to ask:

"Where was it that this shipwreck of yours took place?"

"Down south," he said, vaguely, with a start.

"You are not down south now," I said. "Violence won't do. They would take her away from you in no time. And what was the name of the ship?"

"*Borgmester Dahl*," he said. "It was no shipwreck."

He seemed to be waking up by degrees from that trance, and waking up calmed.

"Not a shipwreck? What was it?"

"Break-down," he answered, looking more like himself every moment. By this only I learned that it was a steamer. I had till then supposed they had been starving in boats or on a raft—or perhaps on a barren rock.

"She did not sink then?" I asked in surprise. He nodded. "We sighted the southern ice," he pronounced, dreamily.

"And you alone survived?"

He sat down. "Yes. It was a terrible misfortune for me. Everything went wrong. All the men went wrong. I survived."

Remembering the things one reads of it was difficult to realize the true meaning of his answers. I ought to have seen at once—but I did not; so difficult is it for our minds, remembering so much, instructed so much, informed of so much, to get in touch with the real actuality at our elbow. And with my head full of preconceived notions as to how a case of "Cannibalism and suffering at sea" should be managed I said—"You were then so lucky in the drawing of lots?"

"Drawing of lots?" he said. "What lots? Do you think I would have allowed my life to go for the drawing of lots?"

Not if he could help it, I perceived, no matter what other life went.

"It was a great misfortune. Terrible. Awful," he said. "Many heads went wrong, but the best men would live."

"The toughest, you mean," I said. He considered the word. Perhaps it was strange to him, though his English was so good.

"Yes," he asserted at last. "The best. It was everybody for himself at last and the ship open to all."

Thus from question to question I got the whole story. I fancy it was the only way I could that night have stood by him. Outwardly at least he was himself again; the first sign of it was the return of that incongruous trick he had of drawing both his hands down his face—and it had its meaning now, with that slight shudder of the frame and the passionate anguish of these hands uncovering a hungry immovable face, the wide pupils of the intent, silent, fascinating eyes.

It was an iron steamer of a most respectable origin. The burgomaster of Falk's native town had built her. She was the first steamer ever launched there. The burgomaster's daughter had christened her. Country people drove in carts from miles around to see her. He told me all this. He got the berth as, what we would call, chief mate. He seemed to think it had been a feather in his cap; and, in his own corner of the world, this lover of life was of good parentage.

The burgomaster had advanced ideas in the ship-owning line. At that time not everyone would have known enough to think of despatching a cargo steamer to the Pacific. But he loaded her with pitch-pine deals and sent her off to hunt for her luck. Wellington was to be the first port, I fancy. It doesn't matter, because in latitude 44° south and somewhere halfway between Good Hope and New Zealand the tail-shaft broke and the propeller dropped off.

They were steaming then with a fresh gale on the quarter and all their canvas set, to help the engines. But by itself the sail power was not enough to keep way on her. When the propeller went the ship broached-to at once, and the masts got whipped overboard.

The disadvantage of being dismasted consisted in

this, that they had nothing to hoist flags on to make
themselves visible at a distance. In the course of the
first few days several ships failed to sight them; and
the gale was drifting them out of the usual track. The
voyage had been, from the first, neither very successful
nor very harmonious. There had been quarrels on
board. The captain was a clever, melancholic man,
who had no unusual grip on his crew. The ship had
been amply provisioned for the passage, but, somehow
or other, several barrels of meat were found spoiled on
opening, and had been thrown overboard soon after
leaving home, as a sanitary measure. Afterwards
the crew of the *Borgmester Dahl* thought of that
rotten carrion with tears of regret, covetousness and
despair.

She drove south. To begin with, there had been an
appearance of organization, but soon the bonds of
discipline became relaxed. A sombre idleness succeeded. They looked with sullen eyes at the horizon.
The gales increased, she lay in the trough and the seas
made a clean breach over her. One frightful night,
when they expected their hulk to turn over with them
every moment, a heavy sea broke on board, deluged the
store-rooms and spoiled the best part of the remaining
provisions. It seems the hatch had not been properly
secured. This instance of neglect is characteristic of
utter discouragement. Falk tried to inspire some
energy into his captain, but failed. From that time he
retired more into himself, always trying to do his utmost
in the situation. It grew worse. Gale succeeded gale,
with black mountains of water hurling themselves on
the *Borgmester Dahl*. Some of the men never left their
bunks; many became quarrelsome. The chief-engineer,
an old man, refused to speak at all to anybody. Others
shut themselves up in their berths to cry. On calm days

the inert steamer rolled on a leaden sea under a murky
sky, or showed, in sunshine, the squalor of sea waifs, the
dried white salt, the rust, the jagged broken places.
Then the gales came again. They kept body and soul
together on short rations. Once, an English ship, scud-
ding in a storm, tried to stand by them, heaving-to
pluckily under their lee. The seas swept her decks; the
men in oilskins clinging to her rigging looked at them,
and they made desperate signs over their shattered
bulwarks. Suddenly her main-topsail went, yard and
all, in a terrific squall; she had to bear up under bare
poles and disappeared.

Other ships had spoken them before, but at first they
had refused to be taken off, expecting the assistance of
some steamer. There were very few steamers in those
latitudes then; and when they desired to leave this dead
and drifting carcase, no ship came in sight. They had
drifted south out of men's knowledge. They failed to
attract the attention of a lonely whaler: and very soon
the edge of the polar ice-cap rose from the sea and
closed the southern horizon like a wall. One morning
they were alarmed by finding themselves floating
amongst detached pieces of ice. But the fear of sinking
passed away like their vigour, like their hopes; the
shocks of the floes knocking against the ship's side could
not rouse them from their apathy: and the *Borgmester
Dahl* drifted out again, unharmed, into open water.
They hardly noticed the change.

The funnel had gone overboard in one of the heavy
rolls; two of their three boats had disappeared, washed
away in bad weather, and the davits swung to and fro,
unsecured, with chafed ropes' ends waggling to the roll.
Nothing was done on board, and Falk told me how he
had often listened to the water washing about the dark
engine-room where the engines, stilled for ever, were

decaying slowly into a mass of rust, as the stilled heart decays within the lifeless body. At first, after the loss of the motive power, the tiller had been thoroughly secured by lashings. But in course of time these had rotted, chafed, rusted, parting one by one; and the rudder, freed, banged heavily to and fro night and day, sending dull shocks through the whole frame of the vessel. This was dangerous. Nobody cared enough to lift a little finger. He told me that even now sometimes waking up at night, he fancied he could hear the dull vibrating thuds. The pintles carried away, and it dropped off at last.

The final catastrophe came with the sending off of their one remaining boat. It was Falk who had managed to preserve her intact, and now it was agreed that some of the hands should sail away into the track of the shipping to procure assistance. She was provisioned with all the food they could spare for the six who were to go. They waited for a fine day. It was long in coming. At last one morning they lowered her into the water.

Directly, in that demoralized crowd, trouble broke out. Two men who had no business there had jumped into the boat under the pretence of unhooking the tackles, while some sort of squabble arose on the deck amongst these weak, tottering spectres of a ship's company. The captain, who had been for days living secluded and unapproachable in the chart-room, came to the rail. He ordered the two men to come up on board and threatened them with his revolver. They pretended to obey, but suddenly cutting the boat's painter, gave a shove against the ship's side and made ready to hoist the sail.

"Shoot, sir! Shoot them down!" cried Falk—"and I will jump overboard to regain the boat." But the captain, after taking aim with an irresolute arm, turned suddenly away.

A howl of rage arose. Falk dashed into his cabin for his own pistol. When he returned it was too late. Two more men had leaped into the water, but the fellows in the boat beat them off with the oars, hoisted the boat's lug and sailed away. They were never heard of again.

Consternation and despair possessed the remaining ship's company, till the apathy of utter hopelessness re-asserted its sway. That day a fireman committed suicide, running up on deck with his throat cut from ear to ear, to the horror of all hands. He was thrown overboard. The captain had locked himself in the chart-room, and Falk, knocking vainly for admittance, heard him reciting over and over again the names of his wife and children, not as if calling upon them or commending them to God, but in a mechanical voice like an exercise of memory. Next day the doors of the chart-room were swinging open to the roll of the ship, and the captain had disappeared. He must during the night have jumped into the sea. Falk locked both the doors and kept the keys.

The organized life of the ship had come to an end. The solidarity of the men had gone. They became indifferent to each other. It was Falk who took in hand the distribution of such food as remained. Sometimes whispers of hate were heard passing between the languid skeletons that drifted endlessly to and fro, north and south, east and west, upon that carcase of a ship.

And in this lies the grotesque horror of this sombre story. The last extremity of sailors, overtaking a small boat or a frail craft, seems easier to bear, because of the direct danger of the seas. The confined space, the close contact, the imminent menace of the waves, seem to draw men together, in spite of madness, suffering and despair. But there was a ship—safe, convenient, roomy: a ship with beds, bedding, knives, forks, comfortable cabins, glass and china, and a complete cook's galley, pervaded, ruled and possessed by the pitiless spectre of starvation. The lamp oil had been drunk, the wicks cut up for food, the candles eaten. At night she floated dark in all her recesses and full of fears. One day Falk came upon a man gnawing a splinter of pine wood. Suddenly he threw the piece of wood away, tottered to the rail, and fell over. Falk, too late to prevent the act, saw him claw the ship's side desperately before he went down. Next day another man did the same thing, after uttering horrible imprecations. But this one somehow managed to get hold of the broken rudder chains and hung on there, silently. Falk set about trying to save him, and all the time the man, holding with both hands, looked at him anxiously with his sunken eyes. Then, just as Falk was ready to put his hand on him, the man let go his hold and sank like a stone. Falk reflected on these sights. His heart revolted against the horror of death, and he said to himself that he would struggle for every precious minute of his life.

One afternoon—as the survivors lay about on the after-deck—the carpenter, a tall man with a black beard, spoke of the last sacrifice. There was nothing eatable left on board. Nobody said a word to this; but that company separated quickly, these listless feeble spectres slunk off one by one to hide in fear of each other. Falk and the carpenter remained on deck together. Falk liked the big carpenter. He had been the best man of the lot, helpful and ready as long as there was anything to do, the longest hopeful, and had preserved to the last some vigour and decision of mind.

They did not speak to each other. Henceforth no voices were to be heard conversing sadly on board that ship. After a time the carpenter tottered away forward; but later in the day Falk going to drink at the fresh-water pump, had the inspiration to turn his head. The carpenter had stolen upon him from behind, and, summoning all his strength, was aiming with a crowbar a blow at the back of his skull.

Dodging just in time, Falk made his escape and ran into his cabin. While he was loading his revolver there, he heard the sound of heavy blows struck upon the bridge. The locks of the chart-room doors were slight, they flew open, and the carpenter, possessing himself of the captain's revolver, fired a shot of defiance.

Falk was about to go on deck and have it out at once, when he remarked that one of the ports of his cabin commanded the approaches to the fresh-water pump. Instead of going out he stayed within and secured the door. "The best man shall survive," he said to himself —and the other, he reasoned, must at some time or other come there to drink. These starving men would drink often to cheat the pangs of their hunger. But the carpenter, too, must have noticed the position of the port. They were the two best men in the ship, and the game was with them. All the rest of the day Falk saw no one and heard no sound. At night he strained his eyes. It was dark—he heard a rustling noise once, but he was certain that no one could have come near the pump. It was to the left of his deck port, and he could not have failed to see a man, for the night was clear and starry. He saw nothing; towards morning another faint noise made him suspicious. Deliberately and quietly he unlocked his door. He had not slept, and had not given way to the horror of the situation. He wanted to live.

But during the night the carpenter, without even trying to approach the pump, had managed to creep quietly along the starboard bulwark, and, unseen, had crouched down right under Falk's deck port. When daylight came he rose up suddenly, looked in, and putting his arm through the round, brass-framed opening, fired at Falk within a foot. He missed—and Falk, instead of attempting to seize the arm holding the weapon, opened his door unexpectedly, and with the muzzle of his revolver nearly touching the other's side, shot him dead.

The best man had survived. Both of them had at the beginning just strength enough to stand on their feet, and both had displayed pitiless resolution, endurance, cunning and courage—all the qualities of classic heroism. At once Falk threw overboard the captain's revolver. He was a born monopolist. Then after the report of the two shots, followed by a profound silence, there crept out into the cold, cruel dawn of Antarctic regions, from various hiding-places, over the deck of that dismantled corpse of a ship floating on a gray sea ruled by iron necessity and with a heart of ice—there crept into view one by one, cautious, slow, eager, glaring, and unclean, a band of hungry and livid skeletons. Falk faced them, the possessor of the only fire-arm on board; and the second best man—the carpenter—was lying dead between him and them.

"He was eaten, of course," I said.

Falk bent his head slowly, shuddered a little, drawing his hands over his face, and said, "I had never any quarrel with that man. But there were our lives between him and me."

Why continue the story of that ship, that story before which—with its fresh-water pump like a spring of death, its man with the weapon, the sea ruled by iron

necessity, its spectral band swayed by terror and hope,
its mute and unhearing heaven—the fable of the *Flying
Dutchman** with its convention of crime and its sentimental retribution fades like a graceful wreath, like a
wisp of white mist. What is there to say that everyone of us cannot guess for himself? I believe Falk began by going through the ship, revolver in hand, to an-
nex all the matches. Those starving wretches had
plenty of matches! He had no mind to have the ship set
on fire under his feet, either from hate or from despair.
He lived in the open, camping on the bridge, commanding all the after-deck and the only approach to the
pump. He lived! Some of the others lived, too—concealed, anxious, coming out one by one from their
hiding-places at the seductive sound of a shot. And he
was not selfish. They shared all alike. But only
three of them all remained alive when a whaler, returning from her cruising-ground, nearly ran over the water-
logged hull of the *Borgmester Dahl*, which, it seems,
in the end had in some way sprung a leak in both
her holds, but being loaded with deals could not
sink.

"They all died," Falk said. "These three, too, afterwards. But I would not die. All died, all! under this
terrible misfortune. But was I, too, to throw away my
life? Could I? Tell me, captain? I was alone there,
quite alone, just like the others. Each man was alone,
Was I to give up my revolver? Who to? Or was I
to throw it into the sea? What would have been the
good? Only the best man would survive. It was a
great, terrible, and cruel misfortune."

He had survived! I saw him before me as though
preserved for a witness to the mighty truth of an unerring and eternal principle.* Great beads of perspiration stood on his forehead. And suddenly it struck the

table with a heavy blow, as he fell forward throwing his hands out.

"And this is worse," he cried. "This is a worse pain! This is more terrible."

He made my heart thump with the profound conviction of his cry. And after he had left me to go on board his ship I called up before my mental eye the image of the girl weeping silently, abundantly, patiently, and as if irresistibly. I thought of her tawny hair. I thought how, if unplaited, it would have covered her all round as low as the hips, like the hair of a siren. And she had bewitched him. Fancy a man who would guard his own life with the inflexibility of a pitiless and immovable fate, being brought to lament that once a crowbar had missed his skull! The sirens sing and lure to death, but this one had been weeping silently as if for the pity of his life. She was the tender and voiceless siren of this appalling navigator. He evidently wanted to live his whole conception of life. Nothing else would do. And she, too, was a servant of that life that, in the midst of death, cries aloud to our senses. She was eminently fitted to interpret for him its feminine side. And in her own way, and with her own profusion of sensuous charms she also seemed to illustrate the eternal truth of an unerring principle. I don't know though what sort of principle Hermann illustrated when he turned up early on board my ship with a most perplexed air. It struck me, however, that he, too, would do his best to survive. He seemed greatly calmed on the subject of Falk, but still very full of it.

"What is it you said I was last night? You know—" he asked after some preliminary talk. "Too—too—I don't know. A very funny word."

"Squeamish?" I suggested.

"Yes. What does it mean?"

"That you exaggerate things—to yourself. Without inquiry, and so on."

He seemed to turn it over in his mind. We went on talking. This Falk was the plague of his life. Upsetting everybody like this! Mrs. Hermann was unwell this morning. His niece was crying still. There was nobody to look after the children. He struck his umbrella on the deck. The girl would be like that for months. Fancy carrying all the way home, second class, a perfectly useless girl who is crying all the time. It was bad for Lena, too, he observed; but on what grounds I could not guess. Perhaps of the bad example. That child was already sorrowing and crying enough over the rag doll. Nicholas was really the least sentimental person of the family.

"Why does your niece weep?" I asked.

"From pity," cried Hermann.

It was impossible to make out women. Mrs. Hermann was the only one he pretended to understand. She was very, very upset and doubtful.

"Doubtful about what?" I asked.

He averted his eyes and did not answer this. It was impossible to make women out. For instance, his niece was weeping for Falk. Now he (Hermann) would like to wring his neck—but then . . . He supposed he had too tender a heart. "Frankly," he asked at last, "what do you think of what we heard last night, captain?"

"In all these tales," I observed, "there is always a good deal of exaggeration."

And not letting him recover from his surprise I assured him that I knew all the details. He begged me not to repeat them. His heart was too tender. They would make him feel unwell. Then, looking at his feet and speaking very slowly, he supposed that he need not

see much of them after they were married. For, indeed, he could not bear the sight of Falk. On the
other hand, it was ridiculous to take home a girl with her
head turned. A girl that weeps all the time and is of no
help to her aunt.

"Now you will be able to do with one cabin only on
your passage home," I said.

"Yes, I had thought of that," he said brightly, almost. Yes! Himself, his wife, four children—one
cabin might do. Whereas if his niece went . . .

"And what does Mrs. Hermann say to it?" I inquired.

Mrs. Hermann did not know whether a man of that
sort could make a girl happy—she had been greatly
deceived in Captain Falk. She had passed a very bad
night.

Those good people did not seem to be able to retain
an impression for a whole twelve hours. I assured him
on my own personal knowledge that Falk possessed in
himself all the qualities to make his niece's future pros-
perous. He said he was glad to hear this, and that he
would tell his wife. Then the object of the visit came
out. He wished me to help him to resume relations
with Falk. His niece, he said, had expressed the hope
I would do so in my kindness. He was evidently
anxious that I should, for though he seemed to have
forgotten nine-tenths of his last night's opinions and
the whole of his indignation, yet he evidently feared to
be sent to the right-about. "You told me he was very
much in love," he concluded, slyly, and leered in a sort
of bucolic way.

As soon as he had left my ship I called Falk on board
by signal—the tug still lying at the anchorage. He
took the news with calm gravity, as though he had all
along trusted the stars to fight for him in their courses.

I saw them once more together, and only once—on
the quarter-deck of the *Diana*. Hermann sat smoking
with a shirt-sleeved elbow hooked over the back of his
chair. Mrs. Hermann was sewing alone. As Falk
stepped over the gangway, Hermann's niece, with a
slight swish of the skirt and a friendly nod to me,
glided past my chair.

Those two met in sunshine abreast of the mainmast.
He held her hands and looked down at them, and she
looked up at him with her candid and unseeing glance.
It seemed to me they had come together as if attracted,
drawn and guided to each other by a mysterious influence. They were a complete couple. In her gray
frock, palpitating with life, generous of form, olympian
and simple, she was indeed the siren to fascinate that
dark navigator, this ruthless lover of the five senses.
From afar I seemed to feel the masculine strength with
which he grasped those hands she had extended to him
with a womanly swiftness. Lena, a little pale, nursing
her beloved lump of dirty rags, ran towards her big
friend; and then in the drowsy silence of the good old
ship Mrs. Hermann's voice rang out so changed that
it made me spin round in my chair to see what was the
matter.

"Lena, come here!" she screamed. And this good-
natured matron gave me a wavering glance, dark and
full of fearsome distrust. The child ran back, surprised, to her knee. But the two, standing before each
other in sunlight with clasped hands, had heard nothing,
had seen nothing and no one. Three feet away from
them, in the shade, a seaman sat on a spar, very busy
splicing a strop and dipping his fingers into a tar-pot,
as if utterly unaware of their existence.

When I returned in command of another vessel some
five years afterwards, Mr. and Mrs. Falk had left the

place. I shouldn't wonder if Schomberg's tongue had succeeded at last in scaring Falk away for good; and, indubitably, there was some vague tale still going about the town of a certain Falk, owner of a tug, who had won his wife at cards from the captain of an English ship.

AMY FOSTER*

AMY FOSTER

KENNEDY is a country doctor, and lives in Colebrook, on the shores of Eastbay. The high ground rising abruptly behind the red roofs of the little town crowds the quaint High Street against the wall whioh defends it from the sea. Beyond the sea-wall there curves for miles in a vast and regular sweep the barren beach of shingle, with the village of Brenzett*standing out darkly across the water, a spire in a clump of trees; and still further out the perpendicular column of a lighthouse, looking in the distance no bigger than a leadpencil, marks the vanishing-point of the land. The country at the back of Brenzett is low and flat; but the bay is fairly well sheltered from the seas, and occasionally a big ship, windbound or through stress of weather, makes use of the anchoring ground a mile and a half due north from you as you stand at the back door of the "Ship Inn" in Brenzett. A dilapidated windmill near by, lifting its shattered arms from a mound no loftier than a rubbish-heap, and a Martello tower squatting at the water's edge half a mile to the south of the Coastguard cottages, are familiar to the skippers of small craft. These are the official seamarks for the patch of trustworthy bottom represented on the Admiralty charts by an irregular oval of dots enclosing several figures six, with a tiny anchor engraved among them, and the legend "mud and shells" over all.

The brow of the upland overtops the square tower of the Colebrook Church. The slope is green and looped by a white road. Ascending along this road, you open a valley broad and shallow, a wide green trough of pastures and hedges merging inland into a vista of purple tints and flowing lines closing the view.

In this valley down to Brenzett and Colebrook and up to Darnford, the market town fourteen miles away, lies the practice of my friend Kennedy. He had begun life as surgeon in the Navy, and afterwards had been the companion of a famous traveller, in the days when there were continents with unexplored interiors. His papers on the fauna and flora made him known to scientific societies. And now he had come to a country practice—from choice. The penetrating power of his mind, acting like a corrosive fluid, had destroyed his ambition, I fancy. His intelligence is of a scientific order, of an investigating habit, and of that unappeasable curiosity which believes that there is a particle of a general truth in every mystery.

A good many years ago now, on my return from abroad, he invited me to stay with him. I came readily enough, and as he could not neglect his patients to keep me company, he took me on his rounds—thirty miles or so of an afternoon, sometimes. I waited for him on the roads; the horse reached after the leafy twigs, and, sitting high in the dogcart, I could hear Kennedy's laugh through the half-open door of some cottage. He had a big, hearty laugh that would have fitted a man twice his size, a brisk manner, a bronzed face, and a pair of gray, profoundly attentive eyes. He had the talent of making people talk to him freely, and an inexhaustible patience in listening to their tales.

One day, as we trotted out of a large village into a shady bit of road, I saw on our left hand a low, brick cottage, with diamond panes in the windows, a creeper on the end wall, a roof of shingle, and some roses climbing on the rickety trellis-work of the tiny porch. Kennedy pulled up to a walk. A woman, in full sunlight, was throwing a dripping blanket over a line stretched between two old apple-trees. And as the bobtailed, long-necked chestnut, trying to get his head, jerked the left hand, covered by a thick dogskin glove, the doctor raised his voice over the hedge: "How's your child, Amy?"

I had the time to see her dull face, red, not with a mantling blush, but as if her flat cheeks had been vigorously slapped, and to take in the squat figure, the scanty, dusty brown hair drawn into a tight knot at the back of the head. She looked quite young. With a distinct catch in her breath, her voice sounded low and timid.

"He's well, thank you."

We trotted again. "A young patient of yours," I said; and the doctor, flicking the chestnut absently, muttered, "Her husband used to be."

"She seems a dull creature," I remarked, listlessly.

"Precisely," said Kennedy. "She is very passive. It's enough to look at the red hands hanging at the end of those short arms, at those slow, prominent brown eyes, to know the inertness of her mind—an inertness that one would think made it everlastingly safe from all the surprises of imagination. And yet which of us is safe? At any rate, such as you see her, she had enough imagination to fall in love. She's the daughter of one Isaac Foster, who from a small farmer has sunk into a shepherd; the beginning of his misfortunes dating from his runaway marriage with the cook of his widowed father—a well-to-do, apoplectic grazier, who passionately struck his name off his will, and had been heard to utter threats against his life. But this old affair, scandalous enough to serve as a motive for a Greek tragedy, arose from the similarity of their characters. There are other tragedies, less scandalous and of a

subtler poignancy, arising from irreconcilable differences
and from that fear of the Incomprehensible that hangs
over all our heads—over all our heads. . . ."

The tired chestnut dropped into a walk; and the rim
of the sun, all red in a speckless sky, touched familiarly
the smooth top of a ploughed rise near the road as I had
seen it times innumerable touch the distant horizon of
the sea. The uniform brownness of the harrowed field
glowed with a rose tinge, as though the powdered clods
had sweated out in minute pearls of blood the toil of
uncounted ploughmen. From the edge of a copse a
waggon with two horses was rolling gently along the
ridge. Raised above our heads upon the sky-line, it
loomed up against the red sun, triumphantly big,
enormous, like a chariot of giants drawn by two slow-
stepping steeds of legendary proportions. And the
clumsy figure of the man plodding at the head of the
leading horse projected itself on the background of the
Infinite with a heroic uncouthness. The end of his
carter's whip quivered high up in the blue. Kennedy
discoursed.

"She's the eldest of a large family. At the age of
fifteen they put her out to service at the New Barns
Farm. I attended Mrs. Smith, the tenant's wife, and
saw that girl there for the first time. Mrs. Smith, a
genteel person with a sharp nose, made her put on a
black dress every afternoon. I don't know what
induced me to notice her at all. There are faces that
call your attention by a curious want of definiteness in
their whole aspect, as, walking in a mist, you peer
attentively at a vague shape which, after all, may be
nothing more curious or strange than a signpost. The
only peculiarity I perceived in her was a slight hesitation
in her utterance, a sort of preliminary stammer which
passes away with the first word. When sharply spoken

to, she was apt to lose her head at once; but her heart was of the kindest. She had never been heard to express a dislike for a single human being, and she was tender to every living creature. She was devoted to Mrs. Smith, to Mr. Smith, to their dogs, cats, canaries; and as to Mrs. Smith's gray parrot, its peculiarities exercised upon her a positive fascination. Nevertheless, when that outlandish bird, attacked by the cat, shrieked for help in human accents, she ran out into the yard stopping her ears,* and did not prevent the crime. For Mrs. Smith this was another evidence of her stupidity; on the other hand, her want of charm, in view of Smith's well-known frivolousness, was a great recommendation. Her short-sighted eyes would swim with pity for a poor mouse in a trap, and she had been seen once by some boys on her knees in the wet grass helping a toad in difficulties. If it's true, as some German fellow* has said, that without phosphorus there is no thought, it is still more true that there is no kindness of heart without a certain amount of imagination. She had some. She had even more than is necessary to understand suffering and to be moved by pity. She fell in love under circumstances that leave no room for doubt in the matter; for you need imagination to form a notion of beauty at all, and still more to discover your ideal in an unfamiliar shape.

"How this aptitude came to her, what it did feed upon, is an inscrutable mystery. She was born in the village, and had never been further away from it than Colebrook or perhaps Darnford. She lived for four years with the Smiths. New Barns is an isolated farmhouse a mile away from the road, and she was content to look day after day at the same fields, hollows, rises; at the trees and the hedgerows; at the faces of the four men about the farm, always the same—day after day,

month after month, year after year. She never showed
a desire for conversation, and, as it seemed to me, she
did not know how to smile. Sometimes of a fine
Sunday afternoon she would put on her best dress, a
pair of stout boots, a large gray hat trimmed with a
black feather (I've seen her in that finery), seize an
absurdly slender parasol, climb over two stiles, tramp
over three fields and along two hundred yards of road—
never further. There stood Foster's cottage. She
would help her mother to give their tea to the younger
children, wash up the crockery, kiss the little ones, and
go back to the farm. That was all. All the rest, all the
change, all the relaxation. She never seemed to wish
for anything more. And then she fell in love. She fell
in love silently, obstinately—perhaps helplessly. It
came slowly, but when it came it worked like a powerful
spell; it was love as the Ancients understood it: an irresistible and fateful impulse—a possession! Yes, it
was in her to become haunted and possessed by a face,
by a presence, fatally, as though she had been a pagan
worshipper of form under a joyous sky—and to be
awakened at last from that mysterious forgetfulness of
self, from that enchantment, from that transport, by a
fear resembling the unaccountable terror of a
brute. . . ."

With the sun hanging low on its western limit, the
expanse of the grass-lands framed in the counter-scarps
of the rising ground took on a gorgeous and sombre
aspect. A sense of penetrating sadness, like that
inspired by a grave strain of music, disengaged itself
from the silence of the fields. The men we met walked
past, slow, unsmiling, with downcast eyes, as if the
melancholy of an over-burdened earth had weighted
their feet, bowed their shoulders, borne down their
glances.

"Yes," said the doctor to my remark, "one would think the earth is under a curse, since of all her children these that cling to her the closest are uncouth in body and as leaden of gait as if their very hearts were loaded with chains. But here on this same road you might have seen amongst these heavy men a being lithe, supple and long-limbed, straight like a pine, with something striving upwards in his appearance as though the heart within him had been buoyant. Perhaps it was only the force of the contrast, but when he was passing one of these villagers here, the soles of his feet did not seem to me to touch the dust of the road. He vaulted over the stiles, paced these slopes with a long elastic stride that made him noticeable at a great distance, and had lustrous black eyes. He was so different from the mankind around that, with his freedom of movement, his soft—a little startled—glance, his olive complexion and graceful bearing, his humanity suggested to me the nature of a woodland creature. He came from there."

The doctor pointed with his whip, and from the summit of the descent seen over the rolling tops of the trees in a park by the side of the road, appeared the level sea far below us, like the floor of an immense edifice inlaid with bands of dark ripple, with still trails of glitter, ending in a belt of glassy water at the foot of the sky. The light blur of smoke, from an invisible steamer, faded on the great clearness of the horizon like the mist of a breath on a mirror; and, inshore, the white sails of a coaster, with the appearance of disentangling themselves slowly from under the branches, floated clear of the foliage of the trees.

"Shipwrecked in the bay?" I said.

"Yes; he was a castaway. A poor emigrant from Central Europe bound to America and washed ashore here in a storm. And for him, who knew nothing of the

earth, England was an undiscovered country. It was
some time before he learned its name; and for all I know
he might have expected to find wild beasts or wild men
here, when, crawling in the dark over the sea-wall, he
rolled down the other side into a dyke, where it was another miracle he didn't get drowned. But he struggled
instinctively like an animal under a net,* and this blind
struggle threw him out into a field. He must have
been, indeed, of a tougher fibre than he looked to withstand without expiring such buffetings, the violence of
his exertions, and so much fear. Later on, in his
broken English that resembled curiously the speech of
a young child, he told me himself that he put his trust
in God, believing he was no longer in this world. And
truly—he would add—how was he to know? He fought
his way against the rain and the gale on all fours, and
crawled at last among some sheep huddled close under
the lee of a hedge. They ran off in all directions,
bleating in the darkness, and he welcomed the first
familiar sound he heard on these shores. It must have
been two in the morning then. And this is all we know
of the manner of his landing, though he did not arrive
unattended by any means. Only his grisly company
did not begin to come ashore till much later in the
day. . . ."

The doctor gathered the reins, clicked his tongue;
we trotted down the hill. Then turning, almost
directly, a sharp corner into High Street, we rattled
over the stones and were home.

Late in the evening Kennedy, breaking a spell of
moodiness that had come over him, returned to the
story. Smoking his pipe, he paced the long room from
end to end. A reading-lamp concentrated all its light
upon the papers on his desk; and, sitting by the open
window, I saw, after the windless, scorching day, the

frigid splendour of a hazy sea lying motionless under the moon. Not a whisper, not a splash, not a stir of the shingle, not a footstep, not a sigh came up from the earth below—never a sign of life but the scent of climbing jasmine: and Kennedy's voice, speaking behind me, passed through the wide casement, to vanish outside in a chill and sumptuous stillness.

". . . . The relations of shipwrecks in the olden time tell us of much suffering. Often the castaways were only saved from drowning to die miserably from starvation on a barren coast; others suffered violent death or else slavery, passing through years of precarious existence with people to whom their strangeness was an object of suspicion, dislike or fear. We read about these things, and they are very pitiful. It is indeed hard upon a man to find himself a lost stranger, helpless, incomprehensible, and of a mysterious origin, in some obscure corner of the earth. Yet amongst all the adventurers shipwrecked in all the wild parts of the world, there is not one, it seems to me, that ever had to suffer a fate so simply tragic as the man I am speaking of, the most innocent of adventurers cast out by the sea in the bight of this bay, almost within sight from this very window.

"He did not know the name of his ship. Indeed, in the course of time we discovered he did not even know that ships had names—'like Christian people'; and when, one day, from the top of Talfourd Hill, he beheld the sea lying open to his view, his eyes roamed afar, lost in an air of wild surprise, as though he had never seen such a sight before. And probably he had not. As far as I could make out, he had been hustled together with many others on board an emigrant ship at the mouth of the Elbe,* too bewildered to take note of his surroundings, too weary to see anything, too anxious

to care. They were driven below into the 'tween-deck
and battened down from the very start. It was a
low timber dwelling—he would say—with wooden
beams overhead, like the houses in his country, but you
went into it down a ladder. It was very large, very
cold, damp and sombre, with places in the manner of
wooden boxes where people had to sleep one above another, and it kept on rocking all ways at once all the
time. He crept into one of these boxes and lay down
there in the clothes in which he had left his home many
days before, keeping his bundle and his stick by his side.
People groaned, children cried, water dripped, the
lights went out, the walls of the place creaked, and
everything was being shaken so that in one's little box
one dared not lift one's head. He had lost touch with
his only companion (a young man from the same valley,
he said), and all the time a great noise of wind went on
outside and heavy blows fell—boom! boom! An awful
sickness overcame him, even to the point of making him
neglect his prayers. Besides, one could not tell
whether it was morning or evening. It seemed always
to be night in that place.

"Before that he had been travelling a long, long time
on the iron track. He looked out of the window, which
had a wonderfully clear glass in it, and the trees, the
houses, the fields, and the long roads seemed to fly round
and round about him till his head swam. He gave me
to understand that he had on his passage beheld uncounted multitudes of people—whole nations—all
dressed in such clothes as the rich wear. Once he was
made to get out of the carriage, and slept through a
night on a bench in a house of bricks with his bundle
under his head; and once for many hours he had to sit on
a floor of flat stones dozing, with his knees up and with
his bundle between his feet. There was a roof over

him, which seemed made of glass, and was so high that
the tallest mountain-pine he had ever seen would have
had room to grow under it. Steam-machines rolled in
at one end and out at the other. People swarmed more
than you can see on a feast-day round the miraculous
Holy Image in the yard of the Carmelite Convent down
in the plains where, before he left his home, he drove
his mother in a wooden cart:—a pious old woman who
wanted to offer prayers and make a vow for his safety.
He could not give me an idea of how large and lofty and
full of noise and smoke and gloom, and clang of iron, the
place was, but someone had told him it was called
Berlin. Then they rang a bell, and another steam-
machine came in, and again he was taken on and on
through a land that wearied his eyes by its flatness
without a single bit of a hill to be seen anywhere. One
more night he spent shut up in a building like a good
stable with a litter of straw on the floor, guarding his
bundle amongst a lot of men, of whom not one could
understand a single word he said. In the morning they
were all led down to the stony shores of an extremely
broad muddy river, flowing not between hills but between houses that seemed immense. There was a
steam-machine that went on the water, and they all
stood upon it packed tight, only now there were with
them many women and children who made much noise.
A cold rain fell, the wind blew in his face; he was wet
through, and his teeth chattered. He and the young
man from the same valley took each other by the hand.

"They thought they were being taken to America
straight away, but suddenly the steam-machine bumped
against the side of a thing like a great house on the
water. The walls were smooth and black, and there
uprose, growing from the roof as it were, bare trees in
the shape of crosses, extremely high. That's how it

appeared to him then, for he had never seen a ship before. This was the ship that was going to swim all the way to America. Voices shouted, everything swayed; there was a ladder dipping up and down. He went up on his hands and knees in mortal fear of falling into the water below, which made a great splashing. He got separated from his companion, and when he descended into the bottom of that ship his heart seemed to melt suddenly within him.

"It was then also, as he told me, that he lost contact for good and all with one of those three men who the summer before had been going about through all the little town in the foothills of his country. They would arrive on market-days driving in a peasant's cart, and would set up an office in an inn or some other Jew's house. There were three of them, of whom one with a long beard looked venerable; and they had red cloth collars round their necks and gold lace on their sleeves like Government officials. They sat proudly behind a long table; and in the next room, so that the common people shouldn't hear, they kept a cunning telegraph machine, through which they could talk to the Emperor of America. The fathers hung about the door, but the young men of the mountains would crowd up to the table asking many questions, for there was work to be got all the year round at three dollars a day in America, and no military service to do.

"But the American Kaiser would not take everybody. Oh, no! He himself had a great difficulty in getting accepted, and the venerable man in uniform had to go out of the room several times to work the telegraph on his behalf. The American Kaiser engaged him at last at three dollars, he being young and strong. However, many able young men backed out, afraid of the great distance; besides, those only who had some money could be taken. There were some who sold their huts and their land because it cost a lot of money to get to America; but then, once there, you had three dollars a day, and if you were clever you could find places where true gold could be picked up on the ground. His father's house was getting over full. Two of his brothers were married and had children. He promised to send money home from America by post twice a year. His father sold an old cow, a pair of piebald mountain ponies of his own raising, and a cleared plot of fair pasture land on the sunny slope of a pine-clad pass to a Jew inn-keeper, in order to pay the people of the ship that took men to America to get rich in a short time.

"He must have been a real adventurer at heart, for how many of the greatest enterprises in the conquest of the earth had for their beginning just such a bargaining away of the paternal cow for the mirage of true gold far away! I have been telling you more or less in my own words what I learned fragmentarily in the course of two or three years, during which I seldom missed an opportunity of a friendly chat with him. He told me this story of his adventure with many flashes of white teeth and lively glances of black eyes, at first in a sort of anxious baby-talk, then, as he acquired the language, with great fluency, but always with that singing, soft, and at the same time vibrating intonation that instilled a strangely penetrating power into the sound of the most familiar English words, as if they had been the words of an unearthly language. And he always would come to an end, with many emphatic shakes of his head, upon that awful sensation of his heart melting within him directly he set foot on board that ship. Afterwards there seemed to come for him a period of blank ignorance, at any rate as to facts. No

doubt he must have been abominably seasick and
abominably unhappy—this soft and passionate adventurer, taken thus out of his knowledge, and feeling
bitterly as he lay in his emigrant bunk his utter loneliness; for his was a highly sensitive nature. The next
thing we know of him for certain is that he had been
hiding in Hammond's pig-pound by the side of the road
to Norton, six miles, as the crow flies, from the sea. Of
these experiences he was unwilling to speak: they
seemed to have seared into his soul a sombre sort of
wonder and indignation. Through the rumours of the
country-side, which lasted for a good many days after
his arrival, we know that the fishermen of West Colebrook had been disturbed and startled by heavy
knocks against the walls of weatherboard cottages, and
by a voice crying piercingly strange words in the night.
Several of them turned out even, but, no doubt, he had
fled in sudden alarm at their rough angry tones hailing
each other in the darkness. A sort of frenzy must have
helped him up the steep Norton hill. It was he, no
doubt, who early the following morning had been seen
lying (in a swoon, I should say) on the roadside grass by
the Brenzett carrier, who actually got down to have a
nearer look, but drew back, intimidated by the perfect
immobility, and by something queer in the aspect of
that tramp, sleeping so still under the showers. As the
day advanced, some children came dashing into school
at Norton in such a fright that the schoolmistress went
out and spoke indignantly to a 'horrid-looking man' on
the road. He edged away, hanging his head, for a few
steps, and then suddenly ran off with extraordinary
fleetness. The driver of Mr. Bradley's milk-cart made
no secret of it that he had lashed with his whip at a
hairy sort of gipsy fellow who, jumping up at a turn of
the road by the Vents, made a snatch at the pony's

bridle. And he caught him a good one, too, right over
the face, he said, that made him drop down in the mud a
jolly sight quicker than he had jumped up; but it was a
good half a mile before he could stop the pony. Maybe
that in his desperate endeavours to get help, and in his
need to get in touch with someone, the poor devil had
tried to stop the cart. Also three boys confessed
afterwards to throwing stones at a funny tramp,
knocking about all wet and muddy, and, it seemed, very
drunk, in the narrow deep lane by the limekilns. All
this was the talk of three villages for days; but we have
Mrs. Finn's (the wife of Smith's waggoner) unimpeach-
able testimony that she saw him get over the low wall
of Hammond's pig-pound and lurch straight at her,
babbling aloud in a voice that was enough to make one
die of fright. Having the baby with her in a perambulator, Mrs. Finn called out to him to go away, and as
he persisted in coming nearer, she hit him courageously
with her umbrella over the head, and, without once
looking back, ran like the wind with the perambulator
as far as the first house in the village. She stopped
then, out of breath, and spoke to old Lewis, hammering
there at a heap of stones; and the old chap, taking off his
immense black wire goggles, got up on his shaky legs to
look where she pointed. Together they followed with
their eyes the figure of the man running over a field;
they saw him fall down, pick himself up, and run on
again, staggering and waving his long arms above his
head, in the direction of the New Barns Farm. From
that moment he is plainly in the toils of his obscure and
touching destiny. There is no doubt after this of what
happened to him. All is certain now: Mrs. Smith's
intense terror; Amy Foster's stolid conviction held
against the other's nervous attack, that the man
'meant no harm'; Smith's exasperation (on his return

from Darnford Market) at finding the dog barking
himself into a fit, the back-door locked, his wife in
hysterics; and all for an unfortunate dirty tramp,
supposed to be even then lurking in his stackyard,
Was he? He would teach him to frighten women.

"Smith is notoriously hot-tempered, but the sight of
some nondescript and miry creature sitting cross-legged
amongst a lot of loose straw, and swinging itself to and
fro like a bear in a cage, made him pause. Then this
tramp stood up silently before him, one mass of mud
and filth from head to foot. Smith, alone amongst his
stacks with this apparition, in the stormy twilight
ringing with the infuriated barking of the dog, felt the
dread of an inexplicable strangeness. But when that
being, parting with his black hands the long matted
locks that hung before his face, as you part the two
halves of a curtain, looked out at him with glistening,
wild, black-and-white eyes, the weirdness of this silent
encounter fairly staggered him. He has admitted
since (for the story has been a legitimate subject of
conversation about here for years) that he made more
than one step backwards. Then a sudden burst of
rapid, senseless speech persuaded him at once that he
had to do with an escaped lunatic. In fact, that impression never wore off completely. Smith has not in
his heart given up his secret conviction of the man's
essential insanity to this very day.

"As the creature approached him, jabbering in a most
discomposing manner, Smith (unaware that he was
being addressed as 'gracious lord,' and adjured in God's
name to afford food and shelter) kept on speaking
firmly but gently to it, and retreating all the time into
the other yard. At last, watching his chance, by a
sudden charge he bundled him headlong into the wood-
lodge, and instantly shot the bolt. Thereupon he

wiped his brow, though the day was cold. He had done his duty to the community by shutting up a wandering and probably dangerous maniac. Smith isn't a hard man at all, but he had room in his brain only for that one idea of lunacy. He was not imaginative enough to ask himself whether the man might not be perishing with cold and hunger. Meantime, at first, the maniac made a great deal of noise in the lodge. Mrs. Smith was screaming upstairs, where she had locked herself in her bedroom; but Amy Foster sobbed piteously at the kitchen-door, wringing her hands and muttering, 'Don't! don't!' I daresay Smith had a rough time of it that evening with one noise and another, and this insane, disturbing voice crying obstinately through the door only added to his irritation. He couldn't possibly have connected this troublesome lunatic with the sinking of a ship in Eastbay, of which there had been a rumour in the Darnford market place. And I daresay the man inside had been very near to insanity on that night. Before his excitement collapsed and he became unconscious he was throwing himself violently about in the dark, rolling on some dirty sacks, and biting his fists with rage, cold, hunger, amazement, and despair.

"He was a mountaineer of the eastern range of the Carpathians, and the vessel sunk the night before in Eastbay was the Hamburg emigrant-ship *Herzogin Sophia-Dorothea*, of appalling memory.

"A few months later we could read in the papers the accounts of the bogus 'Emigration Agencies' among the Sclavonian peasantry in the more remote provinces of Austria. The object of these scoundrels was to get hold of the poor ignorant people's homesteads, and they were in league with the local usurers. They exported their victims through Hamburg mostly. As to the ship, I had watched her out of this very window, reaching

close-hauled under short canvas into the bay on a dark,
threatening afternoon. She came to an anchor, correctly by the chart, off the Brenzett Coastguard station.
I remember before the night fell looking out again at the
outlines of her spars and rigging that stood out dark
and pointed on a background of ragged, slaty clouds
like another and a slighter spire to the left of the Brenzett church-tower. In the evening the wind rose. At
midnight I could hear in my bed the terrific gusts and
the sounds of a driving deluge.

"About that time the Coastguardmen thought they
saw the lights of a steamer over the anchoring-ground.
In a moment they vanished; but it is clear that another
vessel of some sort had tried for shelter in the bay on
that awful, blind night, had rammed the German ship
amidships (a breach—as one of the divers told me afterwards—'that you could sail a Thames barge through'),
and then had gone out either scathless or damaged, who
shall say; but had gone out, unknown, unseen, and fatal,
to perish mysteriously at sea. Of her nothing ever came
to light, and yet the hue and cry that was raised all over
the world would have found her out if she had been in
existence anywhere on the face of the waters.

"A completeness without a clue, and a stealthy
silence as of a neatly executed crime, characterize this
murderous disaster, which, as you may remember, had
its gruesome celebrity. The wind would have prevented the loudest outcries from reaching the shore;
there had been evidently no time for signals of distress.
It was death without any sort of fuss. The Hamburg
ship, filling all at once, capsized as she sank, and at daylight there was not even the end of a spar to be seen
above water. She was missed, of course, and at first
the Coastguardmen surmised that she had either
dragged her anchor or parted her cable some time dur-

ing the night, and had been blown out to sea. Then, after the tide turned, the wreck must have shifted a little and released some of the bodies, because a child—a little fair-haired child in a red frock—came ashore abreast of the Martello tower. By the afternoon you could see along three miles of beach dark figures with bare legs dashing in and out of the tumbling foam, and rough-looking men, women with hard faces, children, mostly fair-haired, were being carried, stiff and dripping, on stretchers, on wattles, on ladders, in a long procession past the door of the "Ship Inn," to be laid out in a row under the north wall of the Brenzett Church.

"Officially, the body of the little girl in the red frock is the first thing that came ashore from that ship. But I have patients amongst the seafaring population of West Colebrook, and, unofficially, I am informed that very early that morning two brothers, who went down to look after their cobble hauled up on the beach, found, a good way from Brenzett, an ordinary ship's hencoop, lying high and dry on the shore, with eleven drowned ducks inside. Their families ate the birds, and the hencoop was split into firewood with a hatchet. It is possible that a man (supposing he happened to be on deck at the time of the accident) might have floated ashore on that hencoop. He might. I admit it is improbable, but there was the man—and for days, nay, for weeks—it didn't enter our heads that we had amongst us the only living soul that had escaped from that disaster. The man himself, even when he learned to speak intelligibly, could tell us very little. He remembered he had felt better (after the ship had anchored, I suppose), and that the darkness, the wind, and the rain took his breath away. This looks as if he had been on deck some time during that night. But we mustn't forget he had been taken out of his knowledge, that he had been sea-sick and battened down below for four days, that he had no general notion of a ship or of the sea, and therefore could have no definite idea of what was happening to him. The rain, the wind, the darkness he knew; he understood the bleating of the sheep, and he remembered the pain of his wretchedness and misery, his heartbroken astonishment that it was neither seen nor understood, his dismay at finding all the men angry and all the women fierce. He had approached them as a beggar, it is true, he said; but in his country, even if they gave nothing, they spoke gently to beggars. The children in his country were not taught to throw stones at those who asked for compassion. Smith's strategy overcame him completely. The wood-lodge presented the horrible aspect of a dungeon. What would be done to him next? . . . No wonder that Amy Foster appeared to his eyes with the aureole of an angel of light. The girl had not been able to sleep for thinking of the poor man, and in the morning, before the Smiths were up, she slipped out across the back yard. Holding the door of the wood-lodge ajar, she looked in and extended to him half a loaf of white bread— 'such bread as the rich eat in my country,' he used to say.

"At this he got up slowly from amongst all sorts of rubbish, stiff, hungry, trembling, miserable, and doubtful. 'Can you eat this?' she asked in her soft and timid voice. He must have taken her for a 'gracious lady.' He devoured ferociously, and tears were falling on the crust. Suddenly he dropped the bread, seized her wrist, and imprinted a kiss on her hand. She was not frightened. Through his forlorn condition she had observed that he was good-looking. She shut the door and walked back slowly to the kitchen. Much later on, she told Mrs. Smith, who shuddered at the bare idea of being touched by that creature.

"Through this act of impulsive pity he was brought back again within the pale of human relations with his new surroundings. He never forgot it—never.

"That very same morning old Mr. Swaffer (Smith's nearest neighbour) came over to give his advice, and ended by carrying him off. He stood, unsteady on his legs, meek, and caked over in half-dried mud, while the two men talked around him in an incomprehensible tongue. Mrs. Smith had refused to come downstairs till the madman was off the premises; Amy Foster, far from within the dark kitchen, watched through the open back-door; and he obeyed the signs that were made to him to the best of his ability. But Smith was full of mistrust. 'Mind, sir! It may be all his cunning,' he cried repeatedly in a tone of warning. When Mr. Swaffer started the mare, the deplorable being sitting humbly by his side, through weakness, nearly fell out over the back of the high two-wheeled cart. Swaffer took him straight home. And it is then that I come upon the scene.

"I was called in by the simple process of the old man beckoning to me with his forefinger over the gate of his house as I happened to be driving past. I got down, of course.

"'I've got something here,' he mumbled, leading the way to an outhouse at a little distance from his other farm-buildings.

"It was there that I saw him first, in a long, low room taken upon the space of that sort of coach-house. It was bare and whitewashed, with a small square aperture glazed with one cracked, dusty pane at its further end. He was lying on his back upon a straw pallet; they had given him a couple of horse-blankets, and he seemed to

have spent the remainder of his strength in the exertion
of cleaning himself. He was almost speechless; his
quick breathing under the blankets pulled up to his
chin, his glittering, restless black eyes reminded me of a
wild bird caught in a snare. While I was examining
him, old Swaffer stood silently by the door, passing the
tips of his fingers along his shaven upper lip. I gave
some directions, promised to send a bottle of medicine,
and naturally made some inquiries.

"'Smith caught him in the stackyard at New Barns,'
said the old chap in his deliberate, unmoved manner,
and as if the other had been indeed a sort of wild animal.
'That's how I came by him. Quite a curiosity, isn't
he? Now tell me, doctor—you've been all over the
world—don't you think that's a bit of a Hindoo we've
got hold of here?'

"I was greatly surprised. His long black hair
scattered over the straw bolster contrasted with the
olive pallor of his face. It occurred to me he might be
a Basque. It didn't necessarily follow that he should
understand Spanish; but I tried him with the few words
I know, and also with some French. The whispered
sounds I caught by bending my ear to his lips puzzled
me utterly. That afternoon the young ladies from the
Rectory (one of them read Goethe with a dictionary,
and the other had struggled with Dante for years),
coming to see Miss Swaffer, tried their German and
Italian on him from the doorway. They retreated, just
the least bit scared by the flood of passionate speech
which, turning on his pallet, he let out at them. They
admitted that the sound was pleasant, soft, musical—
but, in conjunction with his looks perhaps, it was startling—so excitable, so utterly unlike anything one had
ever heard. The village boys climbed up the bank to
have a peep through the little square aperture. Every-

body was wondering what Mr. Swaffer would do with him.

"He simply kept him.

"Swaffer would be called eccentric were he not so much respected. They will tell you that Mr. Swaffer sits up as late as ten o'clock at night to read books, and they will tell you also that he can write a cheque for two hundred pounds without thinking twice about it. He himself would tell you that the Swaffers had owned land between this and Darnford for these three hundred years. He must be eighty-five to-day, but he does not look a bit older than when I first came here. He is a great breeder of sheep, and deals extensively in cattle. He attends market days for miles around in every sort of weather, and drives sitting bowed low over the reins, his lank gray hair curling over the collar of his warm coat, and with a green plaid rug round his legs. The calmness of advanced age gives a solemnity to his manner. He is clean-shaved; his lips are thin and sensitive; something rigid and monachal in the set of his features lends a certain elevation to the character of his face. He has been known to drive miles in the rain to see a new kind of rose in somebody's garden, or a monstrous cabbage grown by a cottager. He loves to hear tell of or to be shown something what he calls 'outlandish.' Perhaps it was just that outlandishness of the man which influenced old Swaffer. Perhaps it was only an inexplicable caprice. All I know is that at the end of three weeks I caught sight of Smith's lunatic digging in Swaffer's kitchen garden. They had found out he could use a spade. He dug barefooted.

"His black hair flowed over his shoulders. I suppose it was Swaffer who had given him the striped old cotton shirt; but he wore still the national brown cloth trousers (in which he had been washed ashore) fitting to the leg almost like tights; was belted with a broad leathern belt studded with little brass discs; and had never yet ventured into the village. The land he looked upon seemed to him kept neatly, like the grounds round a landowner's house; the size of the cart-horses struck him with astonishment; the roads resembled garden walks, and the aspect of the people, especially on Sundays, spoke of opulence. He wondered what made them so hardhearted and their children so bold. He got his food at the back-door, carried it in both hands, carefully, to his outhouse, and, sitting alone on his pallet, would make the sign of the cross before he began. Beside the same pallet, kneeling in the early darkness of the short days, he recited aloud the Lord's Prayer before he slept. Whenever he saw old Swaffer he would bow with veneration from the waist, and stand erect while the old man, with his fingers over his upper lip, surveyed him silently. He bowed also to Miss Swaffer, who kept house frugally for her father—a broad-shouldered, big-boned woman of forty-five, with the pocket of her dress full of keys, and a gray, steady eye. She was Church—as people said (while her father was one of the trustees of the Baptist Chapel)—and wore a little steel cross at her waist. She dressed severely in black, in memory of one of the innumerable Bradleys of the neighbourhood, to whom she had been engaged some twenty-five years ago—a young farmer who broke his neck out hunting on the eve of the wedding-day. She had the unmoved countenance of the deaf, spoke very seldom, and her lips, thin like her father's, astonished one sometimes by a mysteriously ironic curl.

"These were the people to whom he owed allegiance, and an overwhelming loneliness seemed to fall from the leaden sky of that winter without sunshine. All the

faces were sad. He could talk to no one, and had no
hope of ever understanding anybody. It was as if
these had been the faces of people from the other world
—dead people—he used to tell me years afterwards.
Upon my word, I wonder he did not go mad. He didn't
know where he was. Somewhere very far from his
mountains—somewhere over the water. Was this
America, he wondered?

"If it hadn't been for the steel cross at Miss Swaffer's
belt he would not, he confessed, have known whether
he was in a Christian country at all. He used to cast
stealthy glances at it, and feel comforted. There was
nothing here the same as in his country! The earth and
the water were different; there were no images of the
Redeemer by the roadside. The very grass was different, and the trees. All the trees but the three old
Norway pines on the bit of lawn before Swaffer's
house, and these reminded him of his country. He had
been detected once, after dusk, with his forehead against
the trunk of one of them, sobbing, and talking to himself. They had been like brothers to him at that time,
he affirmed. Everything else was strange. Conceive
you*the kind of an existence over-shadowed, oppressed,
by the everyday material appearances, as if by the
visions of a nightmare. At night, when he could not
sleep, he kept on thinking of the girl who gave him the
first piece of bread he had eaten in this foreign land.
She had been neither fierce nor angry, nor frightened.
Her face he remembered as the only comprehensible
face amongst all these faces that were as closed, as
mysterious, and as mute as the faces of the dead who are
possessed of a knowledge beyond the comprehension of
the living. I wonder whether the memory of her compassion prevented him from cutting his throat. But
there! I suppose I am an old sentimentalist, and forget

the instinctive love of life which it takes all the strength of the uncommon despair to overcome.

"He did the work which was given him with an intelligence which surprised old Swaffer. By-and-by it was discovered that he could help at the ploughing, could milk the cows, feed the bullocks in the cattle-yard, and was of some use with the sheep. He began to pick up words, too, very fast; and suddenly, one fine morning in spring, he rescued from an untimely death a grand-child of old Swaffer.

"Swaffer's younger daughter is married to Willcox, a solicitor and the Town Clerk of Colebrook. Regularly twice a year they come to stay with the old man for a few days. Their only child, a little girl not three years old at the time, ran out of the house alone in her little white pinafore, and, toddling across the grass of a terraced garden, pitched herself over a low wall head first into the horsepond in the yard below.

"Our man was out with the waggoner and the plough in the field nearest to the house, and as he was leading the team round to begin a fresh furrow, he saw, through the gap of a gate, what for anybody else would have been a mere flutter of something white. But he had straight-glancing, quick, far-reaching eyes, that only seemed to flinch and lose their amazing power before the immensity of the sea. He was barefooted, and looking as outlandish as the heart of Swaffer could desire. Leaving the horses on the turn, to the inexpressible disgust of the waggoner he bounded off, going over the ploughed ground in long leaps, and suddenly appeared before the mother, thrust the child into her arms, and strode away.

"The pond was not very deep; but still, if he had not had such good eyes, the child would have perished—miserably suffocated in the foot or so of sticky mud at

the bottom. Old Swaffer walked out slowly into the
field, waited till the plough came over to his side, had a
good look at him, and without saying a word went back
to the house. But from that time they laid out his
meals on the kitchen table; and at first, Miss Swaffer,
all in black and with an inscrutable face, would come
and stand in the doorway of the living-room to see him
make a big sign of the cross before he fell to. I believe
that from that day, too, Swaffer began to pay him
regular wages.

"I can't follow step by step his development. He
cut his hair short, was seen in the village and along the
road going to and fro to his work like any other man.
Children ceased to shout after him. He became aware
of social differences, but remained for a long time surprised at the bare poverty of the churches among so
much wealth. He couldn't understand either why they
were kept shut up on week-days. There was nothing
to steal in them. Was it to keep people from praying
too often? The rectory took much notice of him about
that time, and I believe the young ladies attempted to
prepare the ground for his conversion. They could not,
however, break him of his habit of crossing himself, but
he went so far as to take off the string with a couple of
brass medals the size of a sixpence, a tiny metal cross,
and a square sort of scapulary which he wore round his
neck. He hung them on the wall by the side of his bed,
and he was still to be heard every evening reciting the
Lord's Prayer, in incomprehensible words and in a slow,
fervent tone, as he had heard his old father do at the
head of all the kneeling family, big and little, on every
evening of his life. And though he wore corduroys at
work, and a slop-made pepper-and-salt suit on Sundays,
strangers would turn round to look after him on the
road. His foreignness had a peculiar and indelible

stamp. At last people became used to seeing him. But they never became used to him. His rapid, skimming walk; his swarthy complexion; his hat cocked on the left ear; his habit, on warm evenings, of wearing his coat over one shoulder, like a hussar's dolman; his manner of leaping over the stiles, not as a feat of agility, but in the ordinary course of progression—all these peculiarities were, as one may say, so many causes of scorn and offence to the inhabitants of the village. *They* wouldn't in their dinner hour lie flat on their backs on the grass to stare at the sky. Neither did they go about the fields screaming dismal tunes. Many times have I heard his high-pitched voice from behind the ridge of some sloping sheep-walk, a voice light and soaring, like a lark's, but with a melancholy human note, over our fields that hear only the song of birds. And I would be startled myself. Ah! He was different; innocent of heart, and full of good will, which nobody wanted, this castaway, that, like a man transplanted into another planet, was separated by an immense space from his past and by an immense ignorance from his future. His quick, fervent utterance positively shocked everybody. 'An excitable devil,' they called him. One evening, in the tap-room of the Coach and Horses, (having drunk some whisky), he upset them all by singing a love-song of his country. They hooted him down, and he was pained; but Preble, the lame wheelwright, and Vincent, the fat blacksmith, and the other notables, too, wanted to drink their evening beer in peace. On another occasion he tried to show them how to dance. The dust rose in clouds from the sanded floor; he leaped straight up amongst the deal tables, struck his heels together, squatted on one heel in front of old Preble, shooting out the other leg, uttered wild and exulting cries, jumped up to whirl on one foot, snapping his fingers above his head—and a strange carter who was having a drink in there began to swear, and cleared out with his half-pint in his hand into the bar. But when suddenly he sprang upon a table and continued to dance among the glasses, the landlord interfered. He didn't want any 'acrobat tricks in the tap-room.' They laid their hands on him. Having had a glass or two, Mr. Swaffer's foreigner tried to expostulate: was ejected forcibly: got a black eye.

"I believe he felt the hostility of his human surroundings. But he was tough—tough in spirit, too, as well as in body. Only the memory of the sea frightened him, with that vague terror that is left by a bad dream. His home was far away; and he did not want now to go to America. I had often explained to him that there is no place on earth where true gold can be found lying ready and to be got for the trouble of the picking up. How, then, he asked, could he ever return home with empty hands when there had been sold a cow, two ponies, and a bit of land to pay for his going? His eyes would fill with tears, and, averting them from the immense shimmer of the sea, he would throw himself face down on the grass. But sometimes, cocking his hat with a little conquering air, he would defy my wisdom. He had found his bit of true gold. That was Amy Foster's heart; which was 'a golden heart, and soft to people's misery,' he would say in the accents of overwhelming conviction.

"He was called Yanko. He had explained that this meant Little John; but as he would also repeat very often that he was a mountaineer (some word sounding in the dialect of his country like Goorall)*he got it for his surname. And this is the only trace of him that the succeeding ages may find in the marriage register of the parish. There it stands—Yanko Goorall—in the rector's handwriting. The crooked cross made by the castaway, a cross whose tracing no doubt seemed to him the most solemn part of the whole ceremony, is all that remains now to perpetuate the memory of his name.

"His courtship had lasted some time—ever since he got his precarious footing in the community. It began by his buying for Amy Foster a green satin ribbon in Darnford. This was what you did in his country. You bought a ribbon at a Jew's stall on a fair-day. I don't suppose the girl knew what to do with it, but he seemed to think that his honourable intentions could not be mistaken.

"It was only when he declared his purpose to get married that I fully understood how, for a hundred futile and inappreciable reasons, how—shall I say odious?—he was to all the countryside. Every old woman in the village was up in arms. Smith, coming upon him near the farm, promised to break his head for him if he found him about again. But he twisted his little black moustache with such a bellicose air and rolled such big, black fierce eyes at Smith that this promise came to nothing. Smith, however, told the girl that she must be mad to take up with a man who was surely wrong in his head. All the same, when she heard him in the gloaming whistle from beyond the orchard a couple of bars of a weird and mournful tune, she would drop whatever she had in her hand—she would leave Mrs. Smith in the middle of a sentence—and she would run out to his call. Mrs. Smith called her a shameless hussy. She answered nothing. She said nothing at all to anybody, and went on her way as if she had been deaf. She and I alone in all the land, I fancy, could see his very real beauty. He was very good-looking, and most graceful in his bearing, with that something wild as of a woodland creature in his aspect.

Her mother moaned over her dismally whenever the
girl came to see her on her day out. The father was
surly, but pretended not to know; and Mrs. Finn once
told her plainly that 'this man, my dear, will do you
some harm some day yet.' And so it went on. They
could be seen on the roads, she tramping stolidly in her
finery—gray dress, black feather, stout boots, prominent white cotton gloves that caught your eye a hundred yards away; and he, his coat slung picturesquely
over one shoulder, pacing by her side, gallant of bearing
and casting tender glances upon the girl with the
golden heart. I wonder whether he saw how plain she
was. Perhaps among types so different from what he
had ever seen, he had not the power to judge; or perhaps he was seduced by the divine quality of her pity.

"Yanko was in great trouble meantime. In his
country you get an old man for an ambassador in marriage affairs. He did not know how to proceed. However, one day in the midst of sheep in a field (he was
now Swaffer's under-shepherd with Foster) he took
off his hat to the father and declared himself humbly.
'I daresay she's fool enough to marry you,' was all
Foster said. 'And then,' he used to relate, 'he puts
his hat on his head, looks black at me as if he wanted
to cut my throat, whistles the dog, and off he goes,
leaving me to do the work.' The Fosters, of course,
didn't like to lose the wages the girl earned: Amy
used to give all her money to her mother. But there
was in Foster a very genuine aversion to that match.
He contended that the fellow was very good with sheep,
but was not fit for any girl to marry. For one thing,
he used to go along the hedges muttering to himself like
a dam' fool; and then, these foreigners behave very
queerly to women sometimes. And perhaps he would
want to carry her off somewhere—or run off himself.

It was not safe. He preached it to his daughter that the fellow might ill-use her in some way. She made no answer. It was, they said in the village, as if the man had done something to her. People discussed the matter. It was quite an excitement, and the two went on 'walking out' together in the face of opposition. Then something unexpected happened.

"I don't know whether old Swaffer ever understood how much he was regarded in the light of a father by his foreign retainer. Anyway the relation was curiously feudal. So when Yanko asked formally for an interview—'and the Miss, too' (he called the severe, deaf Miss Swaffer simply *Miss*)—it was to obtain their permission to marry. Swaffer heard him unmoved, dismissed him by a nod, and then shouted the intelligence into Miss Swaffer's best ear. She showed no surprise, and only remarked grimly, in a veiled blank voice, 'He certainly won't get any other girl to marry him.'

"It is Miss Swaffer who has all the credit of the munificence: but in a very few days it came out that Mr. Swaffer had presented Yanko with a cottage (the cottage you've seen this morning) and something like an acre of ground—had made it over to him in absolute property. Willcox expedited the deed, and I remember him telling me he had a great pleasure in making it ready. It recited: 'In consideration of saving the life of my beloved grandchild, Bertha Willcox.'

"Of course, after that no power on earth could prevent them from getting married.

"Her infatuation endured. People saw her going out to meet him in the evening. She stared with unblinking, fascinated eyes up the road where he was expected to appear, walking freely, with a swing from the hip, and humming one of the love-tunes of his country. When the boy was born, he got elevated at the 'Coach and Horses,' essayed again a song and a dance, and was again ejected. People expressed their commiseration for a woman married to that Jack-in-the-box. He didn't care. There was a man now (he told me boastfully) to whom he could sing and talk in the language of his country, and show how to dance by-and-by.

"But I don't know. To me he appeared to have grown less springy of step, heavier in body, less keen of eye. Imagination, no doubt; but it seems to me now as if the net of fate had been drawn closer round him already.

"One day I met him on the footpath over the Talfourd Hill. He told me that 'women were funny.' I had heard already of domestic differences. People were saying that Amy Foster was beginning to find out what sort of man she had married. He looked upon the sea with indifferent, unseeing eyes. His wife had snatched the child out of his arms one day as he sat on the doorstep crooning to it a song such as the mothers sing to babies in his mountains. She seemed to think he was doing it some harm. Women are funny. And she had objected to him praying aloud in the evening. Why? He expected the boy to repeat the prayer aloud after him by-and-by, as he used to do after his old father when he was a child—in his own country. And I discovered he longed for their boy to grow up so that he could have a man to talk with in that language that to our ears sounded so disturbing, so passionate, and so bizarre. Why his wife should dislike the idea he couldn't tell. But that would pass, he said. And tilting his head knowingly, he tapped his breastbone to indicate that she had a good heart: not hard, not fierce, open to compassion, charitable to the poor!

"I walked away thoughtfully; I wondered whether his difference, his strangeness, were not penetrating with repulsion that dull nature they had begun by irresistibly attracting. I wondered. . . ."

The Doctor came to the window and looked out at the frigid splendour of the sea, immense in the haze, as if enclosing all the earth with all the hearts lost among the passions of love and fear.

"Physiologically, now," he said, turning away abruptly, "it was possible. It was possible."

He remained silent. Then went on—

"At all events, the next time I saw him he was ill—lung trouble. He was tough, but I daresay he was not acclimatized as well as I had supposed. It was a bad winter; and, of course, these mountaineers do get fits of home sickness; and a state of depression would make him vulnerable. He was lying half dressed on a couch downstairs.

"A table covered with a dark oilcloth took up all the middle of the little room. There was a wicker cradle on the floor, a kettle spouting steam on the hob, and some child's linen lay drying on the fender. The room was warm, but the door opens right into the garden, as you noticed perhaps.

"He was very feverish, and kept on muttering to himself. She sat on a chair and looked at him fixedly across the table with her brown, blurred eyes. 'Why don't you have him upstairs?' I asked. With a start and a confused stammer she said, 'Oh! ah! I couldn't sit with him upstairs, sir.'

"I gave her certain directions; and going outside, I said again that he ought to be in bed upstairs. She wrung her hands. 'I couldn't. I couldn't. He keeps on saying something—I don't know what.' With the memory of all the talk against the man that had been dinned into her ears, I looked at her narrowly. I looked into her short-sighted eyes, at her dumb eyes that once in her life had seen an enticing shape, but seemed, staring at me, to see nothing at all now. But I saw she was uneasy.

"'What's the matter with him?' she asked in a sort of vacant trepidation. 'He doesn't look very ill. I never did see anybody look like this before. . . .'

"'Do you think,' I asked indignantly, 'he is shamming?'

"'I can't help it, sir,' she said, stolidly. And suddenly she clapped her hands and looked right and left. 'And there's the baby. I am so frightened. He wanted me just now to give him the baby. I can't understand what he says to it.'

"'Can't you ask a neighbour to come in to-night?' I asked.

"'Please, sir, nobody seems to care to come,' she muttered, dully resigned all at once.

"I impressed upon her the necessity of the greatest care, and then had to go. There was a good deal of sickness that winter. 'Oh, I hope he won't talk!' she exclaimed softly just as I was going away.

"I don't know how it is I did not see—but I didn't. And yet, turning in my trap, I saw her lingering before the door, very still, and as if meditating a flight up the miry road.

"Towards the night his fever increased.

"He tossed, moaned, and now and then muttered a complaint. And she sat with the table between her and the couch, watching every movement and every sound, with the terror, the unreasonable terror, of that man she could not understand creeping over her. She had drawn the wicker cradle close to her feet. There was nothing in her now but the maternal instinct and that unaccountable fear.

"Suddenly coming to himself, parched, he demanded

a drink of water. She did not move. She had not understood, though he may have thought he was speaking in English. He waited, looking at her, burning with fever, amazed at her silence and immobility, and then he shouted impatiently, 'Water! Give me water!'

"She jumped to her feet, snatched up the child, and stood still. He spoke to her, and his passionate remonstrances only increased her fear of that strange man. I believe he spoke to her for a long time, entreating, wondering, pleading, ordering, I suppose. She says she bore it as long as she could. And then a gust of rage came over him.

"He sat up and called out terribly one word—some word. Then he got up as though he hadn't been ill at all, she says. And as in fevered dismay, indignation, and wonder he tried to get to her round the table, she simply opened the door and ran out with the child in her arms. She heard him call twice after her down the road in a terrible voice—and fled. . . . Ah! but you should have seen stirring behind the dull, blurred glance of these eyes the spectre of the fear which had hunted her on that night three miles and a half to the door of Foster's cottage! I did the next day.

"And it was I who found him lying face down and his body in a puddle, just outside the little wicket-gate.

"I had been called out that night to an urgent case in the village, and on my way home at daybreak passed by the cottage. The door stood open. My man helped me to carry him in. We laid him on the couch. The lamp smoked, the fire was out, the chill of the stormy night oozed from the cheerless yellow paper on the wall. 'Amy!' I called aloud, and my voice seemed to lose itself in the emptiness of this tiny house as if I had cried in a desert. He opened his eyes. 'Gone!' he said, distinctly. 'I had only asked for water—only for a little water. . . .'

"He was muddy. I covered him up and stood waiting in silence, catching a painfully gasped word now and then. They were no longer in his own language. The fever had left him, taking with it the heat of life. And with his panting breast and lustrous eyes he reminded me again of a wild creature under the net; of a bird caught in a snare. She had left him. She had left him—sick—helpless—thirsty. The spear of the hunter had entered his very soul. 'Why?' he cried, in the penetrating and indignant voice of a man calling to a responsible Maker. A gust of wind and a swish of rain answered.

"And as I turned away to shut the door he pronounced the word 'Merciful!' and expired.

"Eventually I certified heart-failure as the immediate cause of death. His heart must have indeed failed him, or else he might have stood this night of storm and exposure, too. I closed his eyes and drove away. Not very far from the cottage I met Foster walking sturdily between the dripping hedges with his collie at his heels.

"'Do you know where your daughter is?' I asked.

"'Don't I!' he cried. 'I am going to talk to him a bit. Frightening a poor woman like this.'

"'He won't frighten her any more,' I said. 'He is dead.'

"He struck with his stick at the mud.

"'And there's the child.'

"Then, after thinking deeply for a while—

"'I don't know that it isn't for the best.'

"That's what he said. And she says nothing at all now. Not a word of him. Never. Is his image as utterly gone from her mind as his lithe and striding figure, his carolling voice are gone from our fields? He is no longer before her eyes to excite her imagination into a passion of love or fear; and his memory seems to have vanished from her dull brain as a shadow passes away upon a white screen. She lives in the cottage and works for Miss Swaffer. She is Amy Foster for everybody, and the child is 'Amy Foster's boy.' She calls him Johnny—which means Little John.

"It is impossible to say whether this name recalls anything to her. Does she ever think of the past? I have seen her hanging over the boy's cot in a very passion of maternal tenderness. The little fellow was lying on his back, a little frightened at me, but very still, with his big black eyes, with his fluttered air of a bird in a snare. And looking at him I seemed to see again the other one—the father, cast out mysteriously by the sea to perish in the supreme disaster of loneliness and despair."

THE SECRET SHARER*

AN EPISODE FROM THE COAST

THE SECRET SHARER

I

ON MY right hand there were lines of fishing-stakes resembling a mysterious system of half-submerged bamboo fences, incomprehensible in its division of the domain of tropical fishes, and crazy of aspect as if abandoned for ever by some nomad tribe of fishermen now gone to the other end of the ocean; for there was no sign of human habitation as far as the eye could reach. To the left a group of barren islets, suggesting ruins of stone walls,* towers, and blockhouses, had its foundations set in a blue sea that itself looked solid, so still and stable did it lie below my feet; even the track of light from the westering sun shone smoothly, without that animated glitter which tells of an imperceptible ripple. And when I turned my head to take a parting glance at the tug which had just left us anchored outside the bar, I saw the straight line of the flat shore joined to the stable sea, edge to edge, with a perfect and unmarked closeness, in one levelled floor half brown, half blue under the enormous dome of the sky. Corresponding in their insignificance to the islets of the sea, two small clumps of trees, one on each side of the only fault in the impeccable joint, marked the mouth of the river Meinam we had just left on the first preparatory stage of our homeward journey; and, far back on the inland level, a larger and loftier mass, the grove surrounding the great Paknam pagoda, was the only thing on which the eye could rest from the vain task of ex-

ploring the monotonous sweep of the horizon. Here
and there gleams as of a few scattered pieces of silver
marked the windings of the great river; and on the
nearest of them, just within the bar, the tug steaming
right into the land became lost to my sight, hull and
funnel and masts, as though the impassive earth had
swallowed her up without an effort, without a tremor.
My eye followed the light cloud of her smoke, now here,
now there, above the plain, according to the devious
curves of the stream, but always fainter and farther
away, till I lost it at last behind the mitre-shaped hill
of the great pagoda. And then I was left alone with
my ship, anchored at the head of the Gulf of Siam.

She floated at the starting-point of a long journey,
very still in an immense stillness, the shadows of her
spars flung far to the eastward by the setting sun. At
that moment I was alone on her decks. There was
not a sound in her—and around us nothing moved,
nothing lived, not a canoe on the water, not a bird in
the air, not a cloud in the sky. In this breathless
pause at the threshold of a long passage we seemed to
be measuring our fitness for a long and arduous enterprise, the appointed task of both our existences to be
carried out, far from all human eyes, with only sky and
sea for spectators and for judges.

There must have been some glare in the air to interfere with one's sight, because it was only just before the
sun left us that my roaming eyes made out beyond the
highest ridge of the principal islet of the group something which did away with the solemnity of perfect
solitude. The tide of darkness flowed on swiftly; and
with tropical suddenness a swarm of stars came out
above the shadowy earth, while I lingered yet, my hand
resting lightly on my ship's rail as if on the shoulder of
a trusted friend. But, with all that multitude of

celestial bodies staring down at one, the comfort of quiet communion with her was gone for good. And there were also disturbing sounds by this time—voices, footsteps forward; the steward flitted along the main-deck, a busily ministering spirit; a hand-bell tinkled urgently under the poop-deck. . . .

I found my two officers waiting for me near the supper table, in the lighted cuddy. We sat down at once, and as I helped the chief mate, I said:

"Are you aware that there is a ship anchored inside the islands? I saw her mastheads above the ridge as the sun went down."

He raised sharply his simple face, overcharged by a terrible growth of whisker, and emitted his usual ejaculations: "Bless my soul, sir! You don't say so!"

My second mate was a round-cheeked, silent young man, grave beyond his years, I thought; but as our eyes happened to meet I detected a slight quiver on his lips. I looked down at once. It was not my part to en-courage sneering on board my ship. It must be said, too, that I knew very little of my officers. In con-sequence of certain events of no particular significance, except to myself, I had been appointed to the command only a fortnight before. Neither did I know much of the hands forward. All these people had been together for eighteen months or so, and my position was that of the only stranger on board. I mention this because it has some bearing on what is to follow. But what I felt most was my being a stranger to the ship; and if all the truth must be told, I was somewhat of a stranger to myself. The youngest man on board (barring the second mate), and untried as yet by a position of the fullest responsibility, I was willing to take the adequacy of the others for granted. They had simply to be equal to their tasks; but I wondered how far I should turn out faithful to that ideal conception of one's own personality every man sets up for himself secretly.*

Meantime the chief mate, with an almost visible effect of collaboration on the part of his round eyes and frightful whiskers, was trying to evolve a theory of the anchored ship. His dominant trait was to take all things into earnest consideration. He was of a painstaking turn of mind. As he used to say, he "liked to account to himself" for practically everything that came in his way, down to a miserable scorpion he had found in his cabin a week before. The why and the wherefore of that scorpion—how it got on board and came to select his room rather than the pantry (which was a dark place and more what a scorpion would be partial to), and how on earth it managed to drown itself in the inkwell of his writing-desk—had exercised him infinitely. The ship within the islands was much more easily accounted for; and just as we were about to rise from table he made his pronouncement. She was, he doubted not, a ship from home lately arrived. Probably she drew too much water to cross the bar except at the top of spring tides. Therefore she went into that natural harbour to wait for a few days in preference to remaining in an open roadstead.

"That's so," confirmed the second mate, suddenly, in his slightly hoarse voice. "She draws over twenty feet. She's the Liverpool ship *Sephora**with a cargo of coal. Hundred and twenty-three days from Cardiff."

We looked at him in surprise.

"The tugboat skipper told me when he came on board for your letters, sir," explained the young man. "He expects to take her up the river the day after tomorrow."

After thus overwhelming us with the extent of his information he slipped out of the cabin. The mate observed regretfully that he "could not account for that young fellow's whims." What prevented him telling us all about it at once, he wanted to know.

I detained him as he was making a move. For the last two days the crew had had plenty of hard work, and the night before they had very little sleep. I felt painfully that I—a stranger—was doing something unusual when I directed him to let all hands turn in without setting an anchor-watch. I proposed to keep on deck myself till one o'clock or thereabouts. I would get the second mate to relieve me at that hour.

"He will turn out the cook and the steward at four," I concluded, "and then give you a call. Of course at the slightest sign of any sort of wind we'll have the hands up and make a start at once."

He concealed his astonishment. "Very well, sir." Outside the cuddy he put his head in the second mate's door to inform him of my unheard-of caprice to take a five hours' anchor-watch on myself. I heard the other raise his voice incredulously—"What? The Captain himself?" Then a few more murmurs, a door closed, then another. A few moments later I went on deck.

My strangeness, which had made me sleepless, had prompted that unconventional arrangement, as if I had expected in those solitary hours of the night to get on terms with the ship of which I knew nothing, manned by men of whom I knew very little more. Fast alongside a wharf, littered like any ship in port with a tangle of unrelated things, invaded by unrelated shore people, I had hardly seen her yet properly. Now, as she lay cleared for sea, the stretch of her main-deck seemed to me very fine under the stars. Very fine, very roomy

for her size, and very inviting. I descended the poop
and paced the waist, my mind picturing to myself the
coming passage through the Malay Archipelago, down
the Indian Ocean, and up the Atlantic. All its phases
were familiar enough to me, every characteristic, all the
alternatives which were likely to face me on the high
seas—everything! . . . except the novel responsibility of command. But I took heart from the reasonable thought that the ship was like other ships, the men
like other men, and that the sea was not likely to keep
any special surprises*expressly for my discomfiture.

Arrived at that comforting conclusion, I bethought
myself of a cigar and went below to get it. All was
still down there. Everybody at the after end of the
ship was sleeping profoundly. I came out again on
the quarter-deck, agreeably at ease in my sleeping-
suit on that warm breathless night, barefooted, a glow-
ing cigar in my teeth, and, going forward, I was met
by the profound silence of the fore end of the ship.
Only as I passed the door of the forecastle I heard a
deep, quiet, trustful sigh of some sleeper inside. And
suddenly I rejoiced in the great security of the sea as
compared with the unrest of the land, in my choice of
that untempted life presenting no disquieting problems,
invested with an elementary moral beauty by the absolute straightforwardness of its appeal and by the
singleness of its purpose.*

The riding-light in the fore-rigging burned with a
clear, untroubled, as if symbolic, flame, confident and
bright in the mysterious shades of the night. Passing
on my way aft along the other side of the ship, I observed that the rope side-ladder, put over, no doubt,
for the master of the tug when he came to fetch away
our letters, had not been hauled in as it should have
been. I became annoyed at this, for exactitude in

small matters is the very soul of discipline. Then I reflected that I had myself peremptorily dismissed my officers from duty, and by my own act had prevented the anchor-watch being formally set and things properly attended to. I asked myself whether it was wise ever to interfere with the established routine of duties even from the kindest of motives. My action might have made me appear eccentric. Goodness only knew how that absurdly whiskered mate would "account" for my conduct, and what the whole ship thought of that informality of their new captain. I was vexed with myself.

Not from compunction certainly, but, as it were mechanically, I proceeded to get the ladder in myself. Now a side-ladder of that sort is a light affair and comes in easily, yet my vigorous tug, which should have brought it flying on board, merely recoiled upon my body in a totally unexpected jerk. What the devil! . . . I was so astounded by the immovableness of that ladder that I remained stock-still, trying to account for it to myself like that imbecile mate of mine. In the end, of course, I put my head over the rail.

The side of the ship made an opaque belt of shadow on the darkling glassy shimmer of the sea. But I saw at once something elongated and pale floating very close to the ladder. Before I could form a guess a faint flash of phosphorescent light, which seemed to issue suddenly from the naked body of a man, flickered in the sleeping water with the elusive, silent play of summer lightning in a night sky. With a gasp I saw revealed to my stare a pair of feet, the long legs, a broad livid back immersed right up to the neck in a greenish cadaverous glow. One hand, awash, clutched the bottom rung of the ladder. He was complete but for the head. A headless corpse! The cigar dropped out of my gaping mouth with a tiny plop and a short hiss quite audible in the absolute stillness of all things under heaven. At that I suppose he raised up his face, a dimly pale oval in the shadow of the ship's side. But even then I could only barely make out down there the shape of his black-haired head. However, it was enough for the horrid, frost-bound sensation which had gripped me about the chest to pass off. The moment of vain exclamations was past, too. I only climbed on the spare spar and leaned over the rail as far as I could, to bring my eyes nearer to that mystery floating alongside.

As he hung by the ladder, like a resting swimmer, the sea-lightning played about his limbs at every stir; and he appeared in it ghastly, silvery, fish-like. He remained as mute as a fish, too. He made no motion to get out of the water, either. It was inconceivable that he should not attempt to come on board, and strangely troubling to suspect that perhaps he did not want to. And my first words were prompted by just that troubled incertitude.

"What's the matter?" I asked in my ordinary tone, speaking down to the face upturned exactly under mine.

"Cramp," it answered, no louder. Then slightly anxious, "I say, no need to call any one."

"I was not going to," I said.

"Are you alone on deck?"

"Yes."

I had somehow the impression that he was on the point of letting go the ladder to swim away beyond my ken—mysterious as he came. But, for the moment, this being appearing as if he had risen from the bottom of the sea (it was certainly the nearest land to the ship) wanted only to know the time. I told him. And he, down there, tentatively:

"I suppose your captain's turned in?"

"I am sure he isn't," I said.

He seemed to struggle with himself, for I heard something like the low, bitter murmur of doubt. "What's the good?" His next words came out with a hesitating effort.

"Look here, my man. Could you call him out quietly?"

I thought the time had come to declare myself.

"*I* am the captain."

I heard a "By Jove!" whispered at the level of the water. The phosphorescence flashed in the swirl of the water all about his limbs, his other hand seized the ladder.

"My name's Leggatt."*

The voice was calm and resolute. A good voice. The self-possession of that man had somehow induced a corresponding state in myself. It was very quietly that I remarked:

"You must be a good swimmer."

"Yes. I've been in the water practically since nine o'clock. The question for me now is whether I am to let go this ladder and go on swimming till I sink from exhaustion, or—to come on board here."

I felt this was no mere formula of desperate speech, but a real alternative in the view of a strong soul. I should have gathered from this that he was young; indeed, it is only the young who are ever confronted by such clear issues. But at the time it was pure intuition on my part. A mysterious communication was established already between us two—in the face of that silent, darkened tropical sea. I was young, too; young enough to make no comment. The man in the water began suddenly to climb up the ladder, and I hastened away from the rail to fetch some clothes.

Before entering the cabin I stood still, listening in
the lobby at the foot of the stairs. A faint snore came
through the closed door of the chief mate's room. The
second mate's door was on the hook, but the darkness
in there was absolutely soundless. He, too, was young
and could sleep like a stone. Remained the steward,
but he was not likely to wake up before he was called.
I got a sleeping-suit out of my room and, coming back
on deck, saw the naked man from the sea sitting on
the main-hatch, glimmering white in the darkness,
his elbows on his knees and his head in his hands.
In a moment he had concealed his damp body in a
sleeping-suit of the same grey-stripe pattern as the one
I was wearing and followed me like my double on
the poop. Together we moved right aft, barefooted,
silent.

"What is it?" I asked in a deadened voice, taking
the lighted lamp out of the binnacle, and raising it to
his face.

"An ugly business."

He had rather regular features; a good mouth; light
eyes under somewhat heavy, dark eyebrows; a smooth,
square forehead; no growth on his cheeks; a small,
brown moustache, and a well-shaped, round chin.
His expression was concentrated, meditative, under
the inspecting light of the lamp I held up to his face;
such as a man thinking hard in solitude might wear.
My sleeping-suit was just right for his size. A well-
knit young fellow of twenty-five at most. He caught
his lower lip with the edge of white, even teeth.

"Yes," I said, replacing the lamp in the binnacle.
The warm, heavy tropical night closed upon his head
again.

"There's a ship over there," he murmured.

"Yes, I know. The *Sephora*. Did you know of us?"

"Hadn't the slightest idea. I am the mate of her——" He paused and corrected himself. "I should say I *was*."

"Aha! Something wrong?"

"Yes. Very wrong indeed. I've killed a man."

"What do you mean? Just now?"

"No, on the passage. Weeks ago. Thirty-nine south. When I say a man——"

"Fit of temper," I suggested, confidently.

The shadowy, dark head, like mine, seemed to nod imperceptibly above the ghostly grey of my sleeping-suit. It was, in the night, as though I had been faced by my own reflection in the depths of a sombre and immense mirror.

"A pretty thing to have to own up to for a *Conway* boy,"*murmured my double, distinctly.

"You're a *Conway* boy?"

"I am," he said, as if startled. Then, slowly . . . "Perhaps you too——"

It was so; but being a couple of years older I had left before he joined. After a quick interchange of dates a silence fell; and I thought suddenly of my absurd mate with his terrific whiskers and the "Bless my soul—you don't say so" type of intellect. My double gave me an inkling of his thoughts by saying: "My father's a parson*in Norfolk. Do you see me before a judge and jury on that charge? For myself I can't see the necessity. There are fellows that an angel from heaven—— And I am not that. He was one of those creatures that are just simmering all the time with a silly sort of wickedness. Miserable devils that have no business to live at all. He wouldn't do his duty and wouldn't let anybody else do theirs. But what's the good of talking! You know well enough the sort of ill-conditioned snarling cur——"

He appealed to me as if our experiences had been as identical as our clothes. And I knew well enough the pestiferous danger of such a character where there are no means of legal repression. And I knew well enough also that my double there was no homicidal ruffian. I did not think of asking him for details, and he told me the story roughly in brusque, disconnected sentences. I needed no more. I saw it all going on as though I were myself inside that other sleeping-suit.

"It happened while we were setting a reefed foresail, at dusk. Reefed foresail! You understand the sort of weather. The only sail we had left to keep the ship running; so you may guess what it had been like for days. Anxious sort of job, that. He gave me some of his cursed insolence at the sheet. I tell you I was overdone with this terrific weather that seemed to have no end to it. Terrific, I tell you—and a deep ship. I believe the fellow himself was half crazed with funk. It was no time for gentlemanly reproof, so I turned round and felled him like an ox. He up and at me. We closed just as an awful sea made for the ship. All hands saw it coming and took to the rigging, but I had him by the throat, and went on shaking him like a rat, the men above us yelling, "Look out! look out!" Then a crash as if the sky had fallen on my head. They say that for over ten minutes hardly anything was to be seen of the ship—just the three masts and a bit of the forecastle head and of the poop all awash driving along in a smother of foam. It was a miracle that they found us, jammed together behind the forebitts. It's clear that I meant business, because I was holding him by the throat still when they picked us up. He was black in the face. It was too much for them. It seems they rushed us aft together, gripped as we were, screaming 'Murder!' like a lot

of lunatics, and broke into the cuddy. And the ship
running for her life, touch and go all the time, any
minute her last in a sea fit to turn your hair grey only
a-looking at it. I understand that the skipper, too,
started raving like the rest of them. The man had been
deprived of sleep for more than a week, and to have this
sprung on him at the height of a furious gale nearly
drove him out of his mind. I wonder they didn't fling
me overboard after getting the carcass of their precious
ship-mate out of my fingers. They had rather a job to
separate us, I've been told. A sufficiently fierce story
to make an old judge and a respectable jury sit up a bit.
The first thing I heard when I came to myself was the
maddening howling of that endless gale, and on that
the voice of the old man. He was hanging on to my
bunk, staring into my face out of his sou'wester.

"'Mr. Leggatt, you have killed a man. You can act
no longer as chief mate of this ship.'"

His care to subdue his voice made it sound monotonous. He rested a hand on the end of the skylight
to steady himself with, and all that time did not stir
a limb, so far as I could see. "Nice little tale for a
quiet tea-party," he concluded in the same tone.

One of my hands, too, rested on the end of the skylight; neither did I stir a limb, so far as I knew. We
stood less than a foot from each other. It occurred
to me that if old "Bless my soul—you don't say so"
were to put his head up the companion and catch sight
of us, he would think he was seeing double, or imagine
himself come upon a scene of weird witchcraft; the
strange captain having a quiet confabulation by the
wheel with his own grey ghost. I became very much
concerned to prevent anything of the sort. I heard
the other's soothing undertone.

"My father's a parson in Norfolk," it said. Evidently

he had forgotten he had told me this important fact before. Truly a nice little tale.

"You had better slip down into my stateroom now," I said, moving off stealthily. My double followed my movements; our bare feet made no sound; I let him in, closed the door with care, and, after giving a call to the second mate, returned on deck for my relief.

"Not much sign of any wind yet," I remarked when he approached.

"No, sir. Not much," he assented, sleepily, in his hoarse voice, with just enough deference, no more, and barely suppressing a yawn.

"Well, that's all you have to look out for. You have got your orders."

"Yes, sir."

I paced a turn or two on the poop and saw him take up his position face forward with his elbow in the ratlines of the mizzen-rigging before I went below. The mate's faint snoring was still going on peacefully. The cuddy lamp was burning over the table on which stood a vase with flowers, a polite attention from the ship's provision merchant—the last flowers we should see for the next three months at the very least. Two bunches of bananas hung from the beam symmetrically, one on each side of the rudder-casing. Everything was as before in the ship—except that two of her captain's sleeping-suits were simultaneously in use, one motionless in the cuddy, the other keeping very still in the captain's stateroom.

It must be explained here that my cabin had the form of the capital letter L, the door being within the angle and opening into the short part of the letter. A couch was to the left, the bed-place to the right; my writing-desk and the chronometers' table faced the door. But any one opening it, unless he stepped right inside,

had no view of what I call the long (or vertical) part of
the letter. It contained some lockers surmounted by
a bookcase; and a few clothes, a thick jacket or two,
caps, oilskin coat, and such like, hung on hooks. There
was at the bottom of that part a door opening into my
bath-room, which could be entered also directly from
the saloon. But that way was never used.

The mysterious arrival had discovered the advantage
of this particular shape. Entering my room, lighted
strongly by a big bulkhead lamp swung on gimbals
above my writing-desk, I did not see him anywhere
till he stepped out quietly from behind the coats hung
in the recessed part.

"I heard somebody moving about, and went in
there at once," he whispered.

I, too, spoke under my breath.

"Nobody is likely to come in here without knocking and getting permission."

He nodded. His face was thin and the sunburn
faded, as though he had been ill. And no wonder.
He had been, I heard presently, kept under arrest in
his cabin for nearly seven weeks. But there was nothing sickly in his eyes or in his expression. He was not
a bit like me, really; yet, as we stood leaning over my
bed-place, whispering side by side, with our dark heads
together and our backs to the door, anybody bold
enough to open it stealthily would have been treated to
the uncanny sight of a double captain busy talking in
whispers with his other self.

"But all this doesn't tell me how you came to hang
on to our side-ladder," I inquired, in the hardly audible
murmurs we used, after he had told me something more
of the proceedings on board the *Sephora* once the bad
weather was over.

"When we sighted Java Head I had had time to

think all those matters out several times over. I had six weeks of doing nothing else, and with only an hour or so every evening for a tramp on the quarter-deck."

He whispered, his arms folded on the side of my bed-place, staring through the open port. And I could imagine perfectly the manner of this thinking out—a stubborn if not a steadfast operation; something of which I should have been perfectly incapable.

"I reckoned it would be dark before we closed with the land," he continued, so low that I had to strain my hearing, near as we were to each other, shoulder touching shoulder almost. "So I asked to speak to the old man. He always seemed very sick when he came to see me—as if he could not look me in the face. You know, that foresail saved the ship. She was too deep to have run long under bare poles. And it was I that managed to set it for him. Anyway, he came. When I had him in my cabin—he stood by the door looking at me as if I had the halter round my neck already—I asked him right away to leave my cabin door unlocked at night while the ship was going through Sunda Straits. There would be the Java coast within two or three miles, off Angier Point. I wanted nothing more. I've had a prize for swimming my second year in the *Conway*."

"I can believe it," I breathed out.

"God only knows why they locked me in every night. To see some of their faces you'd have thought they were afraid I'd go about at night strangling people. Am I a murdering brute? Do I look it? By Jove! if I had been he wouldn't have trusted himself like that into my room. You'll say I might have chucked him aside and bolted out, there and then—it was dark already. Well, no. And for the same reason I wouldn't think of trying to smash the door. There would have been a rush to stop me at the noise, and I did not mean to get into a confounded scrimmage. Somebody else might have got killed—for I would not have broken out only to get chucked back, and I did not want any more of that work. He refused, looking more sick than ever. He was afraid of the men, and also of that old second mate of his who had been sailing with him for years—a grey-headed old humbug; and his steward, too, had been with him devil knows how long—seventeen years or more—a dogmatic sort of loafer who hated me like poison, just because I was the chief mate. No chief mate ever made more than one voyage in the *Sephora*, you know. Those two old chaps ran the ship. Devil only knows what the skipper wasn't afraid of (all his nerve went to pieces altogether in that hellish spell of bad weather we had)—of what the law would do to him—of his wife, perhaps. Oh, yes! she's on board.* Though I don't think she would have meddled. She would have been only too glad to have me out of the ship in any way. The 'brand of Cain' business,* don't you see. That's all right. I was ready enough to go off wandering on the face of the earth—and that was price enough to pay for an Abel of that sort. Anyhow, he wouldn't listen to me. 'This thing must take its course. I represent the law here.' He was shaking like a leaf. 'So you won't?' 'No!' 'Then I hope you will be able to sleep on that,' I said, and turned my back on him. 'I wonder that *you* can,' cries he, and locks the door.

"Well, after that, I couldn't. Not very well. That was three weeks ago. We have had a slow passage through the Java Sea; drifted about Carimata for ten days. When we anchored here they thought, I suppose, it was all right. The nearest land (and that's five miles) is the ship's destination; the consul would soon set about catching me; and there would have been

no object in bolting to these islets there. I don't
suppose there's a drop of water on them. I don't know
how it was, but to-night that steward, after bringing
me my supper, went out to let me eat it, and left the
door unlocked. And I ate it—all there was, too.
After I had finished I strolled out on the quarter-deck.
I don't know that I meant to do anything. A breath of
fresh air was all I wanted, I believe. Then a sudden
temptation came over me. I kicked off my slippers and
was in the water before I had made up my mind fairly.
Somebody heard the splash and they raised an awful
hullabaloo. 'He's gone! Lower the boats! He's committed suicide! No, he's swimming.' Certainly I was
swimming. It's not so easy for a swimmer like me to
commit suicide by drowning. I landed on the nearest
islet before the boat left the ship's side. I heard them
pulling about in the dark, hailing, and so on, but after a
bit they gave up. Everything quieted down and the
anchorage became as still as death. I sat down on a
stone and began to think. I felt certain they would
start searching for me at daylight. There was no place
to hide on those stony things—and if there had been,
what would have been the good? But now I was clear
of that ship, I was not going back. So after a while I
took off all my clothes, tied them up in a bundle with
a stone inside, and dropped them in the deep water on
the outer side of that islet. That was suicide enough
for me. Let them think what they liked, but I didn't
mean to drown myself. I meant to swim till I sank—
but that's not the same thing. I struck out for another
of these little islands, and it was from that one that I
first saw your riding-light. Something to swim for.
I went on easily, and on the way I came upon a flat
rock a foot or two above water. In the daytime, I
dare say, you might make it out with a glass from your

poop. I scrambled up on it and rested myself for a bit. Then I made another start. That last spell must have been over a mile."

His whisper was getting fainter and fainter, and all the time he stared straight out through the port-hole, in which there was not even a star to be seen. I had not interrupted him. There was something that made comment impossible in his narrative, or perhaps in himself; a sort of feeling, a quality, which I can't find a name for. And when he ceased, all I found was a futile whisper: "So you swam for our light?"

"Yes—straight for it. It was something to swim for. I couldn't see any stars low down because the coast was in the way, and I couldn't see the land, either. The water was like glass. One might have been swimming in a confounded thousand-feet deep cistern with no place for scrambling out anywhere; but what I didn't like was the notion of swimming round and round like a crazed bullock before I gave out; and as I didn't mean to go back . . . No. Do you see me being hauled back, stark naked, off one of these little islands by the scruff of the neck and fighting like a wild beast? Somebody would have got killed for certain, and I did not want any of that. So I went on. Then your ladder——"

"Why didn't you hail the ship?" I asked, a little louder.

He touched my shoulder lightly. Lazy footsteps came right over our heads and stopped. The second mate had crossed from the other side of the poop and might have been hanging over the rail, for all we knew.

"He couldn't hear us talking—could he?" My double breathed into my very ear, anxiously.

His anxiety was an answer, a sufficient answer, to the question I had put to him. An answer containing all the difficulty of that situation. I closed the port-hole quietly, to make sure. A louder word might have been overheard.

"Who's that?" he whispered then.

"My second mate. But I don't know much more of the fellow than you do."

And I told him a little about myself. I had been appointed to take charge while I least expected anything of the sort, not quite a fortnight ago. I didn't know either the ship or the people. Hadn't had the time in port to look about me or size anybody up. And as to the crew, all they knew was that I was appointed to take the ship home. For the rest, I was almost as much of a stranger on board as himself, I said. And at the moment I felt it most acutely. I felt that it would take very little to make me a suspect person in the eyes of the ship's company.

He had turned about meantime; and we, the two strangers in the ship, faced each other in identical attitudes.

"Your ladder——" he murmured, after a silence. "Who'd have thought of finding a ladder hanging over at night in a ship anchored out here! I felt just then a very unpleasant faintness. After the life I've been leading for nine weeks, anybody would have got out of condition. I wasn't capable of swimming round as far as your rudder-chains. And, lo and behold! there was a ladder to get hold of. After I gripped it I said to myself, 'What's the good?' When I saw a man's head looking over I thought I would swim away presently and leave him shouting—in whatever language it was. I didn't mind being looked at. I—I liked it. And then you speaking to me so quietly—as if you had expected me—made me hold on a little longer. It had been a confounded lonely time—I don't mean while swimming. I was glad to talk a little to somebody that didn't belong to the *Sephora*. As to asking for the captain, that was a mere impulse. It could have been no use, with all the ship knowing about me and the other people pretty certain to be round here in the morning. I don't know—I wanted to be seen, to talk with somebody, before I went on. I don't know what I would have said. . . . 'Fine night, isn't it?' or something of the sort."

"Do you think they will be round here presently?" I asked with some incredulity.

"Quite likely," he said, faintly.

He looked extremely haggard all of a sudden. His head rolled on his shoulders.

"H'm. We shall see then. Meantime get into that bed," I whispered. "Want help? There."

It was a rather high bed-place with a set of drawers underneath. This amazing swimmer really needed the lift I gave him by seizing his leg. He tumbled in, rolled over on his back, and flung one arm across his eyes. And then, with his face nearly hidden, he must have looked exactly as I used to look in that bed. I gazed upon my other self for a while before drawing across carefully the two green serge curtains which ran on a brass rod. I thought for a moment of pinning them together for greater safety, but I sat down on the couch, and once there I felt unwilling to rise and hunt for a pin. I would do it in a moment. I was extremely tired, in a peculiarly intimate way, by the strain of stealthiness, by the effort of whispering and the general secrecy of this excitement. It was three o'clock by now and I had been on my feet since nine, but I was not sleepy; I could not have gone to sleep. I sat there, fagged out, looking at the curtains, trying to clear my mind of the confused sensation of being in two places at once, and greatly bothered by an

exasperating knocking in my head. It was a relief to
discover suddenly that it was not in my head at all,
but on the outside of the door. Before I could collect
myself the words "Come in" were out of my mouth,
and the steward entered with a tray, bringing in my
morning coffee. I had slept, after all, and I was so
frightened that I shouted, "This way! I am here,
steward," as though he had been miles away. He put
down the tray on the table next the couch and only
then said, very quietly, "I can see you are here, sir."
I felt him give me a keen look, but I dared not meet
his eyes just then. He must have wondered why I had
drawn the curtains of my bed before going to sleep on the
couch. He went out, hooking the door open as usual.

I heard the crew washing decks above me. I knew
I would have been told at once if there had been any
wind. Calm, I thought, and I was doubly vexed.
Indeed, I felt dual more than ever. The steward
reappeared suddenly in the doorway. I jumped up
from the couch so quickly that he gave a start.

"What do you want here?"

"Close your port, sir—they are washing decks."

"It is closed," I said, reddening.

"Very well, sir." But he did not move from the
doorway and returned my stare in an extraordinary,
equivocal manner for a time. Then his eyes wavered,
all his expression changed, and in a voice unusually
gentle, almost coaxingly:

"May I come in to take the empty cup away, sir?"

"Of course!" I turned my back on him while he
popped in and out. Then I unhooked and closed the
door and even pushed the bolt. This sort of thing could
not go on very long. The cabin was as hot as an oven,
too. I took a peep at my double, and discovered that he
had not moved, his arm was still over his eyes; but his

chest heaved; his hair was wet; his chin glistened with perspiration. I reached over him and opened the port.

"I must show myself on deck," I reflected.

Of course, theoretically, I could do what I liked, with no one to say nay to me within the whole circle of the horizon; but to lock my cabin door and take the key away I did not dare. Directly I put my head out of the companion I saw the group of my two officers, the second mate barefooted, the chief mate in long india-rubber boots, near the break of the poop, and the steward half-way down the poop-ladder talking to them eagerly. He happened to catch sight of me and dived, the second ran down on the main-deck shouting some order or other, and the chief mate came to meet me, touching his cap.

There was a sort of curiosity in his eye that I did not like. I don't know whether the steward had told them that I was "queer" only, or downright drunk, but I know the man meant to have a good look at me. I watched him coming with a smile which, as he got into point-blank range, took effect and froze his very whiskers. I did not give him time to open his lips.

"Square the yards by lifts and braces before the hands go to breakfast."

It was the first particular order I had given on board that ship; and I stayed on deck to see it executed, too. I had felt the need of asserting myself without loss of time. That sneering young cub got taken down a peg or two on that occasion, and I also seized the opportunity of having a good look at the face of every foremast man as they filed past me to go to the after braces. At breakfast time, eating nothing myself, I presided with such frigid dignity that the two mates were only too glad to escape from the cabin as soon as decency permitted; and all the time the dual working of my mind distracted me almost to the point of insanity. I was constantly watching myself, my secret self, as dependent on my actions as my own personality, sleeping in that bed, behind that door which faced me as I sat at the head of the table. It was very much like being mad, only it was worse because one was aware of it.

I had to shake him for a solid minute, but when at last he opened his eyes it was in the full possession of his senses, with an inquiring look.

"All's well so far," I whispered. "Now you must vanish into the bath-room."

He did so, as noiseless as a ghost, and then I rang for the steward, and facing him boldly, directed him to tidy up my stateroom while I was having my bath—"and be quick about it." As my tone admitted of no excuses, he said, "Yes, sir," and ran off to fetch his dust-pan and brushes. I took a bath and did most of my dressing, splashing, and whistling softly for the steward's edification, while the secret sharer of my life stood drawn up bolt upright in that little space, his face looking very sunken in daylight, his eyelids lowered under the stern, dark line of his eyebrows drawn together by a slight frown.

When I left him there to go back to my room the steward was finishing dusting. I sent for the mate and engaged him in some insignificant conversation. It was, as it were, trifling with the terrific character of his whiskers; but my object was to give him an opportunity for a good look at my cabin. And then I could at last shut, with a clear conscience, the door of my stateroom and get my double back into the recessed part. There was nothing else for it. He had to sit still on a small folding stool, half smothered by the heavy coats hanging there. We listened to the

steward going into the bath-room out of the saloon,
filling the water-bottles there, scrubbing the bath,
setting things to rights, whisk, bang, clatter—out again
into the saloon—turn the key—click. Such was my
scheme for keeping my second self invisible. Nothing
better could be contrived under the circumstances.
And there we sat; I at my writing-desk ready to appear
busy with some papers, he behind me out of sight of the
door. It would not have been prudent to talk in daytime; and I could not have stood the excitement of that
queer sense of whispering to myself. Now and then,
glancing over my shoulder, I saw him far back there,
sitting rigidly on the low stool, his bare feet close together, his arms folded, his head hanging on his breast—
and perfectly still. Anybody would have taken him for
me.

I was fascinated by it myself. Every moment I
had to glance over my shoulder. I was looking at him
when a voice outside the door said:

"Beg pardon, sir."

"Well!" . . . I kept my eyes on him, and so
when the voice outside the door announced, "There's
a ship's boat coming our way, sir," I saw him give a
start—the first movement he had made for hours. But
he did not raise his bowed head.

"All right. Get the ladder over."

I hesitated. Should I whisper something to him?
But what? His immobility seemed to have been never
disturbed. What could I tell him he did not know
already? . . . Finally I went on deck.

II

THE skipper of the *Sephora* had a thin red whisker all
round his face, and the sort of complexion that goes

with hair of that colour; also the particular, rather smeary shade of blue in the eyes. He was not exactly a showy figure; his shoulders were high, his stature but middling—one leg slightly more bandy than the other. He shook hands, looking vaguely around. A spiritless tenacity was his main characteristic, I judged. I behaved with a politeness which seemed to disconcert him. Perhaps he was shy. He mumbled to me as if he were ashamed of what he was saying; gave his name (it was something like Archbold*—but at this distance of years I hardly am sure), his ship's name, and a few other particulars of that sort, in the manner of a criminal making a reluctant and doleful confession. He had had terrible weather on the passage out—terrible—terrible—wife aboard, too.

By this time we were seated in the cabin and the steward brought in a tray with a bottle and glasses. "Thanks! No." Never took liquor. Would have some water, though. He drank two tumblerfuls. Terrible thirsty work. Ever since daylight had been exploring the islands round his ship.

"What was that for—fun?" I asked, with an appearance of polite interest.

"No!" He sighed. "Painful duty."

As he persisted in his mumbling and I wanted my double to hear every word, I hit upon the notion of informing him that I regretted to say I was hard of hearing.

"Such a young man, too!" he nodded, keeping his smeary blue, unintelligent eyes fastened upon me. What was the cause of it—some disease? he inquired, without the least sympathy and as if he thought that, if so, I'd got no more than I deserved.

"Yes; disease," I admitted in a cheerful tone which seemed to shock him. But my point was gained, because he had to raise his voice to give me his tale. It is not worth while to record that version. It was just over two months since all this had happened, and he had thought so much about it that he seemed completely muddled as to its bearings, but still immensely impressed.

"What would you think of such a thing happening on board your own ship? I've had the *Sephora* for these fifteen years. I am a well-known shipmaster."

He was densely distressed—and perhaps I should have sympathised with him if I had been able to detach my mental vision from the unsuspected sharer of my cabin as though he were my second self. There he was on the other side of the bulkhead, four or five feet from us, no more, as we sat in the saloon. I looked politely at Captain Archbold (if that was his name), but it was the other I saw, in a grey sleeping-suit, seated on a low stool, his bare feet close together, his arms folded, and every word said between us falling into the ears of his dark head bowed on his chest.

"I have been at sea now, man and boy, for seven-and-thirty years, and I've never heard of such a thing happening in an English ship. And that it should be my ship. Wife on board, too."

I was hardly listening to him.

"Don't you think," I said, "that the heavy sea which, you told me, came aboard just then might have killed the man? I have seen the sheer weight of a sea kill a man very neatly, by simply breaking his neck."

"Good God!" he uttered, impressively, fixing his smeary blue eyes on me. "The sea! No man killed by the sea ever looked like that." He seemed positively scandalised at my suggestion. And as I gazed at him, certainly not prepared for anything original on his part, he advanced his head close to mine and thrust his tongue

out at me so suddenly that I couldn't help starting
back.

After scoring over my calmness in this graphic way
he nodded wisely. If I had seen the sight, he assured
me, I would never forget it as long as I lived. The
weather was too bad to give the corpse a proper sea
burial. So next day at dawn they took it up on the
poop, covering its face with a bit of bunting; he read
a short prayer, and then, just as it was, in its oilskins
and long boots, they launched it amongst those mountainous seas that seemed ready every moment to
swallow up the ship herself and the terrified lives on
board of her.

"That reefed foresail saved you," I threw in.

"Under God—it did," he exclaimed fervently. "It
was by a special mercy, I firmly believe, that it stood
some of those hurricane squalls."

"It was the setting of that sail which——" I began.

"God's own hand in it," he interrupted me. "Nothing less could have done it. I don't mind telling you that
I hardly dared give the order. It seemed impossible
that we could touch anything without losing it, and then
our last hope would have been gone."

The terror of that gale was on him yet. I let him
go on for a bit, then said, casually—as if returning to
a minor subject:

"You were very anxious to give up your mate to
the shore people, I believe?"

He was. To the law. His obscure tenacity on that
point had in it something incomprehensible and a little
awful; something, as it were, mystical, quite apart from
his anxiety that he should not be suspected of "counte-
nancing any doings of that sort." Seven-and-thirty
virtuous years at sea, of which over twenty of immaculate command, and the last fifteen in the *Sephora*,

seemed to have laid him under some pitiless obligation.

"And you know," he went on, groping shamefacedly
amongst his feelings, "I did not engage that young
fellow. His people had some interest with my owners.
I was in a way forced to take him on. He looked very
smart, very gentlemanly, and all that. But do you
know—I never liked him, somehow. I am a plain
man. You see, he wasn't exactly the sort for the
chief mate of a ship like the *Sephora*."

I had become so connected in thoughts and im-
pressions with the secret sharer of my cabin that I
felt as if I, personally, were being given to understand
that I, too, was not the sort that would have done
for the chief mate of a ship like the *Sephora*. I had no
doubt of it in my mind.

"Not at all the style of man. You understand,"
he insisted, superfluously, looking hard at me.

I smiled urbanely. He seemed at a loss for a while.

"I suppose I must report a suicide."

"Beg pardon?"

"Sui—cide! That's what I'll have to write to my
owners directly I get in."

"Unless you manage to recover him before to-morrow,"
I assented, dispassionately. . . . "I mean, alive."

He mumbled something which I really did not catch,
and I turned my ear to him in a puzzled manner. He
fairly bawled:

"The land—I say, the mainland is at least seven
miles off my anchorage."

"About that."

My lack of excitement, of curiosity, of surprise, of
any sort of pronounced interest, began to arouse his
distrust. But except for the felicitous pretence of
deafness I had not tried to pretend anything. I had

felt utterly incapable of playing the part of ignorance
properly, and therefore was afraid to try. It is also
certain that he had brought some ready-made suspicions
with him, and that he viewed my politeness as a strange
and unnatural phenomenon. And yet how else could I
have received him? Not heartily! That was impossible for psychological reasons, which I need not
state here. My only object was to keep off his inquiries. Surlily? Yes, but surliness might have pro-
voked a point-blank question. From its novelty to
him and from its nature, punctilious courtesy was the
manner best calculated to restrain the man. But there
was the danger of his breaking through my defence
bluntly. I could not, I think, have met him by a direct
lie, also for psychological (not moral) reasons.* If he
had only known how afraid I was of his putting my
feeling of identity with the other to the test! But,
strangely enough—(I thought of it only afterwards)—I
believe that he was not a little disconcerted by the re-
verse side of that weird situation, by something in me
that reminded him of the man he was seeking—suggested a mysterious similitude to the young fellow he
had distrusted and disliked from the first.

However that might have been, the silence was not
very prolonged. He took another oblique step.

"I reckon I had no more than a two-mile pull to your
ship. Not a bit more."

"And quite enough, too, in this awful heat," I said.

Another pause full of mistrust followed. Necessity,
they say, is mother of invention, but fear, too, is not
barren of ingenious suggestions. And I was afraid he
would ask me point-blank for news of my other self.

"Nice little saloon, isn't it?" I remarked, as if
noticing for the first time the way his eyes roamed from
one closed door to the other. "And very well fitted

out, too. Here, for instance," I continued, reaching over the back of my seat negligently and flinging the door open, "is my bath-room."

He made an eager movement, but hardly gave it a glance. I got up, shut the door of the bath-room, and invited him to have a look round, as if I were very proud of my accommodation. He had to rise and be shown round, but he went through the business without any raptures whatever.

"And now we'll have a look at my stateroom," I declared, in a voice as loud as I dared to make it, crossing the cabin to the starboard side with purposely heavy steps.

He followed me in and gazed around. My intelligent double had vanished. I played my part.

"Very convenient—isn't it?"

"Very nice. Very comf . . ." He didn't finish and went out brusquely as if to escape from some unrighteous wiles of mine. But it was not to be. I had been too frightened not to feel vengeful; I felt I had him on the run, and I meant to keep him on the run. My polite insistence must have had something menacing in it, because he gave in suddenly. And I did not let him off a single item; mate's room, pantry, storerooms, the very sail-locker which was also under the poop—he had to look into them all. When at last I showed him out on the quarter-deck he drew a long, spiritless sigh, and mumbled dismally that he must really be going back to his ship now. I desired my mate, who had joined us, to see to the captain's boat.

The man of whiskers gave a blast on the whistle which he used to wear hanging round his neck, and yelled, "*Sephora*'s away!" My double down there in my cabin must have heard, and certainly could not feel more relieved than I. Four fellows came running out

from somewhere forward and went over the side, while
my own men, appearing on deck too, lined the rail. I
escorted my visitor to the gangway ceremoniously,
and nearly overdid it. He was a tenacious beast. On
the very ladder he lingered, and in that unique, guiltily
conscientious manner of sticking to the point:

"I say . . . you . . . you don't think that——"

I covered his voice loudly:

"Certainly not. . . . I am delighted. Good-
bye."

I had an idea of what he meant to say, and just saved
myself by the privilege of defective hearing. He was
too shaken generally to insist, but my mate, close witness of that parting, looked mystified and his face took
on a thoughtful cast. As I did not want to appear as if
I wished to avoid all communication with my officers,
he had the opportunity to address me.

"Seems a very nice man. His boat's crew told our
chaps a very extraordinary story, if what I am told by
the steward is true. I suppose you had it from the
captain, sir?"

"Yes. I had a story from the captain."

"A very horrible affair—isn't it, sir?"

"It is."

"Beats all these tales we hear about murders in
Yankee ships."

"I don't think it beats them. I don't think it resembles them in the least."

"Bless my soul—you don't say so! But of course
I've no acquaintance whatever with American ships,
not I, so I couldn't go against your knowledge. It's
horrible enough for me. . . . But the queerest part
is that those fellows seemed to have some idea the man
was hidden aboard here. They had really. Did you
ever hear of such a thing?"

"Preposterous—isn't it?"

We were walking to and fro athwart the quarter-deck. No one of the crew forward could be seen (the day was Sunday), and the mate pursued:

"There was some little dispute about it. Our chaps took offence. 'As if we would harbour a thing like that,' they said. 'Wouldn't you like to look for him in our coal-hole?' Quite a tiff. But they made it up in the end. I suppose he did drown himself. Don't you, sir?"

"I don't suppose anything."

"You have no doubt in the matter, sir?"

"None whatever."

I left him suddenly. I felt I was producing a bad impression, but with my double down there it was most trying to be on deck. And it was almost as trying to be below. Altogether a nerve-trying situation. But on the whole I felt less torn in two when I was with him. There was no one in the whole ship whom I dared take into my confidence. Since the hands had got to know his story, it would have been impossible to pass him off for any one else, and an accidental discovery was to be dreaded now more than ever. . . .

The steward being engaged in laying the table for dinner, we could talk only with our eyes when I first went down. Later in the afternoon we had a cautious try at whispering. The Sunday quietness of the ship was against us; the stillness of air and water around her was against us; the elements, the men were against us—everything was against us in our secret partner-ship; time itself—for this could not go on forever. The very trust in Providence was, I suppose, denied to his guilt. Shall I confess that this thought cast me down very much? And as to the chapter of accidents which counts for so much in the book of success, I could only

hope that it was closed. For what favourable accident
could be expected?

"Did you hear everything?" were my first words as
soon as we took up our position side by side, leaning
over my bed-place.

He had. And the proof of it was his earnest whisper,
"The man told you he hardly dared to give the order."

I understood the reference to be to that saving foresail.

"Yes. He was afraid of it being lost in the setting."

"I assure you he never gave the order. He may
think he did, but he never gave it. He stood there
with me on the break of the poop after the maintopsail
blew away, and whimpered about our last hope—
positively whimpered about it and nothing else—and
the night coming on! To hear one's skipper go on like
that in such weather was enough to drive any fellow
out of his mind. It worked me up into a sort of desperation. I just took it into my own hands and went away
from him, boiling, and—— But what's the use telling
you? *You* know! . . . Do you think that if I had
not been pretty fierce with them I should have got the
men to do anything? Not it! The bosun perhaps?
Perhaps! It wasn't a heavy sea—it was a sea gone
mad! I suppose the end of the world will be something like that; and a man may have the heart to see it
coming once and be done with it—but to have to
face it day after day—— I don't blame anybody.
I was precious little better than the rest. Only—I was
an officer of that old coal-wagon, anyhow——"

"I quite understand," I conveyed that sincere
assurance into his ear. He was out of breath with
whispering; I could hear him pant slightly. It was all
very simple.* The same strung-up force which had
given twenty-four men a chance, at least, for their

lives, had, in a sort of recoil, crushed an unworthy mutinous existence.

But I had no leisure to weigh the merits of the matter—footsteps in the saloon, a heavy knock. "There's enough wind to get under way with, sir." Here was the call of a new claim upon my thoughts and even upon my feelings.

"Turn the hands up," I cried through the door. "I'll be on deck directly."

I was going out to make the acquaintance of my ship. Before I left the cabin our eyes met—the eyes of the only two strangers on board. I pointed to the recessed part where the little camp-stool awaited him and laid my finger on my lips. He made a gesture— somewhat vague—a little mysterious, accompanied by a faint smile, as if of regret.

This is not the place to enlarge upon the sensations of a man who feels for the first time a ship move under his feet to his own independent word. In my case they were not unalloyed. I was not wholly alone with my command; for there was that stranger in my cabin. Or rather, I was not completely and wholly with her. Part of me was absent. That mental feeling of being in two places at once affected me physically as if the mood of secrecy had penetrated my very soul. Before an hour had elapsed since the ship had begun to move, having occasion to ask the mate (he stood by my side) to take a compass bearing of the Pagoda, I caught myself reaching up to his ear in whispers. I say I caught myself, but enough had escaped to startle the man. I can't describe it otherwise than by saying that he shied. A grave, preoccupied manner, as though he were in possession of some perplexing intelligence, did not leave him henceforth. A little later I moved away from the rail to look at the compass with such a stealthy gait that the helmsman noticed it —and I could not help noticing the unusual roundness of his eyes. These are trifling instances, though it's to no commander's advantage to be suspected of ludicrous eccentricities. But I was also more seriously affected. There are to a seaman certain words, gestures, that should in given conditions come as naturally, as instinctively as the winking of a menaced eye. A certain order should spring on to his lips without thinking; a certain sign should get itself made, so to speak, without reflection. But all unconscious alertness had abandoned me. I had to make an effort of will to recall myself back (from the cabin) to the conditions of the moment. I felt that I was appearing an irresolute commander to those people who were watching me more or less critically.

And, besides, there were the scares. On the second day out, for instance, coming off the deck in the afternoon (I had straw slippers on my bare feet) I stopped at the open pantry door and spoke to the steward. He was doing something there with his back to me. At the sound of my voice he nearly jumped out of his skin, as the saying is, and incidentally broke a cup.

"What on earth's the matter with you?" I asked, astonished.

He was extremely confused. "Beg your pardon, sir. I made sure you were in your cabin."

"You see I wasn't."

"No, sir. I could have sworn I had heard you moving in there not a moment ago. It's most extraordinary . . . very sorry, sir."

I passed on with an inward shudder. I was so identified with my secret double that I did not even mention the fact in those scanty, fearful whispers we exchanged. I suppose he had made some slight noise

of some kind or other. It would have been miraculous
if he hadn't at one time or another. And yet, haggard
as he appeared, he looked always perfectly self-
controlled, more than calm—almost invulnerable. On
my suggestion he remained almost entirely in the bath-
room, which, upon the whole, was the safest place.
There could be really no shadow of an excuse for any one
ever wanting to go in there, once the steward had
done with it. It was a very tiny place. Sometimes
he reclined on the floor, his legs bent, his head sustained
on one elbow. At others I would find him on the camp-
stool, sitting in his grey sleeping-suit and with his
cropped dark hair like a patient, unmoved convict. At
night I would smuggle him into my bed-place, and we
would whisper together, with the regular footfalls of the
officer of the watch passing and repassing over our
heads. It was an infinitely miserable time. It was
lucky that some tins of fine preserves were stowed in
a locker in my stateroom; hard bread I could always
get hold of; and so he lived on stewed chicken, pâté de
foie gras, asparagus, cooked oysters, sardines—on all
sorts of abominable sham delicacies out of tins. My
early morning coffee he always drank; and it was all I
dared do for him in that respect.

Every day there was the horrible manœuvring to go
through so that my room and then the bath-room
should be done in the usual way. I came to hate the
sight of the steward, to abhor the voice of that harmless
man. I felt that it was he who would bring on the
disaster of discovery. It hung like a sword over our
heads.*

The fourth day out, I think (we were then working
down the east side of the Gulf of Siam, tack for tack,
in light winds and smooth water)—the fourth day, I
say, of this miserable juggling with the unavoidable, as

we sat at our evening meal, that man, whose slightest movement I dreaded, after putting down the dishes ran up on deck busily. This could not be dangerous. Presently he came down again; and then it appeared that he had remembered a coat of mine which I had thrown over a rail to dry after having been wetted in a shower which had passed over the ship in the afternoon. Sitting stolidly at the head of the table I became terrified at the sight of the garment on his arm. Of course he made for my door. There was no time to lose.

"Steward," I thundered. My nerves were so shaken that I could not govern my voice and conceal my agitation. This was the sort of thing that made my terrifically whiskered mate tap his forehead with his forefinger. I had detected him using that gesture while talking on deck with a confidential air to the carpenter. It was too far to hear a word, but I had no doubt that this pantomime could only refer to the strange new captain.

"Yes, sir," the pale-faced steward turned resignedly to me. It was this maddening course of being shouted at, checked without rhyme or reason, arbitrarily chased out of my cabin, suddenly called into it, sent flying out of his pantry on incomprehensible errands, that accounted for the growing wretchedness of his expression.

"Where are you going with that coat?"

"To your room, sir."

"Is there another shower coming?"

"I'm sure I don't know, sir. Shall I go up again and see, sir?"

"No! never mind."

My object was attained, as of course my other self in there would have heard everything that passed.

During this interlude my two officers never raised their
eyes off their respective plates; but the lip of that confounded cub, the second mate, quivered visibly.

I expected the steward to hook my coat on and come
out at once. He was very slow about it; but I dominated my nervousness sufficiently not to shout after him.
Suddenly I became aware (it could be heard plainly
enough) that the fellow for some reason or other was
opening the door of the bath-room. It was the end.
The place was literally not big enough to swing a cat in.
My voice died in my throat and I went stony all over.
I expected to hear a yell of surprise and terror, and
made a movement, but had not the strength to get on
my legs. Everything remained still. Had my second
self taken the poor wretch by the throat? I don't
know what I could have done next moment if I had not
seen the steward come out of my room, close the door,
and then stand quietly by the sideboard.

"Saved," I thought. "But, no! Lost! Gone! He
was gone!"

I laid my knife and fork down and leaned back in my
chair. My head swam. After a while, when sufficiently recovered to speak in a steady voice, I instructed
my mate to put the ship round at eight o'clock himself.

"I won't come on deck," I went on. "I think I'll
turn in, and unless the wind shifts I don't want to be
disturbed before midnight. I feel a bit seedy."

"You did look middling bad a little while ago," the
chief mate remarked without showing any great concern.

They both went out, and I stared at the steward
clearing the table. There was nothing to be read on
that wretched man's face. But why did he avoid my
eyes, I asked myself. Then I thought I should like to
hear the sound of his voice.

"Steward!"

"Sir!" Startled as usual.

"Where did you hang up that coat?"

"In the bath-room, sir." The usual anxious tone. "It's not quite dry yet, sir."

For some time longer I sat in the cuddy. Had my double vanished as he had come? But of his coming there was an explanation, whereas his disappearance would be inexplicable. . . . I went slowly into my dark room, shut the door, lighted the lamp, and for a time dared not turn round. When at last I did I saw him standing bolt-upright in the narrow recessed part. It would not be true to say I had a shock, but an irresistible doubt of his bodily existence flitted through my mind. Can it be, I asked myself, that he is not visible to other eyes than mine? It was like being haunted. Motionless, with a grave face, he raised his hands slightly at me in a gesture which meant clearly, "Heavens! what a narrow escape!" Narrow indeed. I think I had come creeping quietly as near insanity as any man who has not actually gone over the border. That gesture restrained me, so to speak.

The mate with the terrific whiskers was now putting the ship on the other tack. In the moment of profound silence which follows upon the hands going to their stations I heard on the poop his raised voice: "Hard alee!" and the distant shout of the order repeated on the maindeck. The sails, in that light breeze, made but a faint fluttering noise. It ceased. The ship was coming round slowly; I held my breath in the renewed stillness of expectation; one wouldn't have thought that there was a single living soul on her decks. A sudden brisk shout, "Mainsail haul!" broke the spell, and in the noisy cries and rush overhead of the men running away with the main-brace we two, down in my cabin, came together in our usual position by the bed-place.

He did not wait for my question. "I heard him fumbling here and just managed to squat myself down in the bath," he whispered to me. "The fellow only opened the door and put his arm in to hang the coat up. All the same——"

"I never thought of that," I whispered back, even more appalled than before at the closeness of the shave, and marvelling at that something unyielding in his character which was carrying him through so finely. There was no agitation in his whisper. Whoever was being driven distracted, it was not he. He was sane. And the proof of his sanity was continued when he took up the whispering again.

"It would never do for me to come to life again."

It was something that a ghost might have said. But what he was alluding to was his old captain's reluctant admission of the theory of suicide. It would obviously serve his turn—if I had understood at all the view which seemed to govern the unalterable purpose of his action.

"You must maroon me as soon as ever you can get amongst these islands off the Cambodje shore," he went on.

"Maroon you! We are not living in a boy's adventure tale," I protested. His scornful whispering took me up.

"We aren't indeed! There's nothing of a boy's tale in this. But there's nothing else for it. I want no more. You don't suppose I am afraid of what can be done to me? Prison or gallows or whatever they may please. But you don't see me coming back to explain such things to an old fellow in a wig and twelve respect-able tradesmen, do you? What can they know whether I am guilty or not—or of *what* I am guilty, either? That's my affair. What does the Bible say? 'Driven off the face of the earth.'* Very well. I am off the face of the earth now. As I came at night so I shall go."

"Impossible!" I murmured. "You can't."

"Can't? . . . Not naked like a soul on the Day of Judgment.* I shall freeze on to this sleeping-suit. The Last Day is not yet—and . . . you have understood thoroughly. Didn't you?"

I felt suddenly ashamed of myself. I may say truly that I understood—and my hesitation in letting that man swim away from my ship's side had been a mere sham sentiment, a sort of cowardice.

"It can't be done now till next night," I breathed out. "The ship is on the off-shore tack and the wind may fail us."

"As long as I know that you understand," he whispered. "But of course you do. It's a great satisfaction to have got somebody to understand. You seem to have been there on purpose." And in the same whisper, as if we two whenever we talked had to say things to each other which were not fit for the world to hear, he added, "It's very wonderful."

We remained side by side talking in our secret way —but sometimes silent or just exchanging a whispered word or two at long intervals. And as usual he stared through the port. A breath of wind came now and again into our faces. The ship might have been moored in dock, so gently and on an even keel she slipped through the water, that did not murmur even at our passage, shadowy and silent like a phantom sea.

At midnight I went on deck, and to my mate's great surprise put the ship round on the other tack. His terrible whiskers flitted round me in silent criticism. I certainly should not have done it if it had been only

a question of getting out of that sleepy gulf as quickly
as possible. I believe he told the second mate, who
relieved him, that it was a great want of judgment.
The other only yawned. That intolerable cub shuffled
about so sleepily and lolled against the rails in such
a slack, improper fashion that I came down on him
sharply.

"Aren't you properly awake yet?"

"Yes, sir! I am awake."

"Well, then, be good enough to hold yourself as
if you were. And keep a look-out. If there's any
current we'll be closing with some islands before daylight."

The east side of the gulf is fringed with islands, some
solitary, others in groups. On the blue background
of the high coast they seem to float on silvery patches
of calm water, arid and grey, or dark green and rounded
like clumps of evergreen bushes, with the larger ones,
a mile or two long, showing the outlines of ridges, ribs
of grey rock under the dank mantle of matted leafage.
Unknown to trade, to travel, almost to geography, the
manner of life they harbour is an unsolved secret.
There must be villages—settlements of fishermen at
least—on the largest of them, and some communication
with the world is probably kept up by native craft.
But all that forenoon, as we headed for them, fanned
along by the faintest of breezes, I saw no sign of man
or canoe in the field of the telescope I kept on pointing
at the scattered group.

At noon I gave no orders for a change of course,
and the mate's whiskers became much concerned and
seemed to be offering themselves unduly to my notice.
At last I said:

"I am going to stand right in. Quite in—as far as
I can take her."

The stare of extreme surprise imparted an air of ferocity also to his eyes, and he looked truly terrific for a moment.

"We're not doing well in the middle of the gulf," I continued, casually. "I am going to look for the land breezes to-night."

"Bless my soul! Do you mean, sir, in the dark amongst the lot of all them islands and reefs and shoals?"

"Well—if there are any regular land breezes at all on this coast one must get close inshore to find them, mustn't one?"

"Bless my soul!" he exclaimed again under his breath. All that afternoon he wore a dreamy, contemplative appearance which in him was a mark of perplexity. After dinner I went into my stateroom as if I meant to take some rest. There we two bent our dark heads over a half-unrolled chart lying on my bed.

"There," I said. "It's got to be Koh-ring.* I've been looking at it ever since sunrise. It has got two hills and a low point. It must be inhabited. And on the coast opposite there is what looks like the mouth of a biggish river—with some town, no doubt, not far up. It's the best chance for you that I can see."

"Anything. Koh-ring let it be."

He looked thoughtfully at the chart as if surveying chances and distances from a lofty height—and following with his eyes his own figure wandering on the blank land of Cochin-China, and then passing off that piece of paper clean out of sight into uncharted regions. And it was as if the ship had two captains to plan her course for her. I had been so worried and restless running up and down that I had not had the patience to dress that day. I had remained in my sleeping-suit, with straw slippers and a soft floppy hat. The closeness of the heat in the gulf had been most oppressive, and the crew were used to see me wandering in that airy attire.

"She will clear the south point as she heads now," I whispered into his ear. "Goodness only knows when, though, but certainly after dark. I'll edge her in to half a mile, as far as I may be able to judge in the dark——"

"Be careful," he murmured, warningly—and I realised suddenly that all my future, the only future for which I was fit, would perhaps go irretrievably to pieces in any mishap to my first command.

I could not stop a moment longer in the room. I motioned him to get out of sight and made my way on the poop. That unplayful cub had the watch. I walked up and down for a while thinking things out, then beckoned him over.

"Send a couple of hands to open the two quarter-deck ports," I said, mildly.

He actually had the impudence, or else so forgot himself in his wonder at such an incomprehensible order, as to repeat:

"Open the quarter-deck ports! What for, sir?"

"The only reason you need concern yourself about is because I tell you to do so. Have them open wide and fastened properly."

He reddened and went off, but I believe made some jeering remark to the carpenter as to the sensible practice of ventilating a ship's quarter-deck. I know he popped into the mate's cabin to impart the fact to him because the whiskers came on deck, as it were by chance, and stole glances at me from below—for signs of lunacy or drunkenness, I suppose.

A little before supper, feeling more restless than ever, I rejoined, for a moment, my second self. And to find him sitting so quietly was surprising, like something against nature, inhuman.

I developed my plan in a hurried whisper.

"I shall stand in as close as I dare and then put her round. I will presently find means to smuggle you out of here into the sail-locker, which communicates with the lobby. But there is an opening, a sort of square for hauling the sails out, which gives straight on the quarter-deck and which is never closed in fine weather, so as to give air to the sails. When the ship's way is deadened in stays and all the hands are aft at the main-braces you will have a clear road to slip out and get overboard through the open quarter-deck port. I've had them both fastened up. Use a rope's end to lower yourself into the water so as to avoid a splash— you know. It could be heard and cause some beastly complication."

He kept silent for a while, then whispered, "I understand."

"I won't be there to see you go," I began with an effort. "The rest . . . I only hope I have understood, too."

"You have. From first to last"—and for the first time there seemed to be a faltering, something strained in his whisper. He caught hold of my arm, but the ringing of the supper bell made me start. He didn't, though; he only released his grip.

After supper I didn't come below again till well past eight o'clock. The faint, steady breeze was loaded with dew; and the wet, darkened sails held all there was of propelling power in it. The night, clear and starry, sparkled darkly, and the opaque, lightless patches shifting slowly against the low stars were the drifting islets. On the port bow there was a big one more distant and shadowily imposing by the great space of sky it eclipsed.

On opening the door I had a back view of my very own self looking at a chart. He had come out of the recess and was standing near the table.

"Quite dark enough," I whispered.

He stepped back and leaned against my bed with a level, quiet glance. I sat on the couch. We had nothing to say to each other. Over our heads the officer of the watch moved here and there. Then I heard him move quickly. I knew what that meant. He was making for the companion; and presently his voice was outside my door.

"We are drawing in pretty fast, sir. Land looks rather close."

"Very well," I answered. "I am coming on deck directly."

I waited till he was gone out of the cuddy, then rose. My double moved too. The time had come to exchange our last whispers, for neither of us was ever to hear each other's natural voice.

"Look here!" I opened a drawer and took out three sovereigns. "Take this anyhow. I've got six and I'd give you the lot, only I must keep a little money to buy some fruit and vegetables for the crew from native boats as we go through Sunda Straits."

He shook his head.

"Take it," I urged him, whispering desperately. "No one can tell what——"

He smiled and slapped meaningly the only pocket of the sleeping-jacket. It was not safe, certainly. But I produced a large old silk handkerchief of mine, and tying the three pieces of gold in a corner, pressed it on him. He was touched, I suppose, because he took it at last and tied it quickly round his waist under the jacket, on his bare skin.

Our eyes met; several seconds elapsed, till, our glances still mingled, I extended my hand and turned the lamp out. Then I passed through the cuddy, leaving the door of my room wide open. . . . "Steward!"

He was still lingering in the pantry in the greatness of his zeal, giving a rub-up to a plated cruet stand the last thing before going to bed. Being careful not to wake up the mate, whose room was opposite, I spoke in an undertone.

He looked round anxiously. "Sir!"

"Can you get me a little hot water from the galley?"

"I am afraid, sir, the galley fire's been out for some time now."

"Go and see."

He flew up the stairs.

"Now," I whispered, loudly, into the saloon—too loudly, perhaps, but I was afraid I couldn't make a sound. He was by my side in an instant—the double captain slipped past the stairs—through a tiny dark passage . . . a sliding door. We were in the sail-locker, scrambling on our knees over the sails. A sudden thought struck me. I saw myself wandering barefooted, bareheaded, the sun beating on my dark poll. I snatched off my floppy hat and tried hurriedly in the dark to ram it on my other self. He dodged and fended off silently. I wonder what he thought had come to me before he understood and suddenly desisted. Our hands met gropingly, lingered united in a steady, motionless clasp for a second. . . . No word was breathed by either of us when they separated.

I was standing quietly by the pantry door when the steward returned.

"Sorry, sir. Kettle barely warm. Shall I light the spirit-lamp?"

"Never mind."

I came out on deck slowly. It was now a matter of conscience to shave the land as close as possible—for now he must go overboard whenever the ship was put in stays. Must! There could be no going back for him. After a moment I walked over to leeward and my heart flew into my mouth at the nearness of the land on the bow. Under any other circumstances I would not have held on a minute longer. The second mate had followed me anxiously.

I looked on till I felt I could command my voice.

"She may weather,"* I said then in a quiet tone.

"Are you going to try that, sir?" he stammered out incredulously.

I took no notice of him and raised my tone just enough to be heard by the helmsman.

"Keep her good full."

"Good full, sir."

The wind fanned my cheek, the sails slept, the world was silent. The strain of watching the dark loom of the land grow bigger and denser was too much for me. I had shut my eyes—because the ship must go closer. She must! The stillness was intolerable. Were we standing still?

When I opened my eyes the second view started my heart with a thump. The black southern hill of Koh-ring seemed to hang right over the ship like a towering fragment of the everlasting night. On that enormous mass of blackness there was not a gleam to be seen, not a sound to be heard. It was gliding irresistibly towards us and yet seemed already within reach of the hand. I saw the vague figures of the watch grouped in the waist, gazing in awed silence.

"Are you going on, sir?" inquired an unsteady voice at my elbow.

I ignored it. I had to go on.

"Keep her full. Don't check her way. That won't do now," I said, warningly.

"I can't see the sails very well," the helmsman answered me, in strange, quavering tones.

Was she close enough? Already she was, I won't say in the shadow of the land, but in the very blackness of it, already swallowed up as it were, gone too close to be recalled, gone from me altogether.

"Give the mate a call," I said to the young man who stood at my elbow as still as death. "And turn all hands up."

My tone had a borrowed loudness reverberated from the height of the land. Several voices cried out together: "We are all on deck, sir."

Then stillness again, with the great shadow gliding closer, towering higher, without light, without a sound. Such a hush had fallen on the ship that she might have been a bark of the dead floating in slowly under the very gate of Erebus.

"My God! Where are we?"

It was the mate moaning at my elbow. He was thunderstruck, and as it were deprived of the moral support of his whiskers. He clapped his hands and absolutely cried out, "Lost!"

"Be quiet," I said, sternly.

He lowered his tone, but I saw the shadowy gesture of his despair. "What are we doing here?"

"Looking for the land wind."

He made as if to tear his hair, and addressed me recklessly.

"She will never get out. You have done it, sir. I knew it'd end in something like this. She will never

weather, and you are too close now to stay. She'll
drift ashore before she's round. O my God!"

I caught his arm as he was raising it to batter his
poor devoted head, and shook it violently.

"She's ashore already," he wailed, trying to tear
himself away.

"Is she? . . . Keep good full there!"

"Good full, sir," cried the helmsman in a frightened,
thin, child-like voice.

I hadn't let go the mate's arm and went on shaking
it. "Ready about, do you hear? You go forward"
—shake—"and stop there"—shake—" and hold your
noise"—shake—"and see these head-sheets properly
overhauled"—shake, shake—shake.

And all the time I dared not look towards the land
lest my heart should fail me. I released my grip at last
and he ran forward as if fleeing for dear life.

I wondered what my double there in the sail-locker
thought of this commotion. He was able to hear
everything—and perhaps he was able to understand
why, on my conscience, it had to be thus close—no
less. My first order "Hard alee!" re-echoed ominously
under the towering shadow of Koh-ring as if I had
shouted in a mountain gorge. And then I watched
the land intently. In that smooth water and light
wind it was impossible to feel the ship coming-to. No!
I could not feel her. And my second self was making
now ready to slip out and lower himself overboard.
Perhaps he was gone already . . . ?

The great black mass brooding over our very mastheads began to pivot away from the ship's side silently.
And now I forgot the secret stranger ready to depart,
and remembered only that I was a total stranger to
the ship. I did not know her. Would she do it?
How was she to be handled?

I swung the mainyard and waited helplessly. She was perhaps stopped, and her very fate hung in the balance, with the black mass of Koh-ring like the gate of the everlasting night towering over her taffrail. What would she do now? Had she way on her yet? I stepped to the side swiftly, and on the shadowy water I could see nothing except a faint phosphorescent flash revealing the glassy smoothness of the sleeping surface. It was impossible to tell—and I had not learned yet the feel of my ship. Was she moving? What I needed was something easily seen, a piece of paper, which I could throw overboard and watch. I had nothing on me. To run down for it I didn't dare. There was no time. All at once my strained, yearning stare distinguished a white object floating within a yard of the ship's side. White on the black water. A phosphorescent flash passed under it. What was that thing? . . . I recognised my own floppy hat. It must have fallen off his head . . . and he didn't bother. Now I had what I wanted—the saving mark*for my eyes. But I hardly thought of my other self, now gone from the ship, to be hidden for ever from all friendly faces, to be a fugitive and a vagabond on the earth, with no brand of the curse*on his sane forehead to stay a slaying hand . . . too proud to explain.

And I watched the hat—the expression of my sudden pity for his mere flesh. It had been meant to save his homeless head from the dangers of the sun. And now —behold—it was saving the ship, by serving me for a mark to help out the ignorance of my strangeness. Ha! It was drifting forward, warning me just in time that the ship had gathered sternway.

"Shift the helm," I said in a low voice to the seaman standing still like a statue.

The man's eyes glistened wildly in the binnacle light

as he jumped round to the other side and spun round
the wheel.

I walked to the break of the poop. On the over-
shadowed deck all hands stood by the forebraces waiting for my order. The stars ahead seemed to be
gliding from right to left. And all was so still in the
world that I heard the quiet remark "She's round,"
passed in a tone of intense relief between two seamen.

"Let go and haul."

The foreyards ran round with a great noise, amidst
cheery cries. And now the frightful whiskers made
themselves heard giving various orders. Already the
ship was drawing ahead. And I was alone with her.
Nothing! no one in the world should stand now between
us, throwing a shadow on the way of silent knowledge
and mute affection, the perfect communion of a seaman
with his first command.

Walking to the taffrail, I was in time to make out,
on the very edge of a darkness thrown by a towering
black mass like the very gateway of Erebus—yes, I was
in time to catch an evanescent glimpse of my white hat
left behind to mark the spot where the secret sharer of
my cabin and of my thoughts, as though he were my
second self, had lowered himself into the water to take
his punishment: a free man, a proud swimmer striking
out for a new destiny.

EXPLANATORY NOTES

NAUTICAL and foreign terms are listed in the Glossary. In the notes below, the following abbreviations are used:

CEW Norman Sherry: *Conrad's Eastern World* (London: Cambridge University Press, 1966).

LJ   Joseph Conrad: *Lord Jim* (London: Dent, 1946).

NLL Joseph Conrad: *Notes on Life and Letters* (London: Dent, 1949).

SL   Joseph Conrad: *The Shadow-Line* (London: Dent, 1950).

'Typhoon'

1 *title*: before deciding on 'Typhoon', Conrad had considered 'Equitable Division' as a title.

7 *Sigg*: Jucker, Sigg and Co. were teak-merchants in Bangkok (*CEW*, p. 238).

9 *little straws*: i.e. 'little straws show which way the wind blows': small details may have important implications.

16 *Solomon*: the biblical Solomon (who built a navy) 'was wiser than all men' (1 Kings 4: 31); and the famous 'Judgement of Solomon' (initiated by his threat to divide in half a child whose maternity was disputed by two women) has a tenuous connection with MacWhirr's eventual decision to divide equally the coolies' disputed money.

17 *easy life*: the phrase has proleptic irony, in view of Jukes's subsequent ordeal on the *Nan-Shan*.

23–4 *blanked . . . . . blank . . . . . condemned . . . . . crimson*: authorial euphemisms for the swear-words 'blasted', 'blast', 'damned', and 'bloody', which we impute to the engineer and which occasion MacWhirr's subsequent remark, 'A profane man'.

32 *the chapter on the storms*: the following extracts from a seamen's manual may explain both MacWhirr's perplexity and the *Nan-Shan*'s peril. The manual, by James Tait, Master Mariner, is *Tait's Seamanship* (3rd Edition; Glasgow : Brown, 1902); I quote pp. 143–5.

Concise Rules for Revolving Storms.

1. Revolving storms are so named because the wind in these storms revolves round an area of low pressure situated in the centre. They have also local names, and are termed Hurricanes in the West Indies and South Pacific . . . . . ; and Typhoons in the China Sea . . . . .

9. The indications of the approach of a revolving storm are (i) an unsteady barometer, or even a cessation in the diurnal range, which is constant in settled weather; (ii) a heavy swell not caused by the wind then blowing; (iii) an ugly, threatening appearance of the sky.

10. In order to judge what is the best way to act if there is reason to believe a storm is approaching, the seaman requires to know (a) in which direction the centre of the storm is situated; (b) in which semicircle the ship is situated.

11. As these points cannot be determined if a vessel is moving with any speed through the water, the first proceeding should be to 'stop' or 'heave to' . . . . .

12. If an observer faces the wind, the centre of the storm will be from 12 to 8 points on his right-hand in the northern hemisphere and on his left-hand in the southern hemisphere; 12 points when the storm begins; about 10 points when the barometer has fallen three-tenths of an inch, and about 8 points when it has fallen six-tenths of an inch or upwards.

13. If the wind shifts to the right the vessel is in the right-hand semicircle, if to the left in the left-hand semicircle, and, if the wind is steady in direction but increasing in force, she is in the direct path of the storm.

14. If the seaman has reason to think that his vessel is in the direct path of the storm he should run with the wind on the starboard quarter in the northern and on the port quarter in the southern hemisphere until the barometer has ceased falling. If she is in the right-hand

semicircle in the northern hemisphere she should remain
hove to on the starboard tack . . . . . ; if she is in the left-
hand semicircle in the northern hemisphere she should
run with the wind on the starboard quarter . . . . .

17. Should the centre of a storm pass over a vessel, the
wind, after blowing furiously in one direction, ceases for
a time, and then blows with equal fury from the opposite
direction. This makes a confused pyramidal sea, which is
especially dangerous.

(As the *Nan-Shan* is voyaging in the northern hemisphere,
I have deleted some of the references to the southern
hemisphere.) It will be seen that in defiance of standard
procedures (like those of the Hydrographic Department
cited here by *Tait's Seamanship*) MacWhirr directs his
vessel through the centre of the typhoon.

44 *quietness in the enormous discord*: the emphasis on a
small but indomitable voice within the storm may recall
the biblical 'still small voice' after the 'great and strong
wind' (1 Kings 19: 11-12).

confident words on the last day: in 'Henry James' [1905]
(*NLL*, pp. 13-14), Conrad says that when the earth dies,
'if anybody, it will be the imaginative man who would be
moved to speak on the eve of that day without to-morrow
—whether in austere exhortation or in a phrase of
sardonic comment, who can guess?'

when heavens fall, and justice is done: an echo of the
Latin maxim, *fiat justitia ruat cælum*: 'let justice be done,
though the heavens should fall'.

66 *I can steer for ever*: in his heroic devotion to duty,
Hackett resembles Singleton, the old helmsman in *The
Nigger of the 'Narcissus'*.

71 *went on yelling the second*: one of Conrad's occasional
lapses into unidiomatic (Gallicized) word order.

74 *as of girding the loins*: a biblical idiom, as in 'Gird up
now thy loins like a man' (Job 38: 3). (Thus 'girding the
loins' means 'preparing for brave action'.)

86 *a slender hair holding a sword suspended over his head*:
Damocles, flatterer of King Dionysius of Syracuse, was
taught the insecurity of happiness by being made to sit

through a feast while a sword was suspended above his
head by a single hair. In *The Mirror of the Sea* (London:
Dent, 1946), p. 69, Conrad says that once a seaman's ship
has been imperilled, 'A man may be the better for it, but
he will not be the same. Damocles has seen the sword
suspended by a hair over his head . . . . .'

'Falk'

105 *Several of us, all more or less connected with the sea*: this
group clearly resembles the group described at the opening of both 'Youth' and 'Heart of Darkness'. Conrad was
recalling his Thames-side conversations (at locations like
the Lobster Tavern, Hole Haven) with his friends Hope,
Mears, and Keen, who were former seamen.

complained of hunger: together with the subsequent
references ('primeval man', 'scorched lumps of flesh',
'tales of hunger and hunt—and of women', 'break-downs',
the name *Arcadia* and the cargo-steamer with its German
couple), this helps to give the tale a strongly proleptic
opening: the 'inner' narrative is repeatedly foreshadowed
by the 'outer' narrative.

107 *a man of more than fifty . . . . .* : this anonymous narrator
resembles Marlow, who tells the story in 'Youth', 'Heart
of Darkness', *Lord Jim*, and *Chance*, as well as the anonymous captain in 'The Secret Sharer', *The Shadow-Line*,
and 'A Smile of Fortune'.

a certain Eastern seaport . . . . . kingdom: the kingdom is
Siam (now Thailand), its capital is Bangkok, and the
river is the Meinam or Menam (now Chao Phraya).

109 *Diana not of Ephesus*: the Roman goddess Diana was a
chaste huntress; her Greek counterpart, Artemis, was
worshipped at a temple at Ephesus in Asia Minor.

113 *a man who had died suddenly*: the subsequent description
of the narrator's predecessor in command tallies closely
with that given in *The Shadow-Line*. There, the former
captain also plays the violin, resembles 'a wild boar somehow', and manages the ship irresponsibly. Nevertheless,
his real-life counterpart, Captain John Snadden of the
Otago, was apparently conscientious: according to

Norman Sherry, 'far from beging negligent, Snadden was extremely concerned about his ship' (*CEW*, p. 226).

114 *not been favoured by a scratch of the pen for the last eighteen months*: in April 1888, one of the part-owners of the *Otago* complained that Captain Snadden 'never favoured me with a scratch of the pen from the time of leaving Newcastle in August last . . . . .' (*CEW*, p. 226).

the old mate . . . . . was not particularly pleased at my coming: in *The Shadow-Line*, the equivalent mate, Burns, 'expected to be confirmed in his temporary command' and was disappointed that a young captain gained the command instead (*SL*, p. 63). His real-life counterpart, Charles Born of the *Otago*, is described in *The Mirror of the Sea*, pp. 18–20.

115 *the crew was sickly*: in *The Shadow-Line* the crew is stricken with 'tropical fever' and 'choleric symptoms', though in that tale the mate is taken to hospital while the steward remains unaffected by the illness.

a certain Schomberg: the same character appears in *Lord Jim* and *Victory*. Norman Sherry says that the name may have been suggested by that of a German broker, Schomburgk [*sic*], who lived in Singapore (*CEW*, pp. 241–2).

audacious thief, and a first-class sprinter: Conrad is adapting an instance of theft from one of his crew. The *Bangkok Times* reported on 1 February 1888:

A chinese 'boy' employed on the barque *Otago* managed the other day to steal 15 gold mohurs from a sailor on board, and then to abscond. The captain and mate, however, met the juvenile thief a few hours afterwards in Mr Clarke's compound and arrested him. Whilst being conducted to the Bang Rak Police Station, he unfortunately managed to bolt and has not since been seen . . . . . (*CEW*, p. 234).

121 *his pound and a half of flesh*: thus Falk is, metaphorically, fifty per cent more extortionate than Shakespeare's Shylock; and the phrasing ironically beckons, for a moment, the tale's motif of cannibalism.

122 *from early morn to dewy eve. In the last rays of the*

setting sun: Conrad may be distantly recalling Milton's
Paradise Lost, I, 742–5 :

> from morn
> To noon he fell, from noon to dewy eve,
> A summer's day; and with the setting sun
> Dropped from the zenith like a falling star . . . . .

126 *the Great Pagoda*: identified as 'the great Paknam
pagoda' in 'The Secret Sharer'.

127 *enough point in his behaviour to make me . . . . . wonder
audibly what he might mean*: there are various instances
of 'delayed decoding' in the tale. The fictional narrator
is slow to perceive that Falk has been prompted by
Hermann to regard him as a rival suitor; slow to recognize as consequences of the supposed rivalry both Falk's
refusal to tow his ship and the bribery of Johnson; and
slow to infer the reason for Falk's aversion to meat.

129 *tides in the affairs of men which taken at the flood . . . and
so on*:

> There is a tide in the affairs of men
> Which, taken at the flood, leads on to fortune;
> Omitted, all the voyage of their life
> Is bound in shallows and in miseries.
> (Shakespeare, *Julius Caesar*, IV. iii. 216–19)

132 *his wife*: she reappears in *Victory*, with 'silk dress, long
neck, ringlets, scared eyes, and silly grin—all complete'.

149 *Gambril*: he reappears as the elderly helmsman in *The
Shadow-Line* (and survives the tropical illness).

166 *peculiar domestic arrangements*: explained on pp. 177–8;
a meatless cuisine.

170 *that Annihilation which is the worthy reward of us all*:
Buddhists commend, as the best attainable state, Nirvana:
the annihilation of individual existence.

182 *too squeamish*: in 'Heart of Darkness', however, Marlow
recoils in horror from recognition that Kurtz's depravities
may include cannibalism; while, in *Lord Jim*, 'Cannibal'
Robinson is depicted as a senile grotesque. Conrad's
'Author's Note' to *Typhoon and Other Stories* states: 'My
intention in writing "Falk" was not to shock anybody . . . . .

I may safely say that Falk is absolutely true to my experience of certain straightforward characters combining a perfectly natural ruthlessness with a certain amount of moral delicacy' (pp. vii–viii).

Historic instances of cannibalism at sea include the controversial case of Thomas Dudley and Edwin Stephens. After a shipwreck in July 1884, three men and a ship's boy, Richard Parker, endured many days of thirst and starvation in an open boat; eventually two of the men, Dudley and Stephens, killed the boy, whose flesh was then eaten. The survivors were rescued and returned to England. At the subsequent trial, Dudley and Stephens (who had made no secret of their deed) were found guilty of murder; but their death sentences were speedily commuted to sentences of six months' jail. In their defence, it was argued that 'there was an inevitable necessity that one life should be sacrificed in order that the other three might be saved, and . . . . . they were justified in doing so in selecting the weakest' (*The Times*, 7 November 1884, p. 11).

195   *the fable of the Flying Dutchman*: there are many versions of this legend, but their gist is that a Dutch sea-captain, Vanderdecken, commits blasphemy during a stormy voyage and is therefore condemned by the Almighty to sail the seas continually; his vessel, *The Flying Dutchman* itself, becomes a phantom ship with a spectral crew, and imperils voyagers who encounter it. Conrad probably knew the versions by Captain Marryat and Richard Wagner. In the former (*The Phantom Ship*, 1838–9), Vanderdecken's sufferings are terminated by his son's intercession. In Wagner's opera (*Der fliegende Holländer*, 1843), the Dutchman is redeemed by the self-sacrificial love of Senta, a sea-captain's daughter.

  an unerring and eternal principle: 'Falk obeys the law of self-preservation without the slightest misgivings as to his right' (Conrad: 'Author's Note' to *Typhoon and Other Stories*, p. viii).

198   *Wkereas if his niece went . . .*: Hermann's antipathy to Falk is vanquished largely by his aversion to paying for a second cabin.

'Amy Foster'

Ford Madox Hueffer (who changed his name to Ford Madox Ford) claimed that this was originally a short story by himself 'which Conrad took over and entirely re-wrote' (*Joseph Conrad: A Personal Remembrance*; London : Duckworth, 1924; p. 120). In *The Cinque Ports: A Historical and Descriptive Record* (Edinburgh and London : Blackwood, 1900), p. 163, Hueffer stated :

One of the most tragic stories that I remember to have heard was connected with a man who escaped the tender mercies of the ocean to undergo an almost more merciless buffeting ashore. He was one of the crew of a German merchant that was wrecked almost at the foot of the light-house [at Dungeness in Kent]. A moderate swimmer, he was carried by the current to some distance from the scene of the catastrophe. Here he touched the ground. He had nothing, no clothes, no food; he came ashore on a winter's night. In the morning he found himself in the Marsh near Romney. He knocked at doors, tried to make himself understood. The Marsh people thought him either a lunatic or a supernatural visitor. To lonely women in the Marsh cottages he seemed a fearful object. No doubt he was, poor wretch. They warned their menfolk of him, and whenever he was seen he was hounded away and ill-used. He got the name of Mad Jack. Knowing nothing of the country, nothing of the language, he could neither ask his way nor read the names on signposts, and even if he read them, they meant nothing to him. How long this lasted, I do not know; I remember hearing from the village people at the time that a dangerous person was in the neighbourhood. The fear of the cottage folk was real enough. For a fortnight or so hardly one of them would open their doors after nightfall. The police at last got to hear of him, and, after a search of some days, he was found asleep in a pigsty. He had the remains of an old shirt hanging round his neck; and under one arm, an old shoe that he seemed to use as a larder; it contained two old crusts and the raw wing of a chicken. In all the time of his wandering he had not come more than nine miles from the place where he had come ashore.

201   *title*: initially Conrad considered 'The Castaway' and 'A Husband' as titles for this piece.

203   *Brenzett*: the fictional location generally corresponds to south-east Kent (and the Kent–Sussex border) within a 13-mile radius of Dungeness. This area has its expanse of flat land, its long beaches of shingle, its Martello towers, and coastguard stations. The real village of Brenzett, however, lies more than five miles inland, unlike its fictional namesake.

207   *she ran out into the yard stopping her ears*: a proleptic irony, given Yanko's eventual fate.

      some German fellow: the claim 'Without phosphorus, no thought' is usually attributed to Jacob Moleschott of Heidelberg University, author of *Lehre der Nahrungsmittel* (1850).

210   *like an animal under a net*: a major leitmotif in the tale. Cf. p. 224: 'a wild bird caught in a snare'; p. 235: 'as if the net of fate had been drawn closer round him'; p. 239: 'a wild creature under the net . . . . . a bird caught in a snare'; p. 240: 'his fluttered air of a bird in a snare'. (Cf. Ecclesiastes 9: 12.) Gaetano D'Elia has suggested that the tale exploits thematically the ambiguous term 'toil', which means both 'labour' and 'net or snare': see 'Yanko, the Man Who Came from the Sea' in *Conradiana* XI (1979), pp. 165–76.

211   *at the mouth of the Elbe*: at Hamburg in Germany.

227   *Conceive you*: one of Conrad's occasional Gallicisms; instead of the English 'Can you imagine . . . . . ?' or 'Just consider . . . . .', he gives a literal translation of the French 'Concevez-vous . . . . .'.

231   *Goorall*: the Polish word for 'mountaineer' or 'mountain-dweller' is *góral* (and the Ukrainian word for 'mountain' is *ropa*, pronounced goráh).

'The Secret Sharer'

In the 'Author's Note' to *'Twixt Land and Sea*, pp. viii–ix, Conrad stated that the 'basic fact of the tale' was an incident aboard the clipper *Cutty Sark* which 'got into the newspapers'.

This incident, in 1880, was the killing of a black seaman by the *Cutty Sark*'s chief mate, who subsequently escaped but was eventually arrested in London and put on trial for murder. The following extract is from the report in *The Times*, 4 August 1882, p. 4:

John Anderson, 31, seaman, was indicted for the wilful murder of John Francis.....

The accused, it appeared, was chief mate on board a tea clipper called the Cutty Sark, which sailed from the port of London in May, 1880. The deceased, who was a coloured man, shipped as an able seaman, and it was stated that he soon afterwards incurred the displeasure of the prisoner in consequence of his incompetency. About the 9th or 10th of August, 1880, the vessel had just rounded the Cape, and at a quarter to 9 o'clock the prisoner was in command of the watch. The night was dark and dirty, and the watch was occupied in hauling the sail round. The deceased not being competent to perform seaman's duty, had been placed on the forecastle on the look out. The watch on hauling the ropes found that the 'fore lazy tack' was fastened, and the prisoner called out to the deceased to let the tack go. The deceased replied 'Very well,' or, according to the prisoner's version, 'Go to the devil.' Immediately afterwards the deceased let go the lazy tack, but instead of doing so as an able seaman would, he let the end go overboard. The prisoner said, 'That —— has done that out of spite.' The deceased retorted, 'Well, you told me to let it go,' and the prisoner exclaimed 'I will come on the forecastle and heave you overboard, you nigger.' The deceased replied, 'If you come up here I have got the capstan bar waiting for you.' The prisoner then went on to the forecastle and was seen to raise the capstan bar, with which he struck the deceased on the head. The blow knocked the man over the forecastle on to the deck, and he never spoke again. The prisoner said to the watch, 'Did you see that nigger lift the capstan bar to me,' but the men replied that they did not. The prisoner said, 'He will lift no more capstan bars to me, for I have knocked him down,' and he added, 'I have knocked him down like a bullock; he never gave a kick.' The account given by the prisoner was that he did it in self-defence. The captain of the vessel attended to the deceased, but he remained insensible till the following day, when he expired from the injuries he received, and was buried at sea. Before the arrival of the ship at Anger the accused, with the connivance of the captain, made his escape. The vessel proceeded thence to Singapore, and during the passage the captain committed suicide by jumping overboard, having previously dropped into the sea the capstan bar used by the prisoner. At Singapore the matter was reported to a magistrate, who, in due course, instituted an inquiry. The prisoner was arrested in London.

It was stated in cross-examination that the deceased man Francis had on several occasions threatened the prisoner's life, and once he sharpened his knife upon the grindstone for the purpose of carrying his threat into execution.

Mr. EDWARD CLARKE, addressing his Lordship at the close of the case, submitted that the evidence could not sustain the Court charging the prisoner with murder.

Mr. JUSTICE STEPHEN concurred; and

Mr. CLARKE said that, in those circumstances, he could not resist a verdict of manslaughter. The learned counsel addressed the Court in mitigation of punishment, pointing out that the vessel had been under-manned, and that at the time in question the accused had had an important manoeuvre to perform with respect to the sail. The deceased behaved in an insolent and 'lubberly' manner, and it was absolutely necessary that the prisoner should assert his authority.

Numerous witnesses were then called on the part of the defence to show that the prisoner bore an excellent character and was a man whose disposition was humane and kindly.

The jury, by his Lordship's direction, then returned a verdict of manslaughter against the accused.

Mr. JUSTICE STEPHEN, in passing sentence, told the prisoner he had considered the case with anxious attention and with very great pain, because the evidence which had been given showed that he was a man of good character generally speaking and of humane disposition.

He was happy to be able to give full weight to the evidence given in his favour. The deceased had certainly acted in a manner which was calculated to make the prisoner very angry, but it must be clearly understood that the taking of human life by brutal violence, whether on sea or on land, whether the life be that of a black or a white man, was a dreadful crime, and deserving of exemplary punishment. He sentenced the prisoner to seven years' penal servitude.

Another important piece of source material is revealed in Conrad's *The Mirror of the Sea,* p. 19. When describing the character of Charles Born, first mate of the *Otago*, Conrad writes:

It so happened that we both loved the little barque very much. And it was just the defect of Mr. B——'s inestimable qualities that he would never persuade himself to believe that the ship was safe in my hands. To begin with, he was more than five years older than myself at a time of life when five years really do count, I being twenty-nine and he thirty-four; then, on our first leaving port (I don't see why I should make a secret of the fact that it was Bangkok), a bit of manoeuvring of mine amongst the islands of the Gulf of Siam had given him an unforgettable scare. Ever since then he had nursed in secret a bitter idea of my utter recklessness.

Thus, 'The Secret Sharer' adapts and combines some features of the *Cutty Sark* incident with some features of Conrad's captaincy of the *Otago*; and one of its creative motivations is clearly a mixture of psychological compensation and vicarious (imaginative) atonement. At one level, the story says to the Charles Born of memory, 'What you deemed to be reckless manoeuvring had a very good reason, though one that I, the young captain, could not reveal to you at the time.'

241   *title*: in the magazine text, the title was given as 'The Secret-Sharer', which means 'the sharer of a secret' and is therefore less appropriate than the unhyphenated version, which means 'the person who secretly shares'. The latter meaning is made explicit by the text on (for example) p. 295 : 'the secret sharer of my cabin and of my thoughts'. Alternative titles considered by Conrad were:

'The Secret Self', 'The Other Self' and 'The Second Self: An Episode from the Sea'.

243   *barren islets, suggesting ruins of stone walls* . . . . . : these correspond to the 'rocky islets . . . . . like the heaps of a cyclopean ruin' in 'Falk', p. 169. The location is again the Bight of Bangkok, at the north end of the Gulf of Siam.

246   *that ideal conception of one's own personality every man sets up for himself secretly*: attempted fidelity to one's ideal self is a major theme in Conrad's works, which so frequently deal with protagonists who have much to learn and are faced with crucial moral and psychological tests. Here the phrasing ('sets up for himself secretly') gives a further range of meaning to the tale's title.

Sephora: in *Lord Jim* (Chapter 13), Conrad used the same name for a ship which sank off the Spanish coast after a collision.

248   *the sea was not likely to keep any special surprises*: a characterstic example of Conradian proleptic irony.

the singleness of its purpose: the captain is soon to experience duplicity of purpose.

251   *Leggatt*: the name is realistically ordinary; but it is homophonous with 'legate', meaning 'envoy or representative of some great power', and thus has a certain symbolic aptness in the tale; for Leggatt embodies the power to challenge orthodox morality.

253   *a Conway boy*: the *Conway* was a training-ship for cadets, moored in the Mersey at Liverpool. Many of the cadets subsequently became naval officers; and the ex-*Conway* boy could feel that (compared with the average seaman) he belonged to an élite. John Masefield's *The Conway* (London: Heinemann, 1933) makes clear that the trainees were encouraged to be loyal to each other in later life. (Conrad's Lord Jim served on a training-ship whose régime resembles that of the *Conway*.)

My father's a parson: this is one of several links between Leggatt and Lord Jim. Jim, too, was a parson's son, became a fugitive from a maritime scandal, and was sympathetically treated by a sailing-ship's captain.

Furthermore, that captain, Marlow, describes Jim's presence aboard his ship (on another voyage from Bangkok) in terms which partly anticipate features of 'The Secret Sharer':

Jim, for the most part, skulked down below as though he had been a stowaway. He infected me so that I avoided speaking on professional matters . . . . . For whole days we did not exchange a word; I felt extremely unwilling to give orders to my officers in his presence. (*LJ*, p. 201.)

256 *capital letter L*: it becomes, literally, the L for Leggatt.

259 *Oh, yes! she's on board*: in *Nostromo* (Part 3, Chapter 10), Captain Mitchell says: 'I was never married myself. A sailor should exercise self-denial.'

The '*brand of Cain*' *business*: Cain slew his brother Abel, and was condemned by God to be 'a fugitive and a vagabond in the earth'; but 'the LORD set a mark upon Cain, lest any finding him should kill him' (Genesis 4: 8–15).

268 *Archbold:* some critics have suggested that the name bears ironic significance, given that its root meaning, 'pre-eminently bold', is markedly inappropriate for a captain who 'hardly dared give the order' to reef a foresail during a storm. (The suggestion is weakened by the narrator's uncertainty about the name.)

272 *for psychological (not moral) reasons*: an enigmatic phrase which, perhaps, means merely that under Archbold's scrutiny the captain might betray a direct lie by reddening in the face.

276 *It was all very simple*: the captain's belief in its ethical simplicity is unlikely to be shared by the reflective reader. Leggatt has killed a man (whose main offence was merely that of uttering 'insolence') and is prepared to kill again; in his over-reaction during the storm he has broken the laws of the land and the sea.

279 *like a sword over our heads*: like the legendary sword of Damocles, cited in 'Typhoon', p. 86.

284 '*Driven off the face of the earth.*': 'And Cain said unto the LORD, ... Behold, thou hast driven me out this day from the face of the earth . . . . .' (Genesis 4: 13–14).

'*As I came at night so I shall go . . . Not naked like a soul on the Day of Judgment*': cf. 'Naked came I out of my mother's womb, and naked shall I return thither' (Job 1: 12); 'As he came forth of his mother's womb, naked shall he return to go as he came' (Ecclesiastes 5: 15); 'all things are naked and opened unto the eyes of him [God] with whom we have to do' (Hebrews 4: 13).

286 *Koh-ring*: in *The Shadow-Line*, this island on the eastern side of the Gulf of Siam, 'a great, black, upheaved ridge amongst a lot of tiny islets', is invested with apparently uncanny power : it 'seemed to be the centre of the fatal circle' (*SL*, p. 84).

291 *She may weather*: i.e. 'The ship may sail to windward of Koh-ring without needing to tack.' To help Leggatt by taking the ship close to the island, the captain purports to believe that she may safely pass the south point of Koh-ring without changing course. Like the incredulous mate, he knows that she cannot do so.

The vessel's manoeuvres are these. She has been pursuing a roughly south-easterly course down the Gulf of Siam. As the light winds oppose her direct route, the captain has proceeded by tacking, making a zigzag progress which captures the wind now on one side of the ship and now on the other. The latest tack, for twenty hours or so, has directed her mainly easterly, towards Koh-ring; and, in order to reduce the distance to be swum by Leggatt, the captain has let the vessel approach perilously close to the island's rocky coast. If she continues on this course, she will run aground; but, if he attempts to change tack, there is a danger—greatly increased by the darkness—that on losing headway as she faces the wind she will then drift backwards onto the rocks. (Initially the ship is on a starboard tack, which means that the wind is coming over her starboard bow; therefore a sharp right turn, through the wind, is required so as to direct her on a port tack, southwards, away from the island.)

The captain tells the helmsman to 'Keep her good full', i.e. keep the vessel moving with the maximum wind in her sails so that she may have the necessary momentum to preserve headway during the subsequent turn; and by that instruction he deters the helmsman from modifying the course to aid a presumed weathering. At 'Are you going on, sir?', a questioner implies that weathering is now impossible. The warning 'Keep her full. Don't check her way. That won't do now' again restrains the helmsman. The captain orders all hands to be ready on deck, because they will be needed to re-orientate the sails during the new manoeuvre. They are apprehensive, and the mate begins to panic : 'She will never weather, and you are too close now to stay': he thinks that on its present course the vessel will run aground, and that it is too late to change tack. After giving the standard warning of the impending manoeuvre, 'Ready about', the captain orders the mate to see that the headsheets are 'properly overhauled', thus initiating the procedure of variously slackening and hauling the ropes to re-set the headsails. At the command 'Hard alee!', the helmsman turns the wheel so that the rudder is drawn to starboard, thus swinging the vessel to starboard; and the hands then re-angle the mainsail ('I swung the mainyard'). Now, however, the captain's situation is extremely perilous, because in the darkness he cannot tell whether the ship is progressing or, on the contrary, drifting backwards before the wind. If her motion were backwards, the rudder would have to be swung from starboard to port in order to maintain the intended turn (because when a ship goes backwards, the effect of the rudder is reversed). The white hat in the water providentially shows him that the vessel has indeed 'gathered sternway', so he orders the helmsman to 'shift the helm' (i.e. turn the wheel so that the rudder is moved from starboard to port), and accordingly the ship's bows resume their swing in the desired direction. With the wind now coming across the port bow, the order 'Let go and haul' follows : the foreyards (bearing the sails of the foremast) are promptly hauled round to capture the wind, and the ship progresses safely towards open water.

294   *the saving mark*: John Masefield recalled that on the *Conway* the Seamanship Instructor, Wallace Blair, taught the cadets that a white straw hat could be used 'to *mark the sea*' (*So Long to Learn*; London: Heinemann, 1952; p. 71).

a fugitive and a vagabond . . . . . no brand of the curse: a further allusion to Genesis 4: 14-15.

GLOSSARY

abaft: behind, towards the vessel's stern.

'Ach's!': cries of 'Oh!'

'Ach so!': 'Oh, indeed!'

affected (11): made a show of preferring.

aft: towards the vessel's stern.

Alsatian (115): native of Alsatia (Alsace or Elsass), a border-region long disputed by France and Germany.

anchorite: hermit or recluse.

anchor-watch: allocation of one man (or more) to keep watch on deck at night while a vessel is at anchor.

aneroid glass: glass face of the maritime aneroid barometer, which can resemble a clock; its pointer, activated by a vacuum cylinder, registers changes in atmospheric pressure.

answerable (175): responsible for the situation.

arcadian felicity: contentment like that attributed to the pastoral inhabitants of legendary Arcadia in ancient Greece.

articles (76): the contract signed by a seaman on entering a merchant vessel.

ashore (as in 'put my ship ashore', 155): aground, in collision with shore, sandbank, or other obstacle.

athwart: across; at right-angles to the fore-and-aft line of a vessel.

aureole: halo or radiance.

bar (124): shoal or bank of sand or mud opposite a river mouth or harbour entrance.

barque (107): normally a relatively small three-masted ship, often square-sterned, with fore-and-aft rig on the mizzen-mast (the rear mast) but square rig on the foremast and mainmast.

batten (noun): slat of wood or metal which fits staples and thus secures a hatch-cover; *or* wooden slat nailed to a compartment-floor to retain objects.

batten down: fasten down securely by means of battens.

Bedlam: asylum for the insane at London, named after the

Priory of St Mary of Bethlehem which originally occupied the site.

Bengal light: a brilliant light or flare, burning sulphide of antimony, used as a shipwreck signal or to illuminate country at night.

brace: long rope by which a yard (spar bearing a sail) is turned.

billet (10): colloquial term for post or occupation.

black-squad: men of the engine-room.

block: frame containing a roller over which a rope may run.

boatswain (abbreviation: *bosun*): naval foreman; the petty officer on a merchant ship who immediately supervises the work-force and its tasks.

bosun: see *boatswain*.

bow, bows: forward part of a vessel.

bowsprit: spar projecting forward from a vessel's stem.

brass-bound: ornamented with gold braid.

break of the poop: front of the poop deck (raised rear deck), where ladders lead down to the main deck.

bridge: elevated thwartship platform from which the ship is navigated.

bridge-screens: panels to protect bridge-occupants from the weather.

broached-to: swung sideways to windward.

bucolic: rustic.

bulkhead: upright partition between compartments.

bulwark: ship's side above deck-level, protecting the deck.

bummer: sponger or parasitic idler.

bunting: thin material used for flags.

burgomaster: mayor.

calotte: soft round cap.

Cambodje (**Cambodge** in some other editions): Cambodian (now Kampuchean).

capstan: cylindrical device for heaving anchors or raising yards, rotated (if not by steam) by means of capstan bars inserted into its holes.

Capuchin: friar of a Franciscan order.

Carimata: island off the south-west coast of Borneo, 1° 40′ south, 108° 50′ east. Subsequently Karimata.

Celestial: familiar term for Chinaman (China being then 'the Celestial Empire').

centaur: a composite creature (in Greek mythology) with the head and torso of a man but the legs and hindparts of a horse.

chancery: 'in chancery' (p. 60) is a colloquial phrase meaning 'in a tight and uncomfortable grip'.

chock: iron casting through which ropes or hawsers are guided. *But* 'rolling chocks on bilges' (7) are keels on the curve of the hull below the water-line to resist the rolling motion of a vessel.

chronometer: very accurate sea-going clock, fitted with gimbals to neutralize the motion of the vessel.

chucked (151): gave a friendly pat or blow.

chucker-out: barman or doorkeeper ('bouncer') who vigorously ejects unwelcome patrons.

close-hauled under short canvas: with sails reduced in area and hauled close (away from square) so that the ship bears as nearly against the wind as is consistent with retaining the wind's propulsive force.

coal-trimmer: man who stows the coal.

coaming: raised border, to repel water, round the edge of a hatch.

cobble: small fishing-boat with high bows and square stem, usually fitted with a lug-sail (quadrilateral sail).

Cochin-China: region (now included in Vietnam) extending northwards from the Mekong Delta.

coming-to: turning the bows towards the wind.

companion: covered entrance to a stairway; sometimes also a skylight or window-frame through which light passes to a lower deck or cabin.

'Conway' boy: cadet or former cadet of the training-ship *Conway*, moored at Liverpool.

coolies: Chinese labourers.

'coram populo': (Latin:) in the presence of the public.

country (as in 'country wife', 'country ship'): indigenous; native, not European.

crank arrested on the cant (73): shaft-arm halted in a sloping position.

cuddy: on a small vessel (like Falk's), a small cabin; on a larger vessel (like that in 'The Secret Sharer'), a saloon in which the officers take their meals. Hermann's cuddy, intermediate in size, resembles 'a farm kitchen' (113).

cyclopean (169): ancient and immense, built of irregular blocks or unhewn stone. (In legend, the Cyclopes were workmen of Hephaestus.)

davits: small cranes by which a ship's boats are raised or lowered.

deals (195): fir or pine boards.

demurrage of the lighters (148): compensation for undue delay in using the open boats which supply cargo to a ship.

Der verfluchte Kerl (141): (German:) The accursed fellow; the damned oaf.

dodger: canvas wind-shield for the ship's bridge.

drawing nine feet aft (152): requiring a water-depth of nine feet (nearly three metres) towards the stern.

draws over twenty feet (246): has a depth in the water of more than six metres.

dredging with the anchor down (148-9): moving a vessel from one position to another by using a dropped anchor to guide or control its course downstream.

Dumbarton: Scottish town on the River Clyde, near Glasgow; then famed for its shipbuilding industry.

Dutchman (145): (obsolete slang:) Germanic foreigner.

Dutch Uncle: (idiomatic:) person who offers a severe reprimand or admonition.

écarté: card-game for two players in which each player may discard any or all of the cards dealt.

Elbe: German river that flows through Hamburg to the North Sea.

elevated (234): elated by intoxication.

enfilading view: end-to-end view.

Erebus: name (meaning 'darkness') of the gloomy cavern by which, according to classical mythology, the souls of the dead entered the underworld of Hades.

fakir: Indian ascetic, beggar, or magician.

fall: rope which runs through a block to raise or lower a boat. (*Overhauled falls*: ropes arranged to keep their blocks apart.)

fall foul of: become unpleasantly entangled with; clash with.

fauna and flora: animals and flowers; natural enviroment.

fiddle of the stokehold: grating hatch over the boiler room.

Fo-kien: a province (now called Fujian) in south-east China.

forebitts: pair of posts (at the foremast) to which cables are fastened.

forebraces: ropes used to change the setting of a foresail.

forecastle: enclosed area at the foremost end of a ship; a deck is above it and the crew's quarters may be located within it.

forefoot: foremost end of the keel, where it meets the stem.

fore-rigging: ropes of the foremast and foresails.

fore-royal brace: rope of the fore-royal sail (the uppermost sail on the foremast).

foreyards: spars supporting sails on the foremast.

forward (on a ship): towards the vessel's bow (front end).

friction winches: hoisting machines (on which ropes are wound) fitted with a braking device.

Fu-chau: a Chinese port (now Fuzhou) on the Formosa Strait (now Taiwan Strait).

gaskets: canvas bands by which sails are fastened to yards and booms (spars).

German Ocean: North Sea.

gharry: cab drawn by horse or pony.

gimbals: device for keeping an object level, often consisting of two concentric metal rings bearing at opposite points on knife-edges.

gins: pulleys for hoisting cargo.

Good Hope: the South African Cape.

Gottferdam! (142): (partly-phoneticized version of *Gottver-damm!*) Damn it!

gunny-bags: jute sacks.

Hades: the underworld, Hell.

halyards: ropes for hoisting sails and yards. (*Signal halyards:* cords for hoisting signal-flags.)

'Hard alee!': 'Put the helm (tiller) strongly over away from the wind, to re-direct the vessel towards the wind' (preparatory to the new course or tack).

hawse pipe: iron casting (in the bow) through which the anchor-chain runs.

head-sheets: ropes of the fore-and-aft sails in front of the foremast.

helm: steering apparatus, particularly the helmsman's wheel. (*Shift the helm*: turn the wheel.)

'Himmel! Zwei und dreissig Pfund!': 'Good heavens! Thirty-two pounds!'

hooker: mildly derogatory term for a vessel deemed clumsy or inadequate.

Hussars: cavalrymen.

incontinently: impetuously.

inexpressibles: (facetious term for) pants, trousers.

'in extremis': (Latin:) at the point of death; in desperate circumstances.

jalousie: slatted shutter.

Java Head: the western tip of Java, where the Sunda Strait meets the Indian Ocean.

jet (95): black beading.

Joss: Chinese idol.

jury rudder: makeshift rudder, the proper one being lost.

keelson: ship's stringer or inner keel which binds the floor to the outer keel.

Kerl: (German:) fellow, oaf (cf. English 'churl').

Klings: maritime Indians originating from Madras.

Koh-ring: corresponds approximately to Koh Rong (latterly Kas Rong), a large island off the coast of Cambodia (Kampuchea).

lacustrine: lake-side.

land breezes: breezes which blow at night from land to sea (because the sea is then relatively warm).

lascar: oriental sailor.

lead-line: line weighted with lead, used for measuring the depth of water.

leeward: towards the lee: the sheltered side (as opposed to 'windward', the side against which the wind blows).

'Let go and haul': 'Let go the sail-ropes on the windward side and pull the sail-ropes on the lee side.' (This order is given during a tacking manoeuvre when the wind has filled the rear sails and now the front sails need to be swung to capture the wind.)

lighters: open boats used for loading and unloading ships.

limekilns: furnaces in which chalk or limestone is reduced to quicklime.

Lower Hope Reach: four-mile stretch of the River Thames, extending northwards past East Tilbury.

main-brace: rope attached to the mainyard.

maindeck: principal deck of the main hull; uppermost of the decks which span the length and breadth of the ship.

main-hatch: covered opening before the mainmast, giving access to the deck or hold beneath.

mainmast: second mast from the front, located between the foremast and the mizzen-mast.

'Mainsail haul!': 'Adjust the ropes to change the angle of the largest sail!': an order given during the tacking manoeuvre when the wind is nearly ahead; the mainyard is swung to capture the wind for the new stage of the ship's zigzag progress.

mainyard: the lowest yard (horizontal spar) on the mainmast.

manila line: rope made from the fibre (Manila hemp) of the wild banana stalk.

mantle: cloak.

Martello tower: circular fort resembling a squat tower. In south-eastern England, many such forts were erected in anticipation of a French invasion during the Napoleonic period.

mastheads: tops of masts.

Meinam: river (now called Chao Phraya) that flows through Bangkok (now Krung Thep) into the Gulf of Siam (now Gulf of Thailand).

mess money: money for meals.

mess together: take meals together.

midden: refuse-heap, garbage-tip.

mizzen-mast: rear mast on a three-masted vessel.

mizzen-rigging: ropes of the mizzen-mast and of its spars.

monachal: monk-like, ascetic.

mooring-bitts: pair of posts to which mooring-ropes can be fastened.

nap (52): the card-game 'Napoleon'.

narrow seas (15): seas offering numerous navigational hazards.

'nota bene': (Latin:) notice carefully.

off-shore tack: course heading away from shore during the zig-zag manoeuvres of tacking.

olympian: resembling a deity of Mount Olympus.

painter (190): rope in the bow of a boat for securing or towing it.

Paknam: customs port on the Bight of Bangkok.

pallet: rudimentary bed; often merely a straw mattress.

P. & O. boat: vessel of the Peninsular & Oriental Steamship Company.

pâté de foie gras: fat goose-liver paste.

pepper-and-salt suit: suit of mixed black and white material.

pintles: pins or bolts on which the rudder swivels.

Platt-Deutsch: (usually Plattdeutsch:) Low German dialect.

point: division of the compass, being an arc of $11\frac{1}{4}$ degrees. Thus four points off course (31): 45 degrees away from the intended course.

pole-masts: masts bare of yards and sails, as on steamers.

polls (79): heads.

port (side of ship): left side.

ports: openings for light and ventilation.

punkah: large fan, often in the form of a flap raised and lowered manually by means of a pulley.

quarter-deck: rear part of the main deck between the poop and the mainmast.

rack: contraption to torture victims by slowly stretching them. Hence the working of the rack (184): the slow torment.

ratlines: rope rungs to help seamen to climb the rigging.

'Ready about' (293): an order to commence tacking.

reefed foresail: the foresail is the lowest sail on the foremast; it is reefed by being rolled up and secured. On the Sephora (254), when the other sails have been blown away by the gale, the reefed foresail may suffice to enable the ship to be navigated instead of wallowing at the mercy of the winds.

riding-light: white light hanging in the rigging near the bows at night when the vessel is riding at anchor.

right-about: opposite direction; in drill, sometimes a turn preliminary to dismissal; hence sent to the right-about (198): dismissed, rejected.

River Plate: El Río de la Plata, the river which flows between Argentina and Uruguay.

Roads, Roadstead: offshore expanse of water where ships may ride safely at anchor.

rudder-chains: chains leading from the rudder to each of the two rear quarters of the vessel.

running gear: ropes which run through blocks or pulleys and are used to haul spars and sails.

sampan: flat-bottomed oriental boat.

scathless: (usually *scatheless*:) unharmed.

scow: flat-bottomed boat used for local transportation of goods.

siren (196): mythical sea-nymph, part woman and part bird, whose songs lured seamen to death.

slice (55): hooked poker for removing cinders from the grate-bars of furnaces or for stowing coal.

slop-made: ready-made.

slush-slingers: waste-clearers (*slush* sometimes meaning waste from the galley).

sou'-wester: waterproof hat extending over the back of the neck.

sovereign (115): British gold coin worth one pound sterling.

spars: general term for the stout poles used as masts, yards, booms, etc., on a vessel.

spoken them (at sea): hailed them.

'Square the yards by lifts and braces . . . . .' (265): 'Set the yards (the spars which support the sails) so that they are horizontal and at right-angles to the fore-and-aft line of the vessel; use lifts (ropes from each mast-head to its yard-arms) and braces (ropes attached to the ends of the yard-arms) for the purpose.' (*Square by the lifts*: horizontal; *square by the braces*: at right angles.)

stanchion: upright post of wood or metal to support rails, awnings, etc.

stand right in: sail very close to the coast.

starboard (side of ship): right side.

staterooms: private cabins.

stay (verb): head into the wind in tacking. Thus 'you are too close now to stay' (293): 'you are too close to the land to be able to turn the vessel to windward in tacking'. *Put in stays* (291): turned to windward in the tacking manoeuvre.

strop: circle of rope used as a strap (for freight or rigging). *Splicing a strop*: joining two rope-ends by interweaving their strands so as to complete a strop.

Sunda Straits: channel between Java and Sumatra.

Table Bay: bay north of Cape Town in South Africa.

'table-d'hôte': common table (with limited menu and set rate) at a hotel or restaurant.

tack: generally, 'to tack' is to make a zigzag course (when the direct course is opposed by the wind) by angling the yards alternately for each oblique run. More specifically, a vessel 'tacks' when her bows are swung into and across the wind, thus changing the side exposed to it.

taffrail: the rear rail of a vessel.

Talcahuano: Chilean port on the Pacific.

Taotai: provincial officer in a *tao* (circuit or division).

tap-room: room in which beer is served directly from the cask.

Teddington: south-western suburb of London, beside the Thames.

terra-cotta: 'baked earth': reddish-brown composition of clay and sand, hardened by fire.

'thwart-ship: across the ship, from side to side.

tiffin: lunch.

tinker's curse: oath of proverbial worthlessness, allegedly because tinkers curse incontinently.

Tophet: Hell. (Tophet was the name originally of a valley of human sacrifice near Jerusalem, and subsequently, as in Isaiah 30: 33, of the site of God's vengeance.)

towing chock: iron casting (at the bow of a ship) through which the hawser is passed to facilitate towing.

treaty port: port opened by treaty to foreign trade.

trimming . . . . . the stokehold ventilators (23): swivelling the ventilators so that the maximum air-flow is directed down them to the boiler-room.

truck (91): flat circular cap of wood at the top of a mast.

trysail: small triangular or quadrilateral fore-and-aft sail.

turned-to (102): set to work.

'tween-deck: area between decks, particularly between the main deck and the deck beneath.

way (294): motion, progress through the water.

way . . . . . deadened in stays (288): progress arrested as the vessel faces the wind during tacking.

wattle: woven fencing.

weather (verb, 291): sail to windward of an obstacle.

West Hartlepool: coastal town in north-eastern England.

whipping of the fore-royal brace (110): binding of the rope of the fore-royal sail. The 'whipping' is the binding of twine round the end of a rope to prevent its fraying. The fore-royal sail is the uppermost sail on the foremast.

whipping up (21): hoisting by means of a pulley.

windlass: machine for hoisting the anchor.

yard: spar which crosses a mast horizontally and from which a sail can be suspended.

THE WORLD'S CLASSICS

A Select List

SERGEI AKSAKOV: A Russian Gentleman
Translated by J. D. Duff
Edited by Edward Crankshaw

A Russian Schoolboy
Translated by J. D. Duff
Introduction by John Bayley

HANS ANDERSEN: Fairy Tales
Translated by L. W. Kingsland
Introduction by Naomi Lewis
Illustrated by Vilhelm Pedersen and Lorenz Frølich

ARTHUR J. ARBERRY (Transl.): The Koran

LUDOVICO ARIOSTO: Orlando Furioso
Translated by Guido Waldman

ARISTOTLE: The Nicomachean Ethics
Translated by David Ross

JANE AUSTEN: Emma
Edited by James Kinsley and David Lodge

Mansfield Park
Edited by James Kinsley and John Lucas

Northanger Abbey, Lady Susan, The Watsons,
and Sanditon
Edited by John Davie

ROBERT BAGE: Hermsprong
Edited by Peter Faulkner

WILLIAM BECKFORD: Vathek
Edited by Roger Lonsdale

R. D. BLACKMORE: Lorna Doone
Edited by Sally Shuttleworth

KEITH BOSLEY (Transl.): The Kalevala

JAMES BOSWELL: Life of Johnson
The Hill/Powell edition, revised by David Fleeman
Introduction by Pat Rogers

MARY ELIZABETH BRADDON: Lady Audley's Secret
Edited by David Skilton

CHARLOTTE BRONTË: Jane Eyre
Edited by Margaret Smith

Shirley
Edited by Margaret Smith and Herbert Rosengarten

EMILY BRONTË: Wuthering Heights
Edited by Ian Jack

GEORGE BÜCHNER:
Danton's Death, Leonce and Lena, Woyzeck
Translated by Victor Price

JOHN BUNYAN: The Pilgrim's Progress
Edited by N. H. Keeble

FANNY BURNLEY: Camilla
Edited by Edward A. Bloom and Lilian D. Bloom

THOMAS CARLYLE: The French Revolution
Edited by K. J. Fielding and David Sorensen

LEWIS CARROLL: Alice's Adventures in Wonderland
and Through the Looking Glass
Edited by Roger Lancelyn Green
Illustrated by John Tenniel

GEOFFREY CHAUCER: The Canterbury Tales
Translated by David Wright

ANTON CHEKHOV: The Russian Master and Other Stories
Translated by Ronald Hingley

Ward Number Six and Other Stories
Translated by Ronald Hingley

JOHN CLELAND:
Memoirs of a Woman of Pleasure (Fanny Hill)
Edited by Peter Sabor

WILKIE COLLINS: Armadale
Edited by Catherine Peters

The Moonstone
Edited by Anthea Trodd

JOSEPH CONRAD: Chance
Edited by Martin Ray

Typhoon and Other Tales
Edited by Cedric Watts

Youth, Heart of Darkness, The End of the Tether
Edited by Robert Kimbrough

JAMES FENIMORE COOPER: The Last of the Mohicans
Edited by John McWilliams

DANIEL DEFOE: Colonel Jack
Edited by Samuel Holt Monk and David Roberts

Robinson Crusoe
Edited by J. Donald Crowley

THOMAS DE QUINCEY:
The Confessions of an English Opium-Eater
Edited by Grevel Lindop

CHARLES DICKENS: Christmas Books
Edited by Ruth Glancy

David Copperfield
Edited by Nina Burgis

The Pickwick Papers
Edited by James Kinsley

FËDOR DOSTOEVSKY: Crime and Punishment
Translated by Jessie Coulson
Introduction by John Jones

Memoirs from the House of the Dead
Translated by Jessie Coulson
Introduction by Ronald Hingley

ARTHUR CONAN DOYLE:
Sherlock Holmes: Selected Stories
Introduction by S. C. Roberts

ALEXANDRE DUMAS *fils*:
La Dame aux Camélias
Translated by David Coward

MARIA EDGEWORTH: Castle Rackrent
Edited by George Watson

GEORGE ELIOT: Daniel Deronda
Edited by Graham Handley

Felix Holt, The Radical
Edited by Fred C. Thompson

Middlemarch
Edited by David Carroll

JOHN MEADE FALKNER: The Nebuly Coat
Edited by Christopher Hawtree

SUSAN FERRIER: Marriage
Edited by Herbert Foltinek

HENRY FIELDING: Joseph Andrews *and* Shamela
Edited by Douglas Brooks-Davies

SARAH FIELDING: The Adventures of David Simple
Edited by Malcolm Kelsall

GUSTAVE FLAUBERT: Madame Bovary
Translated by Gerard Hopkins
Introduction by Terence Cave

A Sentimental Education
Translated by Douglas Parmée

THEODOR FONTANE: Before the Storm
Translated by R. J. Hollingdale

JOHN GALT: Annals of the Parish
Edited by James Kinsley

ELIZABETH GASKELL: Cousin Phillis and Other Tales
Edited by Angus Easson

North and South
Edited by Angus Easson

GEORGE GISSING: The Private Papers of Henry Ryecroft
Edited by Mark Storey

WILLIAM GODWIN: Caleb Williams
Edited by David McCracken

J. W. VON GOETHE: Faust, Part One
Translated by David Luke

KENNETH GRAHAME: The Wind in the Willows
Edited by Peter Green

H. RIDER HAGGARD: King Solomon's Mines
Edited by Dennis Butts

THOMAS HARDY: A Pair of Blue Eyes
Edited by Alan Manford

Jude the Obscure
Edited by Patricia Ingham

Tess of the D'Urbervilles
Edited by Juliet Grindle and Simon Gatrell

NATHANIEL HAWTHORNE:
Young Goodman Brown and Other Tales
Edited by Brian Harding

ALEXANDER HERZEN: Childhood, Youth and Exile
Introduction by Isaiah Berlin

Ends and Beginnings
Translated by Constance Garnett
Revised by Humphrey Higgins
Edited by Aileen Kelly

HESIOD: Theogony *and* Works and Days
Translated by M. L. West

HOMER: The Iliad
Translated by Robert Fitzgerald
Introduction by G. S. Kirk

The Odyssey
Translated by Walter Shewring
Introduction by G. S. Kirk

WILLIAM DEAN HOWELLS: Indian Summer
Edited by Tony Tanner

THOMAS HUGHES: Tom Brown's Schooldays
Edited by Andrew Sanders

HENRIK IBSEN: An Enemy of the People, The Wild Duck,
Rosmersholm
Edited and Translated by James McFarlane

Peer Gynt
Translated by Christopher Fry and Johan Fillinger
Introduction by James McFarlane

ELIZABETH INCHBALD: A Simple Story
Edited by J. M. S. Tompkins

HENRY JAMES: The Ambassadors
Edited by Christopher Butler

A London Life *and* The Reverberator
Edited by Philip Horne

The Spoils of Poynton
Edited by Bernard Richards

RUDYARD KIPLING: The Day's Work
Edited by Thomas Pinney

The Jungle Book (in two volumes)
Edited by W. W. Robson

Stalky & Co.
Edited by Isobel Quigly

J. SHERIDAN LE FANU: Uncle Silas
Edited by W. J. McCormack

CHARLOTTE LENNOX: The Female Quixote
Edited by Margaret Dalziel
Introduction by Margaret Anne Doody

LEONARDO DA VINCI: Notebooks
Edited by Irma A. Richter

MIKHAIL LERMONTOV: A Hero of our Time
Translated by Vladimar Nabokov with Dmitri Nabokov

MATTHEW LEWIS: The Monk
Edited by Howard Anderson

NICCOLÓ MACHIAVELLI: The Prince
Edited by Peter Bondanella and Mark Musa
Introduction by Peter Bondanella

HENRY MACKENZIE: The Man of Feeling
Edited by Brian Vickers

KATHERINE MANSFIELD: Selected Stories
Edited by D. M. Davin

CHARLES MATURIN: Melmoth the Wanderer
Edited by Douglas Grant
Introduction by Chris Baldick

HERMAN MELVILLE: The Confidence-Man
Edited by Tony Tanner

Moby Dick
Edited by Tony Tanner

GEORGE MEREDITH: Beauchamp's Career
Edited by Margaret Harris

The Ordeal of Richard Feverel
Edited by John Halperin

PROSPER MÉRIMÉE: Carmen and Other Stories
Translated by Nicholas Jotcham

MICHELANGELO: Life, Letters, and Poetry
Translated by George Bull with Peter Porter

MOLIÉRE: Don Juan and Other Plays
Translated by George Graveley and Ian Maclean

GEORGE MOORE: Esther Waters
Edited by David Skilton

JOHN HENRY NEWMAN: Loss and Gain
Edited by Alan G. Hill

MARGARET OLIPHANT:
The Doctor's Family and Other Stories
Edited by Merryn Williams

OVID: Metamorphoses
Translated by A. D. Melville
Introduction and Notes by E. J. Kenney

WALTER PATER: Marius the Epicurean
Edited by Ian Small

THOMAS LOVE PEACOCK: Headlong Hall and Gryll Grange
Edited by Michael Baron and Michael Slater

FRANCESCO PETRARCH:
Selections from the Canzoniere and Other Works
Translated by Mark Musa

EDGAR ALLAN POE: Selected Tales
Edited by Julian Symons

JEAN RACINE: Britannicus, Phaedra, Athaliah
Translated by C. H. Sisson

ANN RADCLIFFE: The Italian
Edited by Frederick Garber

The Mysteries of Udolpho
Edited by Bonamy Dobreaee

The Romance of the Forest
Edited by Chloe Chard

SAMUEL RICHARDSON: Sir Charles Grandison
Edited by Jocelyn Baines

M. E. SALTYKOV-SHCHEDRIN: The Golovlevs
Translated by I. P. Foote

PAUL SALZMAN (Ed.):
An Anthology of Elizabethan Prose Fiction

SIR WALTER SCOTT: The Heart of Midlothian
Edited by Claire Lamont

Waverley
Edited by Claire Lamont

MARY SHELLEY: Frankenstein
Edited by M. K. Joseph

PERCY BYSSHE SHELLEY:
Zastrozzi *and* St. Irvyne
Edited by Stephen Behrendt

SIR PHILIP SIDNEY:
The Countess of Pembroke's Arcadia (The Old Arcadia)
Edited by Katherine Duncan-Jones

CHARLOTTE SMITH: The Old Manor House
Edited by Anne Henry Ehrenpreis

TOBIAS SMOLLETT: The Expedition of Humphry Clinker
Edited by Lewis M. Knapp
Revised by Paul-Gabriel Boucé

Peregrine Pickle
Edited by James L. Clifford
Revised by Paul-Gabriel Boucé

LAURENCE STERNE: A Sentimental Journey
Edited by Ian Jack

Tristram Shandy
Edited by Ian Campbell Ross

ROBERT LOUIS STEVENSON: Kidnapped and Catriona
Edited by Emma Letley

The Strange Case of Dr. Jekyll and Mr. Hyde
and Weir of Hermiston
Edited by Emma Letley

BRAM STOKER: Dracula
Edited by A. N. Wilson

R. S. SURTEES: Mr. Facey Romford's Hounds
Edited by Jeremy Lewis

Mr. Sponge's Sporting Tour
Introduction by Joyce Cary

JONATHAN SWIFT: Gulliver's Travels
Edited by Paul Turner

A Tale of a Tub and Other Works
Edited by Angus Ross and David Woolley

WILLIAM MAKEPEACE THACKERAY: Barry Lyndon
Edited by Andrew Sanders

Vanity Fair
Edited by John Sutherland

LEO TOLSTOY: Anna Karenina
Translated by Louise and Aylmer Maude
Introduction by John Bayley

War and Peace (in two volumes)
Translated by Louise and Aylmer Maude
Edited by Henry Gifford

ANTHONY TROLLOPE: The American Senator
Edited by John Halperin

The Belton Estate
Edited by John Halperin

Cousin Henry
Edited by Julian Thompson

The Eustace Diamonds
Edited by W. J. McCormack

The Kellys and the O'Kellys
Edited by W. J. McCormack
Introduction by William Trevor

Orley Farm
Edited by David Skilton

Rachel Ray
Edited by P. D. Edwards

The Warden
Edited by David Skilton

IVAN TURGENEV: First Love and Other Stories
Translated by Richard Freeborn

VILLIERS DE L'ISLE-ADAM: Cruel Tales
Translated by Robert Baldick
Edited by A. W. Raitt

VIRGIL: The Aeneid
Translated by C. Day Lewis
Edited by Jasper Griffin

The Eclogues and The Georgics
Translated by C. Day Lewis
Edited by R. O. A. M. Lyne

HORACE WALPOLE : The Castle of Otranto
Edited by W. S. Lewis

IZAAK WALTON and CHARLES COTTON:
The Compleat Angler
Edited by John Buxton
Introduction by John Buchan

MRS HUMPHREY WARD: Robert Elsmere
Edited by Rosemary Ashton

OSCAR WILDE: Complete Shorter Fiction
Edited by Isobel Murray

The Picture of Dorian Gray
Edited by Isobel Murray

MARY WOLLSTONECRAFT:
Mary *and* The Wrongs of Woman
Edited by Gary Kelly

ÉMILE ZOLA:
The Attack on the Mill and other stories
Translated by Douglas Parmeé

A complete list of Oxford Paperbacks, including The World's Classics, OPUS, Past Masters, Oxford Authors, Oxford Shakespeare, and Oxford Paperback Reference, is available in the UK from the Arts and Reference Publicity Department (RS), Oxford University Press, Walton Street, Oxford OX2 6DP.

In the USA, complete lists are available from the Paperbacks Marketing Manager, Oxford University Press, 200 Madison Avenue, New York, NY 10016.

Oxford Paperbacks are available from all good bookshops. In case of difficulty, customers in the UK can order direct from Oxford University Press Bookshop, Freepost, 116 High Street, Oxford, OX1 4BR, enclosing full payment. Please add 10 per cent of published price for postage and packing.